Unbroken Bonds

D. W. Hogan

"*Unbroken Bonds* vividly captures the terrible vulnerability of young white women in the United States in the decades before 'reproductive rights' became available to any but the wealthiest of us. Dawn Hogan richly portrays the dozens of ways that sexuality and its consequences endangered the safety and dignity of girls and women when their only source of strength was each other. This novel is a great read. It is also a cautionary tale. If we fail to recognize the truths of Hogan's novel, then girls and women may, quite possibly, be forced to face similar dangers in the future."

—Rickie Solinger, Author of *Wake Up Little Susie:*
Single Pregnancy and Race before Roe v. Wade

"As an adoptee, coming to a place of acceptance I've had to put myself in the shoes of my first mother at the time of my conception to gain a better under-standing of what life was like back then. *Unbroken Bonds* takes its readers on a journey of the essential facts of what many first mothers experience. It shares how extraordinarily difficult our times can be when it comes to unwed and unplanned pregnancy. Dawn shares several sides of the coin, all real and raw glimpses of what first mothers go through. This is a side that needs to be considered among society today. Although times have changed in some regard, we must be awakened in the truths that separation trauma for the adoptee and first mother lasts a lifetime."

—Pamela Karanova, Adoptees Connect, Inc.

"While *Unbroken Bonds* is a novel, the characters might have been your mothers, grandmothers, aunts, sisters, or the girls with whom you went to school. Each of the young women's narratives are carefully crafted, and realistic. Finding it difficult to put the book down, we watch each teenager develop into a unique woman who processes the changes wrought in the decades as they go by and finds strength in her own history and from those who love her. As a birth mother myself, I know the pain and confusion surrounding the relin-quishment of one's child. Dawn Hogan has done meticulous research into the feelings, psychology and aftermath of this experience. I believe this book goes a long way to help the public understand the need for unsealing records and helping first mothers heal the wounds created by the loss of their children."

—Fran Gruss Levin, Author of *The Story of Molly*
***and Me*, and CUB Board Member**

Unbroken Bonds

D. W. Hogan

Woodhall Press
Norwalk, CT

woodhall press

Woodhall Press, 81 Old Saugatuck Road, Norwalk, CT 06855
WoodhallPress.com

Cover design: Asha Hossain
Layout artist: Amie McCracken

Library of Congress Cataloging-in-Publication Data available
ISBN 978-1-949116-53-3 (paper: alk paper)
ISBN 978-1-949116-54-0 (electronic)
First Edition

Distributed by Independent Publishers Group
(800) 888-4741
Printed in the United States of America

This is a work of fiction. All of the characters, organizations, and events portrayed in this novel are either products of the author's imagination or are used fictitiously.

This book is dedicated to Supreme Court Justice Ruth Bader Ginsburg, a small woman with a huge legacy in the fight for equal rights for women. She attended Cornell University during the early years of the Baby Scoop Era. By 1955 she was a young married mother. She understood the need for women to have the power to make personal decisions regarding their reproductive health. Always with wisdom, consistency and dignity, her life's work changed the world, giving a voice to women's issues and opening the door for future generations to become all they aspire to be.

March 15, 1933 – September 18, 2020

Chapter 1

The look on her father's face was one she'd seen far too often. Without warning, he lunged across the kitchen, crashing into the light bulb that hung from the ceiling by a cord and now swung wildly. He pounded his fist on the table. She hated that light. She hated that kitchen, but most of all, she hated her father.

"So you got yourself knocked up, aye, Joanna!" Harris Wilson's words spat anger.

Joanna's brown eyes blinked back the tears she wouldn't allow. She set her jaw to subdue her anger. A wave of nausea swept over her, caused by the bitter aroma of the coffee.

"Who's the father?" Harris's booming voice carried through the two-bedroom apartment and assured he'd wake the adjacent neighbors.

"I'm not gonna tell you," she said through gritted teeth.

"You little tramp!"

"Shhh, Harris, please, you'll wake the babies," her mother started with a fearful visage.

"Don't shhh me, woman!" Harris raged at his wife.

Irene kept her voice low. "It's time for decisions. What're we gonna do?"

"She can't stay here!"

"Maybe she could go to Aunt Vanda's, in Murfreesboro," Irene suggested. Sitting at the far end of the table, Irene frowned. Taking a sip of coffee, she smoothed her gray-brown hair.

"No, that's no good. How's it acceptable for you to bring a bastard into this world?"

"I don't know. How many bastards of yours are out there?" Joanna's words no more than left her mouth when her father's forceful fist struck her. Joanna glared at him. Salty blood warmed her tongue as she licked her broken lip. He tightened his fist as if he might hit her again; instead, he turned and stared out the window at the converging pink hues of the early morning.

Irene ran a rag under the cold-water tap. Hesitant, Joanna accepted the cloth along with the sting it inflicted as she held it to her mouth. Irene returned to her chair and shot Joanna a look begging her not to antagonize Harris. Joanna's last comment alluded to her father's constant philandering. Aside from his drinking, it was the primary source of disharmony within the family.

"I know of a place, the Frances Weston Home, in Knoxville," Harris announced.

"No! Don't send me away!" Joanna begged. Her father was referring to one of those horrible places families hid their pregnant daughters and took away their babies. Joanna intended to keep her baby and raise it with Jack. As soon as Catherine was well, Jack promised he'd leave his wife and marry Joanna.

"We can't afford it!" Irene panicked.

"We ain't payin' for it. I hope the father of your illegitimate brat isn't a deadbeat." Harris drank his paycheck more often than he brought it home. Joanna found his hypocrisy laughable. "He'll be payin' the tab."

His icy tone sent a queasy wave through her stomach and Joanna bolted to the bathroom. Her parents' angry words resonated louder as the argument escalated. At last, she recovered from dry heaves. She rinsed her mouth under the cold running faucet of the porcelain sink, then watched the diluted red swirl vanish down the blackness of the drain.

"This is all your fault!" Her father's hateful words echoed in the hallway. The green flickering of the fluorescent lights on either side of the mirrored medicine cabinet gave a strobe light effect as Joanna examined her swelling split lip. Her jaw ached. Suddenly a crash came from the kitchen. The back door slammed and her mother's footfalls approached.

The woman handed her daughter a piece of ice. Tucking the girl's brown hair behind her ear, she examined the injury.

"You're lucky ya don't have a black eye to go with it. Honestly, Joanna, ya don't wanna provoke him right now."

"I'm not givin' my baby away. You can't make me." With Harris gone, Joanna let the tears come. The girl winced as she put the ice on her lip.

"Ya ain't thinkin' clearly. Ya can't keep it. Ya'd better talk with the man responsible. If he'll give ya the money for a stay in Knoxville, this whole thing'll blow over," Irene bargained. She placed her hand softly on Joanna's shoulder. "Aren't you curious how Daddy knows about a place like that?"

Irene diverted her eyes and withdrew her touch. Joanna caught sight of red marks on her mother's wrist; taking hold, she inspected the ripening bruises left by Harris.

"One of these days he'll kill you. This family makes me sick!" she cried with disgust.

Dew glistened on the October grass as Joanna jogged down the deserted street. Lights were coming on in the homes she passed; the clomping of her saddle shoes kept time with her stride. Too soon, she moderated to a walk, due to the stitch in her side and her ever-present nausea.

She hoped he'd be at his filling station when she arrived. By habit, Jack opened at 6:00 a.m. He was passionate about cars. He loved to work on them, and he loved to race them. Joanna caught racing fever the first time she watched Jack compete at the local amateur track.

She turned the corner onto Delmar; the lights in Jack's Service Station were off. Disappointed, Joanna walked behind the garage with its huge bay doors and sat on the wooden crate where Jack smoked his Camel cigarettes, far away from the gas tanks. The minutes dragged as she wondered what he'd say concerning her parents' decision. Then she felt silly for worrying; he'd fix her dilemma. Next she became uneasy, speculating why Jack was late.

Around six fifteen, Joanna startled at the roar of a car coming around to park at the rear of the station. Jack eased out of his '54 Ford Fairlane, scowling as he approached her.

"You're late, I was worried." Joanna smiled, but was grimacing at the throbbing in her lip.

"Catherine had another episode this morning. I needed to wait for her mother to arrive before I could leave her." The strain on Jack's face made him look older than his twenty-nine years. "What happened to your mouth?"

"My mama told my father about our baby." With the added drama of being a pregnant teenager, Joanna proceeded to describe the earlier confrontation. She trailed behind him as he turned on the lights in the three-bay shop of the garage. The smell of motor oil didn't bother her as much as coffee. By the time she finished her story, she was sobbing. "Jackie, please take me away. Let's go somewhere no one knows us."

"Joanna," Jack Wyatt said with a sigh. "Catherine's in a deep depression right now; I can't leave her. If she learns about you and the baby, she'll kill herself."

Joanna heated with outrage. "Let her! It'd solve a lot of problems."

"I don't want that on my conscience." A vein throbbed at his temple.

"How does your conscience feel about bein' a father?" Joanna crossed her arms. Jack brushed past her to his office and flipped through a 1957 calendar, noting the upcoming race data he'd penciled in. Joanna followed. "You said we'd be together." Joanna pushed aside Jack's grease-stained rolling chair and sat on top of his cluttered desk.

"This is the worst possible timing. What's the place in Knoxville cost?"

"No! You're not considerin' sendin' me away. You sound like you're on their side."

"This isn't a matter of sides; this is a matter of being practical. If things work out, I'll get the details arranged before the baby's born in March and I'll come get you."

Joanna's heart pounded at the thought of living in a home for wayward girls. She took a deep breath. His reassurance and calmness quieted her fears. He'd pay for her disappearance. They'd get married. It'd all work out.

Chapter 2

Jack Wyatt sat behind the worn desk in his gas station. Spread before him were his bankbooks and a scratch pad with columns of numbers. He'd made an anonymous phone call and hyperventilated when he learned they charged $500 for an enrollment at the home beginning in the fourth month of pregnancy. Considering his annual income was $3,000, the cost was a small fortune. The administrator went into detail to justify the fees. She'd used the word *incarceration,* labeling residents felons. Joanna wasn't a criminal; he was the guilty party.

Jack let out a groan. He hated the idea of sending Joanna away, but his first instinct was to protect Catherine. Jack underlined the $500 with enough force that he snapped the pencil lead. Opening the drawer to retrieve another, his eyes locked on a picture of him and Cat, knotted in a hug. It was taken the day she'd learned she was pregnant. They looked outrageously happy.

"Oh, Cat. If only I hadn't accepted Alex's challenge for a drag race," he whispered. He closed his eyes tight. The image of Cat's car wrapped around the tree burned in his memory like a scar. He'd walked away with a few bruises. The case for Cat was far more tragic. When the doctor told him his son was stillborn, Jack wished the accident had taken his own life. When he signed the forms for Catherine's hysterectomy, his hand shook so violently he could barely scrawl his name. According to the doctor, she'd bleed to death without the emergency surgery.

Their baby died, with no future hope for another. The doctors kept Cat heavily sedated after the accident. She never saw her lifeless son. Jack had spent fifteen minutes in a dimly lit private room with the infant he'd all but murdered, but he couldn't bring himself to hold the child. Daniel Aaron Wyatt's interment in the Langley family plot took place with only his grandparents and father attending, while Cat lay unconscious in a hospital bed.

Chapter 3

Catherine Langley Wyatt sat in the window seat of the guest bedroom in the stately seventy-five-year-old house she'd inherited from her grandfather. She loved this house, with all its childhood memories. She thought of the time her granddaddy gave her roller skates and let her try them out on the hardwood floors in the hallways.

Cat circled her arms around her knees, pulling them to her chest. The full skirt of her dress rustled with her movements. When Jack had discovered her with the knife this morning, he'd misunderstood. She'd been hungry and wanted grapefruit to tide her over until Flora arrived. Looking at her scars, she'd remembered the first time she tried to end it all and how much she'd distressed everyone. She regretted the attempt afterward but surviving fixed nothing.

Catherine blamed herself for the accident that killed their baby. She'd encouraged her husband to race. It wasn't until they hit the dangerous curve and started spinning that she screamed, "Jack, slow down!" The car smashed through the guardrail, and Cat's recall ended there.

The guilt she bore overwhelmed her. She tried to kill herself again on the one-year anniversary of the accident. Catherine withdrew to her bed all day and faked sleep when Jack came to check on her. When she heard the shower running, she locked herself in the nursery, took a handful of pills, and swallowed them with whiskey. She wanted to die.

She woke at the asylum, disappointed she'd failed. It crushed her to see Jack sitting by her bed, face in his hands, crying. Cat promised she'd never make another attempt. She didn't want to cause him any more pain; if only she could be rid of her own torment.

Catherine moved the yellow fabric of the curtain; the view overlooked the garden where her mother and Flora were discussing the rosebushes. She cringed, ashamed Jack had called her mother to babysit. Hearing people talk behind her back, seeing them tiptoe around her like she might break, and feeling as if she were sleepwalking through her life had to stop.

Catherine detested taking her antidepressant pills. She wanted her life back, but no one except Flora thought her capable. She'd have to convince her over-achieving mother, Millicent, a well-known member of the Nashville elite. Even before the accident, Cat found it difficult to keep track of her mother's schedule. Now she only half listened when her mother chattered about her charitable projects. When it came to her own daughter's depression, she dismissed discussions in her staunch, businesslike manner by saying, "Hush now, you needn't dwell on such sad things. You should get out more. Come with me to a luncheon." Cat always declined the offer.

In truth, Cat hated to go out in public. The few times she did, all she saw were young mothers strolling with their baby carriages. She experienced actual pain when she saw a pregnant woman shopping in a store. To her, it was the same concept as riding in a car after you learned of a loved one's death and suddenly being hypersensitive to how many cemeteries you passed. They'd always been there, but she hadn't noticed them until it became her emotional focus. She chose the easier path and avoided going out.

Dr. McMahon's car pulled onto the circular drive. He joined the women by the roses; their muffled voices traveled as they entered the house. Her mother's steps and the heavier ones of the doctor thumped up the stairs. Millicent knocked softly.

"Come in," Cat permitted, still sitting by the window.

The doctor entered the room. "How're we feeling today?" Without a word Millicent closed the door and disappeared downstairs.

"I'm fine. Really," Catherine told him. "I wasn't going to hurt myself, I promise." She went on to tell her side of the story. The doctor studied her as she spoke.

When she finished, he assured her, "I believe you."

"Can we try a different medication? I wish I could get off pills altogether!"

"Do you think you're ready?"

"Remember, a couple of weeks ago, we talked about different ways of coping with grief and acceptance?" The doctor nodded. "I've reached acceptance. I'm ready to move on."

"You could begin by joining activities involving children; say, become a Sunday school teacher. You have abundant love to give to children, even if they're not your own."

"That's true," she agreed. "The other day you mentioned adoption. I know I didn't want to talk about it then, but I've been thinking on it a lot."

He smiled at her. "You're getting better."

"I haven't talked to Jack, yet, but I think I'd like to explore the option. What do you think my chances are given my… condition?" She hid her wrists in her sleeves.

"I'm sure a private adoption could be arranged. It'll require more work on your part, but I think you're taking the right steps."

"I'll do whatever it takes. Where do we start?"

"Let's reduce your current medication, see how you feel. Try getting out more. Reach for the goal of having a child in the house."

"Thank you." Cat smiled at him.

"That's the first time I've ever seen you smile. It's pretty; you should do it more often."

Upon returning home, Jack met Dr. McMahon in the kitchen, enjoying a piece of peach cobbler. Flora served the doctor a fresh cup of coffee.

"How's Cat?" Jack asked anxiously.

"She says you misread what you saw and overreacted." The doctor raised his brows and relayed Catherine's version. Jack glanced at the counter; next to the cutting board sat a bowl with grapefruit. Jack turned back to the doctor, who stood and gathered his black bag and hat.

"Actually, Jack, I think Catherine's making good progress. I'm reducing her medication, with the goal of getting her off it completely."

"Is that wise?"

"This is at her request. Your wife seems determined. She needs your love and encouragement more than ever." Jack thanked the man and went upstairs.

He paused at her bedroom door, knocked gently, and called, "Cat? Honey, it's me."

"I'm in the nursery." Her soft voice came from the end of the hall. Jack's heart quickened as he approached. The last time he'd seen her in the nursery, he called an ambulance. This time, he leaned against the doorjamb and observed his wife standing next to the empty crib, as she folded a blanket. Meeting his eyes, she said, "Hi."

Jack gave a slight nod. "How're you doing?"

"I'm good. I need to talk to you." Fatigue showed, but she seemed more lucid than usual.

"Okay." He stepped into the room, supported his hands on the back of the rocking chair.

"I'm sorry for everything I've put you through. I understand why you reacted the way you did this morning. I promised I'd never do that again, and I meant it. Sometimes I think if you'd been anyone else, you would've found yourself a girl-friend and run off by now." She was attempting a joke; Jack swallowed hard. She came to his side. "I guess I'm trying to say, I miss you, Jackie." She slipped her arms around him and laid her head on his chest, surprising him. He hugged her lightly. He hadn't embraced her since the accident; at first, because of her sore-ness. Later, her constant pulling away discouraged him. Eventually, he stopped trying. "I don't want us to be this way anymore," she whispered. "I'm going to get off the pills and start living again. I have work to do, but what would you think about adopting a baby?"

"I hadn't thought about it before," Jack answered honestly, stunned.

"I truly believe adopting a child will help us get back to a normal life," she reasoned, still hugging him. He could smell the sweetness of her hair, recalling how it used to feel to hold her.

"It's a big step." If she'd come to him a year ago with this, he would've jumped at the idea. Now he paled with guilt.

"We can take one step at a time. Let's both think about adoption and see how we feel." She looked at his face. "Will you at least think about it?"

"Yeah. I will. In the meantime, like you said, you have work to do." Feeling on overload already, he feared this latest bit of news might blow the fuses in his brain.

Joanna eased the back door open. She'd planned on sneaking into the apartment, but her mother was elbow-deep in soapsuds, washing the dinner dishes.

"I didn't see Daddy's car. Where is he?"

"Who knows; who cares?" Irene answered and dried her hands on her apron. "Have a seat." Joanna sat at the kitchen table. "Where ya been? I know ya skipped school."

"I was at the movies."

"Did ya talk to your young man?" Irene placed a piece of paper on the table.

"Yes, I did," Joanna snotty-toned. "He promised to take care of it." She looked at the numbers added in her father's handwriting. "Jesus Christ, Mama! It'd be cheaper to send me to a fancy hotel in Florida until this baby's born!"

"Is he gonna be able to shell out the money?"

"I don't know." Joanna shrugged.

"This home takes charity cases, but ya got to work off your bill before ya can leave."

Joanna switched topics. "I'm goin' to Birmingham this weekend with a friend."

"What friend?" Irene challenged with her hands on her hips.

"Mary Atherton," Joanna lied and stomped to her room. In a moment, Irene knocked. "Leave me alone!" Joanna shouted, hugging the pillow, wishing it were Jack.

"You'd better not be runnin' with that fella." Irene's warning came muffled through the door.

"It's not like I'll end up gettin' pregnant this weekend," Joanna shouted back.

Instead of continuing the argument, Irene went into the small living room to make alterations on a dress commissioned by Mabel's dress shop. She'd taken in sewing when they moved to Nashville, fearing her family wouldn't eat otherwise.

Tonight Irene assumed her husband was at a bar. Glad he hadn't come home, she only regretted there wouldn't be much left of his paycheck. He'd probably picked up a woman, too. Better he find someone else than to bring his slobbering drunk ass home and want her. Sometimes she'd imagine the police at her door, telling her he'd died in a drunk-driving accident. She wouldn't cry. She'd be relieved. How he hadn't accomplished it yet was beyond her. Oh, he'd wrecked plenty of cars, totaled several, but always walked away with barely a scratch; drunken, stupid, lucky bastard.

For Irene, a devout Catholic, divorce was unthinkable. Women from her lineage married young and suffered with abusive husbands until one of them died. Mostly the men died first. She wished Harris would hurry and get on with it.

Chapter 4

At 8:00 p.m., Joanna came skipping into the station, a valise in hand. She wore blue-jean pedal pushers and a white, short-sleeved blouse; a red bandanna was tied around her neck.

"Hey, Frankie," she greeted Jack's employee. In his forties and bald, Frankie had the mentality of a ten-year-old. He was simple, but good at pumping gas and ringing up sales.

"Hey, Joanna," Frankie replied, smiling.

"So you got all that, right, buddy?" Jack said, double-checking with his employee.

"Sure, Jack. Put the money and receipts in the bottom drawer and lock it with this key." Frankie showed the key on his lucky-rabbit's-foot keychain. "Open at seven a.m.; close at six at night. Lock the door with this key. And don't take any wooden nickels." Frankie laughed.

Jack smiled. "You're a good man, Frankie."

In high spirits on the long ride to Birmingham, Alabama, Joanna snuggled at Jack's side while the top love ballads of 1956 played on the car radio. She'd be alone with Jack for two nights. He promised to take her shopping and buy her something special. They didn't talk of the home in Knoxville or Catherine's problems. They put reality out of their minds and retreated to their private world. In Jack she found the only real love she'd ever known. Jack, on the other hand, knew of passion. He'd loved desperately before. Joanna brought love back to him.

Arriving at the Holiday Inn after midnight, Jack went into the office to check in while Joanna lay flat in the front seat, giving the illusion Jack was alone. Bathed in the light of the yellow arrow from the sign, Joanna daydreamed of the weekend they'd spend together. Jack had intentionally booked his pit crew at a different motel to limit contact with them away from the track. Jack's best friend Alex, a fantastic driver, had run the time trials for him earlier. When it came to racing, Alex preferred a place in Jack's shadow.

On the back side of the building, Jack and Joanna slipped into the motel room. As soon as they were safely inside, they were in each other's arms, kissing. Jack lowered her onto the white-and-gray-striped bedspread and filled his senses with the taste and feel of her. She clung desperately to him, wanting the security only he could give. The passionate fire between them was the result of the loneliness each harbored in their own soul. Being together filled those voids, briefly.

He woke in the morning to Joanna sitting on the bed next to him, a sweet expression on her face. "What're you doing?" He turned on the brass bedside light.

"Watching you sleep, wonderin' if our baby boy'll look like you."

Jack placed his hand on her warm stomach. He wished he could feel his child move, as he'd done with Daniel. It was too soon. He'd probably never feel this baby move inside her.

"It's a boy," she whispered. "I've seen him in my dreams."

Jack pulled her close. "Seriously, Joanna, I want you to promise me something."

"Anythin'."

"Swear you won't sign any papers giving him away. They'll try to make you at the home, but don't do it. I'll get you and the baby an apartment or something. I need some time."

"I promise. I never will."

"I'll get you out of there before he's born. Even if I have to sell everything I own." She kissed him passionately. They made love again.

As Jack headed for the shower, his friend Alex banged on the door and yelled, "Jackieeee, open up, man!" Alex changed to a knuckle drum solo. Jack wrapped in a towel and put a finger to his lips, signaling to Joanna to be quiet. She rolled her body in the heaps of covers, disguising herself as a pile of blankets. Jack opened the door a crack.

"Let's go get some breakfast!" Alex spoke hyperspeed as usual.

"I'm about to get a shower." Jack made the excuse through a small opening of the door.

"What? Have you got a woman in there, man?" Alex whispered.

"I'll see you at the track this afternoon," Jack told him.

Alex pushed on the door, entering the room. "Well, at least let me use the can." He used the facilities with the bathroom door wide open. All the while, Alex babbled about the time trials. Jack kicked Joanna's bra under the bed, hoping Alex hadn't noticed it on the floor. Alex plopped on the bed next to where Joanna hid.

Jack's heart pounded hard. "Come on, man, you've got to go. I need to jump in the shower." Jack put his hand on his friend's shoulder, giving him a friendly nudge.

Alex walked to the door. "Why don't you come out with me and the guys tonight? There'll be some delicious dames. I'm telling ya."

"No thanks."

"How's Cat these days?" Alex asked, genuinely concerned.

"The same."

"Jesus Christ, Jack! You can't go on living like a monk." Alex shook his head.

"I'm fine. Thanks anyway."

"I didn't mean to torque you off, buddy."

"I'm not. I want to catch up on some sleep."

"I understand. If you change your mind, decide to blow off some steam, I'll set ya up."

Jack laughed, shut the door, and leaning against it breathed relief. Joanna peeked one eye out from under the covers.

"That was close!" she whispered, barely breathing.

"Too close," Jack whispered back. "Why don't you join me in the shower? Then we can get something to eat. I'm starving."

"After breakfast, can we go shoppin'?" Joanna asked, with childlike anticipation.

"Yes, we can go shopping." He loved her enthusiasm and her authentic smile. He wanted to squeeze a lifetime of love into two short days.

Irene rushed to zip the garment bag, which contained the fancy dress she'd completed an hour ago. "Eddie!" she called out. "I'm leaving. Mind the babies now." Turning to the four-year-old, she admonished, "Benny, try to stay out of trouble."

"Where's Joanna? How come she can't do this?" The skinny teenager came into the living room munching on an apple.

"I'm counting on you, Eddie. I'll be back soon. We need the money," Irene scolded. Edmond sat on the worn couch and perused a comic book, ignoring his mother. Irene made it to Mabel Anderson's boutique with mere minutes to spare.

Mabel examined the dress. "This is fine work, Mrs. Wilson."

"Thank you, ma'am," Irene answered modestly. Mabel Anderson's clientele were the affluent women of Nashville. She provided the best dresses at the highest prices in town. The bell above the door jingled, and in walked a classy middle-aged woman with a teenage girl.

"Good afternoon, Mrs. Atherton," Mabel greeted the woman. "How are you, Mary dear?" she asked the sophisticated-looking teen.

"I'm doing well, thank you," the girl answered.

"Your dress is ready, Mary. Let me introduce Mrs. Wilson. She did a beautiful job with your alterations. The dress is exquisite. I know you'll be pleased."

"Delighted to make your acquaintance, I'm Edith Atherton. This is my daughter, Mary."

"Pleased to meet you. Mary, I believe my daughter's a friend of yours." Her name had set off an alarm in Irene's mind. Mary looked confused. "Joanna Wilson?" Irene clarified, suddenly realizing Joanna's blatant lie about being in Birmingham with Mary Atherton.

"Joanna's in my bookkeeping class."

Irene cowered with embarrassment. Of course this girl wasn't a friend of Joanna's. Mary withdrew to try on the dress.

"Mary's in the running for homecoming queen! Mrs. Wilson, would you like to see how the dress looks on her?" The girl's mother beamed with pride.

"Yes, I would." From sewing experience, Irene knew the expense of the dress. She'd wished she were making a homecoming dress for Joanna. But her daughter showed no interest in homecoming dances or high school activities. She envied Mrs. Atherton.

"Mother, help me, please," the girl called from behind the curtain.

Edith stepped into the changing room. "I believe you've gained a few pounds."

"No, I haven't," Mary scoffed.

"Mabel, darling, could you help with this zipper?" Mabel pulled back the curtain, and with a little coaxing it zipped. Mary bounced in front of the three-way mirror. Mabel stepped next to Irene. The dress was too tight across the girl's bust.

"I told you not to eat so much ice cream," Edith told her daughter, turning to the women. "Mary's beau works in his daddy's malt shop. I've told her, she'll lose her girlish figure if she spends too much time there."

"Stop teasing, Mother," the girl exclaimed in a playful tone.

Mabel whispered under her breath to Irene, "Her bosom is bigger than it was two weeks ago. I measured her myself."

"There's a double seam. It'd be simple to give her a skosh more breathing room."

"Show me."

Irene explained that a quarter inch of the first seam could be let out to make the dress more flattering. The women all agreed and Irene completed the adjustment quickly. Mary tried the dress on again and it fit perfectly. The dress shop owner paid Irene a generous bonus. Anxiously, she left the boutique. She was uncomfortable around those high-class city women, and also wanted to stop at the market. Five hungry children counted on her.

As Irene rode the noisy, smoking bus back to her neighborhood, she thought how Joanna would never be homecoming queen; she'd never amount to anything. Sick with disappointment, Irene sensed she'd failed as a mother. She couldn't tell Harris about Joanna's weekend with her boyfriend; he'd beat her bloody. Irene hung her head, not wanting to make eye contact with any of the other passengers, sure they'd see her shame.

Chapter 5

Catherine nibbled on a muffin, reading the Sunday paper. Her father rapped softly on the window of the kitchen door and entered her house without waiting to be invited.

"Hi, Kitten," he greeted, sitting at the table across from her in the bay-windowed breakfast nook. Flora poured a cup of coffee and set it, along with a muffin, in front of him. The housekeeper busied herself in the next room.

"Hi, Daddy."

"Your mother tells me Dr. McMahon's reduced your medication. I'm glad."

"I've been on half a dose for three days now and, honestly, I'm feeling better already." She mustered a small smile to convince him. "Daddy? I've been thinking…"

"Uh-oh. Whenever you say that, it usually costs me money."

"No, I don't need money. I have plenty of my own, but I may need your connections."

"Connections for what?"

"I'm considering adopting a baby." She recognized the look of pain on her father's face. He'd been overjoyed by her pregnancy with Daniel. A wonderful, attentive father, he'd looked forward to becoming a grandfather.

After a moment, he proclaimed, "I think adoption's a wonderful idea. I can make some calls after church and get the ball rolling today."

"No, not today. Maybe in a few months. Jack and I haven't made any decisions yet."

"Where is Jack, anyway?" Wendell asked.

"At a race in Birmingham."

"Damn races," he grumbled, under his breath.

"Don't start, Daddy. I mentioned it to see if you know anyone who can help with a private adoption. I'm nervous about the department of child welfare, given my medical history."

"Poppycock! If you want a baby, I'll get you a baby." He waved his hand dismissively.

"Thanks. I'm doing my best to pull it together. That's why I asked to go to church with you today. It's my first step in rejoining the rest of the world."

"I'm here for you, Catherine. I'll never let you down."

Catherine's anxiety calmed while she was gracefully led on her father's arm into the huge Methodist church. Century-old stained glass colored the sanctuary as they made their way to the Langley family pew. After three years of refusing to be in a crowd, she anticipated the stares of her parents' friends and her father's business associates. Her confidence waned at the glances from her former classmates, though, many of whom had their children in tow. Cat straightened. She'd have to overcome her fears to have children in her life.

When Jack returned home on Sunday afternoon, he found his wife in the parlor, dressed in a navy-blue suit, looking at the current *McCall's* magazine. Her hat and gloves lay on the couch. *She's been out,* he thought. When Cat rose from her chair to greet him, Jack backed away. He feared she might whiff Joanna's lingering scent.

"I'm going to get a shower. I feel grimy from the road."

Standing in the heated mist of the shower, Jack's muscles tightened when Cat's voice came from the doorway.

"I went to church with my father today."

"How'd it go?" He turned his back to her and quickly rinsed off.

"Awkward, but it was okay. We went to the country club for lunch."

Before the accident, Jack's participation in the Langley Sunday ritual had been mandatory. The perception of the perfect upper-class ménage motivated Wendell. Jack complied merely to appear accommodating. Not only was he not invited to Cat's reemergence into society now, though, but he'd been completely unaware of her plans.

Jack finished his shower promptly and turned off the water. Cat handed him a towel. Grateful, he wrapped it around his waist and went into the bedroom they once shared. Catherine trailed behind him, hesitantly taking a seat on the double bed, which had served as a playground for their insatiable passion as newlyweds. Standing in front of the mirror, Jack brushed his wet hair straight back, greaser-style. His wife's reflection watched him.

"Daddy was good today. Although he lied, telling people I'd been traveling extensively. It was silly of him. You know how people talk." Catherine stood and went to the window, taking in the changing autumn leaves. "I saw Daisy Hamilton today. She has a two-month-old daughter. She looks exactly like her..." Her voice broke off. Jack wondered if she'd taken on too much. "Jack, who'd Daniel look like?"

His heart almost stopped. She'd never asked him before. "He... well... he was so small, Cat." Pain stabbed his chest, which relentlessly accompanied the memory of his only moments with his lifeless son. He placed his hand on her shoulder and spoke softly. "He had a tiny bit of hair, dark like yours, and perfect little fingers." Jack swallowed hard against the lump in his throat. "He looked like an angel."

Silence cocooned the room for an uncomfortable length of time, until Catherine turned into the waiting arms of her husband, tears streaking her mascara. She whispered, "I needed to know. Thank you." She let her lips brush his briefly in a kiss. She left the room and went downstairs; next, the back door shut. Jack wiped away his stinging tears. He dressed quickly and joined his wife in the garden.

She wasn't crying but didn't make eye contact when he approached. She traced a rose petal with her fingertip. "My room in the hospital smelled like roses," she mentioned softly. During her recovery Wendell sent fresh roses to her daily. "I haven't liked roses since then. It's a shame. Roses are so lovely." She turned to her husband. His wrinkled brow betrayed his emotional state. "I know you're worried about me. You needn't be."

"It's just... we never talked about this. Now you're a fountain of words," Jack observed.

"I need to talk now. I want to see Daniel's grave. I need to say goodbye so I can finally let all this go." His heart pounded so hard he could hear it in his ears. He hadn't been to the cemetery in a year; she'd only been there once and tried to slit her wrists the next week.

"Are you sure that's such a good idea?"

"I want you to take me next Sunday, right after church."

"How 'bout we see how this week goes; see how you feel?"

"Fair enough." She nodded. "I understand my actions, not my words, will convince you I'm serious about getting better. I'll do whatever it takes for you to have faith in me again."

Jack sighed. "I can't help but worry."

Cat took a deep breath and abruptly changed the subject. "How was the race?" He looked at her blankly. "In Birmingham?"

"Oh," he said, feeling caught in a lie. "I let Alex drive. I got a stomach bug; I went back to the motel and went to bed." He didn't completely lie. He'd gone back to the motel to bed. During his affair with Joanna, he stuck to half-truths; they seemed less of a lie. "I'm still not feeling one hundred percent." Again, it wasn't a fib. It wasn't his stomach ailing him, but the battle being waged in his mind. His wife felt his forehead. She'd touched him more this week than she had since the accident.

"You don't have a fever. Maybe you're on the back side of it," she suggested.

Joanna arrived home to what appeared to be an empty apartment. Thank God, her mother and the rest of them were at evening Mass. The stifling stench of cigarette smoke in the apartment nauseated her. Joanna passed by her parents' bedroom where her father lay passed out on the bed, reeking of alcohol. She quietly closed the door to his room and tiptoed to her bedroom, squeezed past the twins' crib at the end of her bed. Reaching, she retrieved a shoebox from the shelf in the closet and hid the delicate gold music box Jack had bought her on their shopping trip in Birmingham. With the lid open, a lovely tinkling harpsichord played the Platters song, "Only You." She returned the shoebox and crept out of the apartment to sit on the back steps. She filled her lungs with the refreshing, cool air.

It wasn't long before voices of her mother and siblings came from the gangway. Benny whined that his feet hurt. Irene was carrying Linda and Edmond held Lilly. Joanna descended the stairs to meet them at the second floor. She took the baby from her mother.

"Is your daddy home?" Irene asked.

"Passed out in your bedroom, as usual."

When they reached their fourth-floor apartment, Irene instructed, "Eddie, take the babies inside, please. I need to talk to Joanna." Her mother's voice was firm and controlled. Neither Edmond nor Joanna challenged her. The girl leaned against the warped gray railing of the porch and waited. Irene propped herself against the wall, took a cigarette out of her pocket, and lit it. Her mother only smoked when extremely upset.

"Honest to God, girl, I've done the best I can by ya. Ya break my heart."

"What is it I've done this time, Mama?" Joanna hated these melodramas.

"I met your good friend Mary Atherton and her lovely mother at Mabel Anderson's shop yesterday. The dress I've been workin' on was hers. So I know ya weren't in Birmingham with her." Joanna gave her mother a sideways look. "I may not've finished high school, but I didn't fall off the turnip truck yesterday. I know who ya were with and what ya were doin'. I'm tellin' ya, stay away from him!"

"It's not gonna be a problem when ya send me away, is it?" Joanna answered.

"You're goin' to Knoxville Saturday! I don't want ya to see him again."

"Saturday's too soon, Mama! Ya don't understand!"

"I understand plenty. Wise up! He's payin' to send ya away. He doesn't care about ya."

"You're wrong, Mama; he loves me and the baby!" Tears rimmed her eyes.

Irene took a long drag off the cigarette. Letting the smoke out slowly, she watched it drift skyward like a silent prayer. "That's what they all say. If I find out you've been with him, I'll tell your daddy about this weekend and your lie about Mary Atherton. I can't protect ya if you're gonna lie to me." The veins in her mother's temples throbbed.

"If I'd told ya what I was really doin', would ya've let me go?" Joanna reasoned.

"Of course not. Because what you're doin' is wrong. Ya had your fun; now it's over."

"I've got to see him at least one more time, so he can give me the money for Knoxville."

"You'll have to get it early next Saturday morning. I don't trust your daddy with large sums of money here. Tomorrow I'm gonna withdraw you from school; at least you'll be able to continue high school at the home. You can call him from a pay phone on the way back. This is a chance to move on, Joanna. Don't fail!" Irene crushed out her cigarette on the worn floorboards, kicking the butt off the edge. Ten minutes ago, Joanna was basking in the memories of being in Jack's arms; now she'd been forbidden to see him. She ran to the bathroom and vomited.

Across town, Wendell Langley sat behind his mahogany desk in the library of his mansion. A nervous man called Weasel stood before him, an envelope in his shaking hand. Langley didn't know his real name, nor did he care.

"Well, what'd you find out?" Langley asked. Leaning back in his leather chair, he took a sip of scotch from a well-filled glass.

"It's not good news." Weasel's voice quivered. He handed his employer the envelope, scanning the magnificent room with its floor-to-ceiling bookshelves and black marble fireplace.

Wendell broke the seal and let the photographs of his son-in-law with a pretty young woman spill out on his desk. In one, they were holding hands; in another, they were kissing; in a third, they were entering a motel room together.

"Who is she?" Langley asked, red-faced with anger.

"Her name's Joanna Wilson. She's nobody. She's seventeen, goes to Cohn High School, lives in an apartment with her parents."

"Who're her parents?"

"Again, they're nobody. They came from Lynchburg. The dad sells insurance; he's a drunk. Mom raises babies—she's got five kids. They live in a shithole on Forty-Second Street."

Wendell Langley didn't know how this man got his information. He didn't want to know. Weasel was slime; he'd rob his own grandmother's grave if he thought he'd make a buck—but he provided consistently accurate information. Wendell had hired him before, but it only occurred to him last week to have Jack's movements chronicled.

"I want to know if he sees her again." Langley grunted.

"There is one more thing, sir," the thin, fidgeting man interjected. Langley looked up from the photographs. "Your son-in-law took five hundred dollars out of savings the other day."

"Did he buy a car?"

"No, sir. I can't see that he spent it on anything."

"Keep an eye on him. I want to know his every move." The powerful man slid him a wad of bills and sent the informant away.

Fury consumed Wendell as he looked at the photographs again. He placed them back in the envelope then shoved it in the safe, locking away his son-in-law's sin. He should've killed that boy the night of the accident. He always knew Jack Wyatt wasn't good enough for Cat. He'd never be anything but a grease monkey with one dinky gas station, where he played with cars.

Wendell wrestled with his options as to what to do about Jack. He wanted to break every bone in the bastard's body. A convenient car accident could be arranged, and believable, given Jack's history.

Wendell believed staunchly in monogamy; except for one indiscretion when he'd been a much younger man, he'd remained faithful to Millicent. He accepted infidelity as common behavior among many of the men of his status and could overlook such errors in judgment when done with discretion. Jack's careless flaunting of affection for this Joanna person proved his weakness and immaturity.

Wendell opened the ten-foot French doors leading to the back lawn. Stepping out on the terrace, he swallowed the last of the scotch in his glass. He was proud of Catherine's big step out into the world today, honored that she'd chosen him to be at her side. He'd shielded her from questions and would always protect her. His money and power paled compared with his love for Catherine. He'd never allow Jack Wyatt to harm his daughter, not again.

Chapter 6

In the morning, Irene marched Joanna to the high school. She pushed the two babies in a secondhand tandem stroller. The wheel wobbled and squeaked, but it was preferable to carrying the little ones six blocks. Ben dawdled along behind.

"Hurry along now, Bubba," Irene scolded impatiently. Sixteen-year-old Edmond crossed the street to walk with his classmates, embarrassed by his family's hillbilly parade.

Once at the school's main office, Irene filled out the withdrawal paperwork. Joanna sat on a wooden bench, with instructions to keep her siblings occupied while they waited.

"What's the reason for withdrawal? Have you been unhappy with her progress here?" The woman looked in Joanna's direction. Joanna wondered if the school employee noticed her puffy eyes from crying all night.

"We've decided a private Catholic school is better for her." Irene handed over the forms.

"All right." The woman handed Irene a folder. "Give this to the new school. Will she be going to Father Ryan High School?"

"No, St. Frances," Joanna mocked, pushing the baby carriage out the door. The school clerk looked confused; St. Frances Catholic School didn't exist in Nashville.

On the way home, they stopped by a drugstore so Joanna could use the pay phone. Joanna wished Jack wouldn't answer the phone, but he did.

"Make it short," Irene instructed.

"They're taking me to Knoxville on Saturday! My mama wants me to arrange a time early that mornin' to get the money from you," Joanna explained.

"That's fast. She's with you, isn't she?"

"Yes. She knows about Birmingham. I'm grounded."

"I'm sorry. How's five a.m.? I'll meet you at the usual spot."

"I'm sure it'll be fine," Joanna agreed.

"Hang up now," Irene demanded.

"I've got to go," Joanna concluded. A click followed before Jack could say anything else.

Seeking to get his mind off the women in his life, Jack tinkered with the car he'd towed in. He put it on the lift and raised the car six feet off the floor. As he expected, there was a leak in the engine's rear main seal. He grumbled over the pain-in-the-ass job.

"Shit!" he cursed as the socket wrench slipped from his hand and hit him on the head. The familiar *ding- ding* of the bell sounded, and Jack turned his attention to the pumps. He observed his father-in-law's black sedan waiting to be served. Frankie rushed out and talked to the driver as Wendell got out of the backseat. He approached Jack in the service bay.

"Let's step into the office," the older man ordered, leading the way.

"What can I do for you, Wendell?" Jack asked. Shutting the door, he took a seat behind the desk. He took a rag from his pocket and wiped the grease from his hands. Wendell removed a nine-by-twelve envelope from under his suit coat and tossed it on the desk. "What's this?" Jack asked. He pulled out the photographs of Joanna and him, enough to see what they were. He slid them back into the envelope and flung it back at Wendell.

"Your point is?" Jack asked coolly.

"You're lucky I don't rip you limb from limb," Cat's father hissed. "Whatever you have going on with this… girl, it ends now."

"You may have input into Cat's life, Wendell, but you have no say in mine." Jack gave an icy stare, but his hands were sweating.

"You are Cat's life, you little prick! For some reason my daughter loves you, even after everything that's happened. She's finally getting better! This would destroy her. Cat needs your love. I suggest you spend your energy on her."

"I'm not going to discuss my marriage with you," Jack said, bristling.

"You got shit for brains, boy," Wendell spat. "You have absolutely no discretion. If I can so easily obtain pictures like this, don't you think some unscrupulous character could use your cheating to blackmail this family? What if Catherine were to open the mail one day to find these? Not only are you flaunting it in public, but this little piece of ass is underage."

"I'll beat the shit out of your boy if I catch him following me again," Jack threatened. Through the glass windows surrounding his office, Jack saw Frankie, eyes wide with concern.

"End it!" Wendell Langley ordered. "Or I swear to God, if you hurt my daughter again, I'll kill you myself." Langley snatched the envelope containing the photographs and swung open the office door, hitting the half-windowed wall so hard Jack thought the glass might break.

"I don't respond well to threats," Jack retorted defiantly.

"That's not a threat, son, that's a fucking promise," were Langley's last words as he left.

Once the black sedan drove off, Frankie came into Jack's office. "I don't like him."

"Neither do I, Frankie, neither do I."

Joanna spent her last week at home crying in her bed. Irene busied herself with the alterations on a wedding dress commissioned by Mabel Anderson. If Irene wasn't weeping, she was screaming at her kids. Joanna stayed in her room when Harris came home.

"What's with her?" Eddie asked.

"She's sick, leave her alone." Irene's hostile tone sent Eddie out the back door.

By Thursday, lovesick and lonely for Jack, Joanna concocted a plot to get out of the apartment. She initiated her scheme by going into the kitchen and lighting the flame under the teakettle. "I'm makin' myself some tea," she called to her mother. "Do you want some?"

"I reckon I'll have a cup," Irene called back. Joanna let the water come to a rolling boil. Reaching into the cabinet, she took the butesin picrate salve her mother kept for burns and put it in her pocket. Joanna prepared two cups of steaming tea and proceeded into the living room, stopping short and turning one of the cups over, deliberately spilling it, scalding her own arm. She let out a cry of real pain.

Irene jumped and ran to her daughter's side. The two-inch-wide red spot on her forearm blistered immediately. Irene rushed her into the kitchen and put her arm under the cold-water tap, rifling through the cabinets, searching for the burn ointment and not finding it.

"Oh, that's a bad burn, child," she said, her voice full of concern. "You've got to put somethin' on it right away!" Irene retrieved her hidden money coffee can from under the sink and produced coins making a dollar. "Ask the druggist in the pharmacy what to get. He'll know."

Joanna shot out the door without another word. She stopped briefly in the gangway to put salve on her burn. It'd be worth it if she could talk to Jack. She ran as fast as she could, ignoring the sounds of the traffic and the city around her.

Only a few customers were milling around the drugstore. She hurried to the wooden phone booth in the back corner of the store. Shutting the windowed door, shaking with nervous anticipation, she rattled off Jack's number to the operator.

The phone rang twice on the other end. "Jack's Service Station," Jack answered.

"Oh my God, it's so good to hear your voice," she declared.

"You too! What's going on? Where are you?"

"Mama sent me to the drugstore. Jack, I miss you so much."

"Me too, baby," he whispered. "You okay?"

"I'm fine except for missing you! Mama's treating me like a prisoner." She let her misery sound in her voice.

"Listen, you have to be careful. My father-in-law had us followed in Birmingham."

"Why? Does he know about us?"

"Yeah. In a few days, you'll be safely out of town. If you think someone's following you, run like hell, okay?"

"Okay." She got a lump in her throat. "I have to go now."

"Okay, baby. If I don't talk to you before then, I'll see you Saturday. I love you."

"I love you, too. I can't wait." She hurried back home, all the while looking over her shoulder. No one on the street appeared to be following her.

Chapter 7

Joanna quietly descended the gray zigzagging stairs. As expected, Jack waited for her at the end of her street. She jumped into the front seat and kissed him. "I'm glad I can always count on you. Get me out of here."

Jack steered the car away from the curb. "Where'd you like to go?"

"Anywhere. California, Wyoming, it doesn't matter."

"I wish we could." He meant it.

"I can't get over your father-in-law havin' us followed. What did he say to you?"

"He has photographs. My wife's family has a lot of power and influence in Nashville," Jack said, struggling to explain Catherine's social status. "Maybe it'd be better if I showed you." He U-turned in the middle of the street, deviating toward the house he shared with Catherine.

"Nice houses." Joanna gaped at the huge yards and homes that obviously required large sums of money on maintenance alone.

"That's where we live." He pointed to a majestic Victorian on the right. Set back from the street, the house occupied a spacious lot, with picturesque landscaping.

"Wow," she managed as they passed by. "So you're rich?"

"No. I'm not. Catherine's fairly well off. She inherited the house from her grandpa. But it's her money, not mine." Joanna looked suspiciously at him, wondering if he married her for the money. "I never cared about any of that," he stated, as if reading her mind. "It doesn't mean a thing if you're unhappy. It's just stuff. Being happy has nothing to do with money. I could have a chain of stations but rushing around managing them doesn't appeal to me. I'd rather have my one place and work on cars myself. Does that make sense?"

"Yeah. I'd live in a shack, if it meant we'd be together." Her eyes were full of love.

"Maybe with you in Knoxville, Langley's spies will get bored and he'll call them off."

"I hope so, but I can't imagine how I'm gonna make it through the next five months. It was almost impossible to get through this week." She reached over and took his hand.

"It was tough for me, too," he confessed.

"I'll write you every day. I'll send the letters to the station."

"I'll write you, too." Neither one of them knew how to express their tortured emotions. They held each other for comfort. Jack turned right, maneuvering through the neighborhood. He turned onto Love Circle, which became an upward grade. He finally pulled over at Love Park.

Jack pulled her to him and kissed her. Before long, they moved to the backseat where they made bittersweet love, fighting off the cruel reality of their inevitable separation. Afterward, Jack opened the door for her. Taking her hand, he led her to the front of the car, holding her from behind; their bodies knit warmly together as they watched the sky slowly lighten against the background of Nashville. They experienced a spectacular sunrise, highlighted in pinkish purple; the gray churning clouds predicted a coming thunderstorm.

"I want to memorize how it feels to hold you," he whispered in her ear. Tears flowed silently as she leaned into the tenderness of his lips on her face. Stroking her hair, he consoled, "I know, baby. I'm so sorry! This is the best way I know to protect you." Joanna turned her face to his chest and sobbed. "Don't cry," he whispered. "I'll find a way, before the baby's born." Jack rested the side of his face on her hair and breathed in her springlike scent. Finally, time ticked away and they returned to the car. Jack reached under the seat and retrieved an envelope; he handed it to her.

"There's thirty dollars extra; you might need some money."

Hesitating, she confided, "I feel kinda funny takin' this."

"That's my money, not hers! I worked for it." He sounded irritated, "Joanna, you don't understand my situation."

"Tell me your plan so I have somethin' to look forward to," she pleaded.

"Catherine's making progress. When she gets stronger, I'll ask her for a divorce."

"You'll marry me?"

"As soon as I can."

Their time together vanished even as they clung desperately to each second. They kissed one last time. Joanna went to face her fate. She packed all her happy endings in her bag to take with her.

Harris cursed as he sat in bumper-to-bumper traffic, hemmed in by a sea of motorists plotting their way out of Nashville. The clouds, which had threatened rain all morning, let loose now, with huge splattering drops. Joanna, in the back-seat, with her suitcase by her side, occasionally caught her father glaring at her through the rearview mirror. They didn't speak.

Harris lit another cigarette. Joanna rolled down the window next to her, taking an insufficient whiff of fresh autumn rain before her father yelled, "Leave it up!" The four-hour journey to Knoxville was excruciatingly long with him chain-smoking. Joanna silently begged for the trip to end, and at the same time feared the destination.

As they drove into the city limits of Knoxville, Joanna dropped the envelope containing Jack's money over the front seat. The windshield wipers made a rhythmic *whack squeak, whack squeak*. Harris eased the car to a stop at the red light. Inspecting the envelope, he counted the money. Taking some bills out, he slipped them into his breast pocket.

"Hey!" she blurted.

"For pain and sufferin' you've caused this family. You can work off what's missin'. It's the least ya can do." She crossed her arms and scowled at him. He wasn't looking in the mirror now. "I'll do the talkin'. You do what you're told and don't give 'em any grief. As far as I'm concerned, you're dead to me. When you get out, don't come home. You're on your own now. If you mess this up I'll fix it so you never see your mama again. Clear?"

"Perfectly," Joanna scowled. Even with no love lost between them, his steel-cold hatred seared her heart.

Harris turned onto a street with large old homes mixed with 1950s contemporary-style dwellings. When they turned the corner, looming before them was a Gothic-looking stone structure; around it was a stone wall topped by a black iron fence, with vertical bars that came to spearlike points. Harris turned into the driveway. A nun in a rain slicker unlocked the elaborate wrought-iron gate, allowing her father's car to make its way to the mansion.

Joanna swallowed hard; her mouth went dry. She tried to catch a glimpse of the grounds, but the fogged windows and the hard rain blurred the world outside. She wiped her hand on the cold glass to clear the view. To the right of the house sat a flower garden, surrounded by an iron fence. A huge magnolia adorned the left side of the lawn.

As they ascended the front steps to the main entrance, Joanna shook. She looked at the foreboding structure. Just then a loud clap of thunder spooked her into envisioning herself entering a true-life Vincent Price film, complete with a hungry monster disguised as this evil castle.

Harris used the brass lion-head knocker. A short, round nun with a large nose and buggy eyes admitted them. She resembled a blackbird. Harris began to introduce himself, but the nun stopped him.

"Names aren't necessary. The director is expecting you. Please, follow me."

Joanna gawked at the opulent entry hallway and ornate three-story curved staircase. The mahogany railing led her eyes to the domed ceiling with a painted scene of hovering angels, disapproving looks on their artificial faces. The dark wood sucked the light out of the space, except for the windows at the top, illuminating those angry cherubs. Harris and Joanna followed the crowlike nun into an elegant parlor.

"Please, make yourselves comfortable," she instructed, then vanished to the hallway.

Apprehensive, her father removed his hat and chose to sit on the French-style sofa. Joanna stood close to the doorway and surveyed her environment. A shiny baby grand piano occupied a corner of the room. Crowded bookshelves lined one wall. Heavy forest-green velvet drapes framed the windows of a comfortable bay-shaped sitting area. Thick lace panels muted what little daylight the storm clouds allowed.

Joanna stared at the flames dancing warmly in the large fireplace. Her eyes landed on the life-sized oil painting of a woman above the mantel. She assumed it was Frances Weston. The stately woman held a Bible close to her breast, a cross hung around her neck. Sternness permanently expressed on her face. A chill ran through Joanna.

Harris whispered, "This is like a dadgum palace. TV, radio, hundreds of books. You'd think they're applaudin' your behavior."

The round nun reappeared, "Follow me, please."

The administrator, Mrs. Fitch, sat behind her desk. Joanna and her father were ushered to uncomfortable wooden chairs. To Joanna, the room typified a principal's office.

The woman in charge stated, "I took the liberty of completing the paperwork when we spoke on the phone." She donned her reading glasses and quickly scanned the file. "I've got a couple of questions… let's see. Ah, yes, do you have her school transcripts?"

Joanna passed her the forms from Cohn High School. Without inspection, the administrator shuffled them to the bottom of Joanna's folder. She read the prepared information, verifying it without requiring confirmation. "From Lynchburg; seventeen; no known allergies or chronic health conditions." She checked each off as she followed the list.

Harris cleared his throat. "Is there anythin' I need to sign? How long is this gonna take?"

"Just a few more things." The woman turned to Joanna. "Have you had the chicken pox?"

"Yes, ma'am," Joanna answered.

"Okay." She checked off. "Next is the matter of the fee."

Harris recalled, "You mentioned somethin' 'bout receivin' wages, if we're a little short?"

"Yes, by doing extra chores. We understand the financial difficulties associated with your daughter's predicament. Let me show you a breakdown of the charges. Normally, girls are in residence seventy-eight days; Joanna's stay will be longer."

The woman went over everything, starting with the enrollment fee, per-day costs for food, lodging, nursery care, postpartum care for the mother, and counseling. Her father tightened when she continued with the prices for uniforms and high school classes. Harris didn't care about any of this; he wanted to leave and became more rigid with every word.

Mrs. Fitch droned on. "We give full attention to mind, body, and spirit. Plus, we help our girls rebuild their lives with scholarships to trade schools. Many of these unfortunate young women simply need direction; we provide that here." She finished the financials with the charges for foster care for the infant and legal services.

"What if I… I mean, a mother decided to keep her baby?" Joanna found her voice for the first time. Harris shot her a warning glare. "For instance," Joanna clarified.

Harris slid the envelope to the administrator. She counted and frowned. She answered Joanna. "There's additional fees for non-surrender. The government subsidizes the cost starting after the twenty-eighth week, but only if the baby is surrendered. If you truly care about your child, you'll do the right thing. A single mother, foolish enough to raise a bastard, subjects it to a life of poverty and ridicule. Our adoption rate is over ninety-five percent." Joanna felt dizzy. She prayed for it to pass.

Harris justified the payment deficit: "That's all we could scrape up."

"You know, young lady, you should be grateful your father was able to do this much. Many girls are disowned by their families and abandoned by the father of their unwanted baby, forcing them to rely on our generosity." Joanna seethed with the urge to disclose the true source of the cash and the bills in her father's pocket, but fear won out.

Mrs. Fitch turned her attention to Harris, instructing him to sign the forms and pass them to his daughter. Joanna read the first paragraph and Harris snapped, "Just sign 'em!" She absently signed each line where indicated. Her ears were buzzing.

"When you want to visit, please call first. We can arrange a private time."

"No one'll be visitin'," Harris groused rudely.

"So be it. I'll give you a moment to say goodbye." Mrs. Fitch exited the office. A menacing frown accompanied the last look Harris gave Joanna.

She wanted to beg, *Please don't leave me here, Daddy!* But she knew it would prove pointless.

Finally, he put on his hat and without a word walked out of the room, leaving her to face her punishment alone.

Chapter 8

Mrs. Fitch returned to the office. Repositioned behind her desk, she listed the house rules. "None of our ladies use their actual names here. Anonymity makes it less likely anyone will expose your dirty secret outside these walls. Hmm…" The woman studied Joanna. "We'll call you Jean W." Joanna hated the name Jean.

"Divulging the identity of your family or the birthfather to anyone is forbidden. No one wants to know who you are; don't pry into their business. Absolutely no contact with the birthfather is allowed; no phone calls, visits, or mail. Is that clear?"

Joanna's heart skipped a beat. How'd she survive if denied communication with Jack? Mrs. Fitch's expression turned inflexible. "If he cared about you or his child, you'd be married." Joanna wanted to refute her inaccurate assumptions, but the thin tyrant continued.

"Everyone is expected to contribute to the upkeep of our home. You'll be on the kitchen breakfast shift every morning, where Sister Mary Joseph's in charge. To eliminate your tuition balance, you'll work in the laundry on Tuesday evenings High school classes begin at eight thirty a.m. and go until lunchtime on week-days. In the afternoon you'll be in the garment area. Do you know how to sew?"

"Yes, ma'am," Joanna answered. Irene had taught her young.

"The clothing produced is sold to help finance the maintenance of our home, as well as contribute to your vocational training. Dinner is at six p.m. You're to eat well and take proper care of yourself. Evenings are considered free time. You may work on school assignments or enjoy the parlor. The side door is unlocked and leads to the flower garden, which is a favorite spot during pleasant weather. The other doors and gates remain locked. No one is permitted to leave the garden. The property walls and main gate are off limits.

"Lights-out is at nine p.m. Saturdays are different. After breakfast, you'll have group counseling sessions, as well as an individual session every other week. Our medical doctor also gives exams. In the afternoon, you'll work in the garment area.

"On Sundays, except for Mass and essential chores such as meals, you can do as you please. Private family visits are conducted in the parlor, so it's off limits unless you have a prescheduled guest. That's the only area where visitors are allowed, and time is limited to thirty minutes." Joanna half listened as Mrs. Fitch continued to babble on. Finally, the administrator came to a subject piquing Joanna's attention.

"When you mercifully go into labor, you'll go to the hospital wing. Our doctor lives close and delivers all our babies. The nuns are trained practical nurses. Babies remain in the nursery for three to five days and then are placed in foster care while final adoptions arranged. You'll stay in the hospital wing for one week. Once released, many of our girls attend trade school. Our protection makes it possible to start again, as if nothing ever happened. Do you understand the rules?" she asked in conclusion.

Joanna nodded.

"We run a tight ship here. Any young lady who breaks the rules or is disruptive will be transferred to a more stringent facility in one of our affiliate homes. You must understand, we truly want to help you and give you direction. You seem like a smart girl; I'm sure you only want what is best for your baby." Signaling for Joanna to follow, Mrs. Fitch crossed the room and opened the door, startling an eavesdropping nun. The administrator frowned.

"This is Jean, Sister Ruth. Please get her settled."

The fat nun led her to the parlor, where another young lady perched on the sofa. "Wait here," the nun instructed coldly and left the girls alone.

Joanna took a place next to the girl, who attempted to hide her face with her blond curly hair. Joanna decided this little lost soul couldn't be older than thirteen.

"What's your name?" Joanna asked her.

"They told me I'm Missy now," the girl whispered.

"I'm Jean. Did you just get here?" The girl nodded. "Are you scared?" Joanna asked.

"Yes." Missy looked her in the eyes for the first time. "Are you?"

Joanna tried not to swallow hard as she lied, "No, it'll be fine, you'll see."

Within minutes, the nun returned and led the girls up the curved mahogany staircase where the painted ceiling angels scowled at them. Sister Ruth directed them to a hallway on the second floor, then to the third door on the left. Inside, a large room housed six single white iron beds. The heads of each were against the wall with windows, nightstands in between. Joanna picked the bunk next to the one decorated with a pink, stuffed, carnival-prize dog. Missy put her suitcase on the lonely bed on the far left, closest to Joanna's. Then the nun took them to a shower room, made them strip, and vigorously scrubbed them with lye soap. Humiliated, Joanna struggled to cover her girl parts to no avail.

Back in the dorm room, Sister Ruth presented them each with three prison-gray uniforms and commanded in a condescending tone, "Put this on. Laundry is collected every other day. This is an institution, not a country club." The inmates pulled on the hideous smock uniforms.

"Your clothes and personal items go in the cabinet directly opposite your bed. You're excused from the garment area today. Use this time to get settled." The nun stiffly exited the room.

Joanna buttoned the last button of the smock dress. Missy sat on her bed. Her large blue eyes held the expression of a frightened fawn. Joanna opened her cabinet and unpacked, stacking her clothing neatly on the shelves and storing the stationery from her mother on the eye-level shelf next to Jack's music box. She glanced over at her roommate. The girl hadn't moved.

"You want some help puttin' your things away?" Joanna asked.

Missy shrugged.

Joanna opened the girl's cabinet. Silently, they put away her clothes. At the bottom of the suitcase were a stuffed animal and a diary. Missy quickly closed her luggage.

"Did you bring a friend with you?" Joanna smiled hoping to reassure the younger girl.

"Everyone'll think I'm a baby."

"Who cares what anyone else thinks? Let me see." Missy opened the lid a crack and retrieved a stuffed lamb, tattered from too much love.

"What's its name?" Joanna asked.

"Floyd. My grandma made him for me when I was little."

"Do you sleep with him?" Missy nodded. "I think he's sweet. Put him under your pillow. No one's gonna make fun of you. I won't let them." Masking her own anxiety, Joanna suddenly felt protective of this petrified child. Missy hid her comfort toy under her pillow. Abruptly, a bubbly blond-haired girl bounced into the room.

"Hi, we're roomin' together, I'm Rachel."

"I'm Jean, this is Missy."

"If you're ready, I'm supposed to take y'all to Doc Miller, and then you've got appointments with Mrs. Lewis. She's the social worker."

"What does she do?" Joanna asked.

"Asks lots of personal questions, lectures too much, and makes ya feel awful about being here. If ya nod occasionally, she thinks you're listenin' to her." Rachel giggled.

Chapter 9

Joanna waited in the outer office of the clinic. Missy opted to go in for her exam first. After twenty minutes, the door opened and they traded places. Dr. Miller gave her a thorough exam. With her legs in the cold metal stirrups, her face hot, she cringed through this latest violation.

Joanna hated the session with Mrs. Lewis, the counselor, more than her physical exam. Fortunately, the psychologist kept it short. She questioned Joanna regarding her siblings and mother, and finally her father.

"I hate my father; he's a drunk." Joanna hoped her angry tone would end the questions.

"Perhaps you got pregnant to punish him." The counselor's cold blue eyes stared at her through the distorted lenses of her black-framed cat's-eye glasses. Joanna let out a hmph of disgust. "We'll explore that in our next session," Mrs. Lewis stated, ending the meeting.

Rachel escorted them to dinner, giving a tour of their new home along the way. She explained that the three-story U-shaped mansion had been the personal home of Mrs. Frances Weston until her death. In accordance with her will, the house became a refuge for women in need of rehabilitation. Under her son's leadership, the charity expanded to six other homes.

Rachel led them to the other side of the building, on the first floor. They stopped to look through the windowed door of the garment room. "Fifteen of us do the sewin' of the garments. Ten other girls manage the paperwork and purchasin'."

By dinnertime Joanna had received a significant education on the institution she shared with thirty other girls who ranged in age from thirteen to early twenties.

As they entered the dining hall, a line of gray-clad young women moved slowly through the cafeteria-style food service, each taking her tray to a spot at the eight-foot tables. Joanna and Missy joined the procession behind Rachel. A chunky nun behind a counter scrutinized Joanna and passed her a plate of food twice the portion she'd eat at home.

Rachel touted, "The food's the best. Sister Mary Joseph's puts my grandma's to shame." Two girls joined their table directly across from Joanna and Rachel.

"I see our new partners in crime have arrived," the red-haired girl joked.

"Ladies, this is Jean and Missy," Rachel announced.

The brown-haired girl spoke: "I'm Michelle." By the size of her belly, she was full-term.

"Jessie," the redhead said, smiling. "I think Fitch-the-bitch wanted to call me Jezebel but settled on Jessie James instead." All the girls laughed, except for the new arrivals, who weren't privy to the private joke. Missy looked at Joanna for moral support.

"Y'all will be part of our team on the breakfast shift," Jessie explained.

"You gonna eat your roll?" Rachel asked Jessie.

"No, take it, please. I've no intention of gainin' more than fifteen pounds."

"So did Rachel give y'all the nickel tour?" Michelle asked.

Joanna nodded. "But... where do they keep the babies?"

"Above the parlor, on the third floor. But you won't see the hospital wing until you're in labor." Rachel spoke quickly.

In a muffled tone, Jessie explained, "You can only get there by the set of stairs behind Fitch's office or the service elevator."

"I didn't see an elevator," Joanna challenged.

"It's behind the doors to the right of the main stairway. On the third floor, it opens right next to Fitch's apartment."

"You've been in there?" Joanna raised her brows.

"We don't call her an outlaw for nothin'." Michelle tousled Jessie's hair.

"I call it the vulture's nest; she can see most of the grounds from her windows. I wouldn't attempt a stroll by the front fence here."

"Jessie was in one of the other homes. She got caught smuggling in contraband," Michelle explained.

"The other place was nicer. We'd go to the movies or shoppin' on Sunday afternoons. They gave us weddin' rings to wear when we went out. Had I known Fitch'd have this place secured like Alcatraz, I wouldn't've gotten kicked out of the last one."

After dinner, Joanna and Missy made their way to the parlor in the hope of watching TV. They found Jessie at the baby grand piano playing "Unchained Melody" so beautifully, she sounded like a pro. When Jessie finished, they clapped.

"My word, Jessie!" Joanna exclaimed. "You're amazing!"

"What kind of music do you like? I take requests. How 'bout a little Patti Page?" Jessie asked as she played "Doggie in the Window."

"Do you know any Elvis songs?" Missy asked. Without sheet music or missing a beat, Jessie switched to "Love Me Tender." The younger girl's face broadened with a big smile. For fun, Jessie broke into a jazz rift; the girls tapped their feet.

Mrs. Fitch's stern voice barked over the music. "Jessie! I won't tell you again! I don't allow Negro music here!" Immediately Jessie changed to the old Bible Belt classic "Amazing Grace." The matron stormed out, seconds later, slamming her office door. The three girls snickered.

"You must've taken lessons for years," Joanna assumed.

"I never took a formal lesson in my life. I learned from some great musicians. I started playin' when I was five. I can read sheet music but I mostly play by ear."

"You should play in a band," Missy suggested.

"I do. I mean, I did. But I'm sure I won't be in that band again, since the guy who got me in trouble's the lead singer. No, I'm goin' to Nashville. Two things are sure: I ain't goin' home and I refuse to go to one of Fitch's trade schools."

"I thought we weren't supposed to tell anythin' about ourselves," Joanna whispered.

"We aren't supposed to tell our true identity or hometown. We have to talk about somethin'." Jessie closed the lid to the piano and announced, "I've got to pee!"

Joanna inspected the bookshelves and chose *The Nun's Story* by Kathryn Hulme. No surprise, *Peyton Place* wasn't among the selection. Missy and Joanna spent the rest of the evening watching TV. The Wilsons couldn't afford a television; Missy's family must've owned one, because she listed her favorite series. As Jack Benny's show came on, other residents gathered. Some took seats on the couches; a few sat on the floor. Captured by the program, for thirty minutes the Frances Weston Home for girls didn't seem quite so bad.

Chapter 10

Sunday morning, Catherine began the day with purpose. She and Jack would attend church services with her parents, then pay a visit to the cemetery before joining the Langleys at the country club. While she put on her long-sleeved Paul Parnes suit, which hid her scars, she repeated over and over, "I can do this."

Catherine looked at herself in the mirror. She could almost recognize the slightly older, frail, but courageous woman who stared back. She was encouraged by her recent epiphany: At twenty-eight, she enjoyed a life expectancy of another fifty or sixty years; she controlled her future happiness.

After breakfast, Catherine withdrew to the garden and cut a fragrant bouquet of roses; she wrapped them in a damp cloth and newspaper. It was autumn, and this would be the last of the roses. *How appropriate to put these on Daniel's grave.*

Church was the usual spectacle of those in society who came to be seen; the Methodist minister's sermon was much like those she'd heard growing up in this church. Later Catherine escaped, relieved no one asked her how she'd enjoyed the service, because her attention hadn't been on the preacher but on gracefully surviving the day. She'd gotten away with only a few in the flock stopping her to chat.

Jack started the car. Anticipating his question, Cat answered, "Yes, I'm sure I want to go to the cemetery." She turned her gaze out the open car window. The trees looked as if an artist had painted them in oils, selecting the most radiant frost-kissed hues. Catherine breathed in the smell of burning leaves.

Her stomach flip-flopped as they pulled into the cemetery. Jack drove slowly around the curve of the manicured lawns dotted with headstones. Fresh flowers honored many of the graves. Jack eased the car to a stop and came around, opening the door for her.

Taking the roses from the backseat, she touched her husband's hand. "Give me a minute by myself, okay?" Jack nodded. He lit a cigarette and leaned against the car, watching her walk alone to the only headstone in her family's plot that bore the name WYATT. At her little boy's grave, her chest hurt as if it might explode. A trail of tears streamed to her chin.

"My dear, dear Danny, I'm so sorry," she whispered as she knelt, putting the flowers in the vase of his stone marker. Rainwater overflowed with the addition of the <u>bouquet</u>.

"I've grieved so long and so deeply for you. You'll always be in my heart, but I have to make room for other loves. I promise, if I get the chance to be a mom, I'll be the best mother, and you can look down and be proud of me." Cat stood slowly as Jack approached. She wiped away her tears and turned to smile at him. Crossing her arms, she bit her lip.

Jack, looking at the child's grave asked, "Are you going to be okay?"

"Yes. No more falling apart. I promise." Cat put her arms around him. "It's time we forgive ourselves for what happened to him. Letting it eat us up only produces misery."

"It's time to move on," he finally agreed in a hoarse voice.

In Knoxville, Joanna joined her roommates for kitchen duty. "Jean, this is Karen." Rachel introduced a short, brown-haired girl.

Jessie joined in whispering, "See the older chick, gettin' out the dishes? That's Gloria. She's Karen's roommate."

"She keeps to herself." Karen elaborated. "She works all day in Fitch's office. I'll bet that's how she's payin' her way. She infuriates Mrs. Lewis by skippin' group counselin'."

Abruptly, Sister Mary Joseph burst into the room. "All right, ladies, enough chitchat." The girls dispersed and attended their assigned jobs. Jessie poured glasses of milk and juice. Karen filled utensil bins for the cafeteria line.

The heavyset sister waddled across the room and tasked Joanna and Missy to make eighty pieces of toast. She pointed at the counter with four toasters, next to a crate containing loaves of bread. The nun set sticks of butter in front of the toasters. "One of you toasts, the other butters. Count as you go. Toast goes in the metal pan, then to the food line." With the directions complete, the nun trudged to the six-burner stove where Michelle poured scrambled eggs into a heated pan. The girls worked in complete silence, as they did whenever nuns were present.

When they took places to eat, Jessie introduced Nancy, a petite, brown-haired girl with a heart-shaped mouth, who complained, "I hate Sundays, especially Mass."

Jessie agreed, "Mass is bullshit."

"Watch your language, Jessie," an elderly nun barked from three tables away.

"Sister Eugenia," Rachel whispered. "She has the hearin' of a cat! She runs the hospital wing."

Michelle scooted her chair out and struggled to raise her swollen body to stand.

"Are you done?" Karen asked her.

"Everythin' gives me heartburn. I wish this baby'd come already."

"What did Dr. Miller say yesterday?" Jessie passed her toast to Rachel.

"It could be anytime. He's been sayin' that for the last two weeks."

After they completed the kitchen cleaning chores, they attended a mandatory Mass conducted by Father Dominick, an old, partially blind, and most certainly deaf priest. Joanna agonized with the uncomfortable guilt that always accompanied Mass for her.

She studied the solemn faces of those around her. Rachel sat next to her, picking at a loose thread of her smock. Like a fragile porcelain doll, Missy sat perfectly still. In the pew directly in front of her, the irreverent Michelle and Jessie passed notes back and forth.

Class and station in life bore no status in this place; shunned by -society and their families, they were all here for the same reason. So many different faces, yet they were, in many ways, the same. To some, Mass was a choreographed ritual with no meaning or significance; for Joanna, it forced introspection and brought relief when it ended.

The girls filed out of the chapel, taking different directions. Joanna followed her roommates out the side door to a portico with patio chairs. A dying flower garden sprawled at the bottom of the stairs. Jessie pulled a pack of cigarettes from her pocket and lit one. She passed the pack around. Joanna and Missy declined. Karen puffed on the cigarette and coughed, betraying she didn't have a smoking habit.

Michelle waddled out, plopped into a chair, and rested her swollen feet on an unoccupied chair. "This's where you'll find me this afternoon."

"My mama and little sister are comin' to visit at two o'clock. I'd rather Fitch stick bamboo shoots under my fingernails," Rachel announced.

"Bless your heart," Michelle soothed sincerely. Turning to the new girls, she explained, "Rachel's mama told everyone she went to a TB sanatorium."

"My poor sister's gonna grow up believin' TB makes your belly swell."

"My mama's tellin' everyone I'm workin' as a nanny," Michelle chuckled.

"That's funny, because my parents are usin' the excuse I went to my auntie's house to help with her children," Karen said. "What about you, Jean, what story are your folks spreadin' about your disappearance?"

Joanna couldn't adjust to being called Jean. "I don't reckon I know exactly. Mama told the school I'm bein' transferred to a private Catholic high school."

"Not far from the truth," Michelle commented.

"I've got y'all beat," Jessie boasted. "My mama's lie is: I'm in a mental institution. Can you believe it? She'd rather people think I'm a lunatic than pregnant!"

"That's disgraceful," Karen observed.

"I'll never see my mother again. She can go to her grave with this between us!"

Back in Nashville, Mary Atherton stretched and looked at her bedside clock. Her mother had let her sleep past noon. The girl propped on her pillows and smiled as she focused on her blue taffeta dress hanging on the back of her closet door. On the dresser she spotted the tiara she'd worn last night as homecoming queen. The Cohn High Tigers had trounced their opponents in one of the muddiest, most exciting games ever. Mary and her friends had cheered until voiceless.

Mary rolled over and hugged her pillow. She smiled, remembering her boyfriend Tony, their star quarterback, being hoisted by his teammates and carried off the field at the end of the game. Later, Mary and Tony stood side by side as homecoming queen and king.

Mary slid from her bed, grabbed her crown, and swiped the dress from its hanger. She put the crown on her disheveled hair and held the dress as if she were wearing it. She closed her eyes. Pulling her arms tight around her, she swayed, remembering how it felt as she and Tony danced. They'd planned their future: He would attend Mississippi State on a football scholarship, and she'd enroll in nursing school. Tony would go pro and they'd get married.

Light-headed, Mary opened her eyes. She straightened herself upright and looked at her reflection in the mirror. Her crown lay crooked on her head and her hair looked more like a rat's nest than the updo she'd worn last night. Her mother was right: She'd gained weight. Her breasts ached. She attributed that to Tony being too enthusiastic when they'd made love in his car after the dance. Mary pulled off her nightgown and examined herself naked in front of the mirror. Her breasts were much fuller than they had been in the summer, and for the first time in her life she displayed a little pooch of a belly. Was this all part of growing up?

Mary's irregular cycle made no sense, so she didn't keep track. She turned on the shower in the private bathroom adjacent to her bedroom. She hashed over the possibility of pregnancy, dismissing it as she put her head under the hot spray of the shower and inhaled the steam cloud around her.

Chapter 11

Joanna soaked up the warm sunshine on the portico while her fingers worked Missy's curly hair into a braid. Each woven tassel enhanced the young girl's precious childlike facial features.

"You're tellin' me you weren't in love?" Rachel posed the question to Michelle.

"No, I didn't love him." Michelle's wave implied that the notion was ridiculous.

"Then why were you doin' the dirty with him?"

"If you could see his body, you'd know. He's a cop, lived next door. Mama explained the female facts of life to me, but nothin' 'bout guys. Curiosity won out." Michelle licked her lips as if remembering last night's dessert.

Rachel confessed, "My mama told me never to let a boy touch me or I'd get pregnant. I figured once I'd let Sam go to third base, I was already in trouble. Boy, was I dumb."

"It ain't the touchin', honey," Jessie put in.

Michelle continued, "I don't know why I didn't think I'd get pregnant. I guess I thought that happened to other people, not me. He offered to get me an abortion, but that's too risky; I've heard horror stories of girls dyin'! He made me promise not to tell he was the father. If I did, he said he'd deny it and lie 'bout different guys being over and I'd be labeled a slut." Michelle furrowed her brow.

"What'd you tell your parents?" Rachel asked, horrified.

"My dad split when I was seven, so it's just me and Mama. Kevin, the cop, told me to invent a rape story; he knows all the angles. By then I was three months gone. Mama doesn't blame me for this mess. When I go home it'll be like nothin' ever happened." Michelle was glib.

"I was raped, sort of," Nancy revealed.

"What do you mean, *sort of?*" Rachel asked.

"I mean I didn't resist." The girl became flustered trying to explain herself. "I was staying at my best friend Colleen's house 'cause my parents went on a trip. Her dad… a big-shot lawyer, he told me not to tell. He said no one'd believe me. He was right. Nobody did."

"Did you tell your parents it was Colleen's father?" Joanna asked with sympathy.

"Yeah, but not till after my mom took me to the doctor and found out I was pregnant. You wanna know the truth?" Nancy's voice cracked with emotion, "If I wasn't pregnant, I would've kept the whole thing a secret. I was so humiliated."

"Bless your heart," Michelle cooed, looking sadly at Nancy.

Jessie spoke sincerely. "I think friends of the family messin' with kids happens a lot more than people talk about. Ya think ya were humiliated tellin' your parents what happened. Imagine how awful it'd be to testify in a statutory rape case, as the victim."

"That's what Daddy called it, statutory rape." Nancy clapped her hands together, grateful Jessie had reminded her of the exact term.

"How do you know legal stuff?" Michelle acted astonished.

"I can read. I read all kinds of trivial crap that interests me. I think I picked it up in a law journal in my parole officer's waitin' room."

All the girls stared at her with open mouths. Jessie laughed hysterically. "All y'all are too gullible. That's a joke!" She wiped tears formed from laughing. The others laughed with her.

"What 'bout you, Jean?" Rachel asked Joanna.

"My situation's so different. Jack and I are gettin' married. We're keepin' our baby."

Michelle raised her eyebrows. "You're pretty sure; Karen says the same thing."

"You don't believe me!" Joanna crossed her arms, pouting.

"My boyfriend's in college. As soon as he graduates we're gettin' married."

"I think if the fathers were serious, y'all would be married by now. It sounds like pipe dreams to me," Michelle challenged. Karen scowled. Michelle continued, "I'm not tryin' to be mean. I think ya should face reality, that's all."

"Ya don't know anythin' about me," Joanna countered hotly, "and ya sure don't know a thing about Jack. He keeps his promises. Once he's divorced, he'll be with me and our baby."

"He's married." Michelle nodded. "I rest my case."

"His wife's sick. It's complicated." Joanna sensed their disbelief and quit talking.

She rose from her chair to go inside, convinced she had nothing in common with these girls.

"Hey, don't go away mad," Michelle called after her. Joanna kept walking.

Jessie remarked, "Let her be; she'll reach the truth of it on her own. Everyone does."

Joanna ran to the dorm room where she burrowed into her bed, hugged her pillow, and cried. Aching with homesickness, she recalled when she, her brothers, and Mama had lived with Granny. Life was calm on the farm, and Irene had been a young, fun-loving parent.

She closed her eyes, remembering the sweet smell of grass and how magnificent the sky looked, littered with stars on those warm, rural nights. There were creeks to play in and trees to climb. Mama had a contagious laugh.

Fuzzy-headed, Joanna thought of her granny. What a strange bird she'd been. Uncle Henry said she got kicked in the head by a horse. Mama claimed it happened when Granddaddy beat her with a shovel.

Without full consciousness of her current surroundings, Joanna drifted off to sleep and passed into the realm of a disturbing dream. Images of Mama twirling her like a ballerina in Granny's kitchen. Harris calling her a slut; Mama crying, holding an empty blanket. She tossed and turned when in her nightmare Granny, rocking in her time-worn rocking chair, announced, "That girl's got a baby inside her."

Joanna jolted awake in a cold sweat, frozen, haunted by the realistic sensation of the nightmare. She blinked, adjusting to the dim light of the room. She focused on a shadow outline of Missy on the next bed, curled in the fetal position.

"I hope I didn't wake you," the young girl apologized.

"No, you didn't," Joanna said to alleviate the girl's guilt.

"I think it's sweet your baby's father wants to marry you."

"Jack's real special. What about you? Who's your baby's father?"

"I don't know. I don't remember." Missy's eyes filled with tears. Joanna pushed the covers aside and instinctively embraced her.

"You mean like amnesia or somethin'?"

Missy nodded. "The doctor told Daddy something bad happened and I blocked it out. He made it sound like I was a crazy person."

Joanna stroked Missy's head as she sobbed. "Don't cry. Let's talk about something else. You like music, right?" Joanna asked.

"Yes." Missy dried her eyes on her sleeve.

"Look what I have." Joanna switched on the bedside light. She retrieved Jack's music box, wound it, and opened the lid. Joanna watched Missy's frown lines grow into a smile. Then she snapped the lid shut, startled by the silhouette of a nun standing in the darkened hallway.

"I didn't mean to interrupt." The delicate voice came closer. A young nun continued, "Hello, girls, I'm Sister Bridget. All residents on this hallway are under my charge, so if you need anything, you come to me. Okay?"

"Yes, Sister," Joanna answered, thinking how she didn't fit among the dried-up old hags.

"I'm sorry I wasn't here when you arrived. Are you settling in?"

"Yes, Sister." Joanna hoped the nun would leave.

Rachel stepped into the room and plunked on Missy's bed. "Hi, Sister Bridget."

"Hello, Rachel. How was your visit with your mother?" the nun asked cheerfully.

"Awful and my dad won't visit, he's too humiliated."

"I'm so sorry," Sister Bridget sympathized. "Let's go to dinner. It's your favorite, pot roast."

When lights-out arrived, Joanna listened to the creaking of the old house, wide-awake in the darkness. Crushed by overwhelming loneliness, she longed for the warmth of her mother's hug. Joanna's sorrow over Irene's affectionless goodbye yesterday brought misty tears; she was certain their long separation would destroy any chance to rebuild a strong mother–daughter bond. Somewhere, from a distant corridor, came the heartbreak of someone weeping; their hurt made her grief abysmal. She escaped by pulling the pillow over her head.

Chapter 12

The next day held many revelations for Joanna as the normal routine unfolded. During their assigned kitchen duty, Joanna pulled Jessie aside and inquired, "If someone wants to get a letter to their baby's father, how do they do it?"

"Now, why'd ya think I'd know?" she asked, wearing a catlike smile. "Karen can help ya. Follow me." The three girls exited through an unlocked back door.

"Why're we out here?" Joanna shivered in the predawn chill.

"We're waitin' on the milkman," Karen explained. "He comes on Mondays and Thursdays. He delivers all the dairy products." Karen continued in a whisper, the warmth of her breath hanging in the air like a cloud. "He also sneaks in letters from birthfathers, cigarettes, booze, anythin' we want, for a price, of course. If ya wanna write a letter to your honey, he'll mail it for you. Fitch goes through the outgoing mail so you can't send it that way. Rodney, our favorite neighborhood milkman, gets 'round the problem."

"How much does it cost?" No matter the charge, Joanna's first free moment she'd write to Jack.

"It depends on what ya want. If ya send or receive a letter, it's fifty cents. If ya want him to buy somethin' they don't allow, it's the price of the item plus thirty percent."

"A stamp only costs three cents," Joanna complained. "That's highway robbery."

Jessie took a drag off a cigarette. "It's the only way to get anythin' in or outta here."

Joanna hugged herself for warmth as the glow of vehicle headlights bounced on the side of the building. The dairy truck pulled to a stop at the loading dock.

"I'm gonna let y'all get this. I'm freezing." Jessie flicked her cigarette and hurried inside.

"Hey, Karen," the young driver greeted. "Who's the new kid?"

"This is Jean, she's cool."

"I've got five letters and smokes for Jessie. Y'all got the dough?"

Karen dug in her smock pocket and passed him a wad of bills bundled with a stack of letters. He counted the money quickly and handed her the bounty. She tucked the letters in her pocket and the cigarettes under her billowing top. "Thanks, Rod, you're a dream come true," she flirted.

"If you'd stop playin' hard to get, I'd show ya," the skinny kid retorted. He piled the delivery crates on a handcart while Karen checked off the order against the invoice. Rodney pushed the goods up the ramp into the warm, humid kitchen.

When Sister Mary Joseph was distracted at the stove, Karen passed the cigarettes to Jessie. The redhead made a dash for the door, using the excuse never questioned in a maternity home: "I've gotta pee!"

Joanna observed Karen nod to five of the girls in the food line and discreetly hand them napkins containing letters.

On the way to the high school classroom, Joanna linked arms with Karen. Leaning in, she whispered, "You look sad."

Karen reported in a hushed voice, "I haven't had a letter from Stephen in a month."

In the schoolroom, Joanna counted the chairs with bodies in them, twenty-two. They clustered in the defined cliques she'd witnessed in the cafeteria. She and Missy followed their group to the back of the room. Chattering voices filled the air until a man in disheveled clothing appeared. Chairs scraped the floor, students settled, and the room fell silent.

The teacher shoved his black-framed glasses up his greasy nose and smoothed his uncombed hair. Mr. Ehrlichman stepped to the blackboard to write the names of the characters from *Canterbury Tales*. He sat at his desk and in a theatrical voice told everyone to open their literature book to page seventy-five. Obediently the books were dispatched. Deceptively, many of the girls slid paperback novels, or a *True Confessions* magazine, on top of the textbook pages. Some silently wrote notes back and forth. With steady articulation and emphasis in the proper places he proceeded to read Chaucer's epic work to the class. Rachel leaned across the aisle to Karen and Joanna: "I swear, he loves the sound of his own voice."

Karen sat back and breathed a distressed sigh. Rachel caught her vibe immediately and commiserated, "It's so unfair, how they get to go on with their lives and we're stuck in here."

"It's like he forgot all his promises!" Karen pouted.

Ehrlichman slapped a ruler hard on the desk, jarring their attention back to the teacher. "There'll be no talking in this class, or you'll fail." He emphasized his meaning by angrily screeching the chalk across the blackboard in the form of a math equation. "Here's your arithmetic lesson for today. Those of you who're new, pay attention." His voice held a nervous quiver. "*Come to class* plus *be quiet in class* equals *your high school diploma*." The man returned to his squeaky, wooden swivel chair and resumed reading where he'd left off.

Joanna laid her head on the desk and closed her eyes. She focused on Ehrlichman's soothing voice as if she were lounging on the floor with Eddie, listening to the radio at Granny's. Mystery theater programs were her favorite. This teacher possessed the same power to transport her mind's eye to an English tavern. She was disappointed when Mr. Ehrlichman abruptly stopped reading and wrote homework assignments on the board. Joanna ripped a piece of paper from her notebook and feverously copied the teacher's instructions.

Jessie gave Joanna a sympathetic simper. "Homework's bullshit. I turn in a blank piece of paper with my name on it. I have a 4.0 GPA. I'm Einstein. I'll have a diploma when I leave here, so who cares?"

Joanna's mouth dropped open as Rachel added, "It's not like medical school's in my future. The best I can hope for is a clerical job or bein' a beauty operator."

At the conclusion of the midday meal, the girls assigned to Sister Bridget made their way to the garment area. Huge south-facing windows provided abundant natural light. Eight-foot square tables occupied the left side of the room, while twenty industrial sewing machines were lined in rows to the right, with the shipping station at the back.

Rachel took a place at a heavy-duty machine, along with ten girls whose names Joanna didn't know. Jessie and several more workers attended to the fabric stacked on the cutting tables.

"Jean, do you know how to use a sewing machine?" the nun asked.

"Sure, we had one permanently in use in our living room."

"Good, let's put you on the machine closest to Jessie's cutting table; she can show you the process. Missy, Michelle will teach you how we get the garments shipped. The rest of you ladies, we need to get ten outfits completed per day to fill orders in time for the holidays. In four weeks, we have to start on the dresses for the fashion show in January."

"Fashion show?" Joanna asked.

"We put on a fashion show twice a year at the Peabody Hotel in Memphis. I was there last week, making the arrangements and buying the patterns for our spring and summer collection."

"Who are the models?" Joanna inquired.

"We hire them from an agency in Memphis."

"Wouldn't it be funny if we were the models?" Jessie proposed. Grabbing the front of the dress she'd been cutting out, she placed it over her belly and swished around pretending to be on the runway. All the women laughed, including Sister Bridget.

Michelle took Missy by the hand and led her to the finished garments. Joanna joined Jessie at the cutting table, and the redhead explained the pending orders.

"This party dress comes in four different colors. I cut them out according to the size and color ordered, and you sew it. Here's pattern instructions." She handed Joanna the printed directions, which contained illustrations for each step. "Keep the order form with the dress. When it's done, take it to Michelle and she'll ship it out."

"Sounds simple enough," Joanna stated. Accepting her first fabric puzzle, Joanna claimed the heavy-duty sewing machine next to Rachel, who concentrated on her work. Joanna studied her roommate's technique of gunning the machine down a seam and cutting the threads. Rachel flipped the garment over; she stitched the other seam with the skill of a textile factory worker. Joanna familiarized herself with the controls. The power of the device impressed her. The hum of the machines drowned out all other sounds, making the time pass quickly.

At four o'clock, Sister Bridget declared an end to the workday and praised everyone for their efforts, especially Joanna, who had nearly completed her first party dress. Joanna organized her work area and pinned the order form to the dress. She glanced at the name on the shipping label. She was taken aback when she read: MABEL ANDERSON, NASHVILLE, TENNESSEE—the same woman who paid her mother to make alterations. *Small world.* Her mind shifted with excitement; time to write to Jack. Sending a letter out on the next dairy express would establish her only means of communicating with him.

Chapter 13

As the days slipped by, Joanna adjusted to her current strict environment and her new roommates. During the time between dinner and lights-out, each one exhibited her own peculiar habits. Nightly, Jessie would strip to her bra and panties and slather her belly with excessive amounts of lotion, warding off dreaded stretch marks. Rachel often hogged the mirror brushing her hair one hundred strokes. Wetting her head, she'd then roll her damp locks around prickly curlers, which she slept in, rendering her ill-tempered in the morning. Typically, Rachel was disgruntled with her hairdo, considering the effort. Poor Missy suffered with nightmares and often slept with Joanna, seeking comfort.

Joanna continued to be astonished by the relationship the other girls shared with Sister Bridget. Many nights the youngest nun joined in their conversations. Sometimes she played Chinese checkers with Missy or poker with Jessie.

On one such occasion, the lights-out whistle sounded. Sister Bridget bade the girls good night. After a moment's hesitation, Joanna mustered her courage and followed her out into the hallway.

"Sister Bridget?" Joanna called, a decibel above a whisper.

Allowing Joanna to catch up, she whispered back, "What is it, Jean?"

"Can I talk to ya and we keep it between us?"

"Of course," the nun told her.

Placing her arm around Joanna's shoulder, she led the girl to the sparsely decorated corridor, which housed the nuns. The walls were painted a putrid shade of beige, and the polished tile froze Joanna's bare feet. At the far end of the hallway, in front of a twelve-foot stained-glass window, stood a life-sized statue of the Virgin Mary, her hands outstretched to those in need. Bridget made the sign of the cross to the mother of Jesus. Opening the heavy wooden door to her private room, she ushered Joanna in.

"You can speak freely; these walls are thick, which is a blessing. I'm told Sister Ruth snores like a buzz saw." The young nun smiled. Joanna smiled back, glancing around the generic room, void of personal effects. A single wooden bed with a gray blanket occupied one wall. A wooden desk and chair faced an open shelving unit and the sister's hanging habits. Sister Bridget invited Joanna to sit on the bed as she settled for the chair.

"What's on your mind?" Sister Bridget asked warmly.

"I'm worried 'bout Missy. She can't remember how she got pregnant. She's afraid of the dark and has awful nightmares."

"Poor little girl," Sister Bridget mourned compassionately, making Joanna instantly grateful she'd confided in her.

"Could we get her a flashlight? Maybe she'll feel safer."

"Absolutely." Digging through a box on the shelves, she retrieved a flashlight. When she tested the switch, the light sent out an iridescent glow. She turned it off and passed it to Joanna.

"It's selfless, the way you look after Missy."

"I can't help wantin' to protect her," Joanna explained. "I'm afraid her father raped her."

"It's possible, and difficult to prove without a credible witness. Incest cases rarely make it to court," Bridget informed her. "If we show Missy love, if she feels secure, maybe she'll remember and I can intercede."

Joanna nodded, appreciating the nun's honesty. "Sister, can I ask you somethin'?"

"Anything, what is it?"

"Why're ya so nice? The other nuns act like they're herdin' a house full of mangy cats."

Sister Bridget smiled. "Some attitudes are so ingrained, they're impossible to change."

"Their damnation of us is so stupid; if you think about it, the Virgin Mary was an unwed mother. If Joseph had called her a slut and treated her shamefully, he'd've missed the miracle."

Sister Bridget laughed. "I doubt the pope'll make that part of his Christmas Mass. But I get what you're saying and maybe there's the difference; I *do* see the miracle in every baby and birthmother. I know the standard rhetoric is that you're stained and forever condemned. But I don't believe that. My priority is to help you through this time with kindness, not cruelty. I'm certain Our Blessed Mother'd want it that way."

"I'm so glad I was put under your charge and not Sister Mary Joseph's." Joanna rose, as did Sister Bridget, and they came together in an embrace.

"You can always come to me," the nun assured her.

"Thank you," Joanna expressed sincerely.

Peeking out at the hallway, Sister Bridget signaled that the coast was clear. Joanna soundlessly tiptoed back to her room. She knelt by Missy's bed. The wide-eyed girl was curled in a ball, keeping watch for night terrors. Joanna slipped her the flashlight.

"Monsters are afraid of light," Joanna whispered. Missy smiled. Joanna climbed into her bed and watched Missy's covers glow as she tried out her new monster repellent.

A few nights later, a frustrated Rachel camped out in front of the mirror, attempting the easy-to-follow instruction for tomorrow's Lauren Bacall hairstyle. Nancy read a trashy tale from *True Confessions* magazine while Joanna brushed out the braids in Missy's hair.

"Rrrrrr," Rachel growled. A prickly curler hopelessly dangled at the bottom of a fuzzy knot in her hair. "I don't know why this has to be so complicated. I can't see the back of my head to know if I'm doin' it right."

"I'll roll it for you," Joanna offered.

"Would you?" Rachel pleaded.

"Sure." Joanna gave Missy the brush so she could rescue Rachel. She gently untangled the hair, retrieving the curler quickly.

"Wow, that didn't hurt at all. I was expectin' to lose a big chunk of hair."

"I used to roll my mama's hair all the time. When she had the twins, she had me cut it short." Joanna worked quickly on Rachel's curls while Jessie performed her nightly lotion ceremony. Michelle lumbered into the room.

"God, Jessie, I hate you!" Michelle joked.

"Why? What've I done this time?"

"Look at you! Not a mark on you." Michelle raised her nightgown, revealing the claw-scrape symmetry on her stretch-marked belly. "It's not fair! You've got a long waist. My rib bones almost rest on my hips with no room for a baby but out."

"I have four months to go. I might look worse than you in the end," Jessie consoled.

Joanna affixed the last roller to Rachel's head and told her, "Let me style it for ya in the mornin', I think I can make it look cute."

"Okay! Thanks, Jean."

Michelle continued her rant. "All this bull 'bout actin' like this never happened! How on earth can I explain these scars to a man who wants to marry me?"

"Say you used to be obese, and you lost the weight," Nancy suggested.

"I think I'd rather tell him the truth." Miserable, Michelle rubbed her bare swollen belly. "My skin's so tight right now I'm tempted to tell Dr. Miller to take a pin and pop it."

"Ewww, messy," Jessie japed. Giggling erupted in the room.

"I hate bein' pregnant! The end is the worst. Eatin' gives me heartburn; I have to pee all the time; my feet and hands are swollen. I'm so tired, but I can't sleep. When I lie down the baby acts like an octopus doin' cartwheels," Michelle complained.

"An octopus, ya say?" Joanna studied the girl's naked tummy. "Lie down over here." The uncomfortable girl waddled over to her bed, positioned flat on her back. Her flesh instantly shape-shifted, rolling with the motion of the infant inside her.

"May I?" Joanna asked permission to touch her belly.

"Razz my berries," Michelle told her. Joanna placed her hands on the girl and moved them around with the moving of the child.

"I think you're havin' twins," Joanna told her.

"No," Michelle gasped. "Dr. Miller hasn't mentioned twins."

"I don't trust anythin' Doc Miller says," Jessie began. "If he was a talented doctor, he'd work at a fancy city hospital, not deliverin' illegitimate babies in this shithole."

"When ya mentioned an octopus, it reminded me my mama said the same thin' and she had twins." Joanna continued to touch the girl's flesh. "Here, what's this feel like to you?"

Michelle rubbed her hand where Joanna indicated. "A foot."

"That's what I thought, too. Keep your hand there." Joanna felt the other side of her abdomen. The baby wiggled again, as if stretching.

"Wow, look," Jessie pointed out, standing next to Joanna. "You can see the outline of a little foot right here, and another there."

"Unless your baby has three feet, you're gonna have twins," Joanna concluded. "Well, isn't that peachy?" Michelle blurted, disgusted. "Now I get to relinquish two babies, not only one!" During her next visit with Dr. Miller, Michelle presented Joanna's theory. The doctor agreed it was possible, but he doubted it.

Back in Nashville, Mary Atherton lay prostrate on her bed, sobbing into her pillow. As a confidential favor, a doctor from her candy-striper job performed a pregnancy test for her. He confirmed her worst fears today: She was carrying a baby. Two weeks ago, homecoming queen; today a pregnant teenager. Tony swore he'd marry her.

She cried harder now; Daddy's little princess was going to fall off her pedestal and crush him. All his expectations began with her birth, and until now she'd accomplished the goals he set to win his praise.

His occupation as a banker enabled him to spoil her lavishly, when she met the tough standards he demanded. The summer trip to Europe, his promised graduation gift, vanished in the mist of her tears. Cohn High had never allowed a pregnant teen to walk its hallowed halls. Her father's grand agenda including nursing school would have to be put on hold.

Tony soothed her worries by vowing to be a great husband and dad. Drawing on his football experience, his pep talk convinced her: Together they'd juggle college courses, a baby, football, part-time jobs, and her educational goals. First they'd get both sets of parents together and tell them their plans.

With Thanksgiving only weeks away, Mary talked her mother into inviting Tony's family to their house to celebrate the holiday. It thrilled her mother to have the opportunity to put on airs for Tony's parents; granted, she was in the dark about the dubious reason for the get-together.

Mary blew her nose on a tissue. She couldn't sleep. She rehearsed the inadequate words to persuade her parents she and Tony were ready for this adult responsibility. Every scenario she imagined only left her more distressed. Overwhelmed, how could she expect her family to back her now altered future?

Chapter 14

Jack's first letter arrived by dairy express within two weeks of Joanna's initial communication to him, and his notes came once a week consistently thereafter. They were never more than a page, but they were an essential connection to him and the highlight of her miserable life. His reports of the increased mechanic business and his two first-place victories encouraged her. He allocated the prize money for securing an apartment for the three of them. In a brief line he indicated improvement in his wife's condition. But didn't mention a time frame for their divorce. Joanna was on her bed, answering his letter, when Rachel marched in.

"What's up, sugar?" asked Michelle, who'd been resting quietly on her bed.

"I hate this place. I wanna go home." Rachel threw herself on her bed, burying her face in the pillow. With Thanksgiving only days away, Joanna suffered from the contagious gloom infecting everyone. Separated from their families during the holidays for the first time, they agonized over the guilt that they'd landed here.

Michelle closed her eyes as if trying to sleep, but Joanna noticed her recoil in pain.

"Michelle, ya okay?" Joanna abandoned her stationery and went to the girl. Michelle didn't answer. "Are ya in labor?" Joanna asked.

"If I'm not, this is the worst gas pain I've ever had."

"Should we get Sister Eugenia?" Rachel asked, panicking.

"No!" Michelle practically shouted.

"But you're in pain. Shouldn't you be in the hospital wing?" Rachel suggested.

"No, I said!"

"How long've ya been havin' contractions?" Joanna asked her.

"Only a couple of hours. I could be at this all night. Once I go to the hospital wing, I'll be all alone. Please don't get Sister Eugenia, I wanna stay here as long as I can," she begged.

"It's okay. No one's gonna get her unless you tell us to." Jessie stroked Michelle's hair.

"Do you want anythin', some water, or a wet towel for your forehead? Gosh, I feel like we should boil water, like they do in the movies," Rachel nervously rambled.

Michelle laughingly chided, "Rachel, you're such a ditz, but I love ya for it." The other girls chuckled as Rachel blushed and shrugged.

Timing the contractions, they determined they were ten minutes apart. As Michelle writhed again - one, Joanna soothed her. "Don't tighten up. Try to relax; it won't hurt as bad. Here, look at me and breathe like this." Joanna showed her slow, even breaths, stroking her arm. Michelle released the tension in her body and followed Joanna.

When it ended, Michelle asked, amazed, "That helped. How'd ya know what to do?"

"My mama told me," Joanna answered. "All five of us were born at home on my granny's farm. I was with her for the last three."

For the next few hours, Jessie, Joanna, and Rachel tried to make Michelle as comfortable as possible while Missy sat cross-legged on her bed, silently observing. When Michelle complained her back ached, Jessie massaged it for her and Joanna helped her breathe with each contraction. Rachel finally ran to the bathroom for a cold rag to dab the sweat from her forehead. They lost track of time, until Sister Bridget came in to announce lights-out. Immediately the nun started asking questions.

"Her contractions are eight minutes apart," Joanna answered. Michelle begged Bridget to let her stay in the dorm room awhile longer. Following a brief exam to gauge Michelle's dilation, she reluctantly decided to let her remain with her friends for the present.

"You're only halfway," Sister Bridget informed them. "We'll have to turn off the lights or Mrs. Fitch will be in here to investigate. Missy, let me borrow your flashlight."

With the lights out, the girls focused their moral support on Michelle, each cognizant that a similar fate would find her. They passed the time with whispered stories about their families or boyfriends. Hours later, Missy lay sound asleep in

Joanna's bed. The older girls were weary but pumped with adrenaline. Michelle concentrated on noiselessly surviving each contraction.

"I know ya wanna scream, don't ya?" Jessie whispered.

Michelle nodded. "But out of meanness, Eugenia won't give me anythin' for the pain."

"Yeah," Jessie agreed. "What's the story?"

"She gives drugs if it's a difficult labor, but if it's going normally, she won't. She claims it slows the progress. Usually Dr. Miller will give you something," the nun whispered.

"She enjoys seein' the ones she dislikes in pain," Michelle theorized.

"Oh great," Jessie snickered. "I'm really in trouble!"

"Probably," Michelle commented, with a laugh. They all went silent.

Finally Joanna broke the dead air by asking, "What's the deal with Fitch? How come she's so angry all the time? I mean, I know she's a Mrs., so what happened to Mr. Fitch?"

"Trials of a war bride," Sister Bridget explained. "She was a nurse at an army hospital, and she met him at the USO. He was getting shipped overseas in a week; they only knew each other three days and got married."

"Did he get killed in battle?" Rachel asked.

"No, when the war ended he divorced her and married a girl he met in Paris. She's let the bitterness consume her. I feel sorry for her," the nun explained.

"I'm not sorry for her," Michelle jeered hatefully. "She would've driven him away if he'd come back to her. My daddy was military. Whenever he came home on leave, my mama nagged him constantly. Finally, he divorced her and I never saw him again."

"My daddy was in the war," Jessie confided, "He died on D-Day on Omaha Beach."

"I didn't know. I'm so sorry, Jessie," Michelle consoled.

"That's all right. I barely remember him. I was only five years old. It ruined my mama, though. After he was gone, I was nothin' but an inconvenience for her. She got a secretarial job. At night she'd go out and leave me alone at home. At first I was scared, so I'd go to my neighbors; they owned the bar across the alley, where I learned to play piano. Mama'd stagger in drunk on her ass, with Uncle Joe or whoever she brought home. The older I got, the slimier the guys became. They were always there in the mornin'; it doesn't take a brain surgeon to figure out what they were doin'. Ironically, she had the gall to call me a slut!"

"Oh, Jessie, that's terrible," Sister Bridget sympathized.

"No. You know what? It's okay. My mother's gonna die all alone, and I promise you, not one soul on earth will miss her!"

Out of nowhere, Michelle announced, "I love you, Jessie!" The girls hurled together in a hug; they were both in tears.

"I love you, too," Jessie cried in a high-pitched whisper. Missy stretched awake.

Finally, a sobbing Michelle revealed, "I love all y'all. I'll never forget any of you. The hardest part is, I'm never gonna see any of you again. I don't even know who you are. In the future, if I see ya on the street, I'll turn away so ya don't see me and pretend I haven't seen ya, because we can't admit we ever knew each other in this place."

"I won't do that!" Jessie protested.

"I will," Michelle told her, "and I'm such a hypocrite!" Another contraction hit.

"I'll check her after this one's over," Bridget whispered. "She might be getting close." When the pain subsided, the nun checked the girl's progress. "You're at nine. We should go upstairs now."

"No, not yet, please," Michelle pleaded.

"What time is it?" Sister Bridget asked.

Joanna trained the flashlight on the nightstand clock. It was four thirty in the morning; they'd been awake all night. An unsettling scream came from the doorway and Joanna turned the flashlight on Gloria, who, before they could stop her, ran toward the nuns' rooms, yelling for Sister Eugenia.

"No," Michelle wailed. "Don't let her take me! I don't wanna go!" Within seconds, the overhead light flipped on, blinding them. Sister Eugenia yanked Michelle out of the bed, producing back-to-back contractions. As soon as Michelle stood, her water broke, sending a flash flood of amniotic fluid all over the floor. Michelle screamed as the hateful nun put her on the elevator. The scurrying of the nuns and Mrs. Fitch shouting left Joanna stunned.

"Sister Bridget, clean up this disgusting mess," Fitch barked. The other nuns and Mrs. Fitch retreated. Bridget disappeared momentarily but came back with a mop and a bucket.

No one uttered a word until Jessie timidly asked, "You're in trouble, aren't you?" Bridget nodded, continuing to mop. Jessie's lip quivered. "We're sorry."

"Hush now, Jessie," the novice said softly. "I made my own decision. If I'm going to make any beneficial changes here I'm going to fill a file of reprimands before long."

Chapter 15

The morning of Thanksgiving, Mary was jittery. Today was the day! She wanted to warn her father in advance, but Tony thought it best to tell both sets of parents simultaneously.

Tony's parents, large loud Italians, had relocated from New Jersey to Nashville to open a soda shop. They'd been breaking their backs for years to make the business successful. In contrast, Mary's daddy was a reserved businessman, while Mary's mother, a socialite, shopped in the finest stores and mingled with the most influential women in Nashville's high society. Mary regarded them as traditionally southern, and they embarrassed her regularly with their snobbish attitudes. The only commonality between the young couple's families was being Catholic and the impending wedding they'd soon attend.

This dichotomy was reinforced as they awkwardly conversed over dinner. Tony's dad, Anthony, Sr., had a booming voice and broadcast a foreign East Coast accent, which became pronounced when he bragged on his son's football future. Mary's father raised questions pertaining to Tony's academic ambitions. Focusing on education, Gerald Atherton explained that both Mary and her brother, Albert, were expected to obtain college degrees.

"Whatever the kid wants, ya know. It don't matter, as soon as the pros sign him he won't need no more college." Tony's dad talked with a mouthful of food. Mary's mother cringed at his appalling table manners.

Grandma Bernice, who'd come from Knoxville for the holiday, whispered to Mary, "I think your young man is dashing." Mary smiled in agreement.

Tony was the definition of tall, dark, and handsome. As their eyes met, the tension in Mary mounted. By the time her mother brought out the coffee and pumpkin pie, Mary felt as if she might shatter. She gave Tony a pleading look.

He nodded and cleared his throat. "I'm glad we're all together today because Mary and I have an announcement. We've decided to get married."

"We've always suspected you two'd want to marry eventually; you are, of course, talking about a few years from now, when you finish college," Mary's mother clarified casually.

"No, we're thinking next month," Tony disclosed, rubbing his hands together nervously. The shocked expressions on the four parents' faces and sudden enveloping silence made Mary brace herself for the explosion certain to follow.

"Oh my God! She's pregnant?" Tony's mother blurted, waving her hands woefully.

"Yeah," Tony answered.

"How'd you know it's yours?" his father grunted.

Mary's father stood, face reddening, and spoke to defend what little honor Mary retained. "Of course the child is your son's. How dare you come into my house and accuse my daughter..." Tony's father rose from his chair.

Mary's grandmother interrupted, "Let's everyone calm down and be rational." The two men returned to their seats and glared at each other.

"The baby's mine," Tony confessed.

"What about your football scholarship? You're gonna throw it away for this... this... broad?" Anthony, Sr., shot Mary a look of contempt.

"I can still go to Ole Miss. We can get married next month. Mary can stay here with her folks while I'm in college."

"And have everyone talking about how she got herself in trouble? Certainly not!" Mary's mother huffed.

"What if I go to Mississippi State in the fall?" Mary suggested.

"What're you going to live on? Do you know what a baby costs?" Gerald asked.

"Couldn't you help us out, until we're settled..."

"Absolutely not," Gerald said, raising his voice. "You can't marry this boy! Neither of you has any idea of the responsibility involved in raising a child. If you defy me, young lady, I'll cut you off from this family!"

Tony's father continued lecturing his son: "I warned you about girls like her trapping you by getting knocked up."

"That's it!" Mary's father stood, his fists clenched. "Get out of my house. This is a family matter and we'll deal with it privately. Don't ever speak to my daughter again!"

Anthony, Sr., took his wife by the hand and practically dragged her to the front door while pushing his son ahead of him. As the front door slammed, Edith gathered the dessert dishes.

"My God, Mary! How could you do this to us? We've given you every advantage. And this is how you repay us? By giving yourself, like a slut, to that uncouth jock?"

"Mama, it wasn't like that!" Mary cried.

"His family is garbage," her father growled. "I knew that boy was trouble. I hoped you'd wise up and date someone with better breeding. Tony won't finish college; he'll turn out to be low-class swine, like his father." Mary cried into her cloth napkin.

Eventually, they all convened in the living room. The adults embroiled themselves in a heated discussion relevant to Mary's future, ignoring her.

Mary's older brother, Albert, a pre-med Vanderbilt student, suggested, "Dad, I know some interns on campus. They could… you know… do an operation."

"No! I won't be party to murder," Mr. Atherton commanded.

More alternatives were tossed around, until finally Grandma Bernice broke in, "I think she should come back to Knoxville with me. Tell everyone I slipped on those confounded stairs of yours and broke my hip, so she's taking care of me. There's a home for unwed mothers only blocks from my house. She can go there." Bernice explained the benefits of the home. As a volunteer, she helped with the biannual fashion shows and praised their services. "The baby will be surrendered for adoption. When Mary's released, she'll have her high school diploma and can go to nursing school as planned," Bernice concluded. They sealed Mary's future. She'd be going to the Frances Weston Home for Unwed Mothers in Knoxville.

On Sunday afternoon, as her bags were loaded into the back of Grandma Bernice's car, Mary pleaded one more time with her father not to send her away.

"You were my star, Mary. I've never been more disappointed in my life." He slammed the car door and walked away. When they drove out of the city limits of Nashville, Mary sobbed uncontrollably.

"Now, now, it's not as bad as all that," Bernice told her tenderly.

"Yes, it is; my life is over. I wish I was dead!" Mary corrected.

"No, you don't, not really. It seems that way right now, but this is a temporary problem."

"You don't know how I feel!" Mary accused.

"I know exactly how you feel. I've been in the same place you are right now," her grandmother consoled.

"What? You?"

"Yes, me," Bernice admitted. "But I was older than you. At twenty-four I thought I'd be an old maid. I'd been courted by a man for three years and came to believe if I got pregnant he'd marry me. Well, I was wrong. My parents disowned me and I had nowhere else to go. I too wanted to kill myself, and, oh, wouldn't they all be sorry then."

"Does Daddy know this?" Mary asked, astonished.

"No, and I'd appreciate it if you didn't tell him."

"What about Grandpa? Did you tell him?"

"Of course I did. It was your grandpa I turned to out of desperation when I was rejected by my family and boyfriend. He and I were close friends. Your grandpa offered to marry me and raise the child as his own."

The woman's oldest child was Mary's father and she jumped to conclusions. "So my daddy's illegitimate?"

"No, my dear child. I turned him down. I did, however, accept his help to foot the cost of the Weston Home for Unwed Mothers." Bernice continued, "Your grandpa was an extraordinary man and the love of my life. There're a lot of men who'd consider you and me to be damaged goods, but your grandpa never did. I gave birth to a baby girl, whom I let be adopted. Your grandfather and I were married the day I was released. We had forty-five wonderful years before the Good Lord took him."

"Why didn't you get married and raise the baby girl with Grandpa?" Mary asked.

"I couldn't ask him to raise another man's child."

"You loved the father of your little girl, didn't you?"

"I thought I did. But he broke my heart. Hence my decision; I didn't want to look at her every day and be reminded of her father."

"I'll never love anyone the way I love Tony," Mary agonized.

"Maybe not. Maybe you'll find someone you love better," Bernice suggested. Mary sighed. For the first time since she found out about her pregnancy, someone understood.

With the Thanksgiving holiday behind them, the residents of the Knoxville home faced the cold realization that Christmas would soon be upon them, intensifying everyone's gloom. Despite their dismal moods, Joanna felt grateful for the friendship bonds she'd formed with her roommates. She'd never had close girlfriends. Even in Lynchburg, she'd shied away from her peers, embarrassed by the consensus that labeled her family - - *poor white trash.*

At the home, economic status didn't matter. They all shared the same profound sense of loss. It weighed heavily at Michelle's discharge from the home.

According to Fitch's dictum, the girls weren't allowed to talk to her, nor were they told of Michelle's condition or her baby's. Jessie finally broke down Sister Bridget, and they learned that Joanna's inclination was correct: Michelle had given birth to healthy twin girls.

Jessie, Rachel, Missy, and Joanna peered through the parlor window as Michelle got into a taxi. The fees associated with a second baby required her to work off her debt at one of the affiliate homes. Joanna dabbed her eyes with a tissue watching Michelle wave as her cab pulled away. Rachel cried openly. Missy put her arms around Joanna, needing a hug.

"I'm never gonna see her again," Rachel whispered.

"Probably not," Jessie agreed flatly as she stepped away from the window. She spent the next few minutes pecking at the keys on the piano but lacked enthusiasm. Two days later, they watched through the same window as the social workers disappeared with Michelle's babies into a waiting car.

Rachel commented, "Always the same people come to take the babies. What a sad job."

"Are you kiddin' me?" Jessie admonished. "You don't get it! This is a prosperous business. Wealthy couples dish out big bucks to buy a baby. Our families pay a fortune to have us locked up to avoid any embarrassment. And don't get me started on the garment area. Please! This place is a baby factory, supply and demand. A ton of money is bein' made, and everyone's paddin' their pockets. I overheard Fitch talkin' about renovations for the third floor. They'll have sixteen more beds. And if you wanna know the truth, we get somethin' out of it, too. I'll have my high school diploma. Rachel, you'll go on to secretarial school. Jean, you think you're gonna keep your baby, but I'll be surprised if that happens. This place has a ninety-five percent relinquishment rate."

"Well, I'll be part of the five percent," Joanna protested.

"Why do you think we have those bullshit group counselin' sessions? Everything Mrs. Lewis does is to make us feel inadequate. Like the exercise when she made us write the things we couldn't give our babies that adoptive parents can. I'm sick of hearin' I'm a failure!"

In the last session, Mrs. Lewis had berated Joanna because her list included plans with Jack. Lewis shredded her paper an inch from Joanna's face shouting that she was an unwed mother. She had to do it over, omitting wishful thinking regarding her future.

Rachel chimed in, "You're right, Jessie! They'll use any means to make ya give up your baby. I hate when Lewis harps on how, if we loved our babies, we'd do what's best for them. It's not fair to use our love against us. I'm tellin' ya, Jean, if ya resist, they'll push harder."

Joanna didn't want to hear this again. "Jack'll come and get me, and you'll see."

Chapter 16

Flora placed a plate of banana bread in front of Catherine and said, "I say, Catherine, you're lookin' especially lovely this mornin'."

"Thank you, Flora. I feel especially lovely today." Truly, Catherine felt more like her former self every day. By Thanksgiving, she'd been successfully weaned off all the medications. She started volunteering on committees with her mother. Last week, Mabel Anderson and Edith Atherton had enthusiastically recruited her to be on their committee for the New Year's Eve Gala. The black-tie dinner included dancing, champagne, and the ringing-in of 1957. Catherine took pride to be involved in the planning of the celebration and its core purpose of raising funds to benefit local foster homes.

As Catherine sipped her coffee, she envisioned dancing with Jack again; gliding across the floor, he'd always made her feel weightless. She needed a new dress, and only Mabel's shop would be able to supply the attire she had in mind. Catherine smiled. Yes, life was going in the direction she wanted.

"It's time to get up!" Her grandmother yanked the covers off the bed, shocking Mary. Uncompromising, with her hands on her hips, Bernice continued, "I've let you lie in here for three days. No more wallowing in self-pity. Get a bath, wash your greasy hair, and come downstairs."

Mary felt sore and light-headed, as if she'd come out of a coma. Her grandmother had never used this tone before, so Mary complied without objection. Dressed in a clean white button-up shirt and her snug blue-jean pedal pushers, she entered the warmth of her grandmother's kitchen. Sitting at the table, Mary adjusted the towel atop her wet hair. Bernice watched her scoot the food around with the fork.

"Eat. I have some chores I want you to help me with today." Mary moaned. "I can't stand another day of you pouting in a dark room, playing that record over and over."

"'Love Me Tender' was our special song!" Mary informed her.

"I agree with your parents. Right now you think they're being mean. Tony's not right for you… and his father! Well! In time, you'll see the sense of it." Mary tilted her head disbelievingly. "Honey, listen to me. I'm old. I know what I'm talking about. You have to put Tony out of your mind. I truly believed your daddy when he threatened to cut you off. It'd nearly kill him, but he'd do it. I don't want you to go through life without your family," Bernice told her sympathetically.

"I don't know how to stop thinking about him," Mary objected.

"Well, the first thing you do is keep your hands busy and your mind will follow."

After the breakfast dishes were cleared, Bernice led Mary to the attic to scout out donations for the church rummage sale. The cobwebs hanging from the rafters weren't quite as menacing once Bernice flipped on the light. They spent the morning going through dusty boxes of old treasures. Once in a while, Bernice came across something that evoked a memory.

"Oh, I haven't seen this in years," she'd exclaim with joy, and proceed to tell Mary the story behind the box of gems she'd uncovered.

Finally, Mary moved boxes, making a path to an old steamer trunk under the eave. "Grandma, what about the trunk?"

"I don't know if it holds anything to donate." Bernice came over and opened the top. Inside were envelopes with her children's names on them, along with old baby shoes, letters, postcards, and photographs.

Mary lifted a faded photograph of a young woman and asked, "Is this you?"

Bernice stopped sorting through the chest and glanced at the image and laughed. "It sure is. Seems like a hundred years ago. I was your age."

"Wow! You were a knockout!" Mary was astonished.

"Yes, yes I was," her grandmother agreed with a faraway gaze.

"I can't believe you were afraid of becoming an old maid!"

"There were plenty of fellas chasing me. I wanted the one I couldn't win," she lamented.

"Do you have any pictures of your baby's father?" Mary asked.

"No," the old woman said, scoffing. "I burned those before I even went away."

Mary admired the photo again. "Did it take you a long time to get over him?"

"What I felt for him evaporated quickly. When the man you love treats you like a common street walker… well, you can understand how one might become disenchanted."

"Plus, your family disowned you. But you had Grandpa." Mary choked up.

"And you have me." She hugged Mary quickly. "I have something for you, if I can find it." She moved envelopes to the floor and kept digging. Mary held the one with her father's name on it. "Those're old pictures and letters I want them to have after I'm gone. I've put names on the bottoms of the furniture and keepsakes, too, so you each get what I want you to have."

"That's morbid," Mary said.

"No, it's not. It's planning for the inevitable." Bernice smiled. Moments later she located the elusive jewelry box. "Oh good, here it is." Opening it, she took out a medal of St. Nicolas. "I want you to have this." She placed the fine silver chain over the girl's head. "If I was scared or sad, I'd say a prayer to him; it made me feel better. Everything will eventually be all right."

"Thanks," Mary obliged, fingering the gift. She didn't see how this trinket could make things better. Bernice meant well, though, so she gratefully accepted her compassion.

The cold, dreary days of December passed slowly at the Frances Weston Home and mirrored the depression that ran rapidly through its residents. The number of births increased that month, as did the tearful goodbyes of friends who'd be permanently lost to each other.

Karen went into labor in the middle of Mr. Ehrlichman's class. She groaned in pain and the teacher came rushing to her desk. He brushed his oily hair out of his face and asked, "Are you okay? Are you in labor?" Karen nodded. With a glazed look, Ehrlichman kept muttering, "Okay. All right." Returning to the front of the room, he froze.

A girl from another dorm spoke: "Mr. Ehrlichman, should I get Sister Eugenia?"

"Yes. Go get Sister Eugenia," the man answered, getting a grip on reality. Within minutes, Sister Bridget calmly escorted the laboring girl to the hallway.

"Where's Sister Eugenia?" Karen asked.

"She's not feeling well today. So I'll be with you," Bridget reassured her.

"Oh! Thank God!" Karen blurted, genuinely relieved. Ehrlichman, with his hands shaking uncontrollably, instructed the girls to open their literature books and read silently.

For the rest of the day, none of them were able to concentrate on the required tasks. The hours ticked tortuously by as they waited for news on Karen. Finally, after dinner Sister Bridget entered the dorm room.

"Karen had a little boy." The young sister appeared tired.

"Can we see her?" Jessie pleaded.

"No. Mrs. Fitch is with her and she's furious because Karen refused to sign the relinquishment papers unless she was allowed to talk to her boyfriend."

"Did she let Karen call him?" Joanna asked.

Bridget nodded. "Apparently, he'd changed his mind. He couldn't support a family and complete his education. He advised her to put the baby up for adoption."

Jessie lamented, "It always happens; first the letters stop, then they break their promises."

Sister Bridget eyed Jessie suspiciously. "I'm going to pretend I didn't hear about letters from boyfriends." Frustration followed. "I'm trying to make changes for the better around here. But I can't do that if you're going to break the rules!" The nun looked older with a brow-furrowed frown. The girls looked guilty as they faked innocence.

"After she talked to her boyfriend, did she sign the papers?" Joanna asked.

"No. She's insisting she's going to keep her baby."

"No wonder Fitch is fit to be tied," Jessie determined.

"Do you think she's wrong to wanna keep her baby?" Joanna asked the nun.

"No, not to *want* to keep him. I think many women who come here would like to keep their baby, but I don't know if the decision to raise it alone is wise. It'll be a difficult road, especially since her family's rejected her. But Karen has to decide which path is right for her. Maybe if more women kept their babies, the stigma would go away."

"Like that's ever gonna happen," Jessie sneered.

When the day arrived for Karen's discharge, Mrs. Fitch was busy checking in a new girl. Karen showed off her sleeping baby while waiting in the parlor for the taxi to arrive.

"He looks like a porcelain doll," Missy observed, touching the child's tiny fingers.

"He's a good baby, too. He doesn't cry unless he needs somethin'." Joanna asked to hold him. Karen lovingly passed him over. "I named him Patrick."

Jessie, who stood off to the side as if she might contract a flesh-eating disease from the newborn, finally asked in a concerned tone, "Karen, how're you gonna do this?"

"I'll be all right. Sister Bridget made some phone calls and found a boarding-house for us in Chattanooga. The woman who owns it helps unwed mothers get on their feet. Sister also gave me a list of government agencies that provide assistance for women in my situation. The whole time I've been here no one's informed me about the help that's out there, if we keep our babies. Fitch, the nuns, Mrs. Lewis—they don't want us to know our legal rights. Please don't repeat this. I don't want Sister Bridget to get into trouble."

The taxi pulled in front of the building and blew its horn. Joanna gingerly returned Patrick to his mother. Jessie carried Karen's bags as they walked her out. When the taxi began to move, Karen rolled down the window and shouted, "My real name is Katie O'Brien. I'll be at Mrs. Ford's boardinghouse on Front Street. Look me up!" A few seconds later, the yellow cab exited the elaborate front gates.

"She's braver than I gave her credit for," Jessie commented, ascending the front stairs.

"That baby was so cute. Does this mean I can keep my baby, if I want?" Missy asked.

"I doubt it. Karen's eighteen, not a minor. At your age, your parents decide what happens to the baby," Jessie informed her. "I don't want to keep my baby; but they make us feel like dirt, while they hide our options. This place has nothin' to do with what's best for the child; it's about the almighty dollar. I guarantee, Fitch-the-bitch is rakin' in the bucks."

Jack walked into the kitchen and threw his keys on the counter. Mentally preparing for the race as he climbed the stairs, Catherine, dressed in corduroy pants and a sweater, surprised him at the top landing.

"Hey, there," she said, smiling, undaunted by his shock.

"Hey, yourself." He realized this had been their ritual greeting during their courtship.

"What time's the race?" she asked.

"In a couple of hours," Jack answered on the way to his bedroom.

"I was thinking I'd come with you tonight?" she inquired. Jack halted. The last race she attended was the night of the accident.

"It's going to be cold tonight," he rebutted.

"Jack, how many times have I sat in the stands on colder nights than this? I have a hat, gloves, and a thermos of cocoa; I've done this before."

Standing before him was the former Cat; the lovely girl who'd adored him in his youth. Momentarily taken aback by the image, he conceded, "Yeah, sure, I'll be ready to leave in thirty minutes." He entered his bedroom and quickly shut the door.

At the track Catherine appeared in the pit area to give Jack a kiss for luck, which had been their custom, but Jack tensed. Alex crossed his arms, smiling, giving Catherine a nod of approval. Hank and Sam, his pit crew, were grateful for the hot chocolate she provided.

As the drivers started their engines, Jack eyed the cocky driver in the car next to him. Alex had warned him about this new kid, a hotshot named Ritchie Blake.

The race began with the roar of twenty cars speeding into the first corner on the quarter-mile track. By the fifth lap, three cars dropped out with mechanical trouble. Jack hung back in sixth place and watched Blake maneuver into fourth place. Blake tried to edge past the second-place driver several times. When Jack saw his opening on the outside, he hit the gas and shot past Blake, tied for second with a driver from Georgia. Panicking, Blake got reckless. Punching the gas at the wrong time, he went into a slide and careened into Jack's back quarter panel, sending Jack into a skid. The back end of his car hit the wall, sending sparks flying as the metal scraped the concrete for fifty yards until Jack brought the car to a stop.

The stadium cheered when Jack climbed out of the car window and waved at the crowd. Alex got to the wreckage first. "Are you okay, man?" Alex did a quick overall check.

"I'm fine, but my car's fucked!" Jack roared. Alex escorted Jack to the gate where Catherine waited. She hugged him and made her own inspection. He assured her he was fine.

"Let Hank and Sam take care of the car. You need a drink," Alex suggested. Jack didn't argue. Within a half an hour, he and Catherine were in a honky-tonk with Alex buying shots. Noisy and smoky, with music too loud to talk, the two friends got progressively wasted as the night wore on.

In the wee hours of the morning, Cat led her husband up the narrow back stairs from the kitchen. He wobbled but cooperated. Jack rarely got this intoxicated, and was never a mean drunk; he tended to be sappy sweet. Once inside the dark bedroom, he giggled as she took off his shoes and socks. She removed his pants and shirt, leaving him in only his underwear.

As she covered him with the quilt, Jack muttered, "Cat, I have to tell you something."

"I'm sure it'll wait till morning." She kissed his forehead. He was already snoring.

Jack woke with his head pounding and the morning light hurt his eyes. He struggled to recall the events of the night before. His smashed car flashed back first. He remembered the honky-tonk but had no memory of coming home or how he ended up in bed with Cat sleeping next to him. Jack slipped out of bed and painfully made his way to the shower. The whole time his mind searched for the hours he couldn't recall. *Oh God, what if I made love to her last night.*

Chapter 17

Irene Wilson sat at the kitchen table with a blank piece of paper, attempting to compose a letter to Joanna. Over six weeks had passed since Harris dropped her off in Knoxville and the one brief note she'd received from the girl, stating that she was fine and well fed, did nothing to dissuade the mother's anxiety. Irene answered immediately, with a page-long letter, but when her correspondence remained unanswered, she couldn't bring herself to write another.

Irene longed to confide to Joanna the changes that had ensued since she'd left home and to be reassured of her daughter's proper care.

Dear Daughter, she scrawled, hoping the words would flow easily once she began. They didn't. She stared at the page as tears collected in her eyes. What words could she use to accurately convey the terror of Harris's daily tirades? She considered leading with the news of Eddie's after-school job at the grocery store, but she'd have to tell how Harris seized the boy's paychecks, claiming to put them in savings for Eddie to attend trade school. Instead, she suspected he'd been paying off a sizable bar tab or a loan shark. As far as Irene could tell, Harris hadn't touched booze since the day Joanna went away and he'd proclaimed himself Supreme Ruler. Irene didn't believe his sobriety would last. She kept expecting him to come staggering in and pass out. She crumpled the paper, her hands limp. She missed her eldest daughter. How could she put any of this on paper?

Bernice Atherton arranged Mary's belongings in the open suitcase as Mary refolded the same shirt for the third time. "Can't I stay with you until after Christmas?" Mary begged.

"I'm supposed to be at your uncle Matthew's in Charleston day after tomorrow."

The older woman went to answer the ringing phone. "Mary, your parents want to speak with you," she said, her voice carried from the foyer.

"Terrific!" Mary muttered. Descending the stairs, she took the receiver from her grandmother. "Hello, Daddy." Mary sat on the chair at the telephone table. Bernice leaned against the kitchen archway and listened to the one side of the conversation. "Yes, sir... I will. I understand, I will... Okay, bye Dad. Hi, Mom... Yes, I know... I know, I'm sorry," Mary's eyes filled with tears and Bernice stepped forward, ready to take the phone from the girl. Mary raised her hand, blocking her. "Grandma says we need to leave now to make our appointment time... Okay, I will. Bye." As she hung up, Mary let the tears come.

"Now, now! Hush!" Bernice soothed with a hug.

"God! She couldn't leave it alone. No! She had to tell me what a disappointment I am and how I'm not the good girl they raised."

"You're a good girl, Mary. You never gave them a lick of trouble as a child. Your dad feels overwhelmed by this one big bomb you dropped. And you know your mother... Well, Edith can be rather emotional," Grandma defended.

"Emotional! She's psycho! The day after Thanksgiving, she kept me prisoner in my room, lecturing me, calling me a sneaky liar. She said good girls don't enjoy sex; only dirty girls do. She drilled me on where we'd done it, how many times, she wanted details; it was awful!"

"My poor son," Bernice pitied, under her breath. "Listen to me, Mary. Things will be better in time. Now dry your eyes." Bernice stood and, taking Mary by the hand, she directed, "You do have to finish packing." Ascending the stairs, Bernice put her arm around Mary's shoulder. "Not all women feel that way about sex with their husbands. In the right circumstances, it can be a mutually satisfying part of a good marriage."

"You and Grandpa?" Mary dried her tears on her sleeve, giving Bernice an amazed look.

"Oh my, yes! We had a very satisfying relationship that way. And I take offense to being labeled a dirty girl." They both chuckled. Together they collected the belongings she'd take to the Frances Weston Home for Unwed Mothers.

Joanna, Missy and Jessie entered the dorm room to find the new girl with her back to them unpacking her suitcase. "Cool, you've got a record player!" Jessie observed. The girl spun around. "I'm Jessie, and this is Jean and Missy."

Mary looked at Joanna with wide eyes. "I know you! Don't use my real name."

"I won't," Joanna concurred.

"Oh, oh. Come on, Missy, let's go to the parlor and I'll play you a song on the piano." Missy followed Jessie down the hall, their voices echoing off the plaster walls.

Joanna sank on her bed. Mary spoke first, "Well, this is awkward. I guess my name's Marsha now." Mary sorted through her 45 records. "I thought they didn't place girls from the same location together in a home."

"They don't; my dad lied and said I came from Lynchburg," Joanna explained. "Why?"

"I don't know. He can't help himself," Joanna told her. "Don't worry; I won't go back to Nashville and spread stories about you."

"Neither will I; about you, I mean." Mary's lip quivered. "I can't believe this is happening to me." Slumping on the bed, she wept. Joanna handed her a tissue.

"Most of us felt that way at first." Joanna understood.

Mary blew her nose. "I have no idea what this is going to be like or how I should act."

"Some residents keep to themselves; others make friends. On this hallway, we're pretty tight. You'll love Jessie. She keeps us laughin'. Rachel's kinda ditzy, but she's cool. I roll her hair for her every night. She wants to look like Marilyn Monroe tomorrow." Joanna grinned. "If you want, I'll do yours, too." Joanna described the rest of the girls. She finished by saying, "Just be yourself. Except for Sister Bridget, we all lie low around the nuns."

"What if the other girls hate me?"

"You're kidding?" Joanna asked, shocked. "You're so popular at school."

"That's different; I was a cheerleader and homecoming queen."

"Yeah, but you're not like some of the other cheerleaders, like Melinda Peterson and Pookie Lister. They treat everyone like peons. You're not like them," Joanna encouraged.

"Thanks." Mary examined the uniform with disgust. "Now it's complete; I'm a criminal."

"Well, don't beat yourself up. The nuns dish out enough to go around."

"It's comforting to see a familiar face," Mary acknowledged, in a gesture of friendship.

"I'll help you get settled and show you around," Joanna offered. Over the next couple of hours Joanna acquainted Mary, now Marsha, with her new home. They made a pact to keep the secret that they knew each other. Certain Fitch would move one of them to another home, Joanna didn't want to leave the friends she'd made. Mary wanted to stay close so her grandmother could visit often. Jessie and Missy knew, but they'd keep it to themselves.

Catherine stood in front of the three-way mirror in Mabel's boutique, examining the party dress she'd tried on. "Do we have time to have it fitted?" Cat asked.

"I'll have it ready for you by December twenty-eighth," Mabel promised.

"That's perfect," Cat agreed. Mabel marked lines for the alterations.

Catherine's mother, who'd been browsing the store, came over to converse with Mabel. "Did you notice how aloof Edith Atherton acted at the New Year's Gala meeting?"

"Yes. I think she's worried about her mother-in-law. I heard she fell at their house on Thanksgiving Day and broke her hip."

"But did you know they sent their daughter Mary to look after her?" Millicent asked. "You'd think with all their money, they'd hire a private nurse for her."

"I think Mary's going to nursing school after she graduates high school," Mabel offered.

"Maybe they're concerned about hiring staff who might steal from her. Some people don't like strangers in their homes," Cat suggested, remembering her father's discrimination when they interviewed caretakers for her. It took him a while to trust Flora.

"Well, regardless, it's only half the story. The Peterson girl, Melinda, is a friend of Mary's, and apparently Mary had a bad breakup with the football player she's been seeing," Millicent went on. Cat excused herself when Mabel finished her measurements. She suspected she'd been the topic of many a prattle session and no longer cared for gossip.

Three days before Christmas, Nancy went into labor during breakfast chores. Sister Mary Joseph whisked her away to Sister Eugenia before the other girls realized what was happening. Sister Bridget assisted with Nancy during their afternoon sewing enterprise, while Mrs. Fitch consulted with the contractor she'd hired for the renovations to the third floor. This afforded the girls the rare opportunity to work unsupervised.

"I'm gonna do like Michelle, I'll wait till the last minute before I go to that torture chamber," Jessie commented while pinning a pattern piece to orange fabric. Joanna agreed, cutting the threads on a sundress for the fashion show.

Mary finished dressing the mannequin and stepped back to scrutinize the results. Due to her impeccable sense of style, Mary's job was quality control of the finished garments for the show. She inspected the workmanship and dressed mannequins in the outfits to be offered.

At four o'clock, the girls organized their workstations with mixed feelings concerning Mrs. Fitch's edict to close the garment area for a week in observance of Christmas. The high school classes were also suspended until the first of the year, giving the residents more free time; unfortunately, it also provided abundant time to dwell on their homesickness.

On Christmas Eve, Sister Bridget erected a tall, fresh pine tree in the parlor and furnished the girls with craft supplies for homemade ornaments. While the residents created decorations, Jessie played Christmas music on the baby grand piano. With the sweet soprano voice of an angel, Missy sang "Oh Little Town of Bethlehem" while sticking beads with pins attached into a Styrofoam ball. Before long, they were all singing as pleasantly as an all-girls' choir. Sister Bridget smiled, adjusting the strings of colorful lights on the fragrant tree. Soon nuns from all over the building joined them. Mrs. Fitch eventually came out of her office but didn't join the impromptu gathering. Instead she nodded her approval and opted to take a shift with Nancy in the hospital wing, giving Sister Eugenia a respite.

As the women sang and decorated the tree, a common bond flowed among them. Missy's ornaments were the most creative and served as inspiration for the others. Joanna smiled at her little friend, touched by the fact that Missy's pure soul brought some magic to a place filled with so much sorrow. In doing so, she helped to create a peaceful memory none of them would ever forget.

Chapter 18

Christmas morning arrived cold and rainy. Catherine lit the tinder in the living room fireplace. After plugging in the lights of the tree she and Flora had decorated the week previous, she poked at her fire, willing the cozy heat to circulate. Catherine's fuzzy bathrobe would've been more suited for the chill of the morning. However, the long, silky white gown and matching robe were in line with the mood she wished to set.

She placed the silver tray on the coffee table in front of the couch. With the creaking of Jack's movements from upstairs, she fixed his coffee to his preference. She set it next to her cup and shifted the plates of French pastries and fresh strawberries to a balanced presentation on the tray. In a minute, Jack descended the stairs and paused by the oak pillars at the entrance to the living room.

"Merry Christmas, darling. Coffee?" She hoped he'd sit next to her; instead, he took his cup to the armchair next to the fire.

"This looks nice, Cat," he complimented nervously. Catherine retrieved gifts for her husband from under the tree, puzzled when she located a box she didn't recognize.

Jack explained, "That one's for you, from me."

Catherine unwrapped the package to find a beautiful pair of pearl earrings, matching the necklace he had given her the Christmas before the accident.

"I bought those at the same time as the necklace. I was going to give them to you the following Christmas…" Jack stopped short. That would've been Daniel's first Christmas. But during her illness, holidays were ignored. Catherine hugged him and kissed his cheek.

"I love them, Jack. They're perfect," she praised. With a sparkle in her eyes Cat handed him gifts and watched joyfully as he opened them. There were the usual practical presents, new shirts and such. Next, she passed him a cuff-link-sized box. She couldn't suppress the smile of excitement in anticipation of his reaction. Jack lifted the lid. His eyes grew wide, staring at a car key inside. He looked at his wife with a confused expression.

Catherine giggled. "Go look in the driveway."

"What did you do?" He made his way through the foyer and out the front door. Cat stood on the porch beaming, as Jack walked in a circle around his dream car, a red 1950 Barchetta Ferrari race car decorated with a big green bow. Now he stood in the pouring rain as if he were hallucinating.

Catherine turned from thrilled to shocked when Jack retook the porch stairs without even starting the engine. Jack handed her the key. "Cat, that's too generous. I can't accept it."

She pressed the key back into his hand. An uncomfortable vibe emanated from Jack. Before he could object, she expounded, "I don't want to waste any more time dreaming about what we want. It's up to us to make it happen. I'm very happy right now. Please don't tell me something that's going to make me sad." Jack hung his head. Catherine touched his face. "So much love went into my choice to buy the car. I'll be terribly insulted if you refuse to accept it." She slipped back inside.

Jack let out a moan of anxiety. *What the hell do I do now?*

Christmas Day at the home in Knoxville was unlike anything the girls had ever experienced. The gloom of the weather outside contributed to the depressed atmosphere. The home maintained strict rules forbidding visitors on Christmas Day. Fitch also mandated that families could only send one gift.

Joanna and Jessie didn't bother to go and look under the tree, convinced there'd be nothing for them. Missy came bounding into the room and passed around a tin of homemade Christmas cookies.

"My little sister, Lisa made these with the housekeeper," Missy explained.

"You have a housekeeper?" Joanna asked, coaxing the girl to confide about her family.

"Sure, Mrs. Lasky."

"What about your mama?"

"She's kinda sickly; she gets bad headaches a lot. Mom eats meals with us but she doesn't cook. Mrs. Lasky fixes our meals. She loves to bake. Aren't these cookies the best?" Missy spoke as if her mother's incapacitation was a normal occurrence for a household.

"What do the doctors say?" Mary asked, flipping the pages of a first-year nursing school chemistry book, her Christmas present from her father.

"Daddy says she's a hypochondriac."

"Hypo what?" Joanna asked.

"Hypochondriac. It means her being sick is in her head. She imagines it," Missy defined.

"The bizarre world of abnormal psychosis," Jessie commented. "Did your dad send you a psychology book?"

"No, I won't take those classes until later. Missy, how long has your mom been like that?" the future nursing student asked.

"For as long as I can remember. She has good days and bad days. On good days, she'll get dressed and sit on the front porch or watch TV. On bad days she doesn't get out of bed."

"What about your dad, what does he do?" Joanna gently prodded.

"He owns a drugstore; he's a pharmacist. He takes real good care of Mom. He gives her pills, because even though the doctors say it's mental, she still feels real pain. Daddy says her immune system is shot; she gets colds and flu regularly. That's why he gives Lisa and me lots of vitamins, so we don't catch anything and bring it home to her."

"I guess you don't get to have friends in the house, either," Mary said. "I can't imagine. My brother's and my pals regularly hung out at our house."

"I don't really have many friends. Daddy's protective. We don't go to slumber parties. You're the first real friends I've ever had. I mean, here it's like one big sleepover, isn't it?"

"Well, I'm honored to be one of your first real friends." Joanna beamed.

"What about boys? Didn't you have some you liked?" Mary asked.

"I go to an all-girls Catholic school, silly. I don't know any boys."

Rachel surged into the room, rabidly waving a letter from her parents. "My folks said they couldn't afford much for Christmas this year, even for my brothers and sister, because of the price tag here. Mama says she's lookin' forward to me comin' home when I finish secretarial school. I don't think I ever wanna move back home. She sent me a magazine article wrapped in a box like a present. Listen to this, I quote:

"'If you're a working girl, be a working girl and not a would-be siren. Never try to flirt with your boss... he's your bread and butter, and not your honey. Be business-like, not only in your approach to your work, but in your personal appearance, your manners and your deportment. By this, we do not mean that you should try and disguise the fact that you're a woman, but simply that, during work hours, you shouldn't flaunt that fact around like a flirtatious flag.'" Rachel went on to read a ridiculous list of *Don'ts* that were purely commonsense behaviors, finishing exasperated. "She makes it sound like I'm gonna stupidly throw myself at every man I see." She bounced defeated on her bed and pouted.

"At least your family remembered you," Joanna lamented.

"There's presents for you two," Mary said.

Both girls sprang from their beds and ran to the parlor, where two lonely gifts remained under the tree with their names attached. Joanna ripped into the paper of a small box. She opened the note scribed in her mother's hand.

Daughter,

I think of you often. Please don't stay angry with me.

Mama

"She hasn't gotten any of my letters. If she had, she'd know I'm not angry with her! I'll bet my father took them. I'd bet he's forbidden her to write to me." Joanna concluded. Discarding the cotton lining, she lifted a small pewter medallion of St. Nicolas dangling from a tarnished chain. She placed the object around her neck, touching it with her fingertips. "Mama utterly believes in this stuff. She goes to Mass every Saturday and Sunday."

Jessie tore into a long, rectangular box. As she lifted an elegant emerald-green gown from the tissue paper, a card fell on the floor. Joanna retrieved it and read aloud: "'*You're going to wow them with your talent. Love, Santa.*'"

The girls' eyes met, and in unison they said, "Sister Bridget."

Jessie smiled. "Ya know she'll deny any involvement." Yet Joanna could tell, the sentiment deeply touched the normally unaffected girl.

Catherine tried on the formal gown and examined her reflection in the three-way mirror. "Oh, Catherine, you look stunning!" Mabel adjusted the shoulder of the dress for a perfect fit. "Your mother tells me you and your husband are adopting a baby."

"We hope to," Catherine replied kindly, hiding her irritation regarding Millicent's divulgence of personal matters to the shopkeeper.

"You might be interested to know, the dress you're wearing came from a wage home for unwed mothers. Perhaps you'd like to go with me to their fashion show in Memphis next month. It's an excellent charity that places newborns in good homes for adoption, and it also helps the birthmothers by providing job training and support for starting new lives."

"Thank you for the invitation. I'll let you know," Catherine responded.

"It's held at the Peabody; they serve a splendid lunch. All the proceeds go directly to the unfortunate women," Mabel extoled, trying to entice her. "Well, think about it. Perhaps your mother'd be interested as well."

Driving home, Catherine considered attending the fashion show. She'd consult her mother; Millicent stayed abreast of deserving charities.

"A home for unwed mothers," she mulled over aloud. Aware of their existence, Cat couldn't recall a time when such places were ever spoken of in polite conversation.

Chapter 19

Joanna lay on her bed, watching Jessie pace like a caged tiger. Occasionally, the redhead stopped at the window to watch the fat snowflakes falling in a curtain of sparkles.

"If you weren't here, Jessie, how'd you be spending New Year's Eve?" Mary asked.

"Probably playin' piano at a party. Havin' fun," Jessie hypothesized, annoyed.

"We could play Chinese checkers," Missy suggested. "Daddy, Lisa, and I always played board games on New Year's Eve and popped popcorn."

"No," Jessie snapped.

"How 'bout cards?" Joanna offered.

"I don't feel like cards," Jessie snarled.

"If I wasn't here, I'd be at the New Year's Eve Gala with my parents," Mary informed.

"What's that?" Missy asked.

"It's a dinner dance, black tie. They put it on every year to benefit different charities. Ironically, this year they're raising money for local foster homes who place babies for adoption."

Jessie burst out laughing. "Oh, that's rich! The same people who condemn us for bein' knocked up; there they are! All dressed fancy, havin' an elaborate party to benefit our bastards. The same hypocrites who buy our babies!"

Mary agreed. "You're right, Jessie. I never looked at it that way before."

"If I wasn't here, I'd be at Dewey's dad's fishing cabin," Rachel speculated. "We'd go there a lot for kicks. More than likely, my friends have a fire in the fireplace. They'll play some drinkin' games, probably Never Have I Ever. Later, they'll turn on a battery-powered radio to romantic music and dance or neck in the corner." Rachel's voice trailed off.

"How'd you play Never Have I Ever?" Jessie asked as she went to her cabinet, opened a drawer, and dug to the bottom, pulling out a bottle of whiskey and a shot glass.

Rachel explained, "We all sit in a circle; I can start. I say, 'Never have I ever,' followed by somethin' like, 'been to New York City.' Ya go around and if you've ever done the thing and you're the only one that has, ya have to drink and tell the details. If more than one person has to drink, ya don't have to tell the story. You keep goin' around and everyone gets a turn."

"I'm in." Jessie moved her bed closer to Mary's, making room for them to sit on the floor. So Jessie, Mary, Joanna, Rachel, and Missy sat in a circle using Missy's flashlight to see.

Rachel began: "Never have I ever... um,... seen my parents kiss." They went around the circle. Mary had to drink a shot and so did Missy. The youngest shook her head with disgust at the burning liquor. Joanna could honestly say she'd never witnessed any tender moments between her parents. Jessie barely remembered her father.

Next Mary went. "Never have I ever gone steady with more than one boy at a time."

Only Jessie drank. "I did that all the time; ya got to keep your options open or else guys get too possessive."

Joanna took her turn. "Never have I ever seen the ocean." Mary and Jessie had to drink.

Missy's turn came and she said, "Never have I ever kissed a boy, except for my daddy, but he doesn't count." Everyone had to drink.

Jessie went next. "Never have I ever been in love."

Everyone but Missy drank. The game continued for an hour, resulting in Rachel and Mary getting tipsy, whereas Joanna and Missy weren't required to take many shots. Being so young, Missy lacked the experience of the older girls. Joanna's adventures were limited by poverty. Jessie's worldly lifestyle obligated her to drink the most.

Rachel's turn came around again; slurring her words and giggling, she blurted, "Never have I ever, ever given a boy a blowjob."

"What's that?" Missy asked naively. Joanna leaned over and whispered in her ear.

"Oh God, gross!" Missy wrinkled her nose.

The other girls laughed hysterically at their young friend's response. Jessie declared the game over by returning the whiskey bottle to her drawer and staggered over to the window. "Never have I ever played in the snow," she mused absently. She turned, heading for the door.

"Jessie, where're you goin'?" Rachel whispered, following her into the hall. The others were right on their heels.

"I'm gonna go play in the snow," Jessie yelped loudly.

"Shhh, you're gonna wake the nuns," Mary hissed as they tiptoed with Jessie in the lead. When they reached the heavy wooden door to the flower garden, Jessie took a hairpin from one of Rachel's curlers and picked the lock. In seconds they were outside, standing in the freezing air with bare feet, wearing only their pajamas. Jessie skipped down the stairs singing, with her arms outstretched to maximize the feeling of the snowflakes hitting her skin. She twirled in circles like a ballerina. When she became dizzy, she lay in the snow and made a snow angel. Her merriment echoed off the side of the stone building.

"Jessie, come on. It's freezin' out here," Rachel pleaded. Packing a snowball in her gloveless hands, she threw it, missing Jessie by mere inches.

"I know!" Jessie yelled, awakening to sudden inspiration. "We can squeeze through the fence and make a big snowman on the front lawn. No, not a snowman, a snow woman; let's make a big, fat, pregnant snow woman! Fitch'll have a cow!" Jessie cackled out of control.

"She'd also know exactly who did it." Sister Bridget's voice came from the doorway. "Come on, girls; let's go back to bed." Jessie quit laughing and slouched with guilt as they all filed back inside. "Are you trying to get all of us into trouble?" the nun asked Jessie. She took a key from her pocket and locked the door.

"No, Sister, I'm sorry. I was just tryin' to have some fun," Jessie whispered.

Back in the dorm, Bridget chastised, "The snow will still be here in the morning. You can play out there, with coats and shoes. Honestly, girls, you're wearing me out, pushing the limits like this." Exasperated, Bridget left them in the quiet darkness. With the closing of the nun's door at the other end of the hall, they lost all effort to hold back their laughter.

"That was fun," Rachel affirmed. The girls echoed her with uncontrolled giggles.

In the distance, a church bell rang out the stroke of midnight. Jessie said, "Never have I ever gone to sleep before midnight on New Year's Eve."

"Happy New Year, gals," Rachel whispered. They all exchanged the wish and went to sleep. Jessie didn't play outside the next morning. She had a whopper of a hangover and preferred to pull the pillow over her head and sleep through the first day of 1957.

Catherine leaned against the couch and watched the flames in the fireplace. Outside, heavy snow fogged the world past her property line. It was quiet, peaceful, and oddly isolating. Wide-awake, she waited for Jack to come home. Icy road conditions had forced them to leave the party early. Frankie made a panicked call to Jack at the gala; the service station was flooded with calls for towing services.

Thoughts of the evening played like reruns in Catherine's head. The way Jack had gazed at her as she descended the grand staircase. Catherine let her shawl dangle at her side, drawing the eye to her bare left shoulder and sweeping neckline fastened over the right, complimented by the pearl jewelry from Jack. She could tell he found her breathtaking in the formfitting black evening gown. When she reached him, Jack impulsively kissed her on the cheek.

"You look fantastic." Cat blushed shyly at his genuine affection, heightened with hope for an intimate ending to this evening. She sensed the electricity between them when they'd danced. Everyone commented on what a handsome couple they made.

Jack had quickly changed into his insulated jumpsuit as soon as they'd made it home. When he was leaving, Cat stopped him.

"I hate we won't be together for the countdown to midnight," she told him. Before he could object, she instigated the kiss. He'd kissed her back and quickly released her, apologizing for needing to leave. He'd taken her breath away.

Entering the house, Jack took off his coat and hung it on the hook by the back door. He shed his boots, sidestepping the globs of melting snow. Noticing a glow coming from the living room, Jack assumed Cat had left the Christmas tree plugged in. It shocked him to find her sitting on the rug, wrapped in an afghan, with an inviting fire blazing in the fireplace. The lights of the Christmas tree twinkled cheerfully.

"Would you care for a glass of wine?" she asked, showing him a recently opened bottle.

"I'd love one. It's after three; why're you still awake?" He retrieved a wineglass from the liquor cabinet and joined her on the rug. She poured. Jack pointed his feet closer to the fire, making them sting as they thawed.

"Waiting for you to get home. I knew I wouldn't be able to sleep until you got here safe."

The way she studied him made Jack uncomfortable; it had all evening. "It's bitter cold. I wish people'd stay home when it snows like this. They don't know how to drive. They speed fifty miles an hour, slam on the brakes, and spin into a ditch." He shook his head in disbelief. Taking a sip of wine, he shifted for maximum defrost warmth from the hearth. "Oh yeah, that's better."

"How deep is it now?" she asked.

"Maybe two feet and it doesn't appear to be letting up. Frankie's at the station, taking calls; we'll pull their cars out in the morning. If these folks can get to a phone to call me, then they can call a friend to carry them home. Some drunken fool almost ran me over when I was working on the last car I towed. That was it, the rest can wait for daylight."

"Well, I'm glad you're home." Catherine flashed her sweet, sexy smile at him. Her beauty glimmered in the firelight. Jack poured himself another glass of wine.

"It was a great party, wasn't it?" Catherine reflected.

"It was. I hope your charity reached their goal."

"They surpassed it. Mother called me when she and Daddy got home."

Jack's stomach tightened with guilt. "She wanted to make sure I got you home safely."

"Mother's silly, you know," Cat told him.

"Yeah, I know."

They sat in silence for a long time, staring at the flames licking the logs. Cat slowly sipped wine as she fingered the string of pearls still adorning her neck. Jack turned to watch her. Smiling, she looked as beautiful as she had at twenty-two.

"Do you know what I was thinking about, sitting here?"

"No, what?" he asked.

"Our first New Year's Eve, we made love, here on this rug. Do you remember?" Suddenly she looked shy.

Jack turned his face back to the embers. "How could I forget? That seems like a long time ago." He swallowed the last of the wine in his glass.

"Not so long ago, not really." She poured him the remaining wine from the bottle. "I love the pearl earrings. Thank you, again."

"You're welcome. They suit you," Jack said, wrestling with guilt again. If only the gift could redeem him from hell. In the romantic light of the fire, she practically glowed. The old Cat had returned. His feelings for her stirred in him; briefly, he wished he'd never met Joanna. If he'd been faithful, he'd be making love to her now.

"I'm exhausted. Work starts at first light." Jack raised himself off the floor and climbed the stairs to his bedroom. After a quick shower, he tugged on a pair of flannel pajamas. With the fatigue of battling a blizzard, as well as the intoxication of the wine, sleep came quickly and he welcomed it.

Jack's dreams were filled with visions of Catherine, dressed in her party gown, her bare shoulder enticing him. Suddenly the dream changed and they were in their bed. She was holding him from behind and kissing his neck. He could almost feel the warmth of her breath on his face as she whispered, "I love you, Jackie."

It had been so long since he'd experienced a sexy dream. He allowed himself to go with the vivid fantasy. Turning toward Catherine and taking her in his arms, he met her mouth with his. He could practically taste her. This felt too good. She lightly stroked his chest. Her warm tongue found his. In the dim luster from the streetlights, he watched as she lowered her white silk nightgown. She looked like an angel. His body ached for her.

"Don't wake me up," he breathed.

"It's not a dream," she panted. Fully awake now and overwhelmed by the moment, his only thoughts were of Cat and the intensity they were sharing. When it was over, he held her tight, feeling her heart beating in the same quick rhythm as his own. They went to sleep without saying a word.

Chapter 20

Bitter cold followed the snow that greeted the new year and kept the ice from thawing for several days. Rodney the milkman couldn't make his usual deliveries, and the girls who were awaiting letters from birthfathers were getting antsy, especially Joanna. Her melancholy mood irritated Jessie while they worked in the laundry on Tuesday night.

"I don't understand you girls who're so hot to get married," she told Joanna. "I'm never gonna get married. I like my freedom."

"When I'm with Jack, I feel more free than I do anywhere else," Joanna put a load of smock dresses in the huge dryer.

"That's not my experience. Every guy I've dated always wants to control me."

"What about your baby's father?" Joanna arranged the next load in the washer while Jessie folded.

"He was sweet in the beginnin'. We were havin' a great time, until he got possessive, demandin' to know where I was all the time. He kept askin' me to marry him."

"What'd he say about the baby?"

"I didn't tell him. I left him a Dear John letter saying I was goin' to New York." Joanna's eyes went wide. "He was suffocatin' me! We fought a lot! If he knew 'bout the baby, I'd be tied to him for life! Besides, our goals aren't the same. He has the talent, but no drive."

"Jack and I never fight."

"That's not normal. Everybody fights," Jessie objected.

A week later, when the dairy express finally ran again, Joanna received her much-anticipated letter from Jack. He sent her an additional $10, along with an explanation of his race car being out of commission. She cried when she read the change in plans, which required her to give birth at the home. With the racing season shot, he'd be short the money he'd hoped to earn. He promised to fetch both her and the baby from the home upon release. He'd have a cozy apartment for them. This disappointed Joanna, but she understood.

Her roommates were cautiously pessimistic when she told them the news. "You'll see. When Jack comes to whisk me away, you'll believe then," Joanna defended.

Joanna resisted the urge to sink into a depression. Instead she spent her hours daydreaming of the perfect life Jack described. She envisioned yellow curtains in the kitchen and a light-blue nursery for their baby. She imagined their routines: Jack as the provider, working at his gas station, and she as the consummate wife and caregiver. Their weekends would begin with the races. In her fantasy, she'd reserve Sundays for breakfast in bed and picnics at the park. When he grew older, they'd teach their son how to ride a bike. Their life would be flawless.

Joanna and Missy relaxed in the parlor, watching a western on television, while Mary scribbled off a letter to a friend from her cheerleading squad. Her friends in Nashville sent letters to her grandmother's house and for the sake of appearances she answered them, concocting lies about the high school she attended and her recuperating grandmother.

Mary opened the letter from Pookie Lister. Scanning it quickly, she cried, "Oh my God!"

Joanna jumped at Mary's shrillness. "What's wrong?"

"Tony's going steady with Melinda Peterson." Mary hadn't mentioned the name of her baby's father before. "I guess you knew he's the guilty party, right?"

"Yeah, the football player; I figured." Joanna never questioned it.

Struggling to speak, with tears in her eyes, she whispered, "If he can forget about me that easily, I swear I'll kill myself."

"It has to be for show." Joanna talked fast, reassuring her. "Tony has an image to uphold; he'd be uncool to mope after you dumped him. Write him a letter. Mail it dairy express?"

"No, I can't. If I mailed it to his house, his mom'd get it first. There's no one I trust to pass him a message. I'll have to wait. I'm sure he's doing it for appearances' sake." Mary dried her tears, then straightened her shoulders with new resolve.

"Maybe I could ask Jack. I'm sure he'd do it for ya."

"I've heard you talk about him, but I don't remember a Jack at school."

"Oh, ya wouldn't know him; he didn't go to school. His name's Jack Wyatt."

"Catherine Langley Wyatt's husband?" Mary's eyes were wide with surprise. Joanna hadn't considered that because of shared social status, Mary might indeed be acquainted with them. "Wow," Mary gaped, staring at Joanna. "I don't know them very well. Her mom and my mom are always on committees together, and Mr. Langley and my father occasionally have business dealings. I've seen Catherine at events; she used to volunteer a lot, until the accident."

"So ya know 'bout the accident?" Joanna asked.

"Everybody knows. It was tragic," Mary verified. "Catherine became a shut-in."

"You don't think badly of me 'cause Jack's married?"

"We're both here for the same reason. I'm not in any position to judge anyone."

The following Saturday, after the girls had their regular checkups with Dr. Miller, Rachel didn't report to the garment room in the afternoon. Sister Bridget informed them she'd gone into labor. The birth of Rachel's little girl went quickly and mother and baby were fine.

"She's giggly and asking for ice cream," the nun told them as they ate dinner.

"You get ice cream when you get your tonsils out! She's so funny!" Mary chuckled.

Rachel's elation didn't fade over the days of her recovery, and when it came time to say goodbye to the Frances Weston Home, she acted as if it was the best day of her life. Jessie, Joanna, Mary, and Missy stood before her with long faces.

"Oh come on! You should be happy for me!" Rachel urged as she put on a cute blue hat.

"Where're ya going?" Jessie asked her.

"Secretarial school."

"I know that, but where?" Jessie's jaw tightened with irritation.

The blond girl stared at her shoes. Finally, looking at Jessie, she backpedaled, "It's not like I'll ever forget y'all, but I wanna forget this place and start over."

"Oh, I get it, have a nice life; don't look for me." Jessie abruptly headed for the staircase.

"Jessie, don't be that way," Rachel called after her.

"Eat shit, Rachel!" Jessie responded as she continued to the second floor.

Joanna broke the awkward silence left in Jessie's wake by giving Rachel a hug and saying, "I'm gonna miss you! Take care of yourself and keep your hair lookin' pretty."

"Thanks for teachin' me how to do it." Rachel released her. Joanna smiled stiffly.

"I think you'll be a good secretary; you look like one in your suit," Missy told her.

"I think you'll be good at whatever you do, Missy." Rachel patted her on the head.

"Marsha!" Rachel embraced Mary for a final goodbye squeeze.

"Do you have your article on office etiquette?" Mary joked.

"I'm gonna frame it to remind myself. I'll be back at my parents' house if I fail."

"That's the spirit," Mary encouraged. The taxi pulled through the gate and the three girls watched as yet another close friend left their midst, never to be seen again.

Louise Fitch sat behind her desk and chewed at a snagged fingernail, distressed by the impending out-of-town trip to visit her father on his deathbed. A knock broke her concentration.

"Come in," she called.

Sister Bridget entered the room. "You wanted to see me?"

"Yes, Sister. I'm afraid I have to leave town for a family emergency. This couldn't come at a worse time because of the fashion show. We'll have to cancel it."

"Oh no, we can't! The girls are counting on the money for vocational school."

"I'm aware," Fitch barked as she shuffled some folders on her desk.

"Let me handle the show," the nun suggested.

"You can't do it all by yourself."

"I'll have Bernice Atherton with me. You and I've done it with her help for the last two years. I know how everything works."

"I don't know," Fitch considered. "Which girls would you take with you?" The home regularly selected a few of the residents to go to the show. It increased the pity factor and boosted the sales when the benefactors saw the unfortunate birthmothers in person.

"Marsha'd be a great asset with her fashion sense, and Jean's sewing ability would be invaluable if we need any alterations. And of course, Missy, since she sticks so close to Jean."

"Perhaps." Fitch contemplated her unofficial bonus if the show took place as scheduled. "I'm not sure Missy should go; she's from Memphis. What if someone she knows sees her?"

"I'll see to it she maintains a low profile. Besides, from what we know of her family, the only contact she has outside her home is school. She's very sheltered."

She considered the nun's argument. "You'd have to retain complete control of the girls."

"It's only for two nights," Bridget defended.

"Sister Maria Alice will be in charge of the home while I'm gone. I'll allow you to manage the fashion show; you'd better succeed."

"Understood. Everything will run smoothly, I promise."

"It better. I'm taking a huge gamble here. I insist on nothing less than success." Fitch rutted through papers on her desk, signaling the end to the conversation.

"I don't know why any of y'all wanna go. Fitch is usin' ya. '*See the poor pregnant girls.*' I wouldn't be caught dead at her stupid fashion show," Jessie cynically admonished.

"I'm counting on you to provide piano music. I thought you'd relish the chance to get out of here for a couple of days," Sister Bridget countered, using reverse psychology.

"Fitch'd never agree to me bein' there."

"She'll never know. I'm in charge. But you have to promise to behave yourself," the nun skillfully negotiated. The redhead gave her word to stay out of trouble. After having been locked away in the home for months, they all looked forward to the reprieve with excitement.

When Jack came in through the back door, Cat told him, "Dinner's almost ready."

"Give me a few minutes to clean up." Jack habitually showered after work. Catherine removed her apron. Desiring a casual mood for their meal, she wore a simple plaid dress. She'd set the table in the breakfast nook without romantic candles or flowers.

Moments later, Jack took a seat across from her and dug into the fried chicken on his plate. "Wow, you cooked this?" he asked, with his mouth full, obviously impressed.

"Flora gave me her recipe," Catherine explained.

"It's great." Jack took another bite.

"Mother and I are thinking of going to Memphis for a fashion show the third weekend in January, all right?"

"Yeah. Sure," Jack expressed indifferently. He took a second helping of chicken.

Catherine sensed the tension between them. The conversation lagged, and after a few minutes, she softly informed him, "I'm not going to break, Jack."

"You might," Jack warned, looking at his plate.

"No, I won't. I'm ready for things to be like they used to be."

"Things will never be how they used to be." Jack raised his voice and dropped his fork in anger, looking directly at her. "You think you're ready, but for what? Jesus, Cat! You've practically been in a coma for three years; now suddenly you're like a bulldozer, frantically trying to repair the dike that washed away a long time ago. Everything's changed!"

Putting her hand over her heart, Cat said, "I'm sorry, Jack. I've been so preoccupied trying to get my life on track I didn't think about how you're affected. I'm sorry, I promise I won't push you. We can let things happen normally!"

Jack left the table, his back to her. "Normally? I don't even know what normal is anymore!" He paused. "I know you want life to go back to what it was before…"

"I was hoping you'd want that, too," she interrupted.

"We don't always get what we want" were Jack's last words as he left the kitchen.

This shocked Catherine. In all the years they'd been together, he'd never raised his voice or treated her as if he considered her a spoiled child. She mulled his assessment: that their relationship was forever altered. If that were true, then how they proceeded from here would define their marriage in the future.

Chapter 21

Jack paced the concrete floor of his garage. The corner of Joanna's letter received today peeked from his back pocket. Her response to his last letter had been disappointment melded with understanding. He crossed his arms, eyeing the shiny red sports car, Cat's Christmas gift. He'd driven it once, to store it here. He couldn't conceive of running this car in races when leaving his wife to marry his mistress remained the sole purpose for winning. Jack jumped when Alex came in the back door, even though he expected him.

"Damn, she's a beautiful ride," were the first words from Alex. "I'll bet you were blown away. I, of course, knew all about it; who'd you think put it in your driveway, Christmas morning? The way her engine purrs is like a hot dame durin' sex! Have you opened it up yet?"

"No," Jack answered.

Alex looked at him, confused. "You haven't run her at the track? Why not? What about next week's race?"

"I'm not entering. Remember when you asked me if I had someone on the side? Well, I do." Jack explained about Joanna, leaving nothing out. Alex stared blankly at his friend until he finished his story. Without warning, Alex punched Jack in the jaw, hard. Alex danced a circle, rubbing out the pain in his knuckles.

"I guess I deserve that," Jack permitted, massaging his face.

"That's just a taste of what Langley's gonna do to you when he finds out, you stupid fuck! When I'd try to get you out, when Cat was sick, for a one-night stand, it was for somethin' to keep your Wally working and improve your shitty disposition. I wasn't talkin' about a relationship that's gonna ruin your marriage."

"I know. I didn't mean for this to happen," Jack said.

"You can't divorce Cat. You're gonna have to keep Joanna on the side."

"I can't," Jack said solemnly.

"You don't have a choice," Alex told him.

For days afterward, Jack pondered Alex's advice. With Joanna in the home until the birth, he'd borrowed time to break the news to Cat. Regardless, he intended to secure an apartment for them while Cat and her mother went to Memphis for some silly fashion show.

The ride from Knoxville to Memphis took over seven hours, but the girls enjoyed it. Like pet-shop birds freed to fly around the store, laughter punctuated their twittering. Sister Bridget, dressed in street clothes, functioned as ringleader and driver. The girls had also shed their uniforms and now wore regular maternity clothes.

"I don't know how you can stand to be dressed in black all the time," Mary told the young sister. "You look so attractive in your wool suit. What made you want to become a nun?"

Bridget smiled. "I was abandoned at a Catholic orphanage when I was three. I wanted to do something to help others, so I became a nun."

"Do you know anythin' about your parents?" Jessie asked.

"No. The nuns didn't know who left me or why."

"Didn't you ever wonder about your family?" Mary asked.

"Yes, especially when I was getting ready to take my vows. But after much soul searching, I decided God had placed me where He wanted me and dedicated my life to service."

Contemplative silence ensued, until Mary spoke. "That's how it'll be for our babies, isn't it? They won't know anything about us, or why we gave them up. They'll always wonder."

Jessie jabbed, "That's if the adoptive parents even tell them they're adopted. And what if they do? You won't know about it. We're always gonna worry, one day, in the middle of our life, the kid we surrendered is gonna come lookin' for us."

"Those records are sealed, Jessie." Sister Bridget informed her. "The adoptive parents are told little about you, and you're told nothing about them. It protects your privacy in the future."

"It also makes sure we don't change our minds and go lookin' for our babies," Jessie claimed hatefully. "I'm glad. I won't wanna be found twenty years from now."

Bridget parked by the valet booth shortly before 8:00 p.m. and her passengers piled out, excitedly taking in their surroundings. Joanna expected the hotel to look like a medieval castle from Mary's description. Instead, the building had a modern design; she craned her neck to see the red neon PEABODY sign at the top of the building.

When they entered through the heavy glassed revolving doors, Joanna understood Mary's enthusiasm for the Peabody Hotel. Her eyes didn't know where to look as she took in the opulence of the marble-columned lobby with its carved woodwork and stained glass. She'd never seen a ceiling so high. She quickly turned her attention to the lobby fountain.

"Where're the ducks?" she asked Mary, disappointed.

"They're in their pen on the roof. They go back there at five in the evening. The Duckmaster will bring them down again in the morning at eleven. I want to watch from the mezzanine." Mary explained. "If you're on the main floor, someone's always in your way."

Sister Bridget interrupted their conversation by calling, "Come along, girls." Joining her by the luggage cart, they tossed their coats on the top of the suitcases. The nun instructed them to go to the restaurant and charge dinner to their room. She and Bernice had final preparations to discuss. Pocketing their room key, Mary led the way to the elevators in a separate marble alcove.

Jessie stopped them. "Wait, let's take a quick look at the shops." The redhead beelined to the liquor store. The rest looked in the windows of the various merchants. Joanna clutched $5 in her pocket, hoping she might find an inexpensive trinket to keep the memory of this trip. She and Missy came to a stop in front of the closed beauty shop on the mezzanine level and pressed their noses to the window to peer inside.

Mary joined them. "Fancy isn't it?"

"I'll say!" Joanna expressed, "Look at all the services they offer: everything from hair trims and pedicures to facials and massage." The girls reunited with Jessie by the elevators.

"I'm starving," Mary revealed. "We'd better go to the Skyway before they close." Greeted by a maître d' on the top floor of the hotel, Mary requested, "Party of four."

"Right this way, please." The man, dressed in a suit and bow tie, escorted them to an out-of-the-way table, obscured from view of the remaining diners. A waiter replaced the maître d' and treated them kindly, with good service, yet the girls were keenly aware of his discomfort.

Missy's silhouette showed distinctly against the glow of the streetlights on Union Avenue below. Mary lay half asleep in one of the two queen-sized beds. Joanna stretched out in the other, enjoying the luxurious sheets, contently full from the fanciest meal she'd ever eaten. Jessie sat on the couch, sipping the whiskey she'd purchased in the liquor store.

Missy asked, "Do you think Michelle's right about what happens when we go home?"

"Which part?" Joanna sat up.

"That, if I see you on the street, we'd act like we didn't even know each other?"

"I'd never do that to you, Missy!" Joanna assured her. The other girls quickly agreed.

"Good, because I'd never do that to you." Missy continued, "I'm next, you know? Dr. Miller says it won't be long, and I'll never see any of you again."

"Are you afraid to go home?" Mary asked.

"No, not to go home. What if I have nightmares again?"

"You can take your flashlight with you; that might help," Joanna reminded her.

"Tell us about your nightmares," Mary coaxed.

"It's monsters mostly, sometimes snakes crawling on me. A lot of times I can't remember them in the morning, so I put a diary by my bed and started drawing what I could remember."

"Can we see?" Jessie asked.

Missy went to the nightstand, turned on the light, and retrieved the book Joanna had seen their first day at the home. She entrusted it to Jessie, and they all hovered over the pages of the well-drawn creatures haunting Missy's sleep. They marveled at the detail and frightening appearance of the images; monsters resembling fierce dragons and pages of intertwined snakes, poised to strike. The older girls locked eyes in expressions of fear for Missy.

"Missy, do you think it might be your dad who made you pregnant?" Mary asked softly.

"No!" Missy shouted. "No, Daddy'd never do that to me! I know how babies get here, from y'all and Mrs. Lewis. Someone must've raped me, like Michelle told her mom happened to her. It must've been horrifying, that's why I can't remember, just like I can't remember my dreams." Missy sobbed defensively.

"It's okay, honey." Joanna hugged her. "We're concerned for your safety. You're okay."

Missy took a moment to collect herself. With new strength, she proclaimed, "My real name is Priscilla Matthews. Daddy calls me Prissy. I live in Germantown. Daddy's drugstore is only a few blocks from this hotel. Now I want to know your names."

Mary spoke first without hesitation. "I'm Mary Atherton, from Nashville. But I'll be in nursing school here in Memphis this summer. So we can see each other all the time. I promise."

"Oh, I don't know. Daddy might not allow it."

"It's expected girls your age have friends they do stuff with; you can convince him."

"I'm Joanna Wilson, also from Nashville. I'll go back to live with Jack. I'm sure we'll see each other, especially when Jack has races over here."

Jessie went last. "I'm Jessica Devereaux, from New Orleans. I think I'll keep Jessie and change my last name to Diamond as a stage name."

"Jessie Diamond. It has a nice ring," Priscilla said.

Jessie continued, "I'm not sure where I'm goin' after Knoxville. I might visit Karen—I mean, Katie O'Brien—in Chattanooga. Maybe I'll hit Nashville, see what I can find music-wise. We'll stay best friends forever, I promise." The other three added their vow of sisterhood, forever and hugged.

Exhausted and emotionally spent, Prissy yawned as she climbed into the double bed she'd share with Joanna. Before long, she fell asleep; the older girls sat awake in the darkness.

Finally, Mary whispered, "I can't imagine having a father that'd hurt me that way."

"Some dads are worse than others." Joanna sighed.

Mary got philosophical. "Jessie, don't you feel like your dad is your guardian angel?"

Jessie took a swig from the whiskey bottle and let out a painful laugh, "Nope, not at all. I don't believe in God or the hereafter. We get one shot at life and burn out like a shooting star. There's no help from above; you help yourself."

Joanna concluded, "I envy you, Mary. From what you've said, your dad sounds great. I wish I had a dad like him. But mostly, I hope Prissy's father is everythin' she thinks he is."

Chapter 22

A flurry of activity dictated the morning of the fashion show. Bernice Atherton relied on Mary to match the outfits to the hired models. Sister Bridget and Prissy distributed order forms and pens on the tables for their guests, while Joanna fixed Jessie's hair and makeup in the hotel room.

A little before 11:00 a.m., the four young mothers-to-be were excused to view the Duck March. They promised to return to the Skyway Room immediately upon its completion, as at eleven thirty the admittance to the fashion show luncheon began.

The girls assembled by the railing on the mezzanine level, overlooking the crowded lobby, waiting with anticipation for the Duckmaster to make his speech. Joanna marveled at the large number of onlookers excitedly gathered to watch the famous Peabody ducks. They'd had fun, until suddenly Mary grabbed Joanna and pulled her behind a square wooden support pillar.

"Oh my God!" Mary hissed in a panic. "At the table, over there, is Mabel Anderson. She's with the Langleys and Catherine."

"Jack's Catherine? Where?" Joanna peeked out to get a look at her rival.

"Don't look! I think Wendell Langley saw me. God, what if he recognized me?" Mary quickly latched on to Jessie and Prissy, nudging them into a waiting elevator.

"Hey! I thought we were going to watch the ducks!" Prissy complained. As the doors slowly slid shut, Joanna spotted a large man absorbed in conversation with three women who had their backs to her, making it impossible for her to check out Catherine.

As the elevator moved upward, Joanna asked, "That's Wendell Langley, with the cigar?"

Mary nodded. "This is terrible. I can't be seen at the fashion show. I'm sure that's why Mrs. Anderson is here. If those women see me, I'm ruined. Especially Millicent Langley. She'll have the news spread all over Nashville before she even leaves Memphis!"

Conflicting thoughts bombarded Joanna's mind: Why had Catherine come to this fashion show? Joanna remembered Jack's warning about Mr. Langley's surveillance and photographs. Were they in attendance because of her or was all this a bizarre coincidence?

Mary rushed into the Skyway Room hysterical, blurting out to the nun and her grandmother that she must leave the hotel at once. She rambled on, describing impending doom.

Bernice Atherton calmed the excited teenager. "It's going to be all right, child. You stay behind the curtain backstage, and help with the models."

"They've never met me, but I don't think I should be seen, either," Joanna said.

"Maybe it's best if Jessie's the only one our guests meet," Sister Bridget suggested. "You three stay out of sight; I promise, it'll be fine."

Before long, women entered the Skyway, checkbooks in hand, for the fashion show. From backstage, the guests' voices began as a low hum and grew as the room met capacity. Mary paced, rubbing her hands together, formulating an escape plan, while Joanna spied through a small opening in the curtain.

"Jessie sounds great, doesn't she?" Prissy commented on the music coming from the main room. Focused on catching a glimpse of Catherine, Joanna ignored Prissy.

"Where are they?" she asked Mary.

Squinting through Joanna's peephole, Mary said, "Third table to the right of the entrance. Mr. Langley isn't with them. He's probably in the bar."

Joanna looked again, locating them. Her heart beat hard as she took in the beauty of Jack's wife. She watched as Catherine laughed lightly in response to a comment by Mabel. Catherine didn't appear at all sick. Even more distressing, Joanna assessed Catherine as the personification of elegance, health, and beauty. The pregnant girl felt ugly in comparison. She didn't understand: If Jack's wife had recovered, why hadn't he asked for a divorce?

As Bernice Atherton took her place at the microphone and welcomed the women to the luncheon, Millicent leaned over to Mabel and whispered, "Hasn't Edith's mother-in-law made a remarkable recovery from a broken hip? I'd've expected her to be using a cane."

"I'm not surprised," Mabel answered. "She's feisty. She's been mistress of ceremonies at this show for years."

"I had no idea," Millicent commented.

"Remind me to ask after Mary. I hope she'll bring her to my shop in the spring for her prom dress. Edith spends a fortune with me on Mary," Mabel added.

"Has Mary gotten a new beau in Knoxville?"

"I haven't heard. With Mary out of town, I haven't seen much of Edith lately."

The two women continued to whisper between themselves while Catherine paid attention to the redheaded pregnant girl who performed on the piano. Catherine studied the girl's features and the bulge of her swollen little belly. For the first time since the accident, hope replaced pain at the sight of a mother-to-be. Could an unwed mother be the solution to her empty arms? She wondered about the birthmother of the baby she'd adopt; would she be as pretty and talented as the girl at the piano? Mrs. Atherton's opening remarks emphasized that these girls came from all walks of life, many from good homes. Birthmother status didn't matter to Cat, but her father, who promised to handle the details, would consider the baby's background. She needed to persuade Jack. Adopting could mend their damaged relationship.

For the next hour and a half, Jessie entertained the benefactors with the style of a professional musician. She smiled with joy at their applause and graciously accepted their compliments on her musical ability. The other three girls remained hidden behind the velvet curtain, frantically assisting the models with wardrobe changes. A collective sigh of relief went out as the last of the guests departed on the elevators.

Boxing the outfits and organizing the orders consumed the rest of the afternoon. Sister Bridget tallied the paperwork, expressing pleasure with the above-average purchases. When the chores were completed, the nun instructed the girls to return to the hotel room for a nap.

"It's been an exciting day," she told them. "I'll come for you at five and we'll go to the Rendezvous for the best ribs you've ever tasted." She hoped this might lift Mary's glum mood.

Entering their room, Mary threw herself on the bed. "This is the worst day of my life."

"You don't know for sure he saw you," Jessie told her.

"I'll know soon enough; it'll get back to my mother. I can only imagine that hailstorm!"

Joanna went to the phone and spoke into the receiver, "Long distance, please."

"Who're you calling?" Missy asked.

"Jack. I've had a phone sitting right here since yesterday. I can't believe I didn't think of this before." She waited as the call connected. Frankie answered and Joanna asked for Jack.

"Frankie, this is Joanna. Tell him I called?" she asked. "Damn it. Where can he be? I don't know his home phone number or I'd call there! Especially since I know Catherine isn't gonna answer."

"The long-distance operator should be able to look it up," Jessie suggested.

Moments later the phone rang at the other end. Joanna stuttered, "May I... I, speak to Jack?... No, no message." Joanna hung up the receiver. "She must've been the housekeeper. I should've hung up. Where is he?"

Late at night, Joanna stared at the ceiling, blaringly awake. Her deafening anguish should've awakened her sleeping comrades. She slipped silently from her bed and dressed. Carrying her shoes, she tiptoed out of the room and rode the elevator to the roof. Joanna inhaled the cold January air and let her acrid tears escape. The lights of the outstretched city blurred before her.

"Well, fancy meetin' you here." Jessie's voice interrupted Joanna's train of thought. She quickly dried her eyes and cleared her throat.

"I couldn't sleep," Joanna confessed.

"I hope this Jack of yours is worth all this," Jessie warned, lighting a cigarette.

"He is," Joanna assured her.

"Are ya worried he has a new girlfriend, or he's cheating on you with his wife?"

"No, of course not; that's ridiculous," Joanna shot back angrily.

"Is it? If he'll cheat on his wife, he's capable of cheating on you."

"Jessie, I'm not gonna dignify that with a response."

"Hey! Don't get sore with me. I'm just lookin' out for you," Jessie rationalized, staring off toward the faint beat of blues music coming from Beale Street. The red neon light of the PEABODY sign colored their awkward silence. Jessie puffed her cigarette, blowing columns of smoke skyward. Eventually she tried to break the tension by saying, "I can't wait until I have this baby and get the hell out of Knoxville."

"Yeah, then you can go back to not caring about anyone but yourself," Joanna snipped.

Jessie nodded. With a pained frown, she granted, "I'll let ya take a stab at me, if it makes ya feel better, 'cause that's what true friends do. It's not me you're angry with. I hope my gut instinct about Jack is wrong, for your sake. I know I come off as hard, but for the people I care about, I'm all mushy and gooey on the inside."

"Like one of those hard candies that take a while till you get to the creamy filling?" Joanna chuckled, despite her irritation.

"Exactly, but don't tell anyone; it might spoil my image."

"Sorry I snapped at you."

"Don't sweat it, you've got a lot on your mind. You're not alone; I'll always be there for you, if you need me. I'll find Jack's gas station when I get to Nashville."

"Promise?" Joanna hugged her friend.

"I swear. Come on, let's go back to bed. It's cold out here."

A week after the fashion show, the girls were busy with the monumental process of filling the orders. Joanna looked away from her sewing machine when Prissy complained, "My back hurts and I'm sick to my stomach."

"Do you have a fever or a headache?" Sister Bridget felt her forehead.

"Ouch," Prissy winced, rubbing the sore spot of her back.

"You're not sick, you're in labor," the nun announced. "When did this start?"

"Before breakfast."

"We'd better go to the hospital wing and see where you stand," the nun coaxed.

"Can I go, too?" Joanna begged.

"No. Sister Eugenia'd have a conniption fit. With Mrs. Fitch still away, I'll need to be there, which means I'll trust you to work on your own."

"As if we're gonna get anythin' done now," Jessie muttered.

"The busier you are, the faster time will go. I promise, I'll take good care of her."

The girls spent the remainder of the day waiting for news from Sister Bridget. Hours passed slowly with no word. Lights-out came, and the onslaught of darkness made their restlessness maddening. Finally, around two in the morning,

Joanna heard voices coming from downstairs. She and Jessie sneaked from the dorm room and looked over the railing to find Sister Bridget and Sister Eugenia embroiled in a heated discussion, by Fitch's office. As they descended the stairs, Sister Eugenia held a bundle she assumed must be Prissy's baby and she insisted, "My decision is final. This child isn't adoptable."

Sister Bridget continued to negotiate. "Can't you wait until tomorrow, when Mrs. Fitch returns, and see what she says?"

"I know what she'll say. You should be thanking God she's not here, because she'd let the poor little thing die and be done with it! We're not equipped to care for a baby with spina bifida. She has fluid on the brain and is going to have seizures. At least if we take her to the asylum, she'll get the care she needs to make her short life more comfortable."

"But there's a new surgery…" Bridget raised another argument.

"Enough!" The older nun silenced her. "She won't live long enough for the powers that be to approve such a procedure. I'm responsible for the newborns here. With Mrs. Fitch gone, this is my decision and I won't discuss this with you further!"

As they got closer, Joanna asked, "Is that Missy's baby? Did you say it's a girl?"

"Go back to your beds," Sister Eugenia commanded. Joanna and Jessie kept advancing.

"What's wrong? Where're you takin' Missy's baby?" Jessie shouted aggressively.

"Go back to your room. I'll be up in a few minutes," Sister Bridget begged. Joanna and Jessie did as they were told; the five minutes it took for the nun to return seemed like an hour.

As soon as Sister Bridget entered the dorm room, they bombarded her with questions. "Is something wrong with Missy's baby?"

"Where's Sister Eugenia taking it?"

"Is Missy okay?"

The nun turned on the light next to Joanna's bed and sat. The girls gathered around her, eager for answers.

"Missy's fine. She's sleeping. But her baby has a birth defect called spina bifida."

"What's that?" Joanna asked.

"It's where the spine and sometimes the brain don't form properly, right?" Mary guessed.

"That's right. Sister Eugenia says it's the worst case she's ever seen. She's sure

Missy's baby girl won't live but a few days." Sister Bridget rubbed her grief-creased forehead.

"Where did she take the baby?" Mary asked.

"There's an asylum for the mentally ill not far from here, with medical staff better equipped to care for her."

"Do you think what she said is true, about Fitch lettin' babies die if they're not considered adoptable?" Joanna asked.

"No, surely not," Sister Bridget objected, as if it was too outrageous to consider.

"As far as you know. I wouldn't put it past that bitch to commit murder if it affected the cash flow around here. Let's face it: It's more economical to bury a baby than to financially support a retarded child no one wants!" Jessie raised her voice.

"No one's murdered anyone! For pity's sake Jessie, sometimes you… I'm exhausted, and I don't have the energy to debate this with you! Go to bed now and, if I can, I'll let you see Missy in the morning."

Chapter 23

Before breakfast, Sister Bridget came to the dorm room to accompany the girls to the hospital wing for a short visit with Missy. "You can have five minutes. Don't mention the birth defect. She doesn't know, and it'd only upset her."

Mary gasped. "Don't you think she has a right to know?"

"Her family will tell her at the appropriate time." Jessie stared at the nun with contempt. "Jessie, don't give me that look. Please trust me on this."

The rebel challenged, "I don't know if I can trust ya. If I was Missy I'd wanna know."

"If something happens to your baby, I'll tell you. Missy doesn't have a realistic view of things. It's best her family break the news. Now give me your word or you won't see her."

"We promise," Joanna answered quickly, shooting Jessie a warning look.

Once in the room, the drowsy young girl seemed happy to see her friends. "I don't remember much. Sister Bridget gave me some gas and when I woke up, she let me see my baby. Did she tell you it's a girl? She kind of looked like my baby pictures."

"How're you feeling? Do you need anything?" Mary asked, in caregiver mode.

"No, I'm fine. I'm bleeding heavy, but Sister Eugenia says that's normal. She's given me some pain pills so I'm not hurting. I sure am glad Mrs. Fitch's gone. I think she's the mean one and we've been wrong about Sister Eugenia. She's been so kind."

"I'm glad," Joanna soothed.

Two days later, the girls were shocked to learn Prissy's father had taken her home while they attended Mr. Ehrlichman's class. Joanna took it hard. "I can't believe ya let him take her!"

"He's her father; I didn't have any choice," Sister Bridget defended.

"You could've told us. We never got to say goodbye to her!"

"I'm sorry; I didn't know beforehand. He made arrangements with Mrs. Fitch, and I had no idea until he arrived," the nun explained.

Jessie shook her head. "I hope ya can sleep at night, wonderin' if there's somethin' more ya should've done to protect her."

"I'm sorry you feel that way, Jessie. Maybe someday you'll realize I care deeply about you girls. But there's some things even my best efforts cannot change."

"Maybe ya shouldn't bother. You're gonna dedicate your life to this place; years from now you'll be a dried-up, bitter old crow, like the rest of them. I hear all your ambitious talk, how ya hope to make things better. In the end you'll've watched thousands of girls come through and realize your bein' here didn't make any difference."

Sister Bridget looked at the floor. "I'll pray that doesn't happen. I'd sincerely hoped my presence in your life would have a positive effect on you, Jessie. You know, a few times I thought I'd gotten through to you. I guess I was wrong." The young nun left the girl's room.

"Geez, Jessie! You didn't have to be so hard on her," Mary scolded.

"Oh, who cares? I hate this damn place. It's a goddamn prison baby factory!" Jessie screamed in rage. Swiping a hairbrush off the nightstand, she threw it so hard across the room it made a dent in the wall over Prissy's bed.

Cat's fears lightened momentarily when her father joined her in the waiting lounge of the hospital emergency room. He hugged her lovingly and asked, "How're you holding up, Kitten?"

"Oh, Daddy, the doctors are doing everything they can, but he's seriously injured. The attending physician said they'd know more in a few hours. But he isn't holding out much hope Jack's going to make it. I'm so scared, I can't lose him." Wendell held his only child closer. "What did the police say?" Catherine asked Wendell, who'd been to the charred rubble of what remained of Jack's gas station. He'd met with the head investigator to ascertain what they were able to piece together about the explosion.

"They suspect a leaky gas pump. Perhaps he was careless with a cigarette. All indications point to this being a terrible accident," Wendell explained. Catherine nodded her understanding. Wendell went on, "The paramedics claimed Jack reeked of whiskey."

"He's been under a great deal of pressure lately," she defended.

"Well, if he was drunk, it's conceivable he wasn't being careful."

Catherine shook her head. "Jack's always careful, Daddy. I guess it's not important what caused it, as long as the doctors are able to save him."

Sunday afternoon, Joanna sat cross-legged on her bed, writing a letter to Jack. She couldn't imagine why she hadn't gotten any new letters from him in the last two weeks. Being used to Rodney bringing her one every delivery, she felt her anxiety mount with each passing mail drop. Joanna poured her heart out with her pen, pleading with him to write.

Mary visited with her grandmother in the parlor while Jessie, sprawled on her back, stared at the ceiling. The redhead's foul mood initiated with Missy's covertly executed discharge had deepened as her week-away due date approached. Jessie had chosen complaining as her favorite new hobby.

"I wish I could sleep! This brat is killing my back, doing somersaults!" she moaned.

"I know!" Joanna sympathized. "As soon as I lie down, this little guy thinks it's time to play basketball. I don't mind; I like to feel him move."

Jessie rolled over, disgusted. "You're so sappy. I'm fat and miserable."

"You're not near as big as I am, and I've got six weeks to go!"

Mary rushed in, pale and shaking. "What's wrong?" Joanna asked her.

"There's been an accident." Mary clutched a newspaper. Joanna didn't anticipate that the pain Mary displayed was in sympathy for her. "I don't know how to tell you this." Mary took a spot on the bed next to Joanna and put her arm around her. "Honey, Jack's been in an accident." Mary's mother regularly mailed the Nashville newspapers to Bernice, to pass on to Mary; she handed Joanna the week-old front-page with the headline: BUSINESS OWNER CLINGS TO LIFE AFTER EXPLOSION. Joanna's chest went tight; she couldn't breathe. She grew light-headed and her inner ears buzzed loudly. The words of the article became blurry.

"Read it for me," Joanna managed to get out.

Mary read aloud: "'On Thursday night, part of Nashville was shaken when the filling station owned by Jackson Wyatt exploded. Wyatt, a native of Nashville, is listed in critical condition. Investigators from the Nashville Fire Department have concluded their investigation, calling the explosion an accident caused by a leaking fuel tank. The blast jolted the surrounding buildings for several blocks, breaking windows and rattling residents' cupboards.

"'Mira Rodgers, a neighbor, described her fear as the explosion knocked pictures off the walls and broke her lamps and knickknacks. "At first I thought the Russians were attacking, it felt like an atom bomb! When I saw the fireball at the gas station I called the fire department."

"'The estimated costs of this disaster are still being tallied but could reach into the tens of thousands. Fortunately, no one else was injured in the mishap.'"

Joanna's breathing came in short gasps. Staring into space, her eyes filled with tears.

"Don't breathe like that, you're going to hyperventilate. Put your head between your knees and concentrate on getting even breaths," Mary instructed as if she were already a nurse. She rubbed Joanna's back to comfort her.

Once Joanna got her breathing under control, the tears started like they'd never stop. "What's gonna happen to me if Jack dies?" she kept asking Mary.

"He's still alive, Joanna! Try to hold on to that and pray. I'll pray too."

Catherine stuck close to the ICU nurses' station, waiting for the doctor to give her an update. She'd refused to leave the hospital in the ten days since Jack's accident. The staff quickly abandoned their efforts to persuade her to go home.

Flora supplied Catherine with fresh clothes every day and sat beside her for hours. Flora had been a tremendous comfort when the doctors suggested amputating Jack's right leg, crushed by the heavy bay door. "My prayer circle at the Spruce Street Baptist Church is liftin' him up to the Lord. You've got to pray and believe." Flora took her hand and held tight.

"I do. I believe." Catherine fought fiercely with the medical team, insisting they do everything they could to save his leg. Cost didn't matter. If necessary, she'd spend her entire fortune on the best doctors. The surgeons who performed an arduous reconstruction of his shattered limb were amazed: Not only did Jack tolerate the long surgery, but his vital signs stabilized and the doctors replaced pessimism with improving odds, barring infection.

Catherine's first glimmer of hope materialized when he'd begun to come around four days ago. At first, his eyes fluttered. With Jack's leg in traction and his neck in a brace, the doctor kept him heavily sedated against the unbearable pain. Catherine beamed at his side when he finally held his eyes open and focused.

"Hi, darling, glad to have you back. You scared me for a while." Jack tried to sit up, but Catherine placed her hand on his chest, soothing him to lie still as she instructed Flora to summon a nurse. He tried to talk but discovered the tube in his throat. Jack lay back on the pillow, taking comfort in Catherine's calming touch.

He improved every day, and her deepest hope was today they'd remove the tubes and Jack could tell them what caused the explosion.

Dizzy, Jack's body hurt everywhere as he tried to answer the doctor's questions. "Do you know your name?" the attending physician asked.

"Jack Wyatt," he managed to whisper.

"Do you know where you are?"

"Hospital," the injured man responded.

"Can you tell me what happened?" the doctor coaxed.

What was the last thing he remembered? His head pounded as he struggled for the answer. The garage; he recalled being at the garage. But he drew a blank. "I can't remember." Exhausted from the effort, he closed his eyes.

Dr. Stine turned to Catherine and Wendell and reported, "Don't be alarmed. Most people have memory gaps when they suffer a trauma of this type. Sometimes they can recall the accident during the months that follow; many never remember the details. This is completely normal. I'd say, all things considered, Jack's a lucky man. His vital signs are good. I'll have him moved to a private room this afternoon."

"Thank you so much, Dr. Stine." Cat moved to the side of the bed to be closer to Jack.

"How long've I been out?" Jack uttered.

"Off and on for ten days." She offered him a sip of water through a straw. He took it, flinching against the pain of swallowing. He leaned back on the pillow. Cat busied herself, tending to his comfort by adjusting his blanket. The nurse raised the head of the bed slowly, and even with the neck brace, it felt good to be on an incline. The tranquility broke when Jack realized Wendell Langley stood at the end of his bed.

His deep voice seemed to produce a chill in the air. "You're doing much better today. That's good. Well, I think I am going to go now, so our boy here can get some rest. He looks as if he's had a taxing day." Catherine walked her father out.

Once they left, Jack quickly surveyed his surroundings. He didn't see a telephone. Ten days he'd been out; did Joanna know any of this? Poor Joanna, she'd be frantic without his letters. His mind raced, trying to think of a way to get in touch with her.

Chapter 24

Joanna picked at the food on her plate. No matter how she tried, she couldn't swallow the dinner Sister Mary Joseph piled on her tray. She hadn't been able to eat or sleep for the last two weeks. Her eyes were swollen from crying and no one could console her. There'd been no news about Jack, and no way for her to find out anything.

Suddenly a crash, like someone dumping a pail of milk on the floor, made Joanna turn in the direction of the food line. Jessie stood with her hands on her hips, her tray of food upside down next to the puddle of amniotic fluid on the floor under her feet. The redhead declared, "Oh! Damn it to hell!"

Sister Eugenia snatched her before Jessie could react. Joanna strained to see Jessie waving her arms, shouting obscenities, being led to the elevator. The night seemed endless as they waited on a report about Jessie. No word had come at the time of their breakfast chores. Waiting for Rodney's delivery truck, Joanna felt as if she hadn't slept at all. The drowsy sunrise colored the sky a frosty rose when the truck finally arrived. Joanna took the letters from the boy and paid him. Mary checked off the dairy order as he brought in the supplies. Joanna sorted through the letters, finally spotting one in the stack from Jack. Her heart leapt with joy. She wanted to tear into it, but Sister Mary Joseph arrived barking orders, so she stuffed the envelope in her pocket.

Joanna managed to polish off her breakfast, certain this letter contained instructions from Jack. Everything was gonna be alright now!

On the way to Mr. Ehrlichman's class, Joanna and Mary took a detour into the parlor where Joanna quickly pored over Jack's long-awaited note. Mary watched tensely as Joanna's expression went from elation to tears.

"Oh God, Jack! No! Please don't do this to me." Joanna crumpled the letter and threw it into the fireplace where it ignited instantly, sending a bright-orange flame upward, consuming the paper until it turned to flaky ash. Joanna cried hysterically.

"What did it say?" Mary asked, distressed by her friend's emotional reaction.

"He said he can't provide for me now and he's gonna stay with Catherine. I'm to give the baby up for adoption."

"What?" Mary's mouth dropped open.

"He said our affair was a mistake!" Joanna ran to the nearest bathroom, where she violently vomited her undigested breakfast. Mary stayed outside the stall, trying to comfort her.

"Go to class, Marsha," Joanna told her.

"I can't leave you like this!" Mary protested.

"You'll get into trouble if you stay here. I'm goin' to bed. Tell Mr. Ehrlichman I don't feel well. Now go, I'll be all right."

Mary complied, to avoid Ehrlichman's torturous lecture on tardiness.

Even light-headed, Joanna found her way to her room. She hugged the pillow to her chest to stop the stabbing pain in her heart.

Joanna wanted to pull the pillow over her face and scream as loud as she could. Instead she held it tighter and cried tears of loss that came from a deep place inside her. She'd never experienced this type of horrible aloneness; she'd never been more frightened.

Back in Nashville, Irene stretched to view the front sidewalk below her apartment window. Harris's car was still parked at the curb. Every morning, she didn't inhale a breath of peace until he'd left. She'd run downstairs to check the mail, hoping for a letter from Joanna.

This morning, Harris stepped onto the sidewalk as the mailman made his daily round. She couldn't believe her eyes as the postman handed Harris the mail. Harris took one envelope from the pile and returned the rest to the civil servant to deliver. In horror, she watched as he tore it into pieces and let the wind carry bits wherever it may.

"You son-of-a-bitch!" Irene breathed. Taking the stairs as fast as she could, she reached the street as Harris's junky car turned the corner. That was long enough for the letter to be blown in all directions.

Chasing the fragments confirmed Irene's fears, as she recognized the stationery she'd given Joanna. Irene imagined she looked as crazy as her mother, running around gathering the scraps, but she didn't care, even when she stopped traffic to get the pieces littering the street.

An hour later, she'd managed to arrange the shredded puzzle pieces back to the two-page letter, in which Joanna pleaded with her mother to find out information about Jack's condition. Irene hung her head. Maybe it would've been better if she'd let the wind carry it away.

Sloped on his hospital bed, Jack cocked his head toward the spoonful of Flora's homemade vegetable soup Catherine fed him. Flowers and cards cluttered his private room, mostly from Catherine's society friends, some from his crowd at the racetrack. The weeks since the accident lapsed into a ludicrous cycle of doctors, nurses, pills, and shots; all the while, Cat stayed by his side. She'd taken to sleeping on the couch in his room, enabling her to care for him at any hour of the day or night. His physical restrictions required Cat and the nurses to assist him with all his needs, except the one burning constantly in his brain, his obligation to Joanna. He couldn't reach the telephone, arm's length from him on the bedside table. Even if he could, the administrator at the Frances Weston Home wouldn't have allowed him to speak to Joanna.

Alex was the only person he could trust to get word to Joanna. "Did you talk to Alex?" Jack asked Cat, between mouthfuls.

"Yes. He promised to visit you next week."

Frustrated, Jack rested his head on the pillow. His appetite lost, he waved off the next offering of soup. He dreaded the interim, helpless to reassure Joanna.

The second her high school class released, Mary dashed to the dorm room to check on Joanna. "How you feeling, sugar?"

Joanna stirred from light sleep. Rubbing her forehead, she moaned, "I have a headache that'd kill a small child." She hunkered to shade her eyes from the sunlight coming from the window. The pounding of the workmen's hammers on Fitch's third-floor remodel magnified the throbbing in her head.

"Do you want me to get Sister Bridget?" Mary asked, concerned.

"No, please don't. Tell her I'm resting. Can I use your pillow?"

"Sure." Mary passed it to Joanna and tucked her in, pledging to check on her again soon. Joanna pulled the pillow over her head, blocking out all light and sound.

Sleep, what I need is sleep. She closed her eyes. Her memories of Jack relentlessly boiled to the surface; the sound of his voice, his touch. Pain pulsed in her head with every beat of her heart, compounding the misery Jack's letter had wrought.

Our affair was a mistake. I love my wife, his letter had read. Joanna pictured Catherine in her mind. Of course he loved her; she had the beauty of a movie star and the grace of a princess. The only asset Joanna could compete with was the baby; the one thing Catherine couldn't give him. Joanna rubbed her belly, and the child gave a lively kick. What did Jack's letter say, exactly? She regretted tossing it in the fireplace.

Joanna fought her light-headedness. She lay back, staring at the ceiling she prayed, "Please, God, let me sleep and make the pain go away or let me die right now."

Around two in the afternoon, Mary, anxious to check on Joanna, convinced Sister Bridget to accompany her to the dorm room. They soon discovered something terribly wrong. When they attempted to wake Joanna, her skin was clammy. She didn't come around.

"Is she okay?" Mary asked, observing over Sister Bridget's shoulder. As the nun flung the covers off the ailing girl, Mary let out a scream at the sight of the blood-soaked mattress. Her knees weakened; she stabilized her dizziness by holding on to the bedside table.

"Oh sweet Jesus!" the nun prayed, scooping up Joanna with the ease of pure adrenaline.

Keeping step with the nun, Mary ran alongside, petting Joanna's head, and telling her, "It's going to be okay, honey! We're going to take good care of you."

Joanna fluttered her eyes slightly and muttered, "He never even said he was sorry."

In the elevator, the compartment jolted, making its slow ascent.

"What's she talking about?" Sister Bridget asked sternly.

Mary told the truth. "In a letter from Jack, he told her to put the baby up for adoption."

"Not again," the nun agonized. "Jean, please tell me you didn't try to hurt your baby!"

"What?" Joanna asked groggily, and then the question registered. "No, I love my baby."

As the doors of the lift opened, Jessie screamed at Sister Eugenia, "Take off these restraints, you old bat!"

The elderly nun immediately turned all her attention to Joanna after Sister Bridget delivered her to an empty hospital bed. Joanna's blood smeared the young nun's face.

"What happened here?" Sister Eugenia snapped.

"I don't know. I found her like this," Sister Bridget explained.

"Call Dr. Miller, tell him to get here at once!"

Sister Bridget ran to the phone and dialed while Jessie shouted, "What's going on with Jean! Marsha, untie me!"

"Why is Jessie tied down?" Mary yelled.

"She throws things at me. You need to go back downstairs," Eugenia shot back. Examining Joanna, she coaxed, "Come on, now, open your eyes."

Mrs. Fitch stormed into the room, "What's all the commotion?" Her expression turned from anger to shock when she saw Joanna's condition.

"Dr. Miller's on his way!" Bridget reported, rushing back to Joanna's bedside.

"You need to leave, Sister Bridget, and take Marsha with you."

"No. They're both my girls; I want to stay!"

"You're too emotionally involved. Get out." Fitch pushed the nun toward the elevator.

"Don't go! Make that bitch give me some drugs!" Jessie cried, struggling against the straps that pinned her like an insane criminal.

Sister Bridget stepped forward, "Let me help! They need me!"

"I said, get out. If you don't leave this instant, I promise, you'll be back on a bus to the orphanage you came from by nightfall." Sister Bridget caved under Mrs. Fitch's fierceness and led Mary to the elevator. As soon as the doors shut, she broke into tears. Mary hugged her, and they cried together.

Chapter 25

Dr. Miller charged into the room. "What's so urgent?"

"We've got a bleeder!" Sister Eugenia told him. Dr. Miller examined Joanna.

"Get me outta these restraints!" Jessie screamed.

"What's with her?" the doctor asked.

"Eight centimeters dilated," the nun answered.

Jessie screeched hatefully. "Give me somethin' for the pain!"

"Give her some gas," Dr. Miller instructed the nun. "I can't listen to her. We've got a placental abruption here. We've got to do a C-section right now! Jean, can you hear me?" the doctor asked. Joanna's eyes fluttered. "Your baby's in trouble; I'm going to do an operation to deliver it."

"Too soon," Joanna objected.

"No, it'll be okay; you're almost thirty-six weeks. Your placenta has pulled away from the uterus; we need to get the baby out with an operation. Do you understand?"

Joanna nodded and whispered, "Save my baby."

Dr. Miller placed a mask over her nose and mouth. "Breathe deeply, Jean."

The bright surgery lights grew dim and Sister Eugenia argued with Jessie, "You whine for drugs and now you're getting them, you're fighting with me?" As the floating fog clouded her mind, a singular thought prevailed: *Save my baby.*

"I'm bustin' you out!" Alex told Jack, sauntering into the room with his hands mimicking six-shooters. Jack laughed. His friend greeted Catherine with an embrace.

"I'll give you boys some time to play; I'm going to go stretch my legs for a while."

Alex waved as she exited the room. "Damn, she looks great! You, not so much."

"Thanks!" Jack mocked, eager to discuss business before Catherine returned. "I need you to do something for me."

"Anything, you got it, man."

"I need you to go to the Frances Weston Home in Knoxville and talk to Joanna for me. The baby's not due for three more weeks. She needs to know about an apartment I've rented." Jack explained Alex's role in chauffeuring Joanna and the baby to their new home upon release.

Alex hung his head. "Please don't ask me to do this. Anything else, I'll do."

"I can't trust anyone else."

Awkward silence punctuated the tension. Finally, Alex agreed. "I think this is a mistake. But you have a responsibility to this girl. So, I'll do it, on one condition."

"What?"

"You've got to promise you'll think long and hard before you ask Cat for a divorce. You could try telling her the truth, begging forgiveness, and finding a way to make your marriage work."

"Exposing the truth and saving my marriage aren't compatible," Jack defended.

"Of all the marriages I've ever seen, yours was the one I admired the most. I'd hate for you to throw it away, that's all."

Muffled voices prompted Joanna to regain consciousness. Weak and weighed by a heavy covering, with concerted effort she willed her eyes to open. Her mouth was dry and she couldn't feel her feet. Suddenly a baby cried. *Oh, my baby! He's crying he's all right!*

"Here is what you asked for: two birth certificates and one death certificate. Do you want me to fill them out?" Joanna recognized Gloria's voice.

"No, I'll do it," Fitch insisted.

"Whose baby died?"

"Jean's. She lost the placenta," Fitch said emotionlessly.

"That's horrible."

"Go back to the office; there's filing to be done." Fitch spoke abruptly.

Joanna questioned, "My baby?"

"She's coming around," Sister Eugenia alerted.

"Put her back under," Mrs. Fitch demanded.

"My baby, I wanna see my baby!" Joanna managed to utter.

Mrs. Fitch joined the nun next to her bed and disclosed, "Jean, he's dead."

"No, he's crying!" Joanna tried to focus, glancing from Mrs. Fitch to Sister Eugenia. The old nun made the sign of the cross over her breast and administered a shot to Joanna's arm. She winced as the burning medication traveled to the vein in her neck.

"That's Jessie's baby. Your son was stillborn."

"I wanna see him," Joanna begged hoarsely.

"He's right over there, in the crib; you can see him from here," Fitch stated, irritated.

Joanna squinted in the direction the woman pointed. In the dim twilight, she caught sight of a tiny baby wrapped in a blanket, motionless with an ashy-blue skin tone.

Mrs. Fitch strutted away while Sister Eugenia strapped a blood-pressure cuff on Joanna's arm. The medication began to steal her consciousness.

Reaching her hand to her throat, Joanna pulled at the medal of St. Nicholas her mother sent her for Christmas. Breaking the chain, she placed the medaliion in the nun's palm.

"Give this to my baby. I want him to be buried with it." Tears escaped as a trickle to her ears. Sister Eugenia's unreadable stare prompted the grieving girl to beg, "Please?" Sister Eugenia diverted her eyes to the object in her hand and nodded.

A few days later, Mrs. Fitch summoned Sister Bridget to the hospital wing. As the elevator doors retracted, she overheard the tail end of a heated conversation.

"Don't go behind my back on this, or I'll have you transferred to a home for elderly nuns," Mrs. Fitch scolded Sister Eugenia. The older clergywoman glowered, red-faced, as she bustled out of the room, sending a clear warning to the young sister to tread lightly.

"You wanted to see me?" Sister Bridget asked.

"Yes." Mrs. Fitch turned her temper to her new target. "I've packed Jessie's belongings; I want her out of here in the morning. Settle her account and arrange for a cab. She's to have no further contact with the girls downstairs. Is that clear?"

"Yes, ma'am." Duly dismissed, Sister Bridget rode the elevator to the first floor, wondering what had transpired between the administrator and Sister Eugenia.

With the exit of the two nuns, Jessie felt vulnerable. Louise Fitch frowned at her and approached the crib where her helpless infant slept. Fitch jerked the baby off the mattress; placing him on her shoulder, she roughly patted his back.

"Would you like to see your son, Jessie?" she asked, mocking her.

Still tethered to the bed by thick leather straps, Jessie shot a hateful look at the administrator and snarled, "No."

"Oh, come on. Don't you want to hold him and say goodbye?" she taunted, shifting the baby to give Jessie a better view. "Oh, wait, you can't because you're restrained." Fitch laughed.

Jessie turned her face toward the wall, cringing as the child whined. Through clenched teeth, she chided, "You don't have to convince me you're truly evil."

Mrs. Fitch moved into Jessie's line of sight, forcing her to focus on the crying baby. His little face turned beet red. His arms flailed in distress. This time Jessie didn't look away.

"Why don't you tell me how Jean got letters from the birthfather?"

"God, you're such a bitch!" Jessie spat. "You deny the girls who beg to see their babies and throw them in the face of the ones who can't wait to get the hell outta here."

"Did you hear that?" Mrs. Fitch told the struggling baby. "Your mommy hates you. She never wanted you. But thanks to me, you're going to have a good life, with parents who're going to spoil you. You're so lucky, 'cause your mama's a whore and that's all she'll ever be."

Jessie fought against the restraints, intent on freeing herself to attack the administrator. "Tell me how you smuggled in your cigarettes and booze and I'll stop." Jessie set her jaw and glared at the woman. "Your baby only weighed five pounds at birth, Jessie. Did you really think I couldn't smell it on you? I've seen hundreds of girls; just like you, they never amount to anything. Their babies are sickly or brain-damaged; stillborn, some of them. Your baby should've been the one to die, not Jean's. She took good care of herself, while you drank, smoked, and refused to eat so your baby wouldn't scar your body."

The infant in the woman's arms got madder by the second, screaming for Jessie to rescue him. Staring at this tiny tufted-haired stranger, she longed for the child's wailing to end, yet she lacked a maternal bond. Fitch was right, he'd been an inconvenience and she hated him for that. Jessie laid her head back and shut her eyes.

"Tell me!" Fitch shouted.

"Go to hell!" Jessie screamed back. Mrs. Fitch took the child to the changing table. He calmed once he was swaddled in a blanket and a bottle put in his mouth.

"You'll be leaving here tomorrow at nine a.m. Tell the cabbie where you want to go. As for me, this is truly a good riddance. I predict you'll burn out early and die young."

"You casting spells now, witch?" Jessie remained defiant. "Well, you forget I'm from New Orleans, where voodoo lives, and I promise you, Louise Fitch, you'll die a lonely, shriveled-up old hag. In fact, you already are."

Mrs. Fitch abandoned her interrogation of Jessie and skulked out of the room with the infant still in her arms. Jessie peered across the room at a pale Joanna, peacefully sleeping, longing for her to wake. She needed Joanna to know how sorry she was for the loss of her baby and her fairy-tale future. She wanted to say goodbye.

The following Sunday, during their usual visit, Mary implored her grandmother to intercede for her with Mrs. Fitch. "You've got to convince her to let me see Jean. She needs me. Her whole life has fallen apart."

"I'll see what I can do." Compassionately, the older woman set off to talk to Mrs. Fitch.

In a short while, Bernice and Mary were in the elevator, rising to the hospital wing. Noticing a worried expression on her grandmother's face, Mary asked, "What's wrong?"

"It's nothing, dear," Bernice lied.

Mary knew her too well. "Jean's got an infection or something?"

"No, it's nothing like that." The doors opened and Sister Eugenia, who acted as if she'd been expecting them, stepped to the side.

"Jean," Mary whispered, stroking her friend's head. Joanna stirred and opened her eyes.

"How you feelin', honey?" Bernice Atherton asked.

"Better." Joanna strained to sit up, then winced with pain.

Mary came to her assistance. "Slow down. Let me help you." Mary raised the bed slowly, taking Joanna's arm guided her to a sitting position.

"I'm still pretty sore, but Sister Eugenia keeps givin' me pills, so I'm not cryin' all the time. She hates it if I'm cryin'," Joanna explained.

"Your color looks good," Mary complimented.

Joanna furrowed her brow and asked, "Did you get to say goodbye to Jessie?" Mary shook her head. "Me neither. In case she doesn't let me talk to you again, we'd better say our goodbyes now. Fitch told me I'm leavin' here day after tomorrow. She's sendin' me to a kinda halfway house. She asked me what city I preferred; I didn't know what to tell her. I can't go back to Nashville."

"You're in no condition to go anywhere. Look at you; you can't even sit up in the bed!" The girl shot a look at Bernice, understanding the woman's earlier concern.

"Mary's right, child. You're as fragile as an eggshell. How'd you feel about staying at my house until you're strong again?" Shocked, Joanna looked to Mary for an answer.

Mary nodded. "Yes, do it. After my baby's born, we can go to Memphis together."

"What am I gonna do in Memphis?" Joanna asked.

"We'll figure it out later. For now, take Grandma's offer; you need time to heal."

After a brief conversation with Mrs. Fitch, it was settled: Joanna would be staying with Bernice Atherton to recover and await the birth of Mary's baby, only six weeks away.

Chapter 26

When Alex walked into Jack's hospital room, he found him sitting in a wheel-chair. Bruised and bandaged, he looked rough but better than he had two weeks prior.

"Alex!" Catherine rose from the chair. "We're going home tomorrow. Isn't that great?"

"Fantastic." Alex offered to get Jack out of the room. "How 'bout I take you for a spin down the hall? I can flirt with the nurses and see if this ride'll go five miles per hour."

Catherine laughed, "Go, take him."

Alex parked Jack in an unoccupied waiting area. He sat in front of him and reported, "I didn't get to talk to Joanna; she's already gone." Jack looked confused. "The baby came early. He died. I'm sorry, Jack." Jack tilted his head back and closed his eyes. When he turned back to Alex, he breathed shallowly. "I'm sorry, man, I didn't wanna tell ya this."

"I know," Jack grunted vacantly. "Poor Joanna. Where is she?"

"The administrator wouldn't tell me. But she said Joanna never wants to see ya again. It's over, Jack. The baby's gone. Go home with Cat tomorrow. Start over. Look at this as some kinda second-chance gift from God and be happy with the woman you married. Forget all this shit."

"I don't have a choice, do I?"

"She doesn't want you to know where she is. Let her go."

Jack nodded.

✺

The rain plunked as it hit the pane of Bernice's kitchen window, behind Joanna. Silently, she sipped hot tea, while the older woman across the table warmed her hands on a cup of coffee.

Joanna healed well under the watchful eye of Mary's grandmother. The caring lady encouraged, coaxed, and cheered the girl into walking, albeit baby steps, after a few days.

Joanna thoughtfully asked, "What's gonna happen to me now?"

"What do you want to happen?" Bernice returned.

"A month ago, I had a plan. Now I don't know what to do." During Joanna's convalescence, she'd confided in Bernice about Jack and the circumstances of her pregnancy. The wise benefactor always knew the way to guide Joanna through the heartbreak.

"What do you like doing?" Bernice asked her.

"I don't know. That's the problem."

"What about secretarial school?"

"I hated bookkeeping and shorthand," Joanna told her.

"You're a good seamstress," Bernice offered.

"I suppose I could get a job in a factory." Joanna frowned.

"There's any number of things you could do. Be a nanny or a schoolteacher. You could go to culinary school or become a beautician." Bernice listed some of the possibilities.

"A hairdresser!" Joanna gasped. "I used to do that for the girls in the dorm. It was fun. I'd love to work in a shop like the one at the Peabody Hotel." Joanna went on to describe the décor and the services they offered. Bernice smiled at Joanna's enthusiasm.

Catherine joined Jack out on the sunporch. It was a marvelous early-spring day. He'd spent the last hour watching the birds chase one another in the garden. He'd also been thinking what a compassionate caregiver his wife had been.

Squeezing her hand, Jack remarked, "I haven't thanked you properly for standing by me."

"Oh, Jack." She blushed.

"I mean it, you've been outstanding."

"I love you, Jack."

"You must, to put up with me," he chuckled.

"Do you know the only thing that'd make my life happier?" she asked.

"What?"

"If we could raise a child together." His countenance fell with her suggestion. "Jack, are you afraid I couldn't handle adopting a baby?"

"No, not at all," he reassured her. "Look at how you've taken care of me." Jack's mind went to Joanna. The weeks since her tragedy hadn't softened his remorse. The thought of another baby seemed disrespectful. Meeting her eyes, he saw Cat's devotion. "Okay." Jack nodded.

"Okay, yes? We can adopt a baby?" she asked.

Jack gave in. "We can adopt a baby."

She flung her arms around him, kissing all over his face. "Oh, Jackie, I love you! This is going to be so great!"

"I love you too, Cat," he yielded, abandoning the unsalvageable past with Joanna.

Mary watched at a distance as new girls arrived to fill the beds once occupied by her closest friends. She didn't join in when they formed cliques and established their unique versions of dorm room camaraderie.

Mary discarded her never-make-waves persona when she fiercely confronted Rodney and terminated the dairy express. "If I find out you're smuggling anything else in here, I'll turn you in! All you've done is cause harm. It ends today."

"Hey! No skin off my ass, chick," Rodney cackled. Taking a drag off his cigarette, he flicked it into the wet grass. Under his breath he pivoted, "You're a short-timer; there's always a new crop of lovesick girls more than happy to pay me to do their bidding."

The completed renovations to the third floor increased the home's capacity and added to Sister Bridget's responsibilities. Mary watched the nun create a bond with her new charges, easing their fears the way she had with the last batch of girls. Even overworked, she kept watch over Mary's detachment and finally cornered her in the bathroom to speak privately.

"I get the feeling you're avoiding me," Sister Bridget started.

"No, I'm ready for this to be over." Mary scrubbed her teeth with a toothbrush.

"Careful, your gums are sensitive now; you'll make them bleed," the nun told her. The girl rinsed her mouth. "I hate to see you withdraw this way."

Mary softened. "Every time my baby moves inside me, I'm reminded I'm going to miss out on a lifetime of touches. I won't get to see its first steps or be the mommy who cries on the first day of school." Sister Bridget put her arms around her. "It kills me it'll never know how much I love it or how its miraculous existence has changed everything about me." Mary wiped her tears on her pajama sleeve. "Very soon, this child will be born and I'll sign away, forever, my rights as its mother. If Mrs. Lewis believes I can leave here and act like this never happened, someone needs to take back her diplomas, because she's a moron."

Sister Bridget smiled. "Every experience we have in life molds us. Of course you're changed by the life you carry inside you. It's good you recognize there's a grieving period."

"Grandma says it's a path I'll walk and, at each turn, there's a new emotion I'll face."

"Your grandma's a pretty sharp cookie. You're a smart girl, too. You'll get through this."

"Don't take it personally I can't mix with the new girls. The inevitable end is near. It can't come soon enough, in my opinion."

Mary's soon-enough came a couple of weeks later, on a balmy but sunny April day. First thing in the morning, she knocked on Sister Bridget's door.

Mary explained, "I started cramping at two a.m., now I'm pretty sure I'm in labor. Could you call my grandmother? I want her to be here."

Sister Bridget came to Mary a short while later. "Your grandma is upstairs. Are you okay to walk to the elevator?" The girl nodded. Mary felt as if she were sleepwalking, yet her senses were heightened. She found herself grasping at the images and activity around her. The smell of the fresh paint from the third floor, the coldness of the tile beneath her feet, the sounds of the other residents beginning their day: Mary committed these things to memory.

The hours of the morning melted into the pastel hues of twilight before Mary was ready to deliver. Being attentive, Sister Eugenia had given her drugs, dulling the edge of pain. Mary intended to be awake for the birth and strongly objected to using gas.

When Dr. Miller arrived, Mary urgently asked, "I want to push, can I push now?"

"Hold on, let me take a look." Dr. Miller did a quick exam and gave her the command to push. Mary grasped the handrails and, holding her breath, she pushed.

By her side, Bernice cheered her on, "That's it, honey. Bear down."

An hour passed with the laboring girl pushing with each contraction. Exhausted, her hair matted with sweat and her legs shaking, Mary lamented, "I can't do this!"

"You're almost there. Three more good pushes is all you need," Dr. Miller said.

"You can do it, child. Come on," Bernice coached. With the next contraction Mary used all her concentration to push. "You're doing so good! Give a little more, push harder, harder, that's it!" Mary lay back and rested for a minute.

"A few more," Dr. Miller coaxed.

"Two more," Mary clarified. She pushed again, as hard as she could. "It burns! Oh God, it hurts," she cried, through clinched teeth.

"I'm going to give the skin a little snip so you don't tear," the doctor told her.

The sudden slicing pain came with the relief of the burning sensation. With her next push, the child was born and its cries brought tears to her eyes.

"What is it, a boy or a girl?" Mary begged. The doctor looked at Bernice, who nodded.

"He's a healthy baby boy!" Dr. Miller announced and held the pink little body so Mary could get a good look.

"Oh my God, he's beautiful." Mary clasped her hand to her mouth, unable to stop the sobs erupting from an untapped well of emotions within her. Eugenia took the baby from him.

"Lie back now," Dr. Miller instructed. "I'm going to stitch you up like a virgin. On your wedding night, your husband won't know the difference."

Across the room, Sister Eugenia cleaned, weighed, and measured the baby. Once he was diapered and wrapped in a blue blanket, Bernice cradled the child, swaying her body, she soothed his cries. "My goodness, you're sweet." Mary reached out, wanting to hold him.

"It'll only make it harder when you have to sign the papers," Sister Eugenia warned.

"Give me the papers now, and I'll sign them! I'm not going to keep him. I can't. But this is the only time I will ever spend with him," Mary demanded. Sister Eugenia slid the documents in front of Mary; she signed them without reading. Pushing the papers back at the nun, she pleaded, "Let me hold him."

Bernice gently transferred the small bundle to Mary and stood back while the new mother snuggled the baby. She touched the softness of his cheek, looking adoringly in his eyes.

"Hi! I'm Mary. I can't be your mommy, so it's better if you remember me as Mary." The child looked intently at his mother, transfixed on the voice he recognized.

The next few days, unless sleeping, Mary held her son. She loved to rock him as he slept peacefully in her arms. She talked to him, explaining about Tony and how things didn't work out. She told him about herself and why she had to give him away. She told him how much she loved him. The infant always calmed to the sound of her voice and seemed to be taking in all of her meaning.

"He leaves tomorrow. I'm afraid you're going to regret spending so much time with him," Sister Eugenia cautioned compassionately.

"I want him to feel loved for his first few days; it'll give him a good start."

"You did very well with the labor and delivery. You'll be able to have lots more babies."

Mary nodded. Blinking back the tears, she handed the baby to the nun. "I think I'll turn in. I'm kinda tired."

The next morning Mary dressed in her normal clothes for the first time in what felt like a lifetime. She packed her belongings. Lastly, she changed and dressed her son in his leaving clothes. She picked a pale-blue jumper suit with little pockets.

"Today's the big day, little guy. They're going to love you!"

Before she wrapped him snugly in a blue blanket, she unclasped her medallion of St. Nicholas and tucked it into his pocket. With tears in her eyes, Mary kissed her son's soft forehead for the last time and whispered in his ear, "Remember me!"

Chapter 27

"You look great, Joanna. How do you feel?" Mary asked.

"Good. How could I not, with your grandma fussing over me? How 'bout you?" Joanna helped Mary carry her bags to her room.

"Pretty good. I'm a little tired. My boobs hurt and I'm leaking breast milk like a damn cow. The stitches are a nuisance, but all in all, good."

Mary put her suitcase on the bed and looked around the room she'd taken refuge in when the news of her pregnancy had rattled her world. She went to the dresser were a framed photograph of her and Tony from homecoming sat proudly displayed.

"I got to hold him and love on him," Mary reminisced, referring to her baby. Turning toward Joanna, who perched on the bed, she continued, "He had Tony's brown hair and my shaped eyes." Tears streamed down her face, uncontrolled.

"I know. It hurts!" Joanna sympathized; rising, she embraced Mary.

"I never knew anything could hurt this bad."

"I completely understand. There'll be more of this comin', so let it out. Trust me, you'll feel better." Mary couldn't have held back the tears if she'd wanted to.

"Look at me going on like this!" Mary felt suddenly ashamed. "I don't know how you're holding up so well."

"I'm not. But I've had six weeks to deal with my loss. Don't feel like your pain should be less than mine 'cause your baby's still alive. What you're goin' through is almost the same as a death. I'm almost lucky 'cause I have a grave I can visit. My baby's buried in the potter's field at the Catholic church. I put a flower urn with the name WYATT painted on it for a marker." Joanna got a box of Kleenex and the two girls talked for hours consoling each other. Sometime later, Mary sat calmly on the bed and blew her nose on the last tissue in the box.

"Should I get more Kleenex or are ya good?" Joanna half smiled at her.

Mary laughed. "No, I think I'm done."

Bernice appeared in the doorway. "How's it going in here?"

"That was exhausting," Mary confessed, smiling at her grandmother.

"Sometimes a good cry can set a lot of things right. You girls come and help me fix an early dinner."

The few weeks Mary and Joanna spent together at Bernice Atherton's home restored their spirits and prepared them for their burgeoning future. It gave them time to work on their plans.

On a glorious spring day, the three of them took a weekend trip to Memphis. Joanna registered for beauty college, Mary enrolled in nursing school, and the quest for an apartment ensued. They toured three properties and decided on a two-bedroom walk-up, available immediately, with a doughnut shop on the ground floor. Centrally located for both schools, the building resided where a busy avenue intersected a quiet, residential street. The rooms were large and the front room boasted a bay window. Potentially airy and bright, the place pleaded for a good cleaning and fresh paint. The girls signed a lease.

They spent the night at the Peabody Hotel. Bernice woke them early the next morning saying, "Let's go shopping." By the end of the day, they had bought the necessities, from the kitchen utensils and dishes to the dining table and sofas. Bernice splurged on their bedrooms, refusing to let them use any of their own money.

The next morning she took them to the hardware store to buy paint and cleaning supplies. They decided on a pale green for Joanna's room, bright yellow for the dining area and the kitchen. The living room they'd paint warm caramel. Mary chose a frosted blue for her bedroom. Arriving back at the apartment, they made several trips from the car to carry in their purchases. Grandma Bernice walked from room to room prioritizing their tasks.

"My! You two have your work cut out for you. Oh, here you go." Bernice tossed them overalls and some old work shirts. "I'm going back to Knoxville. You girls have two more nights paid at the Peabody. Your bedroom furniture will be delivered tomorrow, so start there first. Once you get the other rooms cleaned and painted, call the furniture store and they'll deliver the rest. I'll come back next weekend with anything you left at my house." The girls looked at each other dumbfounded. What began as a scouting weekend had turned into their move-in day.

Mary examined the work clothes. "Are you throwing us in the deep end of the pool?"

"You can swim. Fixing this place the way you want it will make it a comforting place to be, and that affects attitude. I love you both. Fresh paint, fresh start." Bernice stepped in and kissed each one on the top of the head.

"Bernice, thank you for all this," Joanna said. "You've just been—"

Bernice cut her off. "Oh, stop now, Joanna. You'll embarrass me. You, on the other hand…" She turned to her granddaughter playfully. "You're a spoiled brat! So I'm doing my job right as a grandma. Come here, give us a hug." They group-hugged. "Have fun, girls," Bernice called over her shoulder as she left.

As the door shut, Mary turned to Joanna, surveying the mess. "Where do we start?"

"At the beginnin', I guess," Joanna said with a shrug. In the kitchen, she poured soap into a scrub bucket. Mary blankly stared at her. "What?" Joanna asked.

"I've never done this before. We had a housekeeper," Mary explained.

"We'll work together; come on, grab the broom. Let's do your room."

The hours flew by as the girls cleaned and painted the bedrooms. Joanna scrubbed the bathroom while Mary cleaned the stove and refrigerator. Finally, the midafternoon sun reminded them they hadn't eaten since breakfast.

"Let's go to the doughnut shop," Mary suggested. They were pleased to learn that, in addition to doughnuts, they could get a variety of sandwiches and milkshakes, even pizza. They ordered ham sandwiches and chocolate milkshakes; Mary got a dozen doughnuts at the last minute. "I love the smell of fresh doughnuts," she told Joanna.

"That's good, 'cause you're gonna be smellin' 'em at four a.m.," the young man behind the counter replied. "I'm Stan, Three-A. You're the new tenants in Two-B, right?"

"Yeah, right." Mary smiled. "Mary and Joanna," she introduced, shaking his outstretched hand. Paying for their takeout, she called, "Thanks! See ya 'round, Stan."

After lunch, they cleaned the dining room and moved on to the kitchen. It went well until Joanna accidentally dripped water on Mary's head as they were wiping out the cabinets. Mary shook her sponge at Joanna, which turned into a full-blown water fight, and had them screaming and howling. They drenched each other and the walls. Slipping on the floor, they ended up lying on their backs laughing hysterically. Suddenly a banging noise muzzled them.

"What was that?" Mary asked, startled.

"We must've disturbed one of the neighbors," Joanna giggled. The girls got back to work. Mary washed all the new dishes and organized the cabinets while Joanna cleaned the mess they'd made by wiping the walls and mopping the floor. Hours later, they worked fast on the second coat of paint in the bedrooms, making it back to the Peabody by 11:00 p.m. They showered and fell into bed, exhausted.

Catherine paced, pausing occasionally to stare out the picture window, praying for a car to arrive. The ticking of the mantel clock made the passage of time torture.

"You're going to wear out the carpeting, Kitten," Wendell observed from the armchair.

"Sorry, Daddy." Cat sat on the couch by the window, hoping to gather her poise.

"They're only a few minutes late," Wendell told her.

"Of course," Catherine agreed. "It seems like the last few weeks of this process have been so drawn out. The woman from social services who did the home study made me nervous. She looked at everything in this house."

"You don't have to worry. This is a fine home to raise a child. No woman will ever be a better mother than you, Catherine," he praised.

"Thank you, Daddy."

"Car comin'," Flora announced. Catherine stood, her eyes tracking the black sedan until it parked at the front of the house. Jack entered the room using a cane. Catherine straightened her skirt and gave Jack a *how do I look* expression.

"Don't worry, you're glowing," Jack reassured her. Millicent entered the room and stood next to Wendell. The doorbell rang, and Catherine nodded for Flora to answer.

"Mrs. Wyatt is expecting you." The housekeeper directed the foster mother to the living room. Mrs. Rineholdt entered with a baby bundled in a light-blue blanket in her arms.

"Mrs. Rineholdt, do come in," Catherine greeted.

"Good day." The woman walked directly to Cat, who reached out for the baby. "I have a file here." She opened her shoulder satchel and retrieved an envelope she handed to Jack. "It contains a complete record of his schedule for the last two weeks. He's a good baby, sleeps eight hours at night."

"Thank you so much for everything you've done," Catherine said.

Mrs. Rineholdt nodded. "Well, I'll leave you to get acquainted. Best of luck."

"Goodbye." Catherine focused on the face of the infant in her arms. His dark-blue eyes studied her. Millicent and Wendell stepped forward.

"Let me hold him a minute, darling," her mother instructed. "I hate to rush off, but if we don't, we'll be late for the mayor's dinner." Grandma Millicent held the child briefly. She passed him back to Catherine.

"Daddy, do you want to hold him?" she asked.

"Oh no! Maybe when he's bigger." Wendell backed away.

Catherine turned her attention to the whimpering child in her arms. "What's the trouble?" His eyes widened with curiosity as she spoke. The Langleys made a hasty exit. Apprehensively, Jack leaned in for his first glimpse. The infant's bottom lip quivered and Jack took a wobbly step backward. The baby wailed.

"My goodness," Cat said soothingly. Flora came into the room.

"What's all the fussin'?" Flora asked the baby.

Catherine swayed and spoke sweetly: "Now, now, my love."

"Do you think he's hungry?" Jack asked.

Flora deciphered the schedule from the folder. "He's due for a feedin' in half an hour," she informed them. "My gracious, this woman kept far-flung records. She had him on a strict minute-to-minute schedule."

"Jack, why don't you heat a bottle for him?" Cat suggested. Sitting on the couch, she laid the baby on her lap and told him, "I think you're too bundled. Yes, I do. I think you're hot." He stopped crying and cooed. Flora continued to read Mrs. Rineholdt's file.

"No wonder he's sleepin' so long; she's been puttin' cereal in his bedtime bottle. I never gave none of mine solids till they was at least three months old. Maybe that's some newfangled way by Dr. Spock." Flora shook her head and continued reading. As Catherine unwrapped her son from his blanket, a silver object fell to the floor. The baby kicked his legs, smiling at the feeling of freedom.

"He smiled at me! You have such a pretty smile," Catherine told him. Reaching down, she retrieved the item, examining it. "Isn't that sweet? It's a medallion. This must've belonged to his mother."

"She must've been Catholic," Flora commented.

"Will you put it in the china cabinet? We'll save it for when he's older." Catherine turned her attention to her son. "That's thoughtful of your birth mommy. Did you know, Tommy, Mommy loves baby toes?" Catherine kissed his tiny little sock-covered feet. Thomas Jackson Wyatt made an *mmmmm* sound, as if he was trying to giggle.

Flora took the medallion and headed off toward the dining room, calling over her shoulder, "That Mrs. Rineholdt had a system for ratin' burps! Unbelievable!"

Catherine laughed. "I don't think we'll have to be so rigid, do you, Tommy? No! I think we should have lots of playtime." Jack came back into the room with the baby's bottle and the brand-new parents sat on the couch, watching in fascination every move their infant son made while they fed him his first meal in his new home.

Chapter 28

At four o'clock in the morning, Mary sat next to the open window in the dining room. The cool predawn air made her feel better. Soaked in sweat from the latest distressing nightmare in which someone kidnapped her baby, she went to the refrigerator and poured a glass of milk.

Yesterday had been a fine day until she called her parents to give them her new telephone number, at which time they sprang their plans for their upcoming weekend visit. Mary understood they intended to inspect her living situation.

They rationalized the intrusion by promising to deliver Mary's cherry-red 1954 Bel Air convertible they'd bought for her sixteenth birthday. Dad would drive her car, packed with the rest of Mary's belongings, and Mom would follow in the Rolls-Royce. As a symbol that Mary wasn't welcome back home to live, Edith planned to redecorate Mary's childhood room as a guest bedroom. She hated that she had to deal with her mom to get her car.

"Couldn't sleep, huh?" came Joanna's voice.

"I can go to sleep fine. It's the waking up in the middle of the night that's irritating."

"I know. I do the same thing," Joanna confessed.

In the living room, Joanna turned on the lamp resting on the freshly scrubbed floor. Looking around, Mary surveyed the enormous task still ahead of them. Her parent's impending visit added to the pressure to get this last room in order.

"I'm wide awake. Do you feel like painting?"

"Sure," Joanna agreed. Donning their overalls, they dipped their rollers. While they worked, Joanna kept yawning.

"You could go back to sleep, couldn't you?" Mary asked.

"Naw, but I need coffee." Joanna set down her paint roller and passed through the dining area toward the kitchen. Her terrifying scream sent Mary running to her aid. Joanna gasped, "Stan! What're ya doin' out on the fire escape?"

"Don't scream!" Stan looked rattled, "I use the fire escape every mornin' to go in the back door of the doughnut shop." The banging began again.

"What is that?" Mary asked.

"Old bat Hollan, in Two-A. She pounds her cane on the ceiling at me all the time. She never has a kind word for anyone. I gotta make the doughnuts."

"You scared me to death," Joanna scolded.

"Sorry." He continued to descend the fire escape ladder. Joanna made coffee and the girls returned to painting. A short while later, a horrible screeching coming from the courtyard led them to the open dining room window to investigate. Stan was wheeling a cart, stacked with trays of doughnuts, toward the dumpster.

"Are you throwing all those doughnuts away?" Mary shouted to him.

"Day-old, can't sell 'em," Stan explained.

"That's a waste. Can I buy a few?"

"You can have 'em; come get what ya want." Mary climbed out the window and down the fire escape. The window next door flew open and an old, angry woman stuck her head out.

"What's wrong with you girls, shouting out windows at boys in the middle of the night?" The hateful tenant slammed her window shut. Mary scampered back up the fire escape a minute later with four jelly doughnuts.

"I don't think she likes us," she reasoned, handing Joanna two of the pastries.

"You can't please everyone," Joanna answered, taking a bite. Subsequently, Stan made a habit of bringing the girls doughnuts or dessert a couple of times a week.

The visit from Mary's parents went as anticipated. Fortunately, Grandma Bernice's trip coincided and she acted as a buffer between Mary and her mother.

First, Mary introduced her roommate to her parents. "This is Joanna Wilson; we went to high school together. When I was looking for an apartment, I bumped into her. She's going to school here, too, so we thought, wouldn't it be a gas if we roomed together?"

"I suppose you sprang for all this," Mary's mother accused Bernice, as she rudely ignored the girls and walked from room to room, conducting an inspection.

"I did the same for you and my son when you were first married, as I recall," her mother-in-law reminded her.

"Ah, yes, I'll never forget the lovely turquoise couch," Edith stabbed sarcastically. – Mary's mother had threatened to douse it with lighter fluid and set it ablaze the day she hauled it to the curb for the rubbish truck. Mary couldn't remember a time when the relationship between Edith and Bernice didn't teeter in a fragile balance. She was accustomed to it, though; she pitied Joanna's discomfort. Edith ended her tour with Mary's bedroom. "This is the most godawful shade of blue I believe I've ever seen." her mother howled as she randomly opened Mary's dresser drawers.

"I like it," Mary defended. Bernice shook her head and rolled her eyes.

Edith raised her voice for Bernice's benefit. "I think the purchase of the television's a mistake. You'll waste the whole evening watching some show and you'll study until the wee hours of the morning."

Mary told her, "I'm a night owl, Mom. I always have been."

"Yes, and you're crabby and horrible to get out of bed in the morning."

That evening, Mr. Atherton, who'd been painfully nonverbal all day, took them all to an Italian restaurant for dinner. Upon returning to the apartment, he handed Mary her car keys.

"Your boxes are in the trunk," he explained. "Don't go over the speed limit." Mary felt stung by the coldness from the man who'd once adored her and now couldn't look her in the eye.

"I won't, Daddy," she said, unlocking the trunk. She pulled open the tops of the boxes to view the contents. "Hey, Mom," she called. "Where're my prom dresses?"

"I sold them to a secondhand store. My goodness, you had so much stuff, it took me days and lots of trash bags to clean it out."

"You sold my homecoming queen dress?" Mary furiously yowled. "Where're the things from my shelves?" In particular, she wanted the mementos from her relationship with Tony.

"I threw it away. I was lucky the decorator squeezed me in; he's in such high demand. Here, do you want the money from the dresses?" Edith backtracked and stuffed a wad of bills in one of the open boxes. Mary's face burned bright red.

As her parents pulled away from the curb, she sarcastically shouted, "Thanks a lot."

After they carried in the boxes, Mary vengefully went through them. "I can't believe she got rid of all my stuff! She had no right. Does she believe, by throwing out everything attached to Tony, she is going to rewrite history? In my bedroom, she threw the photo of Tony and me in the wastebasket."

"She does like to express her opinion," Joanna observed.

"Yeah, and woe to anyone who doesn't agree with her. At least with her in Nashville, she won't be breathing down my neck."

The first week of June, school began. Mary and Joanna established a routine. Rising early, Joanna made coffee and showered. By 7:00 a.m., Mary rolled out of bed as Joanna caught the bus to beauty college. Mary's classes commenced at eight; she often cut things close.

Home by four o'clock, Joanna took time to study, then cook dinner. When Mary arrived around six they'd eat, followed by Mary's chore of cleaning the kitchen. Meanwhile, Joanna finished her assignments while listening to the TV. Justifying Edith's warning, Mary typically lounged in front of the television until ten and did homework until midnight. Joanna went to bed at 10:00 p.m.

Joanna wouldn't describe Mary in the morning as "crabby"—more like "unresponsive" until she showered. The girls invested most of their energy on their studies during the week and reserved Sunday afternoons for the latest Hollywood flick at the movie theater. Joanna loved the mysteries, whereas Mary favored drama and romance.

"Those make me think 'bout Jack," Joanna complained, vetoing Mary's movie pick.

"The love stories remind me of Tony, too. But I like to think about him," Mary admitted.

Mary's preoccupation with thoughts of Tony negatively affected her grades. By midsummer, Mary constantly bemoaned the ease with which she'd breezed through high school and the unreasonable amount of work piled on her by the college teachers. Longing for simpler times, she retreated to her memories of Tony rather than concentrating on nursing.

During one of her more fanciful daydreams, she realized she could drive to Ole5 Miss and talk to Tony. He'd be at summer football training. The more she entertained the idea, the more obsessed she became.

For months, Mary passed the time hatching a plot to reunite with her high school sweetheart. Finally, when the college football season kicked off, Mary approached Joanna with her scheme. "I think we need to take a road trip to Nashville this weekend. You haven't had any contact with your mom since we moved here."

"I know. I need to let her know where I am. I'd have to do it without my father findin' out." Joanna eyed her suspiciously. "What's the real reason for goin' to Nashville?"

"Ole Miss is playing Vanderbilt. I might have a chance to catch Tony alone when he arrives for the game."

Joanna frowned. "Do you think that's such a good idea?"

"This has been hanging out there too long. I've got to talk to him. I can't concentrate on anything and I don't think I'll be able to until I see him. Besides, Mother is hounding me to visit, for appearances' sake, you know, the neighbors." Settling the issue, the girls decided to hit the road right after school on Friday night. They'd stay with Mary's parents, in the newly redecorated guest room, formerly Mary's domain.

Jack found Catherine and the baby on the floor in the sunroom, playing in the shadows of the late-afternoon light. Tommy rocked on his hands and knees, blowing bubbles and making humming noises.

"Show Daddy what you can do, Tommy. Come to Mommy." The little boy crawled shakily to Catherine, giggling as she scooped him up, showering him with praise. "You're the smartest little boy in the world."

The new father's lack of experience around infants still made him uneasy when it came to Tommy. As a result, the baby favored Catherine, making Jack feel like an outsider. Even Jack recognized his attitude as childish; Tommy's lack of interest in his father reinforced this notion.

Having to use a cane to get around made it impractical for Jack to carry the boy. When physical therapy no longer returned improvement, Jack adjusted to his limitations. Although he was glad for the end to the monotonous cycle of doctors, X-rays, and therapy, his now unfilled hours gave way to boredom.

"I've been thinking." Jack leaned on the doorjamb. "I need to get back to work. I'm going stir-crazy around here." Cat lifted herself from the floor to a wicker chair. "I can't work on cars anymore. But I could use the insurance money from the station for a down payment on several stations. I'll hire a few mechanics and gas attendants and I'd manage them. Not only in Nashville; maybe Chattanooga, see how it goes. If it works out, open a few more."

"I think that's a great idea!" Catherine agreed. "How much do you need to get started?"

"You know how I feel about that, Cat," he resisted.

"I know and it's silly. You need to get over it. What's mine is yours. I believe in you, Jack." It took skillful persuasion until he finally agreed to go into business with his wife.

Within a few days, Jack engaged in inspecting properties, his head full of blueprints and numbers. He threw himself into his project, wanting more than anything to prove the validity of Catherine's faith in him. For the first time in his adult life, Jack saw his way clear. This time he wouldn't fail.

Chapter 29

Mary arrived at Dudley Field hours before the game. Finding a shady spot near the player entrance, she spread a blanket under the tree. Tucking her legs, she opened her textbook to the pages on hematology... blood. Recalling Joanna unconscious, her mattress saturated with blood, made Mary queasy. She rubbed her head; as a nurse she wondered how she'd cope, seeing that type of scene time after time. Her stomach doing anticipation flip-flops made concentration difficult. After reading the same paragraph four times, she quit. Her mind kept drifting back to the long summer days she'd spent with Tony. The love they'd shared flashed in vivid color. She leaned against the tree, closed her eyes, and took in the woody smell of the warm October day. She imagined the words they'd say and the preordained kiss to follow.

In a short while, the Ole Miss players staggered by. Mary's heart skipped a beat when Tony came around the corner, his head down, deep in thought.

"Hi there, stranger," Mary called, catching the young man's attention.

He stopped abruptly. "Mary? Hi. What're you doing here?"

"Waiting for you, of course," she cooed, flirting.

"I've got to get ready for the game." He pointed toward the locker room.

"I thought you'd be happy to see me." Mary offered, confused by his lukewarm reception.

Tony shifted his weight impatiently. "It's just..."

Mary's face flushed red. "We haven't talked since that horrible Thanksgiving and I thought maybe we should."

"What's there to talk about, huh, Mary? Your family made it clear they thought I was a piece of crap. Your old man didn't give a shit the baby was mine as much as it was yours!"

"Daddy was upset," she tried to explain.

Tony interrupted her. "It doesn't matter!"

"Of course it matters! What about us and how much we loved each other?"

Tony fretted, "I'm a rookie quarterback for the Ole Miss Rebels, don't mess this up."

"I guess it's okay for you to ruin my life, but God forbid I interfere with yours? Don't you want to know about our son?"

"So... it was a boy," Tony pressed his lips together; he nodded and cleared his throat.

"He was born April third at six forty-five p.m. He weighed six pounds, five ounces. He had dark hair and dark-blue eyes. I got to be with him for three days." Mary's chest tightened with emotion.

"Good for you." Tony's voice tremored. "God, you're really something! You show up, wanting sympathy from me. You signed away my rights when you gave up yours. No one asked me what I wanted! My dad has your family pegged: Because you're rich, you call the shots. But you're wrong, you're nothing special."

Mary felt as if he'd kicked the wind out of her. Her heart sank further when Melinda Peterson approached, a Rebel cheerleading uniform draped over her arm. Mary's rival recognized her immediately and quickened her pace.

"Hi Tony, darlin'!" Melinda intruded. Joining them, she kissed him full on the mouth, eyeing Mary hatefully. "Well, well, Mary Atherton, as I live and breathe. I thought you dropped off the face of the earth."

"I'm in nursing school in Memphis now," Mary informed, returning a glare of contempt.

"Did Tony tell ya the news? We're engaged!" Melinda giggled, flashing a ring.

Facing Tony, clenching her teeth, Mary sputtered, "Melinda Peterson? You're kidding?"

Melinda straightened her shoulders and coolly replied, "Wow! You're pitiful. I know all about your trick to trap Tony."

Mary's face betrayed her outrage. "I didn't try to trap him." She turned to Tony. "Who else've you told?"

"No one," he replied, irritated.

Melinda hissed, "Tony's with me now, slut. You'd better stay away or I'll blab to everyone how you were shipped off to a home for unwed mothers."

Shaking her head, Mary whispered, "Tony?"

"Don't come around again." He spoke as if she were a scummy door-to-door salesman.

"Don't worry, I won't. You obviously misrepresented yourself to me, Anthony! I was naive to believe you're a genuine human being. I'm sorry it took me so long to see the real you."

Mary quickly gathered her belongings. Making a straight line to her car, she denied the urge to look back, fearing their mockery would be forever burned in her memory.

From the dime store, Joanna scoped out her old apartment. Harris's car occupied its usual spot. She wished Irene would appear en route on an errand; otherwise she'd wait until her mother faithfully journeyed to Mass. Forty-five minutes passed. Suddenly she spied her father and Eddie exit the street-level door and jump in the family's battered Ford. Waiting until they disappeared into traffic, Joanna dashed across the street and took the stairs by twos. She knocked loudly. Within seconds, Irene appeared, drying her hands on a towel.

"Joanna," she gasped. "Ya can't be here! Your father'll have both of our hides!"

"I'm not staying; I saw him leave with Eddie. I had to come and give you my new address and phone number." Joanna handed her a piece of paper.

"I'm glad you did. Come in, we've got to talk fast; he's takin' Eddie to cash his paycheck. He won't be gone long." She ushered Joanna into the cramped, unchanged living room. Irene parked herself by the window to watch for Harris's return.

"I'm in beauty school now, Mama," Joanna explained. She told her about living with Mary. Irene eyed the girl suspiciously.

"You lied to me about Mary Atherton before."

"It's true, Mama, every word."

"What happened with your baby?" Irene asked. Joanna recounted her tragedy and Irene hung her head. "Oh, child, I'm sorry for the baby, but I'm not surprised he did you thata way. Men aren't worth the dirt God made them from. Uh-oh, here's your father."

Irene escorted the girl to the back door. "Take care of yourself." They hugged quickly.

"I will. I'm gonna be fine," Joanna assured her. The girl swiftly descended the stairs and disappeared out the alley gate. As she navigated through her old community, her mother's accelerated aging worried her. The deep-set wrinkles around her eyes had added twenty years to her appearance. The bruise on Irene's cheek hadn't escaped Joanna's attention. Joanna caught a bus to the Athertons' neighborhood. As she approached the driveway she saw her roommate packing suitcases into the car.

"Hey!" Joanna greeted her. "What's goin' on?"

"I've got to get out of this town. I can't take one more minute!"

"Did your mama do something to make you mad?"

"No more than usual. I'll tell you all about it on the way to Memphis."

Edith joined them. "I don't understand why you have to rush off before dinner."

"I told you, Mom. I have a test on Monday and I study better at my place."

All the way home, Joanna gave Mary her full attention while she listed the myriad emotions pulsing through her; anger, sadness, humiliation, and even relief that her hours of arduous speculation were over. Mary took up smoking that day.

"Am I gonna have to worry 'bout you hurtin' yourself?" Joanna asked, recalling Mary's suicide threat when she first learned about Tony dating Melinda.

"No. I wouldn't do that to you. Could you imagine having to call my parents? I love you too much to ever put you through that."

"Good. I appreciate it."

"I just feel so empty right now! Ya know?"

"Yeah, I do know," Joanna confessed. Mary regretted the trip to Nashville, but Joanna succeeded in her mission to pass contact information to her mother.

After several miles of reflective quiet, Joanna asked, "Ya know what we need to do?"

"What?" Mary braced for some great words of wisdom.

"We need to find Prissy. She'll be back at school at Our Lady of What-cha-ma-call-it."

"Our Lady of Grace," Mary corrected.

"What do we do if her father has switched her school?" Joanna asked.

"Prissy's dad's pharmacy is close to the Peabody. We find it, we find her. Let's blow off school Monday to locate the slimy Mr. Matthews. We can be at Prissy's school in time for dismissal," Mary suggested.

"What about your test?"

"I lied. After my run-in with Tony, I couldn't handle any drama from Mom."

Monday, they cruised the blocks around the Peabody, looking for Prissy's father's business. To their disappointment there were several pharmacies. Outside the first store, Mary told Joanna, "Now act natural, like you're shopping, and make your way to the prescription area and try to find a name. I'll do the same." Three stores later, Joanna expressed impatience. "Come on, we only have a few more left. After we find him we'll go shopping." Whenever Mary was melancholy, her therapy consisted of buying a new outfit. Considering the horrendous outcome of the weekend, it might take a completely new wardrobe to improve her mood.

In the fifth store, Joanna stopped where she could get a look at the man behind the counter. He had blond wavy hair the color of Prissy's. Joanna pretended to be shopping, selecting an item from the shelf in front of her. The pharmacist filled a bottle of pills. His white lab coat had the name GARY MATTHEWS stitched above the pocket. Mary stepped next to her.

"That's him!" Joanna whispered.

They both stared. Matthews suddenly looked up and asked, "Can I help you girls?" Joanna quickly put back the athletic supporter in her hand. Horrified with embarrassment, she blushed bright red as she and Mary broke into hysterical laughter. Joanna bolted for the door while Mary took a different approach.

"Can you recommend a brand of condoms?" she asked, pointing at the shelf behind him.

"Trojans are popular," he answered. "But I only sell them to married women."

"I'm married," Mary lied. She studied him, with contempt, as he took her money.

"You have a nice night." He used a lecherous tone. Mary stepped out to the noisy street to find Joanna waiting in front of the next store.

"What took you so long? I thought you were right behind me."

"I bought some rubbers," she declared, laughing. Joanna cracked up. "I'm sorry, the look on your face was priceless!" When she finally gained composure, she told Joanna, "I got a good look at him. Believe me, he makes my skin crawl."

The girls ate lunch at a diner, then headed off to the dress shops to kill some time. Several hours later, they were sitting in Mary's car in front of the Catholic girls' school, waiting for dismissal. Mary was digging into her retail bags, looking for a scarf, while Joanna picked at a cuticle when the final bell sounded. They straightened in their seats as a sea of girls erupted from the front doors. Like ants in a recently disturbed hill, they took off in all directions. Wearing the same uniform, they all looked alike. Joanna scoured the crowd for Prissy's wavy blond hair.

"There! Walkin' to the corner, two o'clock, that's her!" Joanna barked.

"Are you sure?"

"Yes. Come on." Mary hit the gas, nearly causing an accident by pulling in front of an annoyed man, who laid on his horn.

"Oops!" She waved an apology.

"Turn right at the next corner."

On the residential street Mary slowed and gradually caught up with the girl. Pulling alongside, Joanna grinned as she called, "Hey, little girl, ya want a ride?"

Prissy screamed with elation. "Oh my God! It's so good to see y'all!"

Joanna immediately noticed how Prissy's once childlike body now revealed well-rounded, womanly curves. She'd grown taller, too. Her blood-red lipstick and matching fingernails shocked Joanna.

"That little slowpoke"—Prissy spoke louder—"is my sister Lisa, and if she doesn't hurry up I'm going to leave her behind." The chubby nine-year-old didn't go any faster.

"I was serious, we can give y'all a ride home. Hop in."

Prissy climbed into the back of the car, hollering to her sister to come on. Lisa joined her in the backseat. Prissy directed them to her street, talking nonstop about the boys she'd met.

"I've decided I like boys after all," she told them.

"I thought your father wouldn't let you have friends," Mary inquired.

"I convinced him it's normal for girls in ninth grade to have a social life. I also told him I'm perfectly healthy and don't need to take vitamins anymore. I hate swallowing pills; they make me gag. He's realizing I'm not a child anymore." Mary and Joanna's eyes met, surprised. "This is it, on the right." Mary pulled to the curb in front of a stately home with tall white columns. Joanna handed Prissy a piece of paper with their phone number.

"Come see me when you need a haircut. I have to log a lot of cuts before I can graduate."

"I will," Prissy promised. "And now that I have your phone number, I'll call you and we can catch up." Lisa exited the car without saying anything.

"Bye, Lisa," Mary called.

"Don't pay attention to her," Prissy advised. "She's always like that. She doesn't like to do anything but play with her stupid dolls. She's such a baby." They hugged their goodbyes.

"She seemed good," Mary said, turning the car toward home.

"She looks like she's eighteen, not almost fifteen," Joanna shared her opinion.

"Oh, give her a break. I wore makeup at her age, too."

"She did look good," Joanna had to admit. "My gut instinct says he hasn't touched her since she came back. The whole pregnancy thing probably scared the hell out of him."

"You might be right. I wish I could get one of his so-called vitamins and find out what they really are," Mary reasoned. "What do you make of her sister?"

"Prissy said she's always quiet. If it was a new behavior, I might be worried. I don't know. I hope Matthews hasn't moved on to the younger one."

"Oh God, that gives me chills." Mary shook as if a shiver shocked her spine. "You should've heard the way he said, 'Have a nice night!' Dirty old man."

Joanna sighed heavily. "Well, I'm glad we played hooky today. Now we know where our little Missy-Prissy is, and she can call us if he tries anythin'."

Chapter 30

In the weeks following Mary's confrontation with Tony, Joanna witnessed a change in the girl's behavior. Mary began to spend more time with her nursing school classmates. Many nights she'd skip the dinner Joanna prepared to join them at a dance club.

"Come with us; you'll have a good time." Mary stood at the open dining room window, reasoning with Joanna, who had settled comfortably on the fire escape with a paperback book and a glass of chocolate milk. "Maybe you'll meet a guy," Mary singsonged.

"No, thanks, the last thing I want is a guy," Joanna told her. Suddenly Joanna startled. Stan was standing on the end of her fire escape. He had a habit of popping up. Mary considered him harmless and Joanna too jumpy.

"God, I hate when you sneak up on me," Joanna scolded.

Stan smiled, enjoying her reaction. "Where ya goin', Mary?"

"To a club, but I can't get old stick-in-the-mud to come."

"It sounds like fun. Can I tag along?"

"It's a free country," Mary told him. Stan climbed through their window, and he and Mary left through the front door. Thereafter, Stan turned up wherever Mary hung out.

Unlike Mary, Joanna was content with her path. Scoring at the top of her class, she loved beauty school. Her unrealistic daydream of owning a beautiful salon distracted her from brooding over Jack and the baby.

Prissy kept her word and rang Joanna the week after their reunion. She and Mary made plans a few weeks later to meet their young friend for dinner at a restaurant in Germantown.

Seated in a booth, Joanna asked Prissy, "Where'd you tell your dad you were goin'?"

"I didn't, he wasn't home yet. Mrs. Lasky thinks I'm at a birthday party. I haven't told my dad anything about y'all. He gets angry if I talk about Knoxville, so I don't say anything."

For the next hour, the girls caught up on one another's lives. Prissy expressed the genuine compassion of a woman with some experience regarding Joanna's loss. Joanna couldn't equate scared little Missy with the grown-up young woman she'd become.

With Thanksgiving drawing near, Mary dreaded the requirement she observe the holiday at her parents' home. She begged Joanna, "Please go with me! I'd rather be dead than take part in the Atherton family charade alone this year."

"Why not tell them we're gonna make dinner here, then don't go?"

"Oh, have you learned nothing of my mother's power? My brother, Albert, is bringing his fiancée, Judy. If I don't attend, my mother will be in an uproar and I'll get blamed for ruining yet another one of her sacred holidays. She'll threaten to cut me off."

"I imagine you as crabby without disposable income." Joanna laughed.

"As long as they're paying the bills, I'd better appease them."

"What if they ask why I'm not spendin' the holiday with my own family?"

Mary went to the phone to call her mother. "I'll tell them your family is traveling abroad. Don't worry, my mom's so self-absorbed she rarely considers anyone else unless they can affect her image among her peers. Those of us falling into that category are treated to her relentless badgering and ultimate disapproval."

Joanna got a front-row seat for one of Edith's tirades the night they rolled in for the holiday. Edith wasted no time, waving Mary's nursing school grades around in outrage.

"C's, Mary? C's!" her mother ranted. "I had to double-check the name to make sure they were your grades. You've never gotten C's in your life!"

"Nursing school's hard, Mom. A lot of girls, smarter than me, are getting C's as well."

"I'll bet you're trying to cram until two in the morning. What did I tell you?" Joanna excused herself to the guest bedroom to avoid witnessing the rest of Edith's outburst.

The next morning Edith fussed around the kitchen, demanding Joanna and Mary's help. She took every opportunity to criticize Mary, from scolding her celery-chopping technique to berating her for not setting the table properly.

When her brother, Albert, and his fiancée arrived around 2:00 p.m., Mary's mother opened several bottles of wine and set out a tray of fancy salmon hors d'oeuvres, and they all gathered in the living room. Introductions were made as they sat on Mrs. Atherton's expensive white couches.

Mary leaned over and whispered to Joanna, "Whatever you do, don't get red wine on her sofa; she'll have a brain hemorrhage."

Edith fawned over Judy, complimenting her hairstyle and upscale clothes. Judy's father was the chief of staff at a hospital in Georgia and they were wealthy. Edith put on her best face for the newcomer, while Mary longed to reveal what a fake she was.

Edith instructed Mary to bring out another bottle of wine. Joanna offered to check on the turkey. In the kitchen Mary poured herself another glass of wine. "She better not ask me to carve the turkey. A knife in my hands could be detrimental to her health."

Joanna laughed. "I wish Bernice was here; your mom's better behaved around her."

"Me too. I can't believe her travel schedule; first Uncle Charlie in Richmond, then Aunt Beverly in Tucson. She's considering a trip to Europe, after the home's fashion show. We're not going to see her for a while." Mary left the room to deliver the pricey wine her mother requested and returned to assist Joanna with getting dinner on the table. Mary told her quietly, "Try to avoid Mother's giblet gravy; it's awful. She knows I hate it and yet she continues to make it."

The family gathered and her father offered a prayer. Mr. Atherton set to carving the turkey. Edith intentionally goaded Mary by serving her plate, pouring gravy over her turkey and stuffing. Mary held her tongue and picked at her green bean casserole. She ate rolls, avoiding the lake of gravy, and consumed several more glasses of wine.

Mr. Atherton and Albert discussed his plans for employment after graduation while Edith conferred with Judy on wedding details.

"Of course, Mary, I want you to be one of my bridesmaids," Judy told her.

"She'd be honored," Edith answered for her.

"Albert tells me you're in nursing school," Judy said, trying again to converse with Mary.

"Yes. We're so proud both our children have chosen the medical field," Edith interfered.

Mary scoffed. "Why don't you tell her the truth? I have a C average right now, and Mother threatened to pull the plug on nursing school if I don't improve my grades."

"Mary!" Edith scolded.

"Why put on airs? She'll be part of the family soon. She should know what to expect."

"I think you've had enough wine." Her mother took her daughter's glass, setting it aside.

Mary stood, wobbly on her feet. "What's the matter? Are you afraid I'll say something to embarrass you? Never mind, don't answer." Edith's face turned crimson. "It was nice meeting you," Mary said to Judy. "I'm going to see if I can find an open burger joint. I hate my mother's giblet gravy and she knows it." Mary headed for the kitchen.

Joanna excused herself from the table. "I'll look after her." Joanna kept her voice low as she guided Mary to the back door. "Give me the keys, I'll drive."

"No, I'm okay, I'll drive," Mary protested loudly.

"Come on." Joanna snatched the keys from her. "Let's go before you say somethin' else you're gonna regret." Mary grabbed the last full bottle of wine. Joanna led her to the car.

Joanna eased the car onto the street. Taking the wine, she remarked, "Now I need a drink."

"God! I hate my mother!" Mary yelled. Fortunately, the car windows were shut, so she didn't inform the whole neighborhood.

"I don't guess she's fond of you right now, either," Joanna observed.

"Oh, who cares? I'm so tired of being told what to do; how I should talk, walk, eat. If she goes over proper decorum for a young lady one more time, I swear I'll scream in her face. She's picked on me since we walked in the door. I'm not a puppet she can play with when she wants to put on a good show."

"I know, I was there."

"Where're we going?" Mary suddenly asked.

"I don't know, let's just drive around until you feel ready to go back and face the music."

"We'll run out of gas before that happens." Mary laughed hysterically.

Ultimately, they parked at Love Park, where Jack had taken Joanna the morning she'd left for Knoxville. They took turns sipping from the wine bottle and listening all the injustices in the world. They watched as the day slipped into twilight. The lights of Nashville glowed like a carnival below them. Finally, it was time to go home. Mary stared out the window at the warm lights in the homes, glowing like happy families.

"I'm going to hear how I ruined Thanksgiving two years in a row."

"It wouldn't surprise me."

As they pulled to the stop sign at the bottom of a hill, the Wyatts' home loomed in front of them. The ten cars in the circular driveway signaled a big celebration going on. Mary started to speak, but Joanna cut her off.

"I already know whose house that is." Joanna quickly turned the corner.

"I guess you don't want to pop in and say hi."

"No, not tonight."

"Well, learn from my mistake: Seeing the old boyfriend isn't a good idea."

"I assure you I won't even try. I hope I never see Jack again. My heart couldn't take it."

The next morning, Mary sat across the living room from her father. Her head hung, throbbing with a hangover. Edith had gone to the stores for the annual day-after-Thanksgiving rush. Like Mary, her mother considered shopping an elixir for most ailments.

Before Mr. Atherton could begin, Mary apologized, "I'm sorry, Daddy." It had been so long since her father looked her in the eye. Now his disconnected, icy stare cut her to the core.

"I know she provoked you, but you were disrespectful. We didn't raise you that way."

"No, sir, you didn't," Mary acknowledged.

"It's best if you go back to Memphis today. I expect you to write a sincere apology to your mother before you leave. I expect you to get your head on straight."

Raising objections would only make matters worse, so she simply replied, "Yes, sir."

The rest of the weekend Mary pored over her textbooks, at her desk in Memphis, studying and failing miserably. Her heart wasn't in it. This was her parents' goal, not hers. Her one-sided relationship with them required Mary to concede to gain approval. She was tired of the effort involved in following their demands, when in reality she'd never achieve their expectations. Exhausted, she saw no reason to bother trying.

When Christmas rolled around, Mary diplomatically bowed out of spending it in Nashville by exaggerating her commitment to study during the winter break. Her parents agreed, so for the second year in a row Mary wasn't home for Christmas. Instead she and Joanna prepared their own holiday dinner of roasted pheasant with orange sauce. They exchanged a few gifts and invited Stan to join them when he arrived on the fire escape with a pie. The three of them passed the time with a marathon game of Scrabble. Even though it was in the forefront of their minds, neither Mary nor Joanna mentioned last year's Christmas at the Frances Weston Home for Unwed Mothers. Mary enjoyed the peaceful holiday, and Joanna optimistically predicted 1958 would be her best year ever.

Catherine spooned mashed potatoes into Tommy's baby-bird-like mouth while the room full of family and friends looked on. Alex asked for a second helping of roast and Wendell passed the plate to Jack's best friend.

Jack held the baby while Catherine fed him. "He loves to eat. I can't imagine what he'll be like when he's a teenager."

"He'll eat you out of house and home, like you did me," Jack's father, Phillip, quipped.

Jack flinched. His high school memories were of his mother, sick with cancer, and his father gone on his traveling sales job, peddling goods no one wanted. Jack's recollections were tied with a ribbon of resentment at being alone with her when she'd passed away.

Jack would've preferred to forgo the extended family gathering, but Cat intended to give Tommy childhood memories that'd make Norman Rockwell envious. Her version included a house full of people, scrumptious food, love, and especially grandparents.

Tommy pushed away the spoon. "No more? Okay, let me clean your face." He wiggled as Cat mopped him with a washcloth. "Do you want to open your gift from Grandpa Phillip?"

"Pa," Tommy exclaimed, pointing at Jack's father.

"Okay, Pa, your turn." Jack poked. Phillip followed him to the living room. Using his cane, Jack settled into a chair and Catherine situated Tommy in his lap with Phillip's gift.

Struck with inspiration, she said, "No, wait, let me get my camera." When

Catherine returned with the Rollei, Tommy's chewing on the box made the wrapping paper soggy. "Smile," she cried as she hit the shutter and captured three generations of awkward. "Honey, you need to help him," Catherine instructed.

"I was letting him do it his way. Okay, look, Tommy, what is it?" Jack tore back the paper to reveal a toy tow truck. "Nice touch, Dad. Thanks." Shooting a glance at Catherine, he suspected she'd coached his father. "Look here, buddy, now you have a truck like mine." Jack had five tow trucks now and three service stations.

Soon Tommy grew bored. Crawling to the couch, he pulled himself to stand, raised his arms in the air, and gave out a resounding, "Ta-dah!" Looking over his shoulder at Cat, he clapped his hands.

Catherine clapped as well. "Ta-dah! Look at my big boy!" In his excitement, Tommy took two steps toward her. "Come to me, baby," she encouraged. Raising the camera, she snapped the portrait right before he plopped to the floor, cushioned by his diaper. "Did you see? He walked!" Catherine grabbed Wendell's sleeve.

"He's really something," Wendell acknowledged fondly. That Christmas day in 1957, no one captured a photo of Catherine lifting Tommy and praising him while he giggled. It didn't matter. Those snapshots and a treasure trove more were etched forever in Catherine's heart.

Chapter 31

After the warm glow of the holidays faded, the gray winter sky of Memphis only festered Mary's dark funk. Bored and restless, she rejoined the club scene, partying a couple of nights a week and wildly celebrating on the weekends. On many occasions, in the predawn hours, she'd stumble in and hug the commode until the room stopped spinning.

The nursing student's lack of interest in school gave way to skipped classes and missed homework. Out of concern, Joanna advised Mary to get out of bed and go to class. She met her roommate's crabby morning side. "I'm so sick of people telling me what to do!"

By April 1958, Mary's increasingly promiscuous behavior with unsavory characters she met in the clubs troubled Joanna, although Mary had the good sense not to bring any of them to their apartment and swore she wasn't having sex. Still, Joanna worried her friend might put herself in danger. She contemplated calling Bernice for advice, but Joanna missed the chance.

Early on a Sunday morning Edith called. Joanna understood the gist of the circumstances listening to Mary's side of the conversation.

"When?" Mary asked. "Where was she?. . . Well, what do the doctors say?... No, I understand... I'll leave here as soon as I pack a bag."

Joanna rushed into Mary's room and took out her suitcase. Mary scrambled in seconds later, tossing clothes in a pile. "Grandma had a stroke; I have to go to Knoxville!"

Joanna got her on track. "Here, let me help you. I'll pack for me, too, and drive. I don't think you should be behind the wheel right now."

"You're right. God, she's got to be all right! I can't lose her!"

Once they settled in at Bernice's house, Joanna took over the cooking and household chores, freeing the family to hold vigil at the hospital. For once, Edith behaved, genuinely supporting the family through the dark days when Bernice lay in an unresponsive coma.

One evening, after a long day at the hospital, Mary confided in Joanna, "Daddy's throwing money at them, insisting they bring her out of this. If she survives, she'll be an invalid. I don't want her to die, but I know she'd hate to live that way."

Four days after Bernice Atherton suffered the devastating stroke, the matriarch of the family passed away. Mary was inconsolable. Joanna checked on her right before the funeral.

"How you holdin' up?" she asked.

"I feel like part of me is dead." Mary wiped her nose with a tissue. They watched through the bedroom window as the mailman delivered to the house across the street. Some children passed by on their bikes. Mary stared at them. "Everything's so strange, like the whole world should stop because she's gone, but it just keeps going, doesn't it?"

"It feels disrespectful," Joanna added. "You seem better."

"Yeah, I keep imagining her telling me to dry up and go face what I have to face."

"That sounds like her." They both chuckled.

"Listen, thank you for everything. My dad appreciates all your help," Mary offered.

"It's nothin'. I loved Bernice, too. If you need anythin', let me know."

"What can you do about making this day already over?"

"I'm not that good," Joanna told her.

"I hate the smell of hospitals and funeral homes," Mary confessed.

"This doesn't bode well for someone who's gonna be a nurse."

"Dad hasn't seen my last batch of grades. Trust me, this isn't the time to confess."

A month after Bernice's death, Mary learned the woman had left her a sizable inheritance. Unlike the trust fund her parents had established, which was untouchable until she turned twenty-one or married, she could spend Bernice's money on any of her whims.

Joanna was flabbergasted when Mary came home in a brand-new pristine-white 1958 Ford Thunderbird convertible, flaunting a black-and-white interior. With the canvas top retracted, Mary blew the horn until Joanna met her at the curb. The cranky old woman in 2A rapped her cane on the window at them.

"It'd serve her right if she broke the window," Mary snipped, waving her off.

"What're you gonna do with the Bel Air?" Joanna asked.

"I'll sell it to you," Mary suggested.

"I don't have money for a car."

"Do you have a dollar?" Mary asked.

"Yes, of course I have a dollar."

"Sold, to the girl with the confused look on her face." Mary pointed to Joanna.

"No, Mary, the Bel Air is worth a lot of money," Joanna said, turning to walk away.

"Okay!" Mary called after her. "Five hundred dollars, pay me a dollar now and make payments when you can. I'm not in a hurry."

Joanna reconsidered her offer. "I don't know."

"The Bel Air's a sweet ride," Mary enticed her.

"Then take the new one back and stick with what you have."

"The Thunderbird's sweeter."

With graduation only eight months away, Joanna's grades guaranteed she'd find a secure job in a salon. Mary's flexible payment plan appealed to Joanna and made it possible for her to afford a car. Unable to resist, Joanna Wilson bought her first car. What would Irene say when she possessed a car ten times better than any her father had ever owned?

The infrequent letters Joanna received from her mother told of dresses she'd altered, Ben's high jinks, and the twins' progress. Reading between her mother's fake cheerful lines, Joanna assumed Harris was seizing her paychecks and giving daily beatings to the family. Joanna doubted anything had changed; once a wife-beating drunk, always a wife-beating drunk.

Jack came bounding into the kitchen full of enthusiasm. "Did you see the numbers from the station in Chattanooga?"

"Yes, I did." Catherine greeted him with an excited hug. "It's because you put in the home-style restaurant and the motel with amenities for the truckers! You're brilliant!"

"We need to open one between here and Birmingham. What'd you think?"

"Yes, absolutely. And between Nashville and Memphis? I've heard there're plans for an interstate highway in a couple of years. It'll be heavily used by the trucking lines."

They laid out the strategy and finances for several more truck stops. In the year since adopting Tommy, Jack had become consumed with managing their handful of stations. Catherine encouraged him and bankrolled the start-ups while focusing on her true joy, Tommy. Jack had finally succeeded. The preoccupation with his business decreased the contemplative moments he reflected on the past. He wished he could forget Joanna altogether.

When summer set in, Joanna considered getting a part-time job to help her pay off the balance of her car. Irene had defined *debt* as a curse word. After school one afternoon, Joanna waited at the counter in the doughnut shop, scouring the newspaper want ads, while Stan assembled the sandwich she'd ordered. Neighborhood doughnut shops, like corner bars, cultivate their own set of regular customers. Because of the convenience, Joanna was classified a loyal patron and knew many of the clientele by name.

Sheila, a woman who stopped in every night for a jelly doughnut and a cup of coffee, leaned over and asked, "You're gonna be a hairdresser, aren't you, Joanna? Tell me what you think of my haircut and perm. My mama said if it was rolled any tighter I'd look like a Negro."

"Oh, I don't know." Joanna examined the texture of her hair at the woman's insistence. "I can relax it some, but the key is the set and comb-out. It looks like a fine cut to me. Why don't you pop upstairs when you finish your coffee and let me see what I can do?"

"Order's up, Joanna," Stan called from the cash register. When she handed him the money, Stan asked, "How 'bout you and Mary double with me and my friend Bob on Saturday night?" Joanna didn't want to hurt his pride, but the proposition didn't appeal to her.

Whispering, she replied, "I can't. Didn't you hear I got married?"

"Nuh-uh," Stan uttered disbelievingly.

"Sure did! He's in the army. I met him three days before he shipped out to Southeast Asia. Spur of the moment, we got married the night before he went overseas. Crazy, huh?"

Stan blinked at her, dumbfounded. She chuckled as she took the stairs two at a time to her apartment. That'd keep Stan from playing matchmaker for one of his greasy friends.

Sheila, from the doughnut shop, was thrilled with the results after Joanna fiddled with her hairstyle. "Oh my goodness! You're a miracle worker; I look like Elizabeth Taylor!"

At least your hair does, Joanna thought.

"I'm gonna tell all the gals at work about you."

Sheila spread the word to her co-workers at the button factory. By August, Joanna had a steady stream of clients. She planned to secure a spot in an established salon upon graduation and persuade her existing customers to follow her. Mary didn't mind Joanna making extra money out of the apartment. In the seventeen months they'd been Memphis roommates, the girls had achieved an easygoing coexistence. Mary detested housework and appreciated Joanna's meticulous cleaning of their home. In exchange, Mary tackled the laundry, a chore Joanna had burned out on at the home in Knoxville. She didn't understand Mary's love for ironing.

"It's like therapy, I guess. With a little steam and a hot iron, all the wrinkles come out. Life should be so easy," Mary tried to explain.

They kept no secrets from each other and could generally predict each other's reactions and habits. On an August Friday night, the girls carried out their normal pattern, with Joanna set to watch *The Frank Sinatra Show* and Mary hurrying to meet her pals at a club. Joanna went to bed, anticipating Mary's tiptoed return in the wee hours of the morning. It unexpectedly alarmed Joanna when Mary came crashing into her room.

"Wake up! Look who I brought home!"

"What time is it?" Joanna shielded her eyes from the overhead light.

"Around three a.m., I think."

Joanna adjusted to the brightness and focused on the visitor standing at the door. "Jessie!" Joanna rushed to hug her friend. "You look fantastic!" Jessie's lean figure gave no evidence of having given birth. Her hair was cut in a flattering bob.

"So do you! Curlers in your hair is a stunnin' look."

Joanna explained, laughing, "When you do hair, you have to have good hair. I can't believe you're here! Do you want some coffee?"

"You got anythin' stronger?"

Joanna laughed again. "I got coffee; you two already smell like an ashtray in a winery."

Jessie and Mary sat in the dining room where they could converse over the half wall into the kitchen, where Joanna put on the coffee. "I'll make breakfast. How'd you want your eggs?"

Mary explained finding Jessie. "I was on Beale Street with Cindy and Betty..."

"I thought you steered clear of Beale Street, because of the Negroes?"

"We'd heard a rumor Elvis was going to be there. Lots of white people were around, too."

"His mama died; that's why he's in town," Jessie interrupted.

"I know. That's so sad," Joanna empathized.

"Anyway," Mary continued. "We walked past a club and heard piano music. I thought, *I sure miss Jessie.* We decided to go in; at the piano was the one, the only, Jessie Diamond."

"Thank you, thank you very much." Jessie did her impression of Elvis.

"I tried to call you so you could meet us, but the line was busy."

"Stan called here twice, wantin' to know what club you went to. I took it off the hook."

"When you meet Stan... " Mary started to explain to Jessie.

"And you will meet Stan," Joanna added as strips of bacon sizzled in a hot pan.

Mary went on, "Joanna's married." Jessie had a good laugh by the end of Mary's story.

"You're so bad," Jessie applauded, taking a sip of coffee. Suddenly, the wall vibrated with the familiar rapping from the grouchy neighbor next door.

"Let's have breakfast in the livin' room so we'll be farther away from our shared wall."

Jessie described her visit with Katie in Chattanooga. "She's doin' well; it's been tough. But the lady at the boardinghouse is a big help. Her baby looks like Popeye, not cute!"

"All babies look like Popeye," Joanna said, laughing.

"Mine didn't; mine was beautiful," Mary corrected.

"Well, I guess there're those rare exceptions," Joanna conceded.

Jessie filled in the gaps. "After that, I went to Nashville. I was gettin' steady work. A few days ago, a drummer friend told me 'bout a gig here in Memphis, so I jumped on a bus."

"Where're you staying?"

"I've rented a room close to Beale Street. I'm only there to sleep. It's perfect."

The girls talked until the first light of the new day colored the sky. Mary shuffled off to her room. Jessie crashed in Joanna's bed. The party girls slept while Joanna attended to her scheduled haircuts and rolled hairdos. By midafternoon, the raggedy pair finally came around from their alcohol-induced comas and decided to call Prissy. Mary volunteered to spring for dinner at the Peabody. They planned to hit the club where Jessie headlined.

"I doubt they'll let Prissy in. She's too young," Jessie said.

"You won't believe it when you see her. She looks like an adult," Joanna replied.

"Little Prissy, you're lyin'. I can't wait to see her."

The girls met Prissy a few hours later at the entrance of the Peabody Hotel. They were elated at being together, but disappointed when they learned the Skyway was permanently closed. Instead, they strolled South Second Street to Rendezvous Ribs.

"It's a shame about the Peabody," Joanna mourned, as they were ushered to their table. "Half the shops are gone, even the beauty parlor. What's happened to it?"

"All the modern motels poppin' up everywhere are killing the old businesses because people want what's new," Jessie explained. "I've been travelin' on the Greyhounds since I left Knoxville and all I see are new motels, gas stations, truck stops, and shoppin' centers being built, a lot with futuristic architecture."

"I don't like modern buildings. I prefer the old ones," Joanna said.

"I guess that's progress," Jessie reasoned.

Chapter 32

The realtor pressured him to purchase a piece of land that brought a higher commission than the one Jack wanted. "No, make an offer on the first one. It's the right size for my plans," Jack demanded. Using his cane, he walked over to the window, waiting while the real estate agent crunched the new numbers on his adding machine. This was taking too long for Jack; he'd wanted to be on his way home hours ago.

He watched the traffic and noticed a cherry-red '54 Bel Air as it parallel-parked. The red convertible was his favorite make and model. As the driver got out of the car, Jack unexpectedly darted out the door.

"Hey, what about making a deal here?" the real estate agent called after him.

"I'll get back to you later!" Jack shouted. Crossing the street, he limped after the girl he thought might be Joanna. She walked slowly, distracted, reading a magazine.

"Joanna?" he called, when he got within ten feet of her. The girl stopped instantly, turning, she dropped the beauty journal.

"Jack!" Her eyes went wide and she froze as if her feet were blocks of ice.

"I can't believe it's you!" He wanted to hug her. Then she stiffened and he thought better.

"What're ya doin' here?" Joanna asked, scanning the people on the sidewalks.

"I had some business across the street. I didn't have any idea where you were. I sent Alex to talk to you in Knoxville, but you were already gone. There's so much I need to say to you…"

"Jack, we don't have anythin' to say to each other." Joanna started walking.

"How can you say that?" Jack grabbed her arm. "I know what happened with the baby." A customer exited the doughnut shop, and Joanna tensed under his touch.

"I can't discuss this with you in the middle of the street. I have a life here. My apartment's on the corner. Come on. I'll give you five minutes," she whispered.

In the apartment, Jack's head swiveled as he inspected her home. Joanna clamped her fists to her hips with irritation, and reminded him, "The clock's ticking."

Jack spoke quickly, "I can't tell you how sorry I am for what happened."

"Yeah, me too," she replied sarcastically. "My friends kept tellin' me you were gonna abandon me. But no, Jack'd never do that."

"I didn't abandon you. I sent Alex to tell you about the apartment I rented for us." Jack explained.

"What about the letter you sent tellin' me to give the baby up for adoption?"

"What letter? I never wrote any letter telling you to do that."

"I read about the explosion at the station in the newspaper. Your letter came a couple of weeks later. You said our bein' together was a mistake and you were gonna stay with your wife!"

"Joanna, I swear, I never wrote such a letter."

"It was in your handwritin', Jack!" Joanna cried, confused.

"Oh my God, Langley!" Jack slapped his hand to his forehead. "Forgery's the most obvious answer. He must've found out about the baby."

"Your father-in-law?"

"A forged letter is small time for Langley."

"I saw him at the Peabody Hotel, the January I was livin' in Knoxville."

"What were you doing at the Peabody?" Jack asked. The five minutes she'd granted him had expired, but the conversation continued.

"So our bein' lovers wasn't a big mistake?" she asked, through tears.

"No, of course not! I never would've said that to you, because I've never felt that way. I've been in agony not knowing where you are, not being able to comfort you." He put his arms around her. "I never stopped loving or worrying about you."

She studied his eyes, judging his truthfulness. He kissed her and she went limp with the sensations. She couldn't believe this, Jack was back!

Mary tripped in around 11:00 p.m. to find every window open and Joanna in a bubble bath, bawling. The music box, Joanna's only memento from her time with Jack, lay in landmine pieces, scattered on the hallway floor.

"What's wrong?" Mary asked, concerned.

"I saw Jack today." Joanna explained their chance meeting. "I'm such an idiot!"

"What makes you an idiot?"

"I believed his lines again. We made love. And when we were lying in each other's arms, I asked what this meant for a future together." She sobbed harder. "He said there's no way he'd leave Catherine now. Did you know they adopted a baby?"

"No! My mother didn't tell me. I knew he and Catherine were opening truck stops. I didn't mention it because I didn't think you wanted to know. But a baby; wow, I had no idea."

"I didn't wanna know or ever see him again. I was fine without him. Out of nowhere, he comes along and, stupid me, I fell for his, 'Oh, Joanna I never stopped lovin' you!'"

"How old's the baby?" Mary asked.

"I don't know! I don't care! I told him to get out and never come back. I warned him I'd call Catherine and spill everythin'." Mary sat on the closed lid of the commode, stunned.

Joanna put her face in the washcloth and, in a muffled voice, groaned, "I was so happy in this apartment. Now I wanna move. He's ruined it for me." Mary went to Joanna's room and brought back a nightgown. She went around and closed the windows.

"Sorry it's so cold in here, I opened all the windows to get the stink of him gone!"

"What happened to the music box?"

"I threw it at him. He wants me for a mistress while he stays married to his rich wife."

"Did you hit him with it?"

"Square in the back of his fat head!"

"Good for you," Mary cheered.

A few days later, as Joanna was coming in the street-level door her phone rang. "Joanna, it's Mama."

"Mama, it's so good to hear your voice." Irene rarely called, and suddenly Joanna realized how badly she missed her.

"Ya sound out of breath, child. Ya all right?"

"Yeah, I had to run to catch the phone. How're ya doin'?" Joanna heard muffled crying on the other end of the line. "Mama, what's wrong?"

"I can't take livin' with your father anymore."

"What happened? Did he hurt you again?"

"Eddie ran off and eloped with the little gal he's been seein'; of course she's pregnant. Your father's outta his mind."

"I'm assumin' he's blamin' this on you."

"You know how he is."

Joanna knew his temper far too well. "I don't have much, but I'll share it with you and the babies. I'll come get ya right now."

"No, don't. I have some money put away. I want ya to find a little house for me to rent close to you in Memphis. I'll wire you some money so ya can get things arranged."

"I'll do whatever ya want, Mama. I'm so happy you've finally decided to leave him."

"Find a place we can move into around the first of December. I'll call you in a few days."

"I wish you could be here in three weeks for my graduation."

"I know, I do, too. But I can't. I'll call you again soon."

"Okay, take care of yourself," Joanna told her.

"I'm doin' the best I can," Irene assured. Joanna set to work immediately, circling the promising rental homes in the newspaper classifieds. She spent her free time searching for the perfect place for her family.

Joanna shared the happy occasion of her beauty school graduation with Mary, Jessie, and Prissy. Later, they hit the clubs. They closed out the night with a sleepover at the apartment.

As Joanna drifted into sleep, she thought of her mother and wished she'd been there to see her triumph. She comforted herself with the belief that Bernice had cheered her from heaven. Spitefully, Jack came to mind. She hadn't wanted him there, but she yearned to rub it in his face. She didn't need him or his hollow words. Joanna woke to the smell of coffee and the laughing voices of her closest friends.

"I can't believe y'all let me sleep until eleven thirty," she scolded groggily, coming into the kitchen.

"You deserved to; you've burned the candle at both ends lately. Coffee?" Mary offered.

"God, no! It doesn't even smell good to me. Please don't smoke in the kitchen first thing in the mornin'. It's makin' me sick to my stomach." Joanna took the cigarette dangling from Mary's lips and extinguished it under the tap. Overwhelmed by nausea, she made it to the commode before she vomited.

"I didn't think she drank that much last night," Prissy commented.

"Yeah, but we mixed wine with champagne," Jessie theorized.

"How many glasses of wine did you have?" Prissy asked the redhead.

"Shit, I've no idea. I don't remember how we got here last night." Jessie acted as if she had a headache, yet she seemed in better shape than Joanna.

Mary stood in the doorway of the bathroom as Joanna washed her face. The nursing student stepped forward, rubbed her friend's back, and asked softly, "Do you need to see a doctor?" It hit Joanna what Mary was suggesting.

"Oh God, no! I'm not even late yet. It can't be. It's the stress and the wine and the cigarette smoke, that's all." Her period was due next week; she could design a calendar by its regularity. She shook off her anxiety, sure it would come on schedule.

She signed the lease on a little house for her mother and siblings and used her mama's money for the deposit. It was a fixer-upper, but Irene had lived in worse. The house, a turn-of-the-century, story-and-a-half Victorian, boasted large rooms and a tangled mess of forgotten flower beds in the yard. The owner of the property was fixated on selling the place. Omitting the fact that Irene was incapable of buying, Joanna sweet-talked him into renting.

The house was located three blocks from Joanna's apartment, and had a school a few blocks away. To establish connections for her mother's trade, Joanna placed calls to several boutiques, inquiring after alteration jobs, satisfied with several leads for Irene to explore.

Joanna purposely kept busy while she counted the days. To her dismay, her period didn't come. After a torturous week of worry, Mary scheduled an exam for Joanna with one of the doctors who taught at her school. Before Joanna emerged from his office, she knew the awful truth. She was, once again, pregnant with Jack Wyatt's baby.

Chapter 33

Mary shivered behind the steering wheel of her car. The cold November rain blurred the headlights in the oncoming lanes. Her mouth tasted stale from the liquor she'd downed. She regretted not staying home to watch TV with Joanna.

Mary's heart still raced from running. The high-speed slapping of her windshield wipers had a mesmerizing effect as she concentrated on staying in her lane. Her mind was fuzzy on the details of the night and how she'd been trapped in the alley with Greg or Craig; she couldn't remember his name. She desperately wanted to get home, shower, and hide in bed.

The traffic light at the upcoming intersection turned red and she slowed her car to a stop. Looking at her ripped blouse, angry heat flushed through her. She pulled her coat tight and buttoned it. Impatient with the red light, she fiddled with the radio dial in search of some music to soothe her panic.

He'd seemed like a decent guy earlier in the evening, but he'd turned into an animal once they left the bar. He'd pulled her into the alley and begun groping her. When she protested, his aggressiveness morphed into rage and he pinned Mary against the wall with a choke hold. His other hand yanked down her favorite blue blouse.

The light turned green and Mary eased the gas pedal. Checking her rearview mirror, she saw Stan in his own car, following her. "Thank God for Stan," she breathed aloud. She shuddered to think what'd be happening to her right now if Stan hadn't stepped out of the shadows the moment her attacker brandished a knife.

"Let her go!" Stan had shouted in a faked menacing deep voice. The thug's split second of distraction allowed Mary to kick him in the groin and push him off.

"Run!" Stan shouted. Mary took off as fast as her legs could move. Reaching her car, she turned to see Stan opening the door of his own vehicle, which was parked close to the alley.

I'm almost home. Moderating her breathing toward normal, she pulled into a parking space on the residential street next to their apartment building. Stan parked a few spots behind and quickly got to Mary's car.

"Are you all right?" He guided her to the sidewalk.

"Yeah, I'm fine. God, Stan! If you hadn't come along?" She hugged him tightly.

"Shouldn't we call the police?" he asked.

"No! Promise me you won't tell anyone, especially Joanna," Mary insisted.

"You sure?" Stan frowned.

"Positive! Please do this for me."

"Okay. I'm not sure that's the right thing to do. But I won't say anythin'," he agreed.

The following weekend, the girls were lounging around Mary and Joanna's living room.

"What're you gonna do?" Jessie turned the discussion to Joanna's dilemma.

"I don't know." Joanna closed her eyes, shaking her head.

"I could call Sister Bridget," Mary suggested.

"No!" Joanna yelped. "I'd never go back there."

"You could get lucky, fall down the stairs and lose it," Jessie joked.

"Jessie! That's a terrible thing to say," Joanna scolded.

"I was tryin' to be funny."

"Well, sometimes you're not funny. This baby may not be of my choosin', but I'd never wish it dead. Burying a baby's the hardest thing I've ever done. To be honest, I wanna keep it."

"Have you lost your mind?" Mary cried. "After what Jack's done, you'd raise his child?"

"I don't know." Joanna walked to the window, staring out. "I wish I could understand why my feelings for Jack are so complicated."

"Maybe the same reason your mama's stayed all these years."

"No, it's not like that. Mama's terrified of my father and she hates him."

"And you don't hate Jack?"

"Part of me does. But I can't forget I was the happiest I've ever been with him."

"You gonna tell him you're pregnant?" Jessie asked.

"I don't know."

"I wouldn't."

"You didn't tell your baby's father!" Joanna laughed at the irony.

"For the same reason you shouldn't. You made it clear you never wanna see Jack again. Keep the baby if you want. Thanks to Stan, everyone thinks you're married."

"That's true." Mary laughed. "Get a wedding ring. You ought to stick with the story."

"I borrowed the scenario from Fitch's life. It was meant as a joke. I don't want people to think I did somethin' that stupid. Then what? Pretend I'm divorced?"

"It's better than broadcasting you're an unwed mother," Mary observed.

"Say he was killed in action. You're a widow of a war hero," Jessie suggested.

"It might work." Mary looked at Jessie as if she were a genius.

"Oh, I don't know," Joanna whined. "My priority is to get Mama moved here."

Irene hadn't contacted her lately, and Joanna was concerned; she hoped this didn't signal a change of mind. Finally, a few days later, she received the long-awaited call from Irene.

"Can ya come get us Friday? I'll be ready by nine o'clock in the morinin'. I'm not tellin' him I'm leavin'. He'll kill me if he finds us."

"Why wait? I'll come tomorrow."

"I get paid by Mabel on Thursday."

"He's only gonna take it from you."

"Just part of it; he thinks I work cheap! I've saved almost four thousand dollars over the years."

Astonished, Joanna conceded, "However you wanna do it. I'll be there at nine sharp."

"We'll be ready."

"Mama, be careful."

"I will. See ya Friday."

Presented with the keys to the house, Joanna took it upon herself to do a thorough cleaning of the rooms, which hadn't seen a broom in at least five years. The yard would wait for warmer weather. Mary came by after school to look at the place.

"This is a cute cottage," Mary called from the dining room. Warm light streamed through the street-facing bay window. "I like the built-ins. Granted, it needs work."

"The porch needs fixin'; I put my foot through the boards by the front door." Mary inspected the porch from the window; it wrapped around the house from the front door to a side mudroom entrance. The gingerbread topped posts supporting its roof needed paint.

"There's two bedrooms upstairs and one off the kitchen. Mama's gonna love the kitchen; It's big enough for a table and she can use the whole dining room for sewin'," Joanna gushed. "She's gonna be so happy here, like on Granny's farm. It's takin' extraordinary courage for her to walk out on Daddy."

Despite Irene's careful planning, she never made it out of Nashville Friday. On Thursday morning, Irene sent Benny off to school and walked lightly around Harris and his foul mood until he finally left for work at eight thirty. She dressed her four-year-old twins warmly for the bus ride to Mabel's dress shop. She'd given notice to her employer weeks earlier.

Today Mabel told her, "I hate to see you go. If you need a reference, have them call me."

With her paycheck in hand, Irene went to the bank, and closed her account, taking all of the $4,025 in cash. Nervous about carrying the large amount of money, she went straight home, where she taped the envelope containing her life's savings to the bottom of the dresser drawer in her bedroom. She fed the girls bologna sandwiches for lunch and organized her sewing tools much the same as she'd do between garments. She couldn't pack their suitcases until tomorrow; however, she sorted through the children's belongings, stashing everything they were taking in their bottom bureau drawers. She did the same with her own clothes. She wasn't taking much: a couple of suitcases and her sewing gear.

Inspecting the twin's threadbare winter coats, she went to her bedroom and took some bills out of the envelope. She'd stop at Woolworth's on the way to Benny's school and get them new coats; she didn't want her children looking like beggars.

At the end of the school day, Irene went to the elementary school and withdrew Benny.

When she got home, she trekked into the kids' room and put Benny's school paperwork in the bottom drawer. She made her way to the bedroom she shared with Harris, aiming to put away the change left from shopping. Opening the door, a wave of powerful panic shot through her. Her bedroom had been ransacked. The mattress was flipped off the bed; dresser drawers emptied and thrown across the room. The tape still clung to her hiding place but the envelope was gone! She rushed into the kitchen to the counter where she'd left Harris's money from her paycheck. It was gone, too! Harris had been home and found her money! Digging in the trash can, she found her empty money envelope and a drained whiskey bottle.

She dashed to the living room. Benny was throwing his dirty socks at his sisters.

"Benny! Stop and put on your socks and shoes right now! Girls, get on your coats."

"Where're we goin', Mama?" Linda asked.

"Mama's got to do somethin'. Do as I say, we've got to go!"

Back in the kitchen, Irene retrieved her secret coffee tin of change and dumped it in her purse; she went back to the kids. Ben tried to help Lilly with an inside-out sleeve.

"Give it to me, we'll do it on the way, come along." Irene almost made it to the back door when it flew open and her furious husband stepped through the opening.

"Ya goin' somewhere?" She could smell the whiskey on his breath.

"Just to the market, I'm gonna make chicken and dumplings. I'm outta flour," Irene lied.

"You gonna take all the brats with you?" Angry fire burned in his eyes, terrifying Irene. "Go to your room and don't come out till I tell ya!" Harris shouted. The children fled, shutting themselves safely inside the bedroom. Harris spied the empty coffee can on the counter.

"Another hidin' place? I didn't think of that one." He threw the can at her, hitting her in the head. On her immediately, he slapped and pushed her. "Where'd ya get the money, huh? Joanna send it to ya?" He hit her harder with each question.

"It's mine! I saved it from sewin'," she cried.

"Is that what ya call it? Stealin' money from me, when I'm breakin' my back for this family?" He shoved her so hard against the wall, he knocked the wind out of her. "Where else ya hidin' money?" he yelled. Taking her purse, he spilled the contents on the floor. He bent to examine the pile. Harris snatched the paper with Joanna's address and phone number on it.

"I already knew where she was. The bitch at the home called me at work when she enrolled in beauty school. So ya see, I'd've been there by Sunday to kick the shit out of ya."

Irene took a few steps toward the bedroom where her children were.

"You're gonna leave me with, what? Maybe, twelve dollars in your pocket. I think that's funny." He laughed in a vengeful cackle.

"Harris, please let us go. We're nothin' but a burden to you." She tried another tack.

"You wanna go? Go! But there's a couple of things you gotta do first. Clean up this crap!" Irene scooped the pile strewn from her handbag. He kicked her in the chest; she gasped. "Ya better get all those pennies 'cause that's all you're takin', that and those monsters you created." Irene closed her purse, standing; she backed toward the children's bedroom.

"Please, let us go and we'll be out of your hair," she begged. He lunged and threw her across the room. She landed on the floor next to the couch.

"I wanna know how ya thought it was all right to listen to me bitch about needin' a new fuckin' car and you had the money all along." Irene struggled to stand. He grabbed so hard her arm popped out of its socket. Dragging her down the stairs, he yelled, "Come on, I wanna show ya somethin'. Then ya can go."

He pushed her through the opening of the street-level door and taunted, "What do ya think of my new car?" He slapped the hood of a 1958 Riviera hardtop sedan. "Should we get the kiddies and go for a ride in Daddy's new car?" he taunted her.

"No!" she cried, with tears streaming.

"No? Well, you and me'll take it for a spin." He opened the passenger-side door and dragged her in behind him. "I love the new-car smell." He started the engine and sped off toward the Cumberland River. Irene swallowed hard. Harris pointed out the fine details, like the cigarette lighter and the radio he turned to maximum volume. "He gave me a hell of a deal, 'cause I paid cash." Harris shouted over the radio, laughing hysterically. He pulled a flask from under his seat, taking frequent chugs. Her fear mounted when he blew through the red light, blowing his horn and stepping on the gas.

"Don't ya wanna know where the rest of the money is?" Irene wished he'd go slower so she could jump out. "It's in the glove box." Irene sat like a stone, not taking the bait. "Go ahead, look," he ordered; leaning across her to unlatch the compartment, he lost control of the car.

Eyewitnesses claimed the car must've been traveling eighty miles per hour when it struck the train viaduct. Irene never lost consciousness as the dashboard pinned her all the way in the backseat. Harris's head had broken the windshield, and his brains were splattered everywhere. In the mangled remains of the dashboard, she reached the stack of money bound with a rubber band and put it in her purse. Seconds later bystanders were around the car, gawking at the gore. Irene screamed for them to get her out. A police officer looked in the broken window on the driver's side, where Harris slumped.

"He's dead! Please! Help me get outta here!" Another man took off his jacket and covered her husband's gruesome remains, then joined the cop attempting to pry open the door closest to Irene. She took Joanna's phone number from her purse and, slipping it through the broken window, she begged, "Please, could you call my daughter?"

Chapter 34

Joanna picked at her nail polish in the hospital waiting room. After fifteen minutes, she turned to Mary and pressed, "What's takin' so long?"

"I'm sure he'll be along soon," Mary reasoned, gazing out the window at the lights of Nashville. The sun had set hours ago, but traffic still moved on the streets below.

After a while a police officer approached. "Ladies, are either of you Joanna Wilson?"

"I am. Can you tell me anythin' about my mother? How is she?"

"You'll have to talk to the doctor. I was the first officer on the scene. She was talking during the rescue efforts. That's how we knew to get in touch with you." The police officer provided details gleaned from the witnesses. "Your father was killed instantly. I'm sorry."

"Was he drunk?"

"Your mother said he'd been drinking. Yes."

"What about my brother Benjamin and the twins?"

"Your brother Eddie's with them. He and his wife came from Decatur, Alabama, a couple of hours ago. He was pretty upset; made a scene."

"How'd you mean?" Joanna asked.

"Your mother told me to give you her pocketbook and wedding ring. Your brother became hostile when I wouldn't turn them over to him." He handed the bag to Joanna.

A young doctor came toward them. "Miss Wilson? I'm Dr. Rutherford."

"How's my mother? Can I see her?"

"In a minute. I must warn you; she's in bad shape. She has massive internal injuries and we're not able to control the bleeding."

"Is she gonna be all right?"

"We've done everything we can," Dr. Rutherford bleakly expressed.

"Doctor, I'm Mary, Joanna's best friend, I'm six months short of my LPN. You could fill me in on her condition and let Joanna be with Irene."

"Yes, talk to Mary. Can I see her now?"

"Of course." The doctor called a nurse to take Joanna to her mother. He turned his attention to Mary, who already comprehended the outcome.

"She's going to bleed out, isn't she?"

"Within a couple of hours," the doctor told her sadly. "Her injuries are too severe. The impact alone should've killed her. She's kept herself alive until she could talk to her daughter. It's pretty amazing."

"Take me home," Joanna mumbled when Mary came to her at the ICU.

"We can stay with my parents. I talked to my dad earlier," Mary told her.

"No, please, take me home." The nurse came out with next-of-kin documents for Joanna to sign while Mary used the pay phone to call her parents.

"She wants to go back to Memphis tonight," Mary told her father.

"Are you okay to drive?"

"I'll be fine; I think I'm running on adrenaline."

"Tell her I'm sorry for her loss," her father empathized. Mary knew he was thinking of how Joanna had stepped in when Bernice died.

"I will. Thanks for your support, Daddy, it means a lot. I'll take good care of her."

"I know you will, honey. Drive safe. If I can help, let me know." Mary felt closer to him than she had in years. The loss of Bernice was still fresh for all of them.

Driving home in the middle of the night, the darkness cocooned their car, except for the headlights on the road, cutting their way. Joanna remained silent for the first hour, not crying, just staring out the window. Mary drove without talking, letting Joanna dictate the conversation.

Finally, Joanna broke the stillness by saying, "She knew. I don't know how. She asked me, 'Same father, Jack?' It broke my heart." Joanna's steady voice recalled. "She told me to keep this one; she didn't want me to be alone. She knew she was dyin'." Joanna's voice wavered.

After a long break, Joanna pierced the quiet again. "He found her money, got drunk, bought a car, and killed her. He finally did it; he killed her." Mary understood Joanna didn't want her to respond; she just needed to say it aloud. "I begged her to let me take Benny and the babies, but she told me she wanted Eddie to raise them. She said they don't even remember me. What does Eddie know? He's only eighteen."

"Is there going to be a funeral?" Mary wondered why Joanna was in such a hurry to leave Nashville.

"In Lynchburg. She told me not to attend. If I'm there, Eddie'll cause a ruckus, and that's not how her graveside should be remembered. She'll be buried with her parents, on the farm," Joanna disclosed softly. She didn't mention any arrangements for her father's interment. "The reason Eddie got so belligerent about Mama's purse is 'cause it had the rest of her money in it. She said I was gonna need it more than he will; he's gettin' the life insurance."

After school the next day, Mary didn't go to the apartment; she drove by the rental house and saw Joanna's car out front. "I thought I'd find you here," Mary affirmed, joining Joanna in the sparkling-clean kitchen. The house was chilly with the heat turned off.

"The landlord's meetin' me here in a little while. I didn't tell him I'm gonna back out of the lease. I'm hopin' when he sees how much work I've done, he'll refund the deposit."

"It's much more appealing to future renters now," Mary added.

"I was considerin' movin' in here with them. Now I guess it doesn't matter."

"You're wearing your mother's wedding ring," Mary observed.

"Her last wish was that I keep this baby. That's what I'm gonna do. I'll let everyone think I'm a war widow. But it's the only decision I've made. I'm tryin' to figure out what I'll do about child care while I'm at a salon. It'd be great if I could bring the baby to work."

"Why don't you work from home? You could work around the baby's schedule."

"I thought about that. But the apartment is too small to try to run a business. Plus, Mrs. Holland beat a hole in the wall with her cane because of the customers comin' and goin'."

"You could do it here, in this house. It's perfect for it." Mary rushed into the dining room, continuing to explain her brilliant idea. "This could be your salon. There's plenty of room. You said you wanted to move out of the apartment."

Joanna followed her, considering the possibility. "The bathroom's on the other side of the wall. It'd be easy to put in a shampoo basin. I doubt the landlord'd want major renovations, though."

"So buy the place. If it's yours, you don't need permission."

"A mortgage is risky," Joanna debated, envisioning where she'd put an adjustable hair-cutting chair. "It'd take a lot of work to restore it."

"I'll help you. We can move in here together and work on it, like we did the apartment. I'll pay you rent and even invest in your company. What're you going to call your salon?"

"I still owe you money on the car."

"I see potential here. I'm expecting a return on my investment. It's going to take more than the money your mother gave you to do it right." Mary sounded like Bernice.

Joanna smiled at her. "Dream big, huh?"

"You know, if Bernice were here, she'd encourage you to do it. Besides, I think she'd be happier if I used her money this way, rather than blowing it like I have been."

Joanna chewed on her bottom lip. Quickly she negotiated. "On one condition. We do it legal, with contracts between us."

"My dad can help you get a mortgage and lawyers to finalize it. Say yes!"

Joanna put her hands over her face, took a deep breath, and uttered, "Yes!"

"Yes!" Mary did a victory dance. "Okay, let's look around and find all the repairs the landlord's responsible for. We'll use it as a bargaining tool to get him to sell at a lower price."

An hour later they watched the property owner contentedly walk to his car after Mary skillfully negotiated his price from eleven grand to eight. By the time she finished, the man had even agreed to make the necessary repairs.

She put her arm around Joanna and exclaimed, "Congratulations, you're buying a house."

Chapter 35

Gerald Atherton arranged a mortgage loan at his bank, and Joanna made a small down payment. He gave Mary his blessing to invest her grandmother's money in Joanna's business. She would've done it regardless, but she appreciated his approval.

The girls gave thirty days' notice on the apartment and Joanna took possession of the house on Hollywood Avenue, where the real work awaited her. She spent long hours stripping wallpaper, patching holes, and painting. Mary helped every day after school. Prissy joined them to lend a hand painting the kitchen. Jessie stopped by to supervise.

"Grab a paintbrush. Put on a fresh coat of paint for Joanna's fresh start," Mary ordered.

"Can't, I got a meetin' with a guy at Sun Records."

"Yeah?" Joanna asked.

"I have to audition. But if this works out, I'll get to lay some vinyl with the big boys."

"That'd be so cool." Prissy dipped her brush in the tray of light blue paint.

"You still haven't told us the name of your salon," Jessie reminded.

"I haven't thought of anythin' clever yet."

"How about Hair Repair?" Prissy offered. Joanna rubbed her chin, considering.

"I think you should call it Curl Up and Dye," Jessie suggested. They all laughed.

Joanna asked, "What about Hollywood Hair?"

"Makes sense, you're on Hollywood Avenue." Jessie hoisted herself to sit on the counter.

"It'd have a double meanin'; most of my customers want their hair like Joan Crawford or some other Hollywood name."

"You could get movie posters for the walls," Mary added.

"That's a great idea!" Prissy clapped. It was decided. Joanna planned to open Hollywood Hair by the end of January. She went modern with the décor. Using black fabric she and Mary made the straight-lined curtains and upholstered cushions for the bay window seat. A black rug and round glass coffee table completed her waiting area. She painted the salon walls red.

She commissioned a plumber/handyman, a buddy of Stan's, to create a small powder room for customer use, and put in a salon sink. He installed French doors, which locked off the house from the business. The day her black-and-chrome styling chair arrived far surpassed any Christmas she'd ever known. She got movie posters from the theater as they changed them out.

Jessie pitched in by sending off letters to movie stars, requesting signed photographs. Joanna was thrilled every time she found them in her mailbox. She mounted them with black mats and framed them in chrome. Proudly, she hung them in her salon.

On moving day, ever-reliable Stan arrived with doughnuts and a borrowed truck.

"These last few boxes can go in my car," Joanna told Mary.

"I'll take them," Stan scolded. He'd been mother-henning her ever since she confided in him about her pregnancy.

"I'm fine. I'm pregnant, not an invalid," Joanna corrected.

"Come on, Mary. Get the end of the couch, or Joanna will carry it all by herself."

Mary grabbed the outgoing edge. Navigating the couch down the stairs, she was on the weight-bearing side. She struggled to keep her footing when the old woman from 2A exited her apartment with a clean-cut man, dressed in a pair of jeans and a polo shirt. Seeing their dilemma, the stranger offered his assistance and took over Mary's spot.

"This is my grandson, Lenny. He's a lawyer," the unfriendly neighbor bragged. Mary didn't care who he was; she was happy for another male to handle the bulky furniture. Lenny volunteered to help unload at the Hollywood Avenue destination; he seemed like the decent sort, so they accepted his generosity. He revealed his ulterior motive at the end of the day.

"I'd like to take you to dinner sometime," the lawyer told Mary. Out of a sense of obligation, lacking instant attraction, she finally agreed.

"At least your mom'll enjoy tellin' everyone you're datin' a lawyer," Joanna joked.

"I'm convinced she wants me in nursing school so I'll marry a doctor."

Over the course of the next few weeks, Mary and Lenny dated regularly. "For a lawyer, he's not a good conversationalist," Mary told Joanna while they were watching a variety show.

"You said he wasn't a trial lawyer. What does he do?"

"Wills, estates, family law, and some corporate law. He can't talk about it, though; it's all confidential. Since all he does is work, he doesn't have much to say." Mary rolled her eyes.

On the TV, Dean Martin performed his famous drunk satire. Mary laughed, wiping tears. An Ivory soap commercial cut in and she remarked, "He does that bit so well!"

"I've seen you do a pretty good impression yourself. But not for a while," Joanna noted.

"I wasn't having much fun, especially the morning after. I'm sure I won't be introducing Lenny to any of my club friends." At the heart of the matter, her near-rape experience had scared the hell out of her. "Besides, you've needed me to help with the renovations."

"And… What're you not sayin'?" Joanna raised her left eyebrow.

Mary tucked the throw blanket under her chin. "I'm so close to completing my LPN and I hate it! I've been doing it for my parents."

"So you've decided?"

Mary nodded. "I can't live my life doing something I despise in order to appease them."

"Let me know before you tell them so I can find the nearest bomb shelter, then duck and cover," Joanna laughed, referring to the Cold War drills from their school days.

"Well, I'd better have an alternative plan when I break the news."

"Like what?"

"Maybe I'll skip to the next phase and get married."

"To Lenny?" Joanna gasped.

"Maybe. He's smart, nice, and makes a good living," Mary said.

"You don't love him," Joanna objected.

"People get married for a lot of reasons. Mother's been jealous of her society friends bragging about their daughters' weddings. To hear her tell it, I'm practically an old maid."

"That's not a good reason to marry Lenny," Joanna pointed out.

"I'm going to be married and have a family at some point. Lenny's thirty-one; he's ready now. He might be the best guy I'll ever find. And truthfully, if you take Tony and the other jerks I've met and compare them with Lenny, it's an easy choice."

Joanna cracked up laughing. "Your grandmother-in-law'd be Mrs. Grouchy Neighbor."

"With her cane!" Mary added. Both girls laughed hysterically.

To recruit clients for her beauty parlor, Joanna mimeographed two hundred flyers and she, Mary, and Prissy canvassed the surrounding businesses requesting they display her advertising. Next, the team went door-to-door in her neighborhood, leaving flyers at each house.

The first Monday in February, Joanna hung her framed business license and Hollywood Hair officially opened. In between appointments, she expended her anxious energy scraping the flaking gray paint off the outside of the house.

She took advantage of the mild, springlike weather to apply a fresh coat of warm butterscotch-colored paint to the siding. Stan insisted on taking over after begging Joanna to stop climbing ladders in her condition. By the time they got to the white trim and gingerbread, neighbors were stopping by to compliment the improvements and chat. A few scheduled hair appointments with her.

With the exterior completed, Joanna tackled the chores in the overgrown flower beds. On pleasant days, she'd clear the weed-infested ground. She trimmed the dozens of neglected rosebushes in the side yard, willing them to bloom gloriously come summer.

The roommates still maintained their ritual Sunday-afternoon movie outing. However, Lenny absorbed the majority of Mary's free time. As expected, Mary showed off an engagement ring by March.

"Aren't you happy for me?" Mary questioned when Joanna pursed her lips at the news.

"It's kinda fast, isn't it? I'm happy for you, if this is what you want. I'm gonna miss havin' ya as a roommate." Joanna squeezed her hand and made a show of admiring the ring.

"We'll buy a house close by. We'll see each other every day," Mary promised.

Mary's parents' reacted mildly to her dropping out of school, since she padded it with her impending marriage to a lawyer. They scheduled the wedding for the first Saturday in June, in Nashville. As if lit on fire, Edith took command of the planning.

Lenny's mother, Meredith, proved equally as opinionated when it came to the wedding details. Mary had her own ideas but found out how little weight they carried when they removed Joanna as the maid of honor.

"Your brother's wife should be your maid of honor," Edith ruled, vetoing Mary's choice.

"Your mother's right, family first. With Lenny's five sisters as bridesmaids, your side is complete. Any more than six on a side for the bridal party is garish," Meredith admonished. That was the only detail the two women agreed upon. Mary glumly broke the news to Joanna while presenting the choices for the bridesmaids' dresses.

"I wasn't comfortable with bein' stared at by a church full of people at eight months' pregnant," Joanna said, letting her off easy.

"Which dress do you think is the most hideous?" Mary showed Joanna the samples.

"The Pepto Bismol pink, definitely." Joanna pointed.

"Okay, those are the ones. They gave me the final choice. Take that," Mary spat.

"I'll be with you on your wedding day, whatever you need," Joanna promised.

Mary hugged her for being so understanding. "Planning a wedding is stressful enough, but putting the two mothers together is a nightmare," she confessed.

None of the decisions were going her way—and this applied to Lenny's strong opinions as well. Their first big quarrel concerned the location of their home after the wedding. Mary had her heart set on living close to Joanna, but Lenny wouldn't hear of it. Like many middle-class families, her future husband viewed the changing racial landscape in the city as undesirable.

"The Negroes are taking over. I found a place in the suburbs I put a contract on."

"Without consulting me?" Mary fumed.

"You'll love it. There's tons of kids in the neighborhood and good schools. It's perfect."

On a chilly spring day, they made the long drive, where Lenny presented her with their soon-to-be four-thousand-square-foot home. Its modern floor plan flaunted multiple split levels. The state-of-the-art kitchen, with the space-age-designed appliances, overlooked a family room.

Protective paper covered the carpets and crunched under her feet as she walked from room to room. In the master bedroom, she peered out the window at rows of houses identical to hers, with Bradford Pear saplings. Mary breathed deep; the strong odor of paint made her dizzy.

"The walls are so white," she complained.

"We can have them painted or wall papered any way you want," he compromised. Mary tried to visualize living in this monster house. She glanced around. *Fresh paint, fresh start.*

Prissy pouted, sprawled on the window cushions in Joanna's salon. "It's so unfair. I hate my sister; she's such a tattletale." Mary swung her head to face the girl.

Joanna rerolled the curler on Mary's blond head and scolded, "Would you hold still?" She turned the swivel barber chair so Mary could face Prissy.

"I haven't gone further than second base!" Prissy defended.

"You've got to be careful. Parking with boys can get out of control fast, and the next thing ya know you're hangin' out with Fitch and the crows," Jessie told her, helping herself to the bright-red nail polish on Joanna's manicure station.

"Where's the school he's sendin' ya?" Joanna asked.

"It's Peach Tree Girls Academy in Atlanta. I hate I'm going to miss the wedding."

"They don't let you come home for the summer?" Jessie asked.

"This is a prep school. I'll get to come home on holidays, but it's like military school."

"It's a prestigious academy," Mary put in. "My cousin went there and she's at Vassar."

"I know. But I'll have to start over with new friends."

"You'll do fine," Joanna told her. "What are ya interested in studyin'?"

"Law, I think. Maybe I'll be a paralegal," Prissy hypothesized.

"You're so smart you could become a lawyer," Joanna told her.

"Or a judge; I can see advantages to havin' a close friend who's a judge," Jessie joked.

"Why stop there? How about the first female Supreme Court justice?" Mary added.

Prissy chuckled. "Yeah! Dream big, right?"

Chapter 36

Joanna put her hands on her hips, envisioning her ideal garden. Someday she wanted a quiet courtyard, babbling fountain, and butterfly bushes. Armed with her gardening gloves and shears, she focused on her current task, snipping the dead canes from the ignored blueberry bushes. The kitchen screened door squeaked as Mary stepped onto the back porch.

"You got some grease I can put on those hinges?"

"Yes, but don't. I like the sound. It reminds me of my granny's farm," Joanna replied.

"Stan'd dig out that mess for you, if you asked him," Mary suggested.

"No! They're blueberries. Besides, Stan's already promised to demolish the old garage for me. I'll owe him free haircuts for a year. These bushes require tender lovin' care."

"Don't we all," Mary uttered, plopping on the stairs.

Joanna pulled her gloves off. "I thought you and Lenny were pickin' out furniture today."

"We were. He hated the couch I chose. It's my mother and the turquoise couch, all over again. We argued over investments on the way to the store. I told him I had a bad headache, so he brought me home."

"Do you want some aspirin?"

"I don't really have a headache. Well, I do; this whole wedding's turning into one gigantic migraine. Mother and Meredith are feuding over the guest list now. My father and Lenny are discussing investments for my trust fund. Daddy's transferring the money to an account in both our names. Lenny'll handle the finances once we're married. Women, he claims, don't have a head for such things," Mary lamented.

"But it's your money!" Joanna objected.

"I don't care. He'll be better at taking care of it. You know how I hate to balance my checkbook. Anyway, it's not worth arguing."

Joanna's uneasiness over Mary's pending marriage intensified as the days marched by. She couldn't justify her foreboding, because to listen to Mary tell it, Lenny was the most upstanding man she'd ever met. Joanna kept her reservations to herself, not wanting to cause any friction in Mary's already turbulent relationships.

The following Sunday afternoon, Joanna and Mary walked home from the movie theater. As usual, they were embroiled in a lively analysis of the movie— this time *Some Like It Hot*.

"Doesn't it figure Tony Curtis'd be the saxophone player? I think it's the sexiest instrument, just like him." Mary giggled as they took the path to the house.

"I had three customers last week ask me to do their hair like Marilyn Monroe as Sugar Kane Kowalczyk. I figured I'd better go see the movie." Joanna stuck her key in the lock and jumped when a room full of people yelled, "Surprise!"

Gawking, she recognized Jessie and Stan in the crowd. The faces of her customers and neighbors came into focus. Balloons and streamers hung from the ceiling, and gifts were piled in the center of the room.

"What've you done?" She squeezed her roommate in disbelief.

"Me? This is all a surprise to me," Mary lied unconvincingly.

Jessie came forward. "Here, have a seat. I don't want the excitement to put you in labor."

"I had no idea you were plannin' this!" Joanna had never seen so many gifts in one place and they were all for her baby: everything from blankets and diapers to stuffed animals and one-piece sleepers. A regular Friday customer, Mrs. Thatcher, gave her a basket full of practical items; pacifiers, baby soaps, nail clippers and diaper pins, as well as coupons for free babysitting.

"You call me anytime. I can't tell you how much I admire you for raising a child on your own. My mother helped me when my husband went off to war; I feel so fortunate he came home to me." The middle-aged neighbor's voice wavered.

Awkward silence choked the room. Everyone knew the story of Joanna's poor departed husband through the rumor mill and, out of respect, rarely mentioned it. Joanna said softly, "You've all been so wonderful. I don't know what to say. Thank you doesn't seem adequate."

"Oh! Don't get all mushy on us now," Jessie pivoted. "Let's play some games."

"I don't know if I wanna play your kinda games," Joanna laughed, teasing her.

"No whiskey involved, honest; just your standard boring baby shower stuff."

Joanna swallowed the lump in her throat and enjoyed the day set aside exclusively for her. Laughter filled her little house on Hollywood Avenue. They feasted on a potluck-style buffet featuring spiral ham, an assortment of casseroles, deviled eggs, and a sheet cake. At dusk, her guests conveyed their well wishes and made their way home, leaving Joanna, Jessie, Mary, and Stan to get the house back in order.

"This can wait. We have something to show you." Mary led the guest of honor upstairs. Opening the nursery door. Joanna put her trembling hand to her lips, marveling at the crib and changing-table boxes. A rocking chair and dresser completed the ensemble.

"Wow, y'all're too much!" Joanna exclaimed.

"This is from, me, Jessie, Stan and Prissy, 'cause we love you."

"I love y'all too. Thanks so much."

She hugged each of them, even Stan, who blushed and pledged, "I'll come by tomorrow and put together the crib and stuff." He took off, and the girls attacked the task of cleanup.

Later, Joanna relayed an earlier conversation. "Ann Keeler told me the last trimester's the worst. I feel bad. I hate they all think I'm someone I'm not."

"Why?" Jessie countered. "You didn't tell them about your dead husband; Stan did that."

"It's still a lie," Joanna told them.

"Nothin' stoppin' ya from tellin' them the truth. But why should ya? The whole world isn't entitled to know your business," Jessie said. Turning to Mary, she asked, "Have you told Mr. Fancy-Pants Lawyer about your stay at the Frances Weston Hotel?"

"No, I haven't had the courage," Mary admitted. "Mother's advised me to go to my grave with that information. As far as Lenny knows, I'm a virgin."

Jessie blurted laughter. "Did you tell him you were?"

"No. He assumes and I didn't correct him," Mary clarified.

"So you and he haven't danced the light fantastic yet?" the redhead asked.

Mary shook her head. "He's been a real gentleman. Besides, Dr. Miller assured me my husband wouldn't know the difference on our wedding night."

"Pretend like it never happened; you sound like Mrs. Lewis," Joanna observed.

"Mrs. Lewis's doctrine reflects the views of society. This is a second chance for me. Telling him won't change the past, but it could sabotage my future," Mary stated.

"Mary's right," Jessie concurred. "Let people think what they want; they're happier that way."

"We're all going through big changes right now, all four of us. Prissy's off in Atlanta, I'm getting married, you with the baby coming…"

Jessie interrupted: "Which is why I called this meeting today. I have an announcement to make. I have an audition Thursday, with Twentieth Century Fox, in Hollywood, California."

Astonished, Joanna screamed. Hugging Jessie, she asked, "How'd this happen?"

"Well, a month ago, I was talkin' to this guy at a club…"

"Of course," Joanna remarked, sarcastically.

"He liked the way I played the piano. It turns out he's an assistant for a hotshot at Fox. He promised to get me an audition for a spot in the orchestra for an upcomin' movie soundtrack. Yeah, right, I thought, but you got to give him credit for usin' that line to get in my panties. Two weeks ago, I got a phone call from a secretary and they're flyin' me out."

"This is so excitin'!" Joanna cheered, pride beaming on her face.

"The thing is, even if I don't get the job, I'm gonna stay, kick around a bit."

"Oh, so you're leavin', and we won't see you for a while." The true meaning hit Joanna.

"Don't get so glum, chum," Jessie teased. Then she added, more seriously, "I'd hate myself if I didn't try."

"Of course, you've got to do this. But you won't be here when my baby's born."

"Yeah, I tried to compensate for that with the shower," Jessie apologized.

"It softens the blow. You'll do well in Hollywood. You're gonna miss Mary's weddin'."

Mary chimed in, "It's okay, Joanna, I've known for a couple of weeks; turns out, she doesn't do funerals, either."

Jessie shrugged. Feigning a look of innocence, she announced, "All right, chicks, this heavy discussion and all those cheesy shower games have made me thirsty. God, I need a drink."

"You need a manicure before your audition," Joanna offered.

"We'll do it tomorrow. I'll be over first thing in the mornin' to help with the nursery. Get to bed early. You've had an excitin' day."

"Thanks again for the shower, it was the best," Joanna told her.

"I had so much help from your great neighbors. This little undertaking is perfect for you. Settle into it and enjoy your life for a change." Jessie kissed Joanna on the top of the head then turned to Mary. Hugging her, she inquired, "Love you too. We good?"

"Of course, love you," Mary told Jessie. "Be careful!" she called to the redhead.

"Always. See ya in the mornin'." Jessie waved from the yard.

"What was that about?" Joanna asked.

"You know Jessie. She thinks I'm jumping from the frying pan into the fire. She's never even met Lenny. She has a bad attitude regarding marriage in general," Mary explained.

Joanna doubted that was the whole story. She had her own reservations about Mary's impending nuptials, but she didn't waste her breath. Once her roommate reached a decision, Joanna couldn't change her mind.

Chapter 37

Joanna didn't accompany Mary to the wedding shower in Nashville. She understood; Joanna had booked appointments for prom season. Mary took solace that she'd be with her at the wedding.

The shower morphed into a grand formal affair. The luxurious buffet and lavish decorations testified to Edith's extravagance. Mary instantly regretted picking the nauseating color for the bridesmaids, as everywhere she turned, splashes of Pepto Bismol pink dominated. Seventy-five women crowded the garden of the Atherton home.

Surrounded by cheerful acquaintances, Mary felt disconnected. The atmosphere resembled a political gathering, lacking the intimate warmth of Joanna's baby shower. Forcing a pleasant smile for the guests, Mary realized she had nothing in common with these people anymore. It seemed so phony.

The next morning Edith woke her daughter early and escorted her to the dining room. "We have a lot of work to do; gifts need to be opened and thank-you notes sent promptly."

"Do we have to do this today?" Mary said, hoping for an out. She dreaded the prospect of an entire day of her mother dictating thank-you notes.

"You must get the shower acknowledgments out now, or you'll be buried when the wedding gifts arrive."

"Let's get this over with," Mary grumbled. Taking pen in hand, she transcribed her mother's words onto elegant cards as her mother opened each gift.

When only a third of the presents were opened, Mary grew impatient. "Can we make the messages shorter? This is taking forever."

"Proper thank-you notes are essential. You'll understand when you have to write them for yourself." Edith ripped into the gift from Joanna, Prissy, and

Jessie and mumbled, "Well at least at your new home in the suburbs, you'll meet a better class of people."

"My friends are the better class of people," she admonished, infuriated.

Edith waved off her daughter's annoyance. "Write whatever you want to your friends; they sent you feather dusters, Ajax, and other cleaning supplies." Edith disapprovingly wrinkled her forehead when her daughter burst into laughter.

"Private joke… They know I hate cleaning house."

"See! Everything's a crass joke with that crowd."

"It's all right, Mother, you don't understand. Let's move on to the next gift," Mary deflected, still chuckling. Cutting off the impending lecture meant a speedier end to this chore.

By midafternoon, only a few packages remained. Mary anticipated freedom with each stroke of her pen. Edith read the card attached to the gift from Mr. and Mrs. Jackson Wyatt.

"You've invited them to the wedding?" Mary asked with such alarm, she startled Edith.

"Of course I did. I couldn't invite the Langleys and not include Catherine. I've already received their RSVP. Why're you acting like this?"

"This wedding has turned into a three-ring circus and I'm the one on the high wire." Mary rose from the table and headed for the door.

"Come back here and finish the last of these notes!"

"Finish them yourself. I'm going back to Memphis."

On the drive home, Mary cried and banged her fist on the steering wheel, agonizing over how to break this latest development to Joanna. When she pulled into the driveway, she found Joanna crocheting on the front porch, sitting in one of her repainted secondhand wicker chairs.

"I didn't expect you till tomorrow," Joanna said.

"I had to get out of there." Mary settled beside her. "I didn't know you crocheted."

"I don't. Mrs. Thatcher tried to show me, but mine doesn't look like hers." Joanna pulled the yarn, unraveling her work. "Your eyes are puffy; have you been cryin'?"

"This dream wedding is a nightmare," Mary sulked. "You can't come to my wedding."

"Why not?" Joanna was upset now.

"Because my mother invited Catherine and Jackson Wyatt, who graciously accepted."

"If Jack saw me, all he'd have to do is the math."

"I'm sorry!" Mary implored.

"It's not your fault; you didn't invite them." Joanna nodded, trying to feel as sensible as she sounded. "Doris Day is comin' on. Maybe she can cheer us up."

The following weeks went by in a blur for Mary. Before she knew it, she viewed herself in the bride's room mirror, in her wedding dress, her head spinning from the maddening chatter of her future sisters-in-law. Her mother and Meredith were bickering over the boutonnieres.

An hour later, standing before the priest, she exchanged vows and became Mrs. Leonard Hollan. A receiving line followed; family, friends, and acquaintances filed past her, with hugs and good wishes. Edith repeatedly whispered in her ear, reminding her to smile and unclench her fists. When the Langleys approached, Mary stiffened involuntarily.

"Congratulations!" Millicent beamed at the girl. "Catherine sends her regrets, dear; her little Tommy's running a fever. She wouldn't dream of leaving her baby when he has the sniffles." Mary stared at her blankly; Joanna had missed her wedding for nothing.

Mr. Langley shook her hand next, saying, "Best wishes." He didn't look her in the eye.

On July 2, Joanna Wilson gave birth, via scheduled C-section, to a six-pound, ten-ounce baby girl she named Hope Irene Wilson, listing the father as one John Wilson, deceased.

Joanna's elation at the birth of her daughter was bittersweet when Dr. White explained it'd be virtually impossible for her to have any more children due to excessive scarring. "That's okay," she accepted softly. "I wasn't plannin' on havin' more babies." Joanna lightly brushed blond wisps of hair on the child's tiny forehead to one side.

By the middle of August, Joanna got back to working six days a week, with her daughter in a bassinet in the salon. Her customers begged to hold the infant. Before long Hope became the darling of the block.

By October, Joanna breathed easier on the financial front, due in part to her increasing sales of Avon products. The catalogs gave the ladies reading material while under the dryer, and they all clamored for the free samples.

The toughest part for Joanna was the long days on her feet and seemingly endless nights with a three-month-old baby. Even though Joanna loved her daughter above all else, she fought exhaustion, in the middle of the night, when she'd used every tactic she knew to soothe the crying infant to no avail. Joanna would sob in her bedroom while Hope fussed in her crib. In those moments Joanna grieved for Irene, wishing she had her gift for mothering.

One Sunday afternoon, Joanna sat on the floor, still in her pajamas, filling in the form for her next Avon order, when someone knocked on the door. She peeked through the curtains. Mary stood on the porch, looking like Grace Kelly, with her hair tucked in a sophisticated twist. She hadn't seen Mary in a month and didn't expect her today.

"Chick, you look like hell," were Mary's first words.

Joanna laughed. "Did you just step off a Hollywood backlot? I hate you, come in."

Mary lifted the baby, who been lying on a blanket on the floor, chewing on a toy.

"Go get a shower. We're going to the movies. Mrs. Thatcher will watch Hope." Joanna ran off to take a long, hot shower, a luxury she'd almost forgotten since Hope came along. When she reemerged, Hope vocalized sweet baby gurgles as Mary bathed her in the kitchen sink. Seeing Joanna, Mary asked, "Feeling better?"

"Much. Great showers are proof there's a God."

"So you've been praying to the shower deity?" Mary set the baby on a towel.

"Yes, and He heard my prayer, and it was good." They both laughed.

"Well, I think He pulled off a miracle; you look a million times better than when you opened the door. Hey, look in the bag. I brought something for Hope," Mary revealed, diapering the baby. Joanna pulled a frilly dress from the grocery bag.

"My goodness, this's beautiful, so fancy! We don't go anyplace she'd wear such a thing."

"Take her for a walk in the stroller. That's special enough for Princess Hope." Mary slipped the baby into a comfortable sleeper.

"This must've cost a fortune. Won't Lenny be angry?"

"I didn't buy the dress; I made it," Mary touted proudly. "Lenny works a lot. I got bored one day and bought myself a sewing machine. I have two more dresses on the cutting table for her, not quite this fancy."

"You could have your own business makin' these dresses," Joanna suggested.

"No, I did it for fun. Besides, when my baby comes, in June, I'll be too busy to sew."

"Your baby! June?" Joanna hugged her.

"That's right. We get to raise our kids together. Lenny's ecstatic. He wants a boy." Mary handed Hope over to Joanna.

The doorbell rang and Mary ran to greet Mrs. Thatcher. "Where's my little doll baby!" the neighbor called. She usurped the baby. "You've had your bath, haven't you, young lady? You two run along now. Why not have dinner out, too?"

"I don't wanna impose," Joanna said.

"It's not an imposition. I love babies. This one's my special girl, yes she is," the woman twittered adoringly.

At the theater, Joanna and Mary watched *The Best of Everything*. They had popcorn and Cokes, like old times. After the movie, they decided on hamburgers at a malt shop.

"Do you think that movie was true, the way women are treated in the business world?"

"I don't know. I've never worked in an office," Joanna told her.

"Well, quite a few women work at Lenny's office, secretaries, paralegals, and clerks."

"You worried Lenny's cheating on you?"

"No. I guess the movie made me glad I'm not a working woman."

"So how is married life, anyway?"

"Boring mostly. We're busy on the weekends with parties. I've been meeting some of his colleagues and their wives. I'm hosting my first dinner party in two weeks, sixteen people."

"You hate to cook," Joanna reminded her.

"I hired a caterer my next-door neighbor recommended."

"So you're making friends?"

"I don't know. The women on my street have children. So they're cliquish. Maybe once my baby comes, I'll feel like I belong. Right now, it's lonely."

"Things must be goin' well with marriage if you're pregnant," Joanna guessed.

Mary lowered her voice to a whisper. "We've been married four months now, and honestly, I thought as newlyweds we'd be doing it like rabbits. Tony and I couldn't keep our hands off each other. Lenny and I've had sex only eight times. I'm amazed I'm pregnant. Weirdly, during it, the room has to be pitch dark."

"That's strange," Joanna offered.

"If I'd had a few serious relationships, would they be so different from one to the next?"

"Don't ask me. The only serious relationship I've had is Jack. You should ask Jessie."

"She called the other day," Mary said, changing the subject. "She's got a spot in an orchestra for a movie soundtrack. Oh, and get this, some guy cast her in a dish-soap commercial. They'll show her washing dishes in a sink full of suds, then close in on her hands playing the piano, and she says, 'Use Palmolive and your hands will stay lovelier than if you didn't do the dishes.'"

"That's hysterical! Jessie's never washed a dish in her life. Is she sleepin' with him?"

"Probably! You're right, I should ask her take on sex. I can't talk to him, he thinks I'm this naive girl; he's teaching everything. With Tony, it was fun. With my husband, it's strange. And worst of all, I'm not attracted to him." Mary smiled. "Anyway, now that I'm expecting, he's not interested. Oh my gosh, look at the time! I'd better be getting back. I have to iron Lenny's shirts for next week. But we'll do this again real soon," Mary promised.

Joanna doubted they'd see each other anytime soon. They lived separate lives now, and she missed the old times. The autumn days ambled into the crisp air of winter and Joanna continued the Sunday movie tradition by herself, taking Mrs. Thatcher's offers to babysit. Joanna understood the notion of change. She and Prissy exchanged letters regularly. Mary and Jessie preferred the telephone. She accepted this as the natural progression of life. Still, it saddened her that their evolution had resulted in the four friends drifting apart.

Chapter 38

Mary was blessed with a good-natured baby girl on June 15, 1960. Disappointed, Lenny expressed confidence the next one would be a boy. She named her Marguerite, nicknaming her Meg. Edith swooped in to lend a hand when they came home from the hospital. Mary healed quickly, mainly to get her mother to go back to Nashville.

The new mother doted over her little girl. Meg thrived on being entertained in a windup swing, while Mary held complete conversations with her and sewed adorable baby outfits. Mary balanced the house and the baby and experienced happiness she'd never known. The neighbors' attitudes grew warmer with the birth of Mary's daughter. They shared parenting advice and invited her to teas. However, it made Mary uncomfortable; they reminded her of the Melinda Petersons of the past.

No one was more surprised than Mary to find out she'd conceived again when Meg turned six months old. Her once manageable life collided with her hormones. Lenny's career consumed his time. Preoccupied with her own day-to-day chores, Mary didn't care. She hated that her babies were going to be so close in age and she'd have two in diapers.

Her mother lectured her on the wisdom of spacing out her children. Mary's defense rested on Lenny's devotion to the Catholic ideology on birth control. He hadn't stepped in a church since their wedding, and Mary felt powerless. She regretted not ironing out myriad issues before the marriage.

By the middle of this pregnancy, Mary had trouble sleeping. She lay awake in the middle of the night, staring at the ceiling, pondering the what-ifs in life. What if she'd married Tony; where would she be now if she hadn't married Lenny?

Always, in the back of her mind, dwelled the little boy she gave away. He'd turn four in April. She wondered about his happiness. She fantasized about the adoptive mother contacting her and granting her a window into his life.

When Joanna called with the details for Prissy's high school graduation, Mary needed an event to look forward to. Prissy's final exams were the last week of May. The next week she'd be home in Memphis. They'd carpool for the graduation in Atlanta, on Friday. Jessie planned to fly in, too. They'd be together again and the anticipation was electrifying.

Jack Wyatt barely made it in the door before Tommy came running, hugging his good leg, yelling, "Teach me to ride my bike, Daddy." Jack laughed at the boy's enthusiasm.

"Please, Daddy," Catherine joined the chorus. Tommy's fourth-birthday present gleamed bright red in their driveway, his first two-wheeler. "I made him wait until you got home."

"Okay. Let me put my briefcase down."

Tommy raced out the front door to the waiting challenge.

Catherine kissed Jack hello and asked, "How do things look in Birmingham?"

"Construction is coming along. If the rains hold off, we could open in July."

"Take the camera," Catherine instructed.

Jack snapped pictures, while Catherine ran alongside the bike with the boy. His damaged leg prohibited his participation in many of the activities that normally fell to a dad. The bike wobbled, but Tommy regained his balance. Jack painfully recalled Joanna's letters, and her fantasy of teaching their son to ride a bicycle. A lump formed in Jack's throat as Tommy hit his rhythm and cried, "Let go, Mom."

The boy broke free and pedaled to the end of the long driveway. Jack snapped the shutter. Joining her husband, Cat put her arm around him. Noticing the glisten of emotion, she shared, "I know, I feel that way, too. I'm so proud of him."

The boy stopped at the street and hollered, "I can do it." He climbed to the seat and, with shaky balance, managed to push the pedals. Seconds later, he breezed past his parents, pedaling toward the other end of the driveway.

"Don't go in the road!" Catherine called after him.

"I won't," Tommy promised.

"I'm going to start dinner," Cat decided.

"I'll keep an eye on him," Jack vowed, ascending the porch stairs with his wife. He took a seat on the wooden glider with the best vantage point. He loved Tommy. He'd brought so much joy to their home. Yet a barrier existed that kept a close relationship with the child out of his reach. Was it punishment for the two boys buried in separate cemeteries? If he didn't make promises, he wouldn't disappoint the boy.

The laughter of the former roommates filled the living room of Joanna's home. Jessie, center stage, recounted her adventures in California and presented Joanna with autographed pictures of the stars she'd met. "I was at Warner Bros. studio for an audition one day—you know me, late as usual. I turned the corner and ran smack into Troy Donahue! I spilled my coffee all over his shirt."

"Oh my God, was he mad?" Prissy asked, giggling.

"No! He was nice about it. I apologized, babblin' like an idiot, offerin' to pay for the dry cleanin'. He said, 'You're in a hurry, an audition maybe?' I told him yes. He wished me luck and told me not to worry about dunkin' him in coffee. He's even dreamier in person."

Each one of them had their stories to tell, filling in the spaces since they'd been apart. Prissy's tales were of her academy chums. She announced her acceptance into Vanderbilt, where she intended to begin her undergraduate studies in the fall and then attend law school. They were thrilled by her news.

Around ten o'clock Prissy let out a contagious yawn and Joanna offered to make coffee. "No, I'm going to head home. I'll be back tomorrow for the haircut you promised me."

"You can spend the night here," Joanna offered.

"Thanks. I didn't get a chance to talk to Lisa earlier. If I go now, maybe she'll be awake."

The youngest girl hugged her goodbyes. Joanna and Mary tiptoed upstairs to check on their daughters, who were sound asleep in the crib. In the living room, Jessie turned on the radio, selecting her favorite Memphis blues station. She entered the kitchen in search of more wine.

The three remaining friends settled into the comfort of Joanna's living room for quiet conversation. Mary described living with an esoteric lawyer, "He has an office at home I'm forbidden to enter. He claims his work is confidential. So I'm not supposed to ask questions and he never tells me about his clients."

"I'd have a problem with a room in my house that's off limits to me," Jessie remarked.

"He stays out of my sewing room, so it's fair. I don't want him snooping in my things."

"Why? What're you hidin'?" Jessie asked.

"Newspaper articles about Tony," Mary and Joanna chimed in unison.

"I thought he was gettin' married?" Jessie asked.

"He did, two months ago. A pro team on the East Coast signed him. So Melinda's found her pot of gold at the bottom of a goalpost," Mary reported.

"Well, don't dwell on it too much," Jessie offered. "Your hormones are whacked out right now, so you're hypersensitive."

Suddenly, Joanna jumped from her seat to investigate a banging on the door. "What on earth?" When she opened the door, there stood Prissy, supporting her twelve-year-old sister, who appeared to be drunk. Making eye contact, Prissy burst into tears.

"What's wrong?" Joanna ushered them into the living room.

"I caught him!" Prissy hysterically wailed. "He was touching her. She's so out of it! He drugged her or something!" Mary led Lisa, who was naked under a blanket, to Joanna's bedroom. She put a T-shirt on her and tucked her in bed. From the other room, she could hear Prissy describe the horrific experience.

"I shoved him against the bookcase and it fell on him. I grabbed Lisa and we drove straight here! I didn't know what else to do!"

"We need to call the police and an ambulance," Mary asserted, joining the group. The other women agreed. Within a few minutes a squad car arrived, followed by paramedics. They transported Lisa to the hospital, where she'd be examined and observed overnight.

Prissy launched into the longest night of her life. The probing questions from the police were difficult for the girl, but with the support of her friends, she kept her composure.

"We've sent a patrol car to bring Mr. Matthews in for questioning, okay? I'll take your statement here, but you may have to come to the station," explained a compassionate female police officer, Detective Mercer. She was professional and well trained for this type of situation. A male police officer came into the house and interrupted the deposition; Jessie, sensing more bad news, followed the female civil servant to the door.

"It's a real tragedy." The man chronicled their fellow officer's attempt at taking Prissy's father into custody. "He'd already shot his wife in the head and was burning pictures in a trash barrel in the backyard. He shot at our guys. They returned fire, killing him." Jessie put her hand to her lips, suppressing a gasp, for Prissy's sake.

Mobilizing their emotional reserves, Prissy's friends cared for her as the painful days of the investigation dragged on and revealed the sickening depth of her father's depravity. Lisa's medical exam confirmed she'd been violated. The scene at the Matthews home unsettled even the veterans on the force. Evidence in the form of pornographic photographs, which Matthews had been unable to destroy, corroborated Prissy's story. Those photos also disclosed the truth of the sexual abuse Prissy had unknowingly endured. Lisa's lab reports from the hospital confirmed that their father had spiked their orange juice.

The emotional weight of these revelations threatened to crush Prissy; she blamed herself for not protecting her sister. She also brooded over the guilt she felt for not protecting her mother, whom her father had also kept drugged. Mary, fearing for the girls' mental health, suggested Prissy and Lisa see a psychiatrist for a healthy perspective. They didn't attend the graduation in Atlanta; Prissy's emotional state dictated they skip the event.

Prissy and Lisa stayed with Joanna during this difficult time. With the help of their therapist, the molested girls were able to find some closure to this chapter of their life. Due to the lack of family willing to take responsibility for Lisa, Prissy petitioned the court for guardianship of her sister; the only alternative would place the girl in the foster system. Impressed by her maturity and conviction, the judge granted her motion and assigned a caseworker to monitor their situation and report back to him.

At first Prissy thought she might go to college in Memphis. Joanna offered them a home, as long as they wanted. Ultimately, Prissy decided to go on to Vanderbilt.

On the day the two Matthews sisters departed for Nashville, Joanna helped put their suitcases in the car. "You call me anytime, day or night." Joanna hugged Prissy tightly.

"I will. I'll call often. We're going to be fine."

"I know you'll do better than fine; you'll be fantastic!" Joanna told her with pride.

Mary Atherton Hollan gave birth to a son on September 17, 1961. They named him Paul. Mary's life consisted of endless chores and many nights with little sleep, as Paul turned out to be a colicky and sickly child. There were repeated doctor visits for ear infections and the croup. Most nights she fell asleep with him in the rocking chair assuring they both got some rest. Lenny was consumed with his career and rarely around.

Chapter 39

As America moved into a time of extreme turmoil, the women who'd resided in Knoxville came of age along with the nation. They watched in fear as the East Germans built the Berlin Wall and held their breath in October 1962 when the world came close to nuclear war during the Cuban Missile Crisis. In the spring of 1963, they listened as a black minister from the South spoke in Washington, DC, to a crowd of over 250,000. The rally called for equal rights. They couldn't escape the undercurrent of hate that swept through the Deep South like a sickness.

It angered Joanna to see the images come out of Birmingham, of police attacking black children with dogs and fire hoses. In September, the bombing of a church in that same city frightened her to the core. If it could happen in Birmingham, it could happen in Memphis. She cried with the masses when President John F. Kennedy was assassinated.

Prissy was enthusiastic about President Johnson's 1964 Civil Rights Act being signed into law. "It's so exciting to see Jim Crow laws abolished and new civil rights legislation passed. It proves America can change for the better."

"As long as they can enforce the new laws," Joanna amended. "No piece of paper is gonna change the hearts and minds of some of the good-ol'-boys who're more than happy to pull the sheets off the line when it suits 'em. I saw it myself, as a kid, in Lynchburg. The Klan terrorized the colored folks. Every time, the lawmen did nothing, claimin' they couldn't prove who'd been involved. Everyone knew full well who those bullies were, but they were too afraid of becomin' targets themselves. It was sickenin'."

"It's different now, Joanna. These're federal laws that can't be ignored."

"Tell Alabama's George Wallace," Joanna corrected. "Till men like him are voted out, I'm afraid real change isn't gonna happen." Depressed by her own pessimism, Joanna changed the subject. "How's Lisa doin'?"

"She's doing well. Her grades are pretty good, and she's made a few friends. We're both still going to therapy. That's helped. She's coming out of her shell more. As for me, school is going to take eight years. Some people can get through law school in seven."

"It's okay if it takes you a little longer; you've got a lot on your shoulders. I'm proud of you," Joanna encouraged.

"Thanks. I'm doing the best I can."

In December, Mary gave birth to another boy, Luke. For this baby, Lenny's mother came to help. However, having Meredith around was worse than having Edith hovering.

"You'd've thought World War Three had begun when I packed her bags and told her to leave," Mary told Joanna during a phone conversation. "I couldn't take any more. She was supposed to be here to help, but all she did was bark orders and tell me I'm doing everything wrong. Lenny took his mother's side and forced me to call her and apologize. Which I did, only to get him off my back. It doesn't matter, I didn't mean a word of it."

"That's awful," Joanna sympathized.

"The saddest part is my kids will never get to have the kind of relationship I had with my grandmother. It breaks my heart, but I don't want my kids around either one of our mothers."

"At least you have your dad," Joanna rationalized.

"That's true. He adores my kids and spoils them despite my mother. I'm sorry to complain, when you'd give anything to have your mom there for Hope."

"She's too little to know she's missin' out on extended family. With any luck, she won't miss somethin' she's never had." Still, Joanna dreaded the day when Hope began asking questions about not having a daddy or other family.

During the summer of 1965, a colored family moved in three doors down from Joanna. The tension ran high in the predominantly white neighborhood as house after house listed for sale. Joanna went by the Johnsons' home to introduce herself as she'd done with all new neighbors. Apprehensive, Tilley Johnson opened her door to Joanna and Hope, but soon relaxed when Hope and her two youngest children became fast friends and ran off to play.

"I made this banana bread; it's still warm." Joanna offered a basket to her neighbor.

"That's very kind of ya. Would ya like to come in? I'll put on a pot of coffee," Tilley suggested. Joanna accepted the invitation and followed her through to the kitchen.

Joanna liked the Johnsons; they were hardworking and excellent parents. Tilley had a night job in housekeeping at St. Joseph's Hospital and George drove a garbage truck for the city. Tina was Hope's age. The middle son, Darryl, was eight and George, Jr., was fourteen.

In no time, Tina and Hope were inseparable. Joanna could always count on the two girls to be upstairs in the playroom enjoying a dollhouse Joanna had purchased at a yard sale and lovingly restored. Other days the girls watched television. The Johnsons didn't own a television, and Tina thought it boring; she'd rather play school and always functioned as the teacher. To the children, the summer seemed endless, but for the parents the school year came too quickly.

"I hope we done right pickin' Hollywood Elementary," Tilley confided in Joanna. They sipped lemonade while the girls chased butterflies in the yard. "I knew they'd take Tina, 'cause of their grade-a-year policy, letting in a new crop of first-graders every year, but they flat-out refused Darryl's transfer. So I went to the superintendent and it took some fast talkin', but he let him in when I told him that havin' a smart student like Darryl'd make their desegregation look on track. They ain't givin' no transfer to Douglas High School for Junior. He'll have to ride the city bus south to Melrose High School."

"Hollywood's a good little school; I'm glad they let your younger ones enroll."

"It's powerful important our children get a good education. That's why we come here from Birmingham."

"Your kids are so smart. I heard Tina readin' to Hope the other day and I was amazed," Joanna complimented.

"She reads like a third-grader. My grandma never learnt to read; she always said, 'Child, if ya can read, ya can do anythin'.' I want my kids to have the opportunities we ain't had. My husband had to quit school at thirteen and get him a job after his daddy was lynched in Alabama."

"Oh, Tilley! How awful! I'm so sorry for him." Joanna's hand went to her heart.

"Happens all the time. Can't do this or go there 'cause you colored." Tilley frowned.

"I can't imagine what it's like for ya. I wish I could." Joanna took Tilley's hand.

Tilley squeezed Joanna's gently. Tears rimmed in her eyes. "No you don't. You'd have to experience it youself to understand how it feel and I don't wish that for you. Our options was limited by Jim Crow, but my kids… It'll happen in their lifetime. Some ways it already is."

Tina and Hope giggled in stereo as they danced in a circle, holding hands like two little fairies, Hope's blond pigtails bouncing in time with Tina's colorfully beaded dark braids. Both mothers smiled at the sweetness of their play.

"Hope's so excited Tina's in her first-grade class," Joanna relayed.

"So's Tina. It's all she talk 'bout. Memphis hasn't had any ruckus at the schools, not like in Little Rock. I sure hopes they ain't picked on. Kids can be so mean," Tilley said.

"It's hard to imagine children this young with cruel hearts toward others. Hatred isn't born in them, it's learned in the home," Joanna theorized.

"I seen that hate turn violent. George, Jr., got a concussion and his arm broke walkin' in the Children's Crusade, couple years ago. We worshiped at the Sixteenth Street Baptist Church, where those little girls were killt. It easy could've been one of mine."

"That's frightening. Again, I can't even imagine." Joanna shook her head.

The first week of school went off with no incidents of angry adult segregationists shouting ugly remarks at minority students. However, taunting by mean-spirited bullies in the higher grades occurred. Joanna was shocked when she received a phone call from the principal informing her Hope had been in a fistfight and requested she come to the school immediately. Joanna dashed to the elementary school, where she found her daughter sitting on a long wooden bench outside the office.

"What happened?" she asked.

"Ricky Keeler pushed Tina and called her a Nigger. So I punched him."

"I know you were stickin' up for your friend, but you can't get into fights at school. If somethin' like this happens again, you tell your teacher and let her handle it."

"Oh, I don't think it'll happen again. Ricky has a black eye," Hope explained matter-of-factly. Joanna refrained from laughing, not wanting to contradict the seriousness of the predicament. Ricky never laid a hand on Tina again, but the harassment by many of the other children would've made the neighbor child's first few years in the public schools unbearable if not for the courage and self-respect instilled by Tilley and George Johnson.

Chapter 40

As a twenty-six-year-old mother with three small children and a mostly absent husband, Mary found life exhausting. Just when she thought she couldn't be more tired, she again became pregnant. This time she gave birth to another daughter, Renee. The hospital nursing staff were caring for the new baby.

Mary reclined on the thick hospital sheets. Her chest ached at the thought of Jessie, Joanna, and Prissy, together again in Nashville, attending Lisa's high school graduation. Mary found it hard to believe Lisa was old enough to be going off to Berkeley. She felt miserably left out. Isolated in the dimness of the hospital room, she let her tears fall freely as she grieved over her own discarded opportunities and her lost passion for life. She dreaded going home with a new baby and facing days that brought her little joy.

"How's she doing?" Joanna asked Jessie, who came in the salon door after visiting Mary and the new baby at the hospital.

"She's dancing at her own Boo-Hoo Ball." Jessie slid into the styling chair.

"I was afraid of that." Joanna swept the hair on the floor into a dustpan. "She wasn't happy about this baby."

"I know. And that husband of hers! He made a grand entrance while I was there. After all these years, this is the first time I've actually met the guy. I'll be honest, I don't like him."

"I'm not a fan, either. It'd be one thing if he made Mary happy, but he doesn't," Joanna expounded. "And I think he discourages her friendship with us. She hasn't admitted it, but she never invites me out and we hardly ever talk on the phone anymore."

"Do you think she told him about Knoxville?" Jessie asked.

"No. I'm sure she hasn't. That's crazy."

"I don't know." Jessie's tone questioned the absurdity. "The way he looked at me, it was as if he knew all my secrets."

"Smug and condescendin'?" Joanna asked.

"Yeah, but it's more than that."

"He's like that with everyone, even her," Joanna said. She changed the subject. "I wish you'd stay another week."

"I can't. I'm under contract for a greeting-card commercial. I'm also gonna audition for some movie roles." Two years earlier, Jessie had purchased a condominium in Culver City. For the first time in her adult life, she'd set down roots, and she was thriving in Hollywood.

At the end of January 1968, the Vietnam War intensified on the televisions in American homes with the Tet Offensive, and signaled the beginning of a year that changed the United States forever. The voices of opposition to the war were getting louder, dividing the country. Joanna sided against the war. She saw the widening gap between the affluent and the laborers, the blacks and the whites, the haves and the have-nots.

She considered herself to be a have-a-little. The Wilsons, like many people, were barely keeping their heads above water financially. She used coupons, shopped sales, bought their clothes at yard sales and thrift stores. Joanna collected Green Stamps and turned them in for the towels she used in her salon. Irene's lessons on how to pinch pennies paid off for Joanna. Still, she worried a catastrophe might wipe her out. She knew they weren't the only ones struggling and endeavored to be grateful for what she had.

George and Tilley Johnson were also having a hard time. Even with both of them working, they were living paycheck-to-paycheck. George, Jr., now seventeen, wanted to get a job to help. Unwavering, his father forbade it, insisting he concentrate on graduating.

Joanna knew George Johnson to be a mild-mannered man, slow to anger and the first neighbor to lend a helping hand. She had sensed his uneasy tension since the summer when race riots and violence threatened to undermine the progress being made for racial justice.

"My husband got strong feelin's supportin' civil rights. He wants life to be different for our kids, but bein' a father, his nature's to protect them. After what happened to Junior in Birmingham… well, he don't wanna leave 'em fatherless neither," Tilley explained to Joanna.

In February, George's resolve to stay out of demonstrations broke when the sanitation workers went on strike. Dressed in her blue hospital uniform, Tilley and Joanna sat at the table, drinking coffee and talking in low tones.

"I wish he'd stay outta this, but he's such a strong, proud man… qualities I love 'bout him," Tilley told her. "I reckon he's got to support the strike. The disrespect he's endured is shameful. If there's one thing that riles George, it's bein' called *boy*. But he's kept his mouth shut to hold his job. It's the wages and danger that can't go on."

"I heard on the news about those two workers being killed in the compacter." Joanna bristled at the ghastliness.

"They's black. If'n they be white, it'd be different. Thing about this strike, George don't get paid if he don't work." Tilley nervously tapped her finger against the side of the coffee mug. "I'm gonna have to work extra shifts at the hospital or get a second job if this goes on long."

"Can I do anythin'?" Joanna asked, concerned.

"Help me with Tina, like you doin' tonight. I don't want her home alone when I goes to work. George and my boys gonna be at meetin's and petition drives every night. Tonight they makin' protest signs sayin', I AM A MAN."

"Having Tina here's easy. I'll sign the petition. Heck, tell George I'll put one in my salon for my customers to sign, too. If you need any groceries or anythin', please let me know."

"Thank you," Tilley said.

The garbage amassed quickly as the Memphis mayor took a hard stance on the strike, labeling it an illegal work stoppage that endangered public health. The city replaced the strikers with new hires. Less than half of the city's garbage trucks were making pickups.

Tilley worked extra hours at the hospital. Tonight George was at home with the children. Joanna learned of the Johnsons' struggles when Hope described Tina's lunch as an apple and a half a buttered-bread sandwich. There'd been a march earlier and sirens. Joanna assumed there'd been trouble.

"Go down -and see if Mr. Johnson wants to watch the evening news," Joanna told her daughter. He'd often come over to watch how their cause was being reported by the media. Hope quickly put on her coat and took off out the door.

Joanna set the table for six and checked on the casserole browning in the oven. In her pantry, she put together a box with her home-canned peaches, a jar of peanut butter, and other staples. She rolled the television into the kitchen when her daughter returned with the neighbors.

George, Sr., held a washrag in his hands and occasionally wiped his bloodshot eyes. "Tear gas," he explained when he saw Joanna's concern. Junior looked the same. Church leaders admonished the high school students to join the marches.

Joanna set the casserole on the table. "Please." She motioned the neighbors to join.

"This is mighty nice of you," George said.

"There's plenty to go around." Joanna took her place next to Hope. The news skewed the events of the day in favor of the mayor's perspective as they ate the filling meal.

"They're only telling half the story!" Junior disputed hotly. "They never said anything about the woman who got her foot run over by a police car! That's what started it!"

"Son, violence whips up quick in these type protests. We gotta check our tempers. The marches gotta be peaceful and dignified, like Reverend King says."

"Do you think Dr. King will come to Memphis?" Joanna asked regarding the rumors.

"I hope so. If he does, maybe Washington'll take notice."

"Somethin's got to be done," Joanna interjected. "Mayor Loeb is diggin' in his heals."

"That's right," Junior agreed. As dinner ended, they switched off the TV. Tina and Hope cleared the dishes. Joanna walked with Mr. Johnson out onto the back porch.

"Junior'll be back in school tomorrow," he told her. "He can't have but four absences or they'll expel him for truancy. If he don't go to college, he's gonna be sent to Vietnam."

Joanna sighed. "They say we're fightin' communism to ensure human rights. It's such hypocrisy when Washington refuses to enforce freedom and equality here."

"There's thousands of young Negro men fightin' in Vietnam; lowers the numbers can demonstrate here, I wager," George theorized.

"This is so wrong." Joanna felt powerless to effect any change. As George, Sr., prepared to leave, she handed him the box of food she'd put together.

"I'm not one that's good about takin' charity," he objected.

"It's not charity, it's neighbor helpin' neighbor, like you and Junior cuttin' the dead branches out of my tree last summer," Joanna pressed, resolved not to take no for an answer.

"You're good people, Miss Wilson."

"You too, Mr. Johnson."

Weeks went by with no resolution to the strike, and racial tensions escalated. The city slowly collected the trash. The marches continued. On March 22, an unseasonal snowstorm forced a scheduled march's cancellation. Joanna was giving Mrs. Thatcher a perm when snow shovels scraped the sidewalk in front of her house. Bundled in their parkas and scarves, George, Jr. and Darryl were shoveling her walk.

"Isn't that kind! Do you think they're gonna ask you to pay them?" her customer asked.

"No, it's just neighbor helpin' neighbor," Joanna explained.

"Don't you worry letting those Negro children run through your house the way you do could hurt your business? Some folks aren't as understanding as I am, you know?"

"Truly, if that's how they feel than I'd rather they go elsewhere! The Johnson children are good kids. You won't find a harder-workin' family," Joanna said passionately. She knew Mrs. Thatcher was right. She'd already lost a couple of clients.

On March 28, George, Jr., walked in his second protest for the sanitation workers. He proudly stood on one side of his father, while Tilley supported him on the other side. Darryl and Tina were in school. Joanna went through her day with uneasy concern for her friends. Later sirens sped toward Beale Street. It was · happening again.

Rumors were flying that the National Guard was coming. The city of Memphis issued a curfew from 7:00 p.m. to 5:00 a.m. When Tilley arrived at the salon in the early afternoon, she told Joanna stories of looting and vandalism, including firebombs.

"Dr. King was there. But soon it got violent and they hightailed him out. I didn't see how it started. 'Fore I knew what's happenin', windows're being busted with the sign sticks, and police're beatin' anyone they could grab."

"Where're your husband and son?" Joanna desperately asked.

"They gone to march headquarters. George wants to hear 'bout plans for the next march."

"Oh, Tilley!" Joanna groaned, knowing she'd worry during her shift at the hospital.

The next march was indeed a peaceful demonstration as three hundred protesters walked, carrying signs, down Main Street. National Guardsmen lined the route, bayoneted weapons pointed at the crowd. Store owners stood inside their shops, many with baseball bats ready to protect their property should looting begin. The march proceeded without incident. Dr. King publicly promised he'd return to Memphis to lead a peaceful march.

A few days later, President Johnson announced he wouldn't run for office in the next election. Joanna couldn't blame him; in her opinion, being the leader of a country in so much turmoil had to be the worst job in the world.

Martin Luther King, Jr., made good on his promise and returned to Memphis on April 3. Injunctions were handed down by the court to prevent a scheduled march on April 8. Despite the threat of tornadoes, the Johnson family joined hundreds at Mason Temple to listen to the Nobel Prize–winning preacher's sermon, which later became known as his "Mountaintop Speech" and was, sadly, the last he'd ever give.

It was after six thirty the next evening, while Joanna mopped the floor in the salon, that a furious banging rattled her front door. She dropped her mop and opened the door to find Tilley, crying, Darryl by her side.

"Dr. King's been shot! He's at St. Joseph's Hospital; they sent us all home. There's police and newspeople ever'where." Tina and Hope came running downstairs; Tilley hugged Tina close. Joanna led them to the living room and turned on the television.

"Where's George and Junior?" Joanna asked.

"We don't know where Junior is. His daddy's lookin' for 'im." Tilley looked terrified.

At seven thirty, Walter Cronkite announced that Reverend King had died. Soon reports came in of sporadic violence erupting in cities all over the country. The Wilsons sat on the couch, numb, watching the TV as events of the evening unfolded.

"The whole world's lost its mind," Joanna muttered. Unexpectedly, the phone rang.

Mary didn't bother to say hello. "You and Hope need to come out here by me. It's not safe to be in Memphis tonight!"

"No, I can't. Tilley's here. Don't worry about us, we're okay."

"Are you sure?" Mary asked, concerned.

"Stan's on his way over. I thought it'd be good to have a male around who's older than eleven," Joanna explained.

"That's sensible. My offer still stands, if you change your mind."

"Thanks. Love you."

"Love you too; be safe," the suburban friend advised as she disconnected.

Stan made it to Joanna's house a few minutes later. The tension created by the sirens from emergency vehicles was palpable.

Tilley paced the living room, "I feel like I can't sit still. Where are they?"

"George'll find him." Joanna encouraged with a hug. Suddenly the sound of breaking glass gave them a fright. The screeching of spinning tires and the holler of voices made everyone bolt outside to investigate. The taillights of a truck glowed, and the jeering from those who rode in the bed echoed off the houses as they sped out of sight.

Their attention quickly turned to the Johnsons' home where the front window had been smashed and the word COON spray-painted on their siding.

Darryl seethed. "White trash!" he spat.

"If you got any wood, I can board up the window," Stan offered.

"In the garage. Darryl, help him. We'll paint the siding tomorrow," Tilley instructed.

As the mothers led the girls back to Joanna's house, Hope asked, "Why do people have to be so hateful, Mama?"

"Because they're ignorant," Joanna answered. Once inside, they sent the girls upstairs.

"I'll make some fresh coffee," Joanna offered, feeling helpless. Tilley followed her into the kitchen and once again paced, wringing her hands. Darryl and Stan returned a short while later. The middle school boy parked himself in front of the television.

Stan took Joanna aside. "I've got a shotgun in my car. Let's turn on the porch light and I'll sit out there."

"No guns! Your being out front should be deterrent enough. I'll bring you some coffee," Joanna offered. The hours passed slowly; the mothers put the children to bed, the girls in Hope's room and Darryl on a pallet in the playroom. Tilley made dozens of phone calls to determine if anyone had seen her men. Meanwhile Joanna stayed close, hoping for good news. Finally, shortly after midnight Stan came through the front door with Tilley's husband and son.

"Thank God!" Joanna breathed.

"I been worried sick!" Tilley scolded, examining Junior's beaten and bruised face.

"I'm sorry, Mama."

"He got in a scuffle with some white boys, but he come out okay," his father explained.

As Tilley put on her coat, Joanna told her, "Let's not wake Darryl and Tina. I'll send them home after breakfast. Hope won't be goin' to school tomorrow, I imagine you're gonna do the same."

Tilley nodded. "Thank you," she said simply, but gave Joanna a hug, expressing her relief. Twelve days later the sanitation strike ended, and George Johnson returned to his job. The events of that spring became a permanent stain on the legacy of Memphis, Tennessee.

Chapter 41

Mary folded yet another load of laundry. "This sure wasn't what I thought my life was going to be like," she told the cat who jumped on the warm dryer. Meg yelled at Paul, while Luke shouted something about spilling a glass of milk.

"I'll be up in a minute," she hollered, arranging a basket of whites.

Stomping as she ascended the stairs, Mary screamed at her older two children, "Paul Michael, go clean your bedroom! Marguerite! Set the table for dinner."

Entering the kitchen, she found a puddle of milk in the middle of the floor and Luke sitting at the table with the last doughnut in his hand.

"There were four doughnuts left! Did you eat them all?"

"I'm hungry." He shoved an oversized bite in his mouth.

"Goddamn it Luke, I'm ready to make dinner and you're eating sweets! Get out of my kitchen before I blister your butt," she growled. Grabbing a sponge, she attempted to clean the spill only to be interrupted by three-year-old Renee crying when Luke stepped on her doll.

"You're being mean! Go to your room!" She swatted him on the butt with a fly swatter. Renee continued to moan. "All right, that's enough! Y'all're wearing me out!"

Going back into the kitchen, she finished mopping the mess. Mary felt like she'd explode at the next little thing. She dropped hot dogs on a cookie sheet with some tater tots, and burned her hand putting it in the oven. She wanted to scream or throw something. Gritting her teeth, she went to the phone and dialed Joanna.

"What're you doing?" Mary asked as Joanna answered the phone.

"I'm baggin' Avon orders. How 'bout you?"

"Making dinner."

"We ate an hour ago. I take it Lenny isn't home again tonight?"

"Nope. Honestly, I'm glad he's not. My kids are being monsters today. For the life of me, I can't remember why I thought being a mom was a great idea. It must be a full moon."

Joanna laughed. "You wanna talk about it?"

"I need your help with something." Mary poured herself a glass of wine.

"Okay?"

"I need you to drive me somewhere and watch Renee on Monday." She stretched the extra-long phone cord out to the back porch and took a big gulp of wine. She continued in a whisper, "I have to get an abortion."

"Oh, honey!" Joanna sympathized.

"I can't have another baby! Half the time I don't feel like I can deal with the four I've got. My doctor won't do it, but he gave me the name of a doctor in Memphis."

"You haven't told Lenny, have you?"

"No. I can't. Abortion'd be out of the question."

"Abortion's illegal," Joanna told her.

"It's also a mortal sin. I'll probably go to hell," Mary agonized.

"I can rearrange my appointments. What time do you need me?" Joanna asked.

"Early, as soon as I get the kids off to school. I need to get back home before they're due in the afternoon. I wouldn't ask you, but I'm not supposed to drive afterward."

The following Monday Joanna drove her to the home of the doctor who'd do the procedure and took Renee to a nearby park for the next hour. When she headed back to get Mary, she found her walking several blocks away.

"You okay?" Joanna whispered so as not to wake Renee, who was in the back-seat.

Her face wet with tears, Mary shook her head. She flicked her cigarette to the ground and got into the car. Joanna pulled back into traffic.

"I know I'm going to regret this," Mary confessed.

"You did what you felt you had to do."

Mary gave a short laugh and shook her head. "I couldn't go through with it. A girl was screaming in the other room. The place was filthy."

"Wow!" Joanna put on her turn signal and switched lanes.

"I couldn't do it," Mary repeated. She wiped away her tears and blew her nose.

"Why're you crying, Mommy?" came Renee's small voice.

"I'm not, baby. Mommy's got a cold," Mary said, attempting a cover-up.

The expectant mother did catch a cold the next week, as well as a bad case of depression, which lasted long after the birth of her daughter Kimmy. Between school activities, extracurricular ball teams, and dance lessons for the older children, Mary's sanity unraveled. She had no time for herself, no time off from responsibility, and no passion. As a result, she numbed herself with alcohol to make it through the day.

Mary's feelings for her husband went from complacency to contempt. His lack of involvement with his family infuriated her. Their marriage became sexless after the birth of Kimmy, and Lenny spent the whole week in the city, only coming home on weekends.

"He comes waltzing in here like the king of the castle, giving me orders. I swear, things are better when he's away," she told Joanna during a phone conversation. "I can't even stand the way he chews his food."

Joanna let out a sympathetic laugh. "Jesus! You make me glad I'm not married."

In the summer of 1969, Hope learned her first lesson in loss when the Johnson family moved back to Alabama. Tilley's mother was ill, and it fell on her to look after the woman. Tina and Hope said their tearful goodbyes on the sidewalk, promising to write and stay best friends.

Hope moped for weeks, but Joanna understood; she missed Tilley, too. Thankfully, one afternoon Hope came home with a little girl she'd met at the park. Allison was a pretty, blond-haired child with a contagious laugh. Hope had a knack for amusing Allie, and their giggles were a welcome addition to Joanna's home.

Allie's father was a general contractor, and they'd recently moved to the neighborhood. A widower, he relied on his sister Jane, a teacher at the nearby Catholic school and a regular client of Joanna's, to watch Allie.

Joanna first met Mark Rhodes the same afternoon Allie appeared. He came to collect his daughter right after Joanna set a dinner of fried chicken in front of the girls. She offered him a plate. He accepted, and a friendship formed between the two single parents. They established early on that neither of them was interested in romantic relationships. Mark broached the subject one evening after bringing Hope home from the movies.

"Hope wants to show me something," Allie called as the two girls bounded upstairs.

"They could be a while," Joanna chuckled, offering him a glass of iced tea. The two adults made themselves comfortable in the wicker chairs on the front porch.

"How come you never got married again after your husband was killed?" Mark asked.

"Oh, I don't know," she speculated. "It's always been just me and Hope." She turned the question to him. "What about you? How long've you and Allie been on your own?"

"Since the day after she was born. My wife… a blood clot killed her. One day she's a happy new mom and the next day I was planning her funeral."

"Oh! I'm sorry. That must've been so hard."

"It was," he confirmed. "My mother helped with Allie. Mama died last winter, so we moved here, to be closer for my sister to help. Which is funny, because Allie's over here more than she's at Jane's. I get your meaning on it being just the two of you. That's the way it is for Allie and me. Having her gave me a reason to get up in the morning after her mom died."

Mark shuttled the girls around on the weekends to the movies or birthday parties. He also came in handy as a repairman when something broke at Joanna's house. Since she refused to accept payment for babysitting, Mark insisted on building her a new garage. He painted it to match her house and detailed it with gingerbread, for a carriage-house look. Joanna was thrilled.

Hope's unhappiness with school during her last year at Hollywood Elementary concerned Joanna. In first grade, there were seven black students in her school; by fifth grade, Hope was among the only three remaining white students in her class. The Wilsons understood how the Johnson children must have felt as the minority. The Supreme Court–ordered desegregation in Memphis schools failed miserably when, in response, white families moved to neighboring Shelby County or put their children in private schools.

Hope begged Joanna continually to put her in the private Catholic school Allie attended. Finally, she gave in. Recalculating their budget, Joanna made cuts to afford the tuition. They were back to eating a lot of beans, rice, and spaghetti.

But Hope enjoyed school again. Joanna felt like a failure for jumping ship with the rest of the white middle class that didn't have the courage of the thirteen little first-graders who'd broken the color line a decade earlier.

"Pookie Lister called me last week," Mary told Joanna one Sunday when she came into Memphis to meet her for lunch. "Tony broke his neck during training! A linebacker tackled him and he landed wrong. His days of football glory ended the split second he hit the ground."

"Oh my God!" Joanna breathed.

"Tony's having a hard time accepting life in a wheelchair. He's living in Nashville with his parents. I'm not surprised Melinda left him. I never saw her as someone with staying power when things got rough." Mary's voice cracked with emotion.

"Unlike you," Joanna replied.

"I asked Lenny if he wanted a divorce; he said he'd turn it into a bloodbath, if I filed."

"So you're officially separated?"

Mary snorted. "No. He doesn't want anyone at the firm to know he's moved into a condo in the city. He told the children he's traveling continually for his job. He comes by the house for a day or two every other week and still expects me to do his laundry. Lenny's not fooling anyone; the kids tell me all the time, he only comes around for show."

"What a prick. Have you talked to your father?" Joanna asked.

"I can't. Dad considers divorce worse than being a pregnant teenager. I'm trying not to accomplish all of his worst fears for me." Joanna raised an eyebrow. "Don't give me that look. I'm happier with this arrangement. I've hired a housekeeper. It lets me enjoy the kids' activities without the house getting out of control."

When Prissy graduated magna cum laude and passed the bar exam on her first try, she took a job in the state prosecutor's office. Joanna was elated when Prissy called to announce she'd gotten married. Joanna predicted it from the first day Prissy had mentioned William Nelson. He was a handsome young lawyer, a colleague she worked closely with and admired a great deal.

"We didn't want a big wedding. The justice of the peace was sweet, especially since Judge Cramer is Will's mentor," Prissy explained. "As soon as we get a break, we're going to go see Lisa at Berkeley and tour California. Jessie offered to meet us in Carmel."

"It sounds wonderful," Joanna told her.

Prissy and Will's trip didn't happen the way they anticipated. Prissy hadn't been able to get in touch with Lisa for weeks, and the school informed her that her sister had dropped out. She blamed herself for not recognizing the clues something was awry. In the past, when Prissy called and left a message, Lisa always called her back. This time Lisa couldn't be found.

Prissy filed a missing persons report and waited. Months later they were horrified when the police found Lisa living in a flophouse with a group of strung-out hippies. Sadly, Lisa was pregnant and spaced out on hallucinogenic drugs. The newlyweds wasted no time getting on a plane to the West Coast and took Lisa to a hospital. After days of begging, they convinced her to come back to Nashville.

Lisa gave birth to a remarkably healthy baby girl she named Summer. Lisa turned out to be a pathetic mother, in Prissy's opinion. When Summer was only three months old, Lisa began randomly disappearing for days on end, returning without explanation or apology. This threw Prissy and Will's life into turmoil, as they tried to balance their careers and care for Summer.

"We've hired a nanny," she told Joanna after the fifth time Lisa took off. "I've got a full caseload right now and so does Will. I can't drop everything because she's split again."

"I thought things were better after she went to rehab?" Joanna questioned.

"They were for a little while, but she flaked out on me again. I'm doing everything I can to help her and half the time I feel like she's throwing it back in my face."

"Have you asked her to sign over Summer to you? This has got to be confusin' for that child."

"I've pleaded. She uses her baby as a pawn to get what she wants out of me. Frankly, I'd be worried to death if, one of these times, Lisa takes her with when she leaves. God knows what could happen to her." Prissy knew all too well how a drug-using mother could damage their children in the most heinous ways. She'd prosecuted many cases of child abuse and neglect. "Legally, there're steps I could take. But she's my sister. I wish she'd get her shit together."

Finally, by the spring of 1973 Prissy and Will had to take legal action. Lisa tripped off to Florida for six months, then came back threatening to take the now three-year-old Summer and leave the state. Prissy warned her she'd have her declared an unfit mother. Two weeks later, without warning, their attorney phoned informing them Lisa had signed papers legally giving them custody of Summer, ending the struggle but alienating the two sisters for life.

Chapter 42

Catherine sat next to Wendell on the bleachers at the ballpark while Tom warmed up in the batter's box. It was a beautiful spring day, warm sunshine and the sweet smell of honeysuckle gently carried on the breeze.

"Why isn't Jack here today?" Wendell accused.

"He wanted to be. He's in Mobile at our truck stop. This oil shortage has him traveling a lot. We've both had some sleepless nights lately," she explained.

"The whole oil shortage is politically driven, Cat. Hang tough, it'll work itself out."

"Tell that to the customers who were paying thirty-eight cents a gallon last year and now pay fifty-five cents." She paused, studying him. "You feeling okay, Daddy? You look tired and your color's a little ashy. When was the last time you saw the doctor?"

"I had a physical a couple of months ago. I'm healthy as a horse," he grumbled.

"And stubborn as a mule." She patted him on the back lovingly. "I'll bet he scolded you about smoking and fattening foods."

"If you can't enjoy life, what's the point?" He puffed his cigar.

Tom Wyatt came to bat. On the second pitch, he slammed a line drive, which the left fielder chased; Tom held at second base. The next batter struck out and retired the side.

"Maybe next inning," the grandfather muttered. Later, when Tom approach the batter's box, he nodded at his grandfather. Wendell gave him a thumbs-up, then cursed under his breath when the pitcher intentionally walked the boy.

❧

"I need to ask you a favor," Mark said while he and Joanna cleared a spot with rakes and pickaxes for the flagstone courtyard he'd offered to help her with.

"I'm a little obligated to say yes to whatever it is, at this point, since you're not charging for materials or labor." Joanna laughed.

"Graduation from middle school's a big deal to Allie. Would you take her to buy a dress? Jane offered, but Allie pretended to stick her finger down her throat at my sister's ideas."

Joanna smiled. "That sounds like Allie. I'll be happy to take her."

"Thanks. I know as much about teenage fashion as I do about handling her mood swings. One minute she's bubbly, the next she's bawling over some boy named Leon."

"Leon Harper." Joanna knew the situation. "Cutest boy in the eighth grade. Allie's madly in love. He won't give her the time of day."

"Her exact words were, 'He doesn't know I exist.' I'm not sure how to deal with this."

"Don't worry, it's merely a crush. I doubt she's settin' herself up to chase unavailable men. Besides, you should be glad she isn't like Hope. I'm not too happy about the punks she's bringin' around." The boys had started to notice Hope in fifth grade. Now at almost fourteen, Hope's voluptuous figure not only attracted the horny teenagers, but also generated honks and lewd comments from grown men when they saw her walking on the street.

Mark turned the conversation back to the landscaping project. "This looks good. Now we have to level it." Joanna worked for weeks to get her backyard project finished for the barbecue graduation party she'd organized for Hope and Allie.

When the day finally came, the girls, adorned in pale-blue caps and gowns, graduated from middle school in a formal ceremony. The day turned into a potluck with twenty families celebrating in Joanna's backyard. The smell of mouthwatering southern barbecue filled the neighborhood. The feast consisted of everything from ribs, chicken, hot dogs, and hamburgers to fruit bowls, salads, watermelon, and homemade ice cream.

The day was perfect for a yard party, with the temperature at eighty and a light breeze. Best of all, Jessie had flown in for a weeklong visit. Prissy's little family came and so did Mary and her children. The afternoon went by in a blur for Joanna as she made sure the guests were enjoying themselves.

By nine in the evening, the four old friends were the only ones left at the house. Mark and Will took all the children to the movie theater to see *The Golden Voyage of Sinbad*, finally giving the women some much-needed girlfriend time.

"If not for Will, I don't think I would've survived Lisa's shenanigans. It's funny, we weren't going to have children. Now we can't imagine our lives without Summer," Prissy admitted.

"You haven't heard from Lisa since she gave you guardianship?" Jessie asked, pouring herself another frozen margarita from the pitcher on the picnic table.

Prissy shook her head. "I don't even know where she is. Maybe if I'd protected her better when she was young, she wouldn't be like this now."

"Jesus! Prissy, what more could you have done?" Joanna admonished.

Prissy sighed. "Her behavior's classic from child sexual abuse victims."

Mary interjected, "You're the only one who knows if you've used all the emotional resources you can afford." Everyone's attention turned to Mary. The tone of her voice abruptly halted the conversation. Crickets chirped in the distance. The patio candles, flickered in the breeze.

"Are we talkin' about your exhausted emotional resources?" Joanna asked.

"I'm trying to decide if I've done something crazy," Mary put forward.

"Do tell," Jessie coaxed disbelievingly.

"My parents took the kids to Mass on Easter and I went to see Tony."

"What prompted this?" Joanna asked, blindsided.

"His mother called me and begged me to talk to him. He's been paralyzed over four years and he's not moving forward. I could go into detail, but the bottom line is he's suicidal."

"How's it your problem?" Jessie asked. "When you saw him last, he was shitty to you."

"I know." Mary stopped Jessie. "He apologized. He was crying; it was pitiful. In my heart, I know I'm going to follow through with the promise I made him."

"Which was?" Joanna asked.

"That I'd try to find our son. Our baby is the only one he'll ever have."

"How do you plan to do that? The adoption records are sealed," Joanna reminded her.

"There're ways to get information besides court documents; I plan to go talk to Sister Bridget, casual-like. People let things slip when they're comfortable with the conversation."

"Why do ya wanna open Pandora's box?" Jessie questioned.

"I'm simply going to see what I can find out."

"I want to go with you," Prissy chimed in. "You do realize the Frances Weston

Home violated our rights, as well as using psychologically soul-crushing tactics and coercing most of the girls into signing away their babies." Prissy sounded like a lawyer.

"This is what I'm sayin', Pandora's box," Jessie warned.

"So you never think about your baby boy?" Mary asked.

Jessie defended herself. "I think about him sometimes. I think of Fitch holdin' him as if he was yesterday's garbage and how helpless I felt. I vowed I'd never feel that way again. If you go pokin' around, you're liable to rouse shit you can't handle. What about your husband?"

"He won't find out. We barely talk these days. What'd you do if your son came looking for you? He'd be sixteen now, old enough to look for answers," Mary shot back.

"I'd talk to him; he'd see I'm not mother material," Jessie replied offhandedly.

"Well, I think about it all the time. I want to find him before he finds me. I'm tired of feeling like something's stalking me," Mary told them.

"This explains why you haven't had time to talk lately," Joanna scolded.

"With five kids, I meet myself coming and going." Joanna frowned at Mary. "Okay, I knew you wouldn't approve," Mary admitted. "I've got to do this. Tony promised that if I help him, he'll straighten up, go back to school. But it's not only for Tony; it's for me, too. There isn't a day that goes by I don't think of our baby. I'll feel better if I know he has a good life."

"What if he doesn't have a good life?" Jessie asked.

"Then I'd want to know. Maybe I can make it better."

"Well, the next time you conjure an insane idea, fill me in as you go. It's not like I've ever been able to talk you out of anythin' once your mind is set," Joanna huffed.

The next morning Prissy and Mary left for Knoxville. Will and Summer went back to Nashville, while Joanna and Jessie hung out at the house with Hope and Mary's brood. The kids were playing in the sprinkler while Joanna and Jessie played cards at the picnic table. They were surprised when Mark and Allie came from the side yard.

"I didn't expect to see you today," Joanna told Mark as Allie ran to be with Hope.

"I thought you wanted me to take a look at your car," he reminded her.

"I do. The keys are in my purse on the counter," she told him. Mark headed to the house.

In a moment, he came back out, keys in his hand. "Got 'em." He started across the yard, calling to his daughter, "Allie, your swimsuit's in the car, girl."

"What's the story on Mark, the widower?" Jessie asked. "He's pretty handy, huh?"

Joanna could almost read Jessie's dirty mind. "It's not like that, Jess. Our daughters have been best friends for the last four years."

"Do you mean to tell me you haven't jumped his fine ass? Oh my God, have you taken a good look at his body? I could take a bite out of that!"

"Jessie!" Joanna shook her head.

"So he's available?"

"Don't, Jessie; he's not one of your disposable one-night stands. He's not like that."

"You're awful familiar with him," Jessie commented.

"Whaddaya mean by that?"

"I mean, he walks in and out of your house pretty comfortable. You let him go through your purse—most husbands don't have that privilege. Do you really expect me to believe there's nothin' goin' on?"

"Nothing."

"How much time do you spend with him?"

"I see him pretty much every day. Allie's over here most of the time. We go to the movies on Sunday afternoons, like Mary and I used to. We're close friends. Nothing more."

"And he isn't seein' anyone?" Jessie asked.

"No."

"What does he do for sex?"

"I don't know!" Joanna laughed. "And don't you dare ask him."

"Seems like a huge waste to me," Jessie concluded.

Chapter 43

After seven hours in the car, Prissy and Mary arrived at the Gothic house that had once been their prison. A chill ran down Mary's spine and landed in the pit of her stomach, just like sixteen years earlier. Sister Bridget opened the door, hugging them. She ushered them into the administrator's office. It was her office now since Mrs. Fitch had finally retired.

"I couldn't have a lawyer walk into my office at a more perfect time. I have quite a mess and inspectors coming next month. I need some legal advice." Sister Bridget went on to explain that after going through her predecessor's books, she'd found irregularities.

"Do you think Fitch was cooking the books?" Mary asked.

"Could be, but I need a lawyer and an accountant's opinion before I make accusations."

"I'll be happy to help you," Prissy offered.

"Me too," Mary joined in.

Sister Bridget pulled out her files and showed them what she had so far.

"I think we should go back further in her records, randomly pick some years, and identify a pattern," Prissy suggested. Sister Bridget gave them access to the dusty file room on the third floor while she checked in a new girl. Prissy pulled financial records from boxes for the years when Mrs. Fitch oversaw the home. Mary opened the cabinets containing the residents' folders, which were filed by year.

"Good Lord, Prissy! Look at all the girls that've come through here. It's staggering."

"Multiplied by hundreds of homes for unwed mothers, and the number of adoptions is in the hundreds of thousands. All those records are sealed; there's fuel for a firestorm. Places like this are definitely one of America's dirty secrets."

"Finally! Here it is," Mary exclaimed, locating her folder under 1957. "My baby went to a foster home in Nashville, Mrs. Rineholdt." She copied the address and put it in her pocket. Her file went back in the drawer before Sister Bridget returned.

"Have you found anything yet?" the sister asked.

"Yes, I think I've figured out one way she was siphoning money. Look here," Prissy revealed. "When I left here in January 1957, there were thirty-three girls in residence. Fitch's records show thirty-five. If she was inflating the numbers, she could've gotten more money from the state. Now look at this receipt for fence repairs. See how this nine and that nine don't match? Looks like she altered a one to a nine. She could've pocketed eight hundred dollars."

Sister Bridget frowned. "I didn't want to be right. So where do we go from here?"

"I think you have enough to launch an investigation. I can run this by a friend in the Justice Department since this involves government funding. In the meantime, follow the money and see where she committed fraud by claiming nonexistent residents."

"That's not the only problem I have. I've found serious safety violations. Our enrollment is down and I don't anticipate enough inflowing cash to bring this place back to compliance."

"Do you think it's because of legalized abortion?" Prissy asked.

"Maybe a little, but we've had a steady decline in the last five years, mainly due to society being more accepting of teenage pregnancy. A lot more girls are keeping their babies."

"Attitudes have changed drastically since we were here," Mary added.

"That's a change for the better as far as I'm concerned," Sister Bridget agreed. She suggested they continue their discussion over dinner at a nearby restaurant.

A short while later, they sat across from the nun who had aged, but still retained a youthful sparkle to her eyes. Their conversation turned to the other nuns who'd been at the home.

"Sister Mary Joseph passed away four years ago, Sister Ruth transferred to the home in Atlanta, and Sister Eugenia went to a nursing home last year. She's ninety-two and has dementia. She says crazy things these days. I still visit her every week."

"What kind of crazy things?" Mary asked.

"She screams she's lost something and gets angry if you try to help her find it."

"It doesn't sound like she'll be much help with a case against Mrs. Fitch," Prissy told her.

"No, she isn't coherent. She's paranoid someone's trying to kill her but won't say who."

"I can guess," Mary surmised.

"Mrs. Fitch, I know," the nun concurred. "She knows things none of the rest of us were privy to. But there's days she can't remember her own name."

"That's too bad; you could use more witnesses to corroborate your claims," Prissy lamented. The next day the two women drove back to Memphis.

"We're going to Nashville tomorrow. Prissy's going to hand over the evidence to a friend in the Justice Department. I'm going to find the foster home where my baby went," Mary reported to Jessie and Joanna. "I've arranged for a nanny to watch my kids while I'm gone."

"You gonna stay with your parents?" Joanna asked.

"No, I'll be at Prissy's. I'm not ready to face their condemnation at present."

"With any luck we can issue subpoenas for Fitch's personal financial records, as well as the records of the companies who provided services to the home. If Sister Bridget's right, Fitch will be facing serious jail time for fraud and embezzlement," Prissy announced.

Jessie laughed. "I wanna be in the courtroom for that."

Joanna crossed her arms and let out a sigh. Mary hugged her. "I know you're worried for me. But whatever I discover, it can't be worse than not knowing."

Mary found herself on the other side of Nashville from her childhood home. She drove down the residential street, looking at the house numbers until she pulled to the curb in front of a home undergoing renovations. Scaffolding was wired to the house like braces on a child's teeth. A man ripping wood on a table saw by the garage cut off the power as Mary approached.

"Excuse me, sorry to interrupt. Is this Mrs. Rineholdt's house?"

"Used to be. I'm the new owner, Emmett Tango," he said. "Mrs. Rineholdt died a while back. What a mess. She was a pack rat; junk and papers I'm still burnin'."

"Papers? What kind of papers?" Mary asked hopefully.

"I guess this place used to be a foster home. There were rooms of files on the kids."

"What'd you do with the files?" Mary asked.

"I've been burning them in the furnace when I get extra time," he said offhandedly.

"Do you mind if I take a look?" Mary asked, fearing her records were already destroyed.

"Knock yourself out. Hey, take anything you want; it's less I'll have to burn." He showed her to the basement entrance and Mary descended the stairs with her heart beating in her throat. She pulled the cord of a dangling bulb. It illuminated the space of the eighty-year-old unfinished basement. Exposed floor joists overhead resembled the bones of an ancient beast. Boxes stood stacked on one side of the now quiet furnace, while other boxes had collapsed, spilling their contents on the floor. Mary saw boxes labeled 52 and 55, deciding that this indicated the year.

Mary desperately looked for the box labeled 57. Her heart sank when she spotted it, empty, behind the pile of papers littering the floor. In a last-ditch effort, she poked through the pile—then almost screamed when she found one from January 1957. With renewed hope, she grabbed empty boxes and collected the papers on the floor.

It took weeks for Mary to go through the documents. None of the birthmothers' names were included, and there were endless records of diaper changes, eating schedules, and sleeping habits. She used the color of ink, dates, and type of paper to piece together the puzzle on each particular child, separating them into files that made sense.

Prissy nearly dropped the phone when Mary's high-pitched enthusiasm came through the earpiece: "I think I found him. I'm coming to Nashville. I don't want Joanna to know anything until I know for sure."

"Why not?" the lawyer asked.

Mary lowered the boom: "Because I think Catherine and Jack Wyatt adopted my son." Prissy sat at her desk as Mary explained the evidence. "The Wyatts were given a baby boy on Sunday, April twenty-first. I've put together two weeks of records that match when my baby arrived at the foster home."

"Oh, this is dangerous," Prissy warned. "What if Catherine Wyatt won't talk to you?"

"I've already phoned her. I'm going to her house tomorrow. I didn't get specific; I mentioned I knew she'd adopted a child and I wanted to ask her about the experience."

"How can you be sure this is your baby?" Prissy asked.

"Mrs. Rineholdt kept extensive notes on each child, the outfit they were wearing, and any possessions given to the adoptive parents. You'd be surprised how many birthmothers gave their babies a stuffed animal or a trinket. I gave mine a medal of St. Nicolas."

"The Wyatts' baby was in possession of a medallion," Prissy said, connecting the dots.

~

The next day in the Wyatts' living room Catherine handed Mary a china teacup. "Tom grew up knowing he's adopted."

"Was he ever curious about his birth parents?" Mary added a cube of sugar to her tea.

"We've all been curious. I've wondered who gave him his dark hair and brown eyes." *That'd be Tony*, Mary thought. Catherine continued, "And an even bigger concern is the health issues that run in those families. I recently lost my father to a massive heart attack. It's important to know if your child's predisposed to certain diseases."

Mary nodded. "I'm so sorry to hear about Wendell; I didn't know."

"I'm curious, are you here because your daughter's pregnant and you're considering adoption? Or is it because you relinquished a baby?" Catherine asked compassionately.

"One I surrendered," Mary confessed, producing the file, convinced it corresponded to her son. "I have reason to believe I may be Tom's birthmother."

"Oh, Mary," Cat sympathized. "I wish I could tell you that's true, but it's not."

"When's Tom's birthday?" Mary asked, confident for a match.

"April first, 1957."

"April Fools' Day? My son was born on April third. Maybe there's an error."

"Here, let me show you something." Mary followed Catherine to the dining room, where the adoptive mother searched through a box on the table.

"What's this?" Mary asked.

"Paperwork from my father's safe. Here it is," she answered. Retrieving an envelope, she produced Tom's original birth certificate. "Even though it was a closed adoption, my father was very resourceful, as I'm finding out."

The mother's name on the document was Jessica Devereaux. "Jessie?" Mary proclaimed. She looked at the birthdate: April 1, 1957. "This is wrong! Jessie's baby was born February seventeenth."

"Did you know his mother?" Catherine asked hopefully.

"The file I have says Tommy had a St. Nicholas medallion. Do you have it? Can I see it?"

"Of course." Catherine went to the china cabinet and handed it to Mary. With trembling hands she examined it. It had a cheap dime-store chain with a broken clasp.

The back door slammed, and a young man's voice called, "Mom?"

"I'm in here, honey," Cat returned. In an instant, a tall, handsome teenager stood in the archway to the dining room.

"Oh, sorry to interrupt," he apologized. Mary's heart skipped a beat as she looked into the eyes she recognized. They were Joanna's eyes. "The guys and I are going to the batting cages."

"Okay. Who's driving?" Catherine asked.

"I am." He left the room.

"Be careful, dinner's at six thirty." Catherine turned her attention back to Mary, who stood as frozen as Lot's wife, paralyzed by shock, punished for looking back. "Mary? Are you all right?"

"Yes," Mary snapped back to the present, "I must be mistaken. I'm so sorry."

"Do you know where Jessica Devereaux is?" Catherine asked expectantly.

"Yes. Let me talk to her first. Do you have a copy of your adoption papers handy?"

"Right here," Catherine handed an envelope to Mary. The document seemed standard, until she came to the signature of the lawyer who'd handled the adoption. The rush of shock hit again. Signed in black ink was the name Leonard Hollan, her husband.

Chapter 44

"I have a bad feeling, Catherine," Flora warned after Mary made a hasty exit. Cat inspected the envelopes in the box her father's lawyer had dropped off. She'd looked through them briefly the other day, but the pain of losing Wendell was still too fresh. Cat set aside the stocks, bonds, and investments. Finally, she came to a file halting her search. She let the photographs of a young woman fall to the table.

"Sometimes it's better to let sleepin' dogs lie," Flora advised.

Cat examined the photo of a girl with long brown hair, holding hands with Jack. On the back, scrawled in her father's handwriting, was the word *Weasel* and a phone number.

"Do you know who she is?" Catherine asked.

"No. But seein' how friendly she is with Jack, I could guess."

Cat went to the phone and dialed the number.

"Spanky's," a gruff voice answered, with music in the background.

"Is Weasel there?" she asked, taking a chance.

"He doesn't usually show up till six," the voice answered.

"Thanks." Cat disconnected. She located Spanky's in the phone book. It was a neighborhood bar in a seedy section of town. "Can you make dinner? I'm going to get to the bottom of this."

"I'll take care of the cookin', but maybe you oughta talk to Jack before you go runnin' off, puttin' yourself in danger." Flora spoke too late; Catherine had already made her way upstairs.

Catherine entered the smoke-filled cavern of Spanky's Pub. Dressed in jeans and a leather jacket, with too much makeup on, she fit in at this dive. At the bar she ordered a stiff drink.

"Do you know where Weasel is?" The bartender nodded his head in the direction of a corner table. "Thanks." Giving the barkeep a tip, she made her way over to the booth. Without waiting for an invitation, she sat at the table and asked, "Can I buy you a drink?"

Looking up with the sleepy eyes of a drunk, he answered, "Sure."

"My name is…" Catherine started.

"I know who you are, Mrs. Wyatt. Wendell Langley was your old man," he said coherently. "What I don't know is why you wanna buy me a drink."

"That's simple. I need information, and you're the person who can give it to me."

"Anything's possible, for a price." Cat pulled the photographs from her oversized handbag. Weasel looked at them and nodded. She placed money on the table with her hand covering most of it; with a shift of her eyes, she told him to spill what he knew.

"Seeing your old man's dead, God rest his soul, and he can't break every bone in my body…" Weasel paused. "Her name's Joanna Wilson. This was a long time ago… whoa, let me think… 1956. Your father had me tail your husband. Jack was keeping company with her."

Catherine breathed shallowly. "She looks pregnant; is the baby Jack's?"

"Yes." Catherine took her hand off the money and the informant snatched it like a rodent after cheese, stuffing it into his pocket without counting it. "I don't think you wanna know the rest of the story." The man's hands trembled.

"Yes, I do." She took more money from her pocket and laid it on the table.

"Jack sent her to a home for unwed mothers. Your father was furious and I'm not certain, but the next thing you know, Jack's gas station explodes."

Blinking back tears, she asked. "What happened to the baby?"

"I honestly don't know," Weasel told her. "I didn't hear from your father again until six months later when he asked me to find Joanna."

"But this picture here is dated April 1959. She's obviously pregnant again."

"Yes, ma'am, I took that photo. I was told she'd married a military man, killed in Southeast Asia. I couldn't confirm it. In July that year she had a baby girl. She has a beauty parlor in her home in Memphis, Hollywood Hair."

Catherine wrote the information on the back of the photograph. Her mind was doing the math: Had Jack gone to Memphis in October 1958? That's when they purchased the land for the truck stop. She raised her hand off the wad of bills; Weasel ignored the money.

"I told your father I confirmed she was a war widow. But I didn't. I watched her for over a year. Jack didn't come around at all. He wasn't cheating on you in 1959. I didn't wanna be responsible for anyone getting hurt." The informant reluctantly pulled out the money he'd taken earlier and put it in front of her. "I don't want your money; all you're buying is heartbreak." The frail man put on his hat and left the bar.

Catherine gulped her drink and ordered another. Sickening realization raced through her as she processed the truth.

Immediately after having tea with Catherine Wyatt, Mary and Prissy drove to Knoxville to talk to Sister Eugenia. She was seated in her bed when they entered her room. "Hi, Sister Eugenia, it's Mary. Do you remember me?" she asked, coming to the woman's bedside. Prissy took a seat in a chair by the window. The elderly nun examined Mary through cloudy eyes.

"You're one of the girls from the home. Mary, you had a sweet baby boy!"

Mary shot a hopeful glance at Prissy and continued. "That's right! I'm so glad you remember. Do you remember Jessie? She's a redhead. She and I were there at the same time."

"Jessie's a bad girl, like a wildcat." The old nun put out her hands like claws and made a hissing sound. She seemed to forget Mary and with trembling hands spooned a glob of chocolate pudding out of the Snack Pack, barely getting it to her mouth.

"Do you remember Joanna and what happened to her baby?" Mary asked.

"I like chocolate pudding the best," the white-haired woman declared.

"Me too." Mary tried to engage her again. "Jessie didn't like Mrs. Fitch. Did you?"

She scowled and shook her head. "Evil woman. God's just, He'll punish her for murder."

"Who did she murder?" The nun stared straight ahead still scowling. "Did she murder Joanna's baby?" Mary asked softly.

"She sold him," the old woman confided, staring directly at Mary now.

"Did she murder Jessie's baby?" Mary held her breath.

"She choked him with his own umbilical cord."

"She told Joanna it was her baby," Mary finished.

"Someone with lots of money bought that baby," the nun confirmed. "Don't know who, someone powerful, who could squish me like a bug."

"Did anyone else know?" Prissy chimed in, hoping for a credible witness.

"The fancy lawyer and the foster home knew."

Mary's head throbbed. She'd suspected Lenny's knowledge of the switch when he processed the adoption; this added kidnapping, and accomplice to murder, to his crimes.

"There's more than fifty babies buried in the woods. She killed them all, 'cause they was sickly and not adoptable. Evil woman!" Sister Eugenia confessed.

"Sweet Mother of God," Mary whispered, making the sign of the cross over her chest.

"Why didn't you tell anyone this before?" Prissy asked angrily.

"I wrote it in a notebook; gave it to the Virgin Mary. Don't tell. She'll kill me to keep me silent." Wide-eyed, the nun looked around, expecting murderous Louise Fitch to appear.

After leaving the nursing home, Prissy and Mary went directly to Sister Bridget and relayed their conversation with Sister Eugenia.

"Babies buried in the woods? Sounds far-fetched," Sister Bridget challenged.

"There's only one way to find out; you got a shovel?" Mary asked, defiantly.

Sister Bridget wrinkled her brow, "It's my responsibility. I'll call the sheriff."

"Is it possible Dr. Miller was in on it, too?" Prissy asked the nun.

"I'd hate to think so. He doesn't seem like the type of man who'd do that. He's retired now. He and his wife live in the same house they've had for the last twenty years."

"It's late; we should talk to him in the morning," Mary suggested.

Prissy updated the nun on the investigation under way. "Louise Fitch's financials should be coming through any day. They've allocated four investigators."

Bridget let out a heavy sigh. "I'll meet with the bishop tomorrow. I'm sure he's going to want this handled quietly without casting a shadow on the church. I've discovered she was charging families for services covered by Catholic Charities and the government. The fees here were double those of other homes. I feel bad I didn't realize what Mrs. Fitch was doing. If I'd paid attention, maybe I could've done something."

"You're doing something now," Prissy told her.

After leaving the home, the former residents got a room at the first motel they saw. Mary lay staring at the ceiling above her bed while Prissy phoned an investigator in Nashville. When she ended the call she told Mary, "They're getting the ball rolling to investigate Lenny. If he's capable of baby selling, he's probably guilty of other crimes."

"What am I going to tell my kids?" Mary lamented, covering her face with her hands. "I never understood why Lenny discouraged my friendship with Joanna and Jessie. He must've realized the connection from the beginning."

"Which means he probably figured out you met them in Knoxville," Prissy deduced.

"He never let on. What a cool liar he is," Mary marveled. She switched gears. "We need to let Jessie know what's going on."

"What we need is a confession from Fitch. I'll book all three of us flights to Florida after we talk to Jessie," Prissy said.

When Cat arrived home, Tom was in the den watching *The Carol Burnett Show*.

"What's with the outfit, Mom?" the teenager asked, noticing her slumming style.

"Where's your father?" Catherine ignored his question.

"He's in the garage with Uncle Alex; something's wrong with the timing in my car," the boy explained, turning his attention back to the TV show.

Taking the photographic evidence from her purse, she made her way to where the two men were closing the hood of her son's 1967 red Ford Mustang.

"Good news! We got it running with precision now." Alex smiled with pride.

Catherine slapped the photographs on the hood of the car and, looking directly into Jack's eyes, demanded, "Tell me about Joanna Wilson."

Jack diverted his eyes to the pictures Wendell had threatened him with. Putting his hands on his hips, Jack exhaled heavily.

"Oh shit," Alex breathed. Her husband's friend took a few steps toward the door.

"Don't you dare go anywhere. Something tells me you know all about this!" Catherine barked. Alex stopped and waited for Jack to answer.

"It was a long time ago, Cat," Jack began.

"I can see that by the date stamp, October 1956."

"You were sick back then. I was lonely," Jack started to explain.

"She was carrying your baby, wasn't she?" Catherine pointed at the picture of the smiling, pregnant girl. Guilt flashed on Jack's face. "That's just great! Here I was, begging you to adopt a child, and you were hiding away an underaged girl in a home for unwed mothers. What happened to the baby, Jack?"

"The baby died," he barked angrily. Catherine, taken aback by his answer, flushed red while Jack continued with a more even tone as he told her the whole story.

"If you were in the hospital, how did you find out?" Cat asked, scornfully.

"I sent Alex to Knoxville to talk to her, but she was already gone," her husband answered. Catherine turned to Alex, who nodded confirmation. She crossed her arms, trying to decide where to vent her wrath next.

"Don't be angry with Alex, Cat. You should know, he punched me in the face when I first told him about Joanna." Cat looked at Alex, who shrugged in his own defense.

"Did you ever see her again?" Catherine asked, fuming.

"Once, a couple of years later. I haven't seen her since," Jack answered honestly.

"When you bought the property for the truck stop in Memphis? October 1958?"

"I saw her on the street. We talked, she told me herself what'd happened with the baby."

"Did you have sex with her?" Jack didn't answer. "Did you fuck her?" Cat demanded.

"Yes," Jack painfully admitted. "I never saw her again."

"So, you're telling me you didn't know she gave birth to a daughter in July of 1959?" Catherine produced the later picture of Joanna, pregnant with Hope.

"I don't know anything about this." Jack examined the photograph.

"Is Joanna Wilson's daughter yours?" Catherine asked.

"It's possible," Jack conceded.

"I want you out of my house tonight," Catherine ordered, enraged.

"Out of the house?" Jack's mouth dropped open.

"I can understand you finding comfort or solace, or whatever you want to call it, when I was sick. But after everything we've been through? In the fall of 1958 I was one hundred percent supporting you." Catherine's voice cracked with emotion. "You need to get off my property." She left the photographs on the hood of the car and went back into the house.

Alex looked at Jack with disbelief. "Are you going to punch me again or give me a place to stay until she's had time to cool off?"

Chapter 45

"Dr. Miller confirmed it was your baby who died, not Joanna's. He's willing to testify in court," Prissy told Jessie, who drove the rental car from the Tampa airport. Mary, in the front passenger's seat unfolded a Florida state map, acting as navigator for the journey.

"That bitch murdered my baby and let Joanna grieve for a son whose been livin' with his father all these years!" Jessie darkened with anger.

"In Fort Myers we need to stop by the Lee County Sheriff's Department. There'll be an arrest warrant and police backup. I'll wear a wire and we'll talk to her first," Prissy explained.

"I wanna wear the wire and be the one to take her down," Jessie objected.

"That's fine." Prissy shrugged.

"Knowin' Fitch, she won't wanna miss rubbing my face in it," Jessie speculated. By the time they were following the sheriff's deputies out to Captiva Island, it was pouring rain.

"This sucks!" Jessie had the windshield wipers on full blast and still had trouble seeing the road for the deluge. The police cars pulled to a stop next to a long lane surrounded by thick, Florida foliage. When an officer ran back to their car, Jessie opened the window.

"We'll hang back and listen and record. The house is at the end of the road," he directed.

"Are you sure you can hear with this thing between my boobs?" Jessie asked, tilting her head to speak directly into the microphone. The cop in the car gave a thumbs-up.

"We've heard every word you've said since we left the station," the drenched police officer confirmed, chuckling.

"Great!" Jessie bristled sarcastically. "I guess I can't take back my comment about your partner's nice ass. Seriously, if she pulls a gun, I expect y'all to bust in like the Kool-Aid man."

"We've got you covered," he assured her. Jessie closed the window and proceeded to a cul-de-sac with several brightly painted beach houses.

"Hey, over there, L. FITCH is on the mailbox," Prissy said, pointing. Huddling together under an umbrella, the three friends took the path to the stairs of a wraparound porch, which overlooked a spectacular view of the Gulf of Mexico on a good day. At the sunroom door, they didn't knock but rushed in. Louise Fitch, shrouded with an afghan, hunched on the wicker couch.

"Are you receiving guests this afternoon?" Mary looked at the woman hatefully.

"Come in. I don't get many visitors these days," the former administrator answered.

"Except for delivery boys," Jessie muttered, observing the discarded take-out containers littering her dirty house. She stared at the old, huddled-in-a-heap tormentor. Fitch's thinning hair indicated sickness. Through the open French doors, dirty dishes piled high in the sink and junk overtook every horizontal surface. A cat chased a palmetto bug bigger than the roaches Jessie had stomped in the worst dives she stayed.

"I have to say, you look like hell." Jessie spoke as if paying a compliment. The redhead cleared away the newspaper on the couch next to Mrs. Fitch and sat.

"Lung cancer. I suppose cancer treatment's closer to being in hell than anyplace on earth. Except the Frances Weston Home for Unwed Mothers," Fitch answered coldly.

"I didn't know you smoked." Jessie pointed at the overflowing ashtray.

"Everyone smoked during World War Two. I'd quit when I took the job at the home; that's how I could always smell it on you. It was the cigarettes I confiscated from your cabinet that got me started again." The older woman chuckled at the irony, then coughed as if choking on her own lungs. Once she recovered, she said to Prissy and Mary, who were still standing by the door, "Where're my manners? Please, make yourselves comfortable. There's wine in the refrigerator. By this time of day you'll be dying for a drink," she offered Jessie.

"Sure, why not," Jessie replied. Going to the kitchen, she came back with four Dixie cups and poured for everyone.

Mrs. Fitch tossed hers back like a seasoned drinker and started, "Now that we have the pleasantries out of the way, I've been informed I'm being investigated for improprieties at the home in Knoxville."

"How much did you get for sellin' Joanna's son?" Jessie asked, getting right to the point.

"Ten thousand," Mrs. Fitch answered, pouring herself another glass of wine.

"Why'd you do it?" Mary asked naively.

"To buy this place and retire in sunny Florida." The rain beat hard on the sunroom roof.

"Who was the buyer?" Prissy asked.

"I don't know. I was paid for putting the brat in Mrs. Rineholdt's foster home in Nashville. I don't know where she placed him. I only dealt with the lawyer."

"Leonard Hollan?" Mary asked.

"Yes," the sick woman answered, coughing again.

"Why didn't you just switch babies? Why'd you have to murder mine?" Jessie asked.

"You've been talking to Sister Eugenia. Your son was sickly; probably brain-damaged from the alcohol you drank on the sly. He'd've been impossible to place. Joanna didn't intend to surrender her baby, but if the boy was dead… well, she'd never cause me any more trouble."

Red-faced, Jessie narrowed her eyes. "What gives you the right to play God?"

"Somebody had to. God sure as hell wasn't looking out for me, you, or your babies! I guarantee, Joanna's son has a better life than she'd ever provide. I did him a favor."

"That wasn't your decision to make," Jessie corrected.

"Sure it was. And I made it based on what was best for everyone involved." The rain torrent slowed and then stopped. A gusty wind tugged at the exhausted storm clouds.

"How many did you murder because they weren't perfect?" Prissy demanded angrily.

"Eugenia's tattling again? If I'd been there the night your baby was born, I'd've put her out of her misery, instead of suffer in an institution." Prissy tensed as if she might pummel Fitch.

"Somehow, I was expectin' it to be harder to get you to spill your guts," Jessie told her.

"It doesn't matter. They tell me I've got two months to live. I'll never see the inside of a courtroom. Besides, basing this on the ravings of a crazy old nun doesn't make much of a case."

"That's where you're mistaken. Sister Bridgett has called in the sheriff's department. They're investigating the woods behind the house as we speak," Prissy gloated.

"Dr. Miller will testify Jessie's baby died, not Joanna's," Mary told her.

"He didn't see me wrap the cord around the baby's neck. There's a big difference between stillborn and proving I choked the brat."

"That may be true," Jessie allowed, smiling. "But now we have a recorded confession of baby brokering." The redhead unbuttoned her blouse to show Fitch the wire. "I think you guys have enough to issue the arrest warrant," Jessie said into the microphone. The sun broke through the clouds, producing a sunset painted purple with rims of orange, like fire in the sky.

"I'll scream entrapment," Mrs. Fitch warned.

"It doesn't matter," Jessie heckled her. "Like you said, you'll be dead in two months. I'm gonna make sure you spend it in a jail cell, not sitting here enjoying the sunsets." The two officers entered the house and read Louise Fitch her Miranda rights.

"Give me a minute to change my clothes," she stipulated, hoisting herself from the couch, revealing her plaid flannel pajamas. The cops exchanged wary expressions. "Look at me. Do you think I'm a flight risk?" Mrs. Fitch shuffled off toward her bedroom.

Mary, Jessie, and Prissy took an early flight on the Fourth of July, 1973, from Tampa to Memphis. When they arrived at Joanna's, she was in the kitchen, cooking.

"Jessie!" Joanna hugged her. "When'd you get back in town?"

"This morning." Jessie returned her hug.

"Well, this is a surprise. I wasn't sure you two were comin', since I haven't talked to you in a week." Joanna turned back to the preparation of the crowd-sized bowl of potato salad for her annual Independence Day backyard barbecue.

"Where's Hope?" Mary asked.

"She spent the night at Allie's. Mark and the girls'll be here soon. I'm glad y'all're early, I could use your help. I've got twenty people comin' this afternoon," Joanna rambled, oblivious to her friends' serious demeanors.

"Joanna, honey, we have to tell you something," Mary said gently.

Joanna stopped what she was doing and turned to Mary. "Did you find your baby?"

"No. Let's go into the living room. I think you should sit down," Mary instructed with a grave face. Jessie and Prissy took chairs opposite the couch where Joanna and Mary sat.

"I didn't find my son, I found yours," Mary began. The blood drained from Joanna's face as her three friends revealed what they'd discovered and played the audio confession from Louise Fitch.

"I don't know whether to faint or puke," Joanna gasped, holding on to the cushion of the couch. "That son-of-a-bitch has been raisin' my son all these years!"

"Joanna, I don't think they know you're Tom's birthmother. The birth certificate has Jessie's name on it. It looks like Catherine's father is the one responsible," Prissy told her.

"You're sure the St. Nicolas medallion was mine?" Joanna asked.

"Positive," Mary answered.

"But the birth dates are wrong?"

"Lenny was taken into custody last night," Mary stated. "He's singing like the canary coward he is. He confessed Langley changed the date. April Fool's Day; the joke was supposed to be on Jack."

Prissy went on to explain, "They denied Lenny bail because, when they went to arrest him, he was packing and had a plane ticket to Argentina. Apparently someone tipped him off."

Joanna looked sympathetically at Mary. "This is gonna destroy your life."

"My life's been a mess for a long time. This is going to get it back on track. I'm more concerned for you. All this is going to come out in court; Catherine and Jack will be told."

"Which also means he's sure to find out about Hope," Joanna added miserably. "Oh God, this can't be happenin'." Joanna glanced at her wristwatch. "Mark and the girls are gonna be here any minute. I don't want this brought up around anyone today. I need some time."

"Of course not," Mary confirmed. "Come on, we'll help you get things ready for the BBQ."

Within a few hours, the guests in the backyard of the house on Hollywood Avenue were enjoying the festive atmosphere. Music played and the smoky smell of the charcoal grill filled the air. Joanna carried a plate of hot dogs to Mark, who expertly flipped hamburgers.

"Are you okay, Joanna? You look kinda pale," Mark asked.

"I got some distressin' news today, and I don't wanna talk about it right now," she whispered. Neighbors and clients filled her yard, as well as Hope and Allie's schoolmates. Stan assisted the teenagers in erecting a volleyball net while the adults were relaxing in lawn chairs or working to get the food buffet ready.

Jessie, who'd been standing in the side yard smoking a cigarette, came to Joanna and inquired, "Some guy's pulled up in front; you expectin' anyone else?" Joanna followed her around the house as a man came through the wrought-iron gate at the front walk.

"Oh my God! It's Jack," Joanna hissed. Immediately she marched toward him. Seeing her, Jack turned his direction to the side yard; limping, he met her halfway.

"What're you doin' here? I told you I never wanted to see you again!" she rebuked angrily.

"I'm here about what you didn't tell me. I want to see my daughter!" His anger matched hers. Joanna lunged forward, pushing him hard in the chest.

"She's my daughter, not yours." Their voices were getting louder with each exchange.

"You kept her from me. How could you do that?"

"Hey, guys," Jessie jumped in. "This isn't the best time or place to do this."

"You're right; it's fourteen years past time. I want to see my daughter," Jack reiterated.

Using his cane, he sidestepped the women and headed for the backyard. Joanna stopped him again, pushing him harder than the first time. "I wanna see my son," she growled. Jack looked at her confused. "Your father-in-law purchased him for his daughter like some doll off a shelf. You've been raisin' your own son all these years, you stupid son-of-a-bitch."

"What?" he asked, stunned.

"Yes, Mother, what're you talkin' about?" Hope's voice shattered the moment like a pane of glass. "You told me my father died a war hero! You lied to me!" All conversation among the guests in the yard had ceased; their attention focused on Joanna and Jack. Hope ran for the house, using the side mudroom door to make her escape.

"Hope!" Joanna called. The teenager slammed the door. Joanna turned to Jack ·

and screamed, "Why is it, every time I see you, you fuck up my life?" She ran into the house.

Jessie, thinking fast, took Jack by the arm. "Let's you and I take a walk; there's some heavy shit goin' down and you might as well hear it from me." Prissy and Mary followed them.

Allison ran to Mark. "Daddy!" she pleaded. Mark looked around as the party spontaneously began to dismantle. Neighbors gathered their lawn chairs and children. Mrs. Thatcher covered the food and handed it to the guests who'd brought it.

"Help Mrs. Thatcher with the food." Mark turned to Stan. "Hey, man, will you keep an eye on the grill? When the burgers are done, give them to Allie; she'll put them away."

"Sure thing," Stan said, seeming glad to have a reason to hang around.

Mark walked through the house to the front porch, where he joined Joanna's friends and Jack. He shook Jack's hand and politely introduced himself, "Mark Rhodes."

Jack responded, "Jack Wyatt." The two men sized each other up.

Hope's tirade at her mother could be heard through the open window. "All the times I asked about him, you lied to me!"

Joanna's muffled response couldn't be understood as she tried to calm the girl. Jack, who'd seemed to be ready for a fight a few minutes ago, was now subdued, while Jessie told him about the impending investigation.

"How did you find out about Hope?" Mary probed. Jack told his version, including Cat kicking him out. "I didn't realize Mr. Langley could be so calculating," Mary confessed.

"You have no idea," Jack answered sadly.

"Well, this is a tangled web of shit, if I've ever seen one," Jessie said.

Mark chimed in, "It may be best to talk to Hope another day, when things've calmed down." Jack agreed and gave them Alex's apartment phone number. Defeated, Jack limped to his car. He paused to look back at Joanna's house before getting in and driving away.

A few minutes later, Joanna emerged through the front door. Her eyes were red from crying. "Hope wants to spend a few days at your house with Allie, all right?" she asked Mark.

"Sure, no problem," the father answered.

Chapter 46

Jessie went back to California, Prissy returned to Nashville, and Mary retreated to the suburbs to try to explain to her children why their daddy was in jail. On Sunday afternoon, Mark knocked gently on Joanna's kitchen screen door. She waved him in.

"What're you doing?" he asked, looking around her messy kitchen. Pots and pans littered the counter; the cabinet doors were open. At the sink, she vigorously scrubbed the bottom of a saucepan. Her disheveled hair drew attention to her puffy-red, been-crying eyes.

"Whenever I'm upset, I clean. I haven't scoured these pans in a long time," she answered.

"Well, you're wearing a hole in that one." Mark quipped.

"How's Hope?" she asked, drying the pan with a towel.

"She's all right. Still angry," Mark answered.

"Is she ever gonna speak to me again?" Joanna's voice quivered.

"Eventually. I'd give her a few more days, though."

Joanna's eyes glistened with regret. "I've received a steady stream of phone calls since Thursday, and I can tell you, I've lost some friends. Stan's particularly upset. I haven't spoken to Mrs. Thatcher. A lot of people are standin' in judgment of me right now. I wondered how long it was gonna take before you came around."

"I'm not here to judge you, Joanna," Mark consoled, comforting her with a hug. Joanna put her arms around him and a torrent of tears let loose.

"I shouldn't've lied to her. It's not disgraceful to be a single mother anymore."

"I know why you did it," he reassured her. "You were in a bad spot in 1959. She'll come around." Mark glided his index finger under Joanna's chin, gently raising her face to see her eyes. "As for those people who're judging you harshly, forget them. Sometimes it's good to know who your true friends are."

Swallowing the lump in her throat, Joanna whispered, "It occurred to me, over the last few days, aside from my relationship with Hope, yours was the one I was in most fear of losin'."

Without warning, Mark lowered his lips to hers, kissing her gently. With her heart racing, she returned his kisses, finally admitting to herself the feelings for Mark she'd ignored for years.

Breathlessly, Mark moved his mouth away. "You're not going to lose me, Joanna. I'm in love with you and I have been for a long time."

"Why didn't you tell me?"

"You were so guarded, I felt like you wouldn't let me in."

"I don't have any walls built now. You don't think I'm a terrible person?"

"God, no! You were a kid."

"As bad as this has been, there's a certain amount of relief to have the weight of such terrible lies lifted off my shoulders." Mark nodded in understanding. "As long as we're bein' so honest," she continued, "I suppose I should tell you, I love you, too."

Mark tucked a stray hair behind her ear. "I know you're vulnerable right now. I'd never take advantage of you. All I've wanted to do, since Thursday, is find a way to fix everything."

"I'm grateful," she told him honestly. She kissed him tenderly and laid her head on his chest. With his arms encircling her, Joanna felt safe.

A few days later Hope came back home. The adults tactfully tried to explain the change in their relationship to the girls.

"We care for each other," Mark revealed. "So we're going to spend more time together."

"You mean, like boyfriend and girlfriend?" Allie asked.

"Yes. How do you feel about that?" Joanna looked from Allie to Hope.

"Cool with me," Allie said, turning to Hope. "If they get married, we'll be sisters."

"Terrific," Hope snapped, annoyed. She got off the couch and tromped to the stairs.

"I thought you'd be happy to see me datin' for the first time in your life," Joanna called.

"Why do you care what I think? You've never worried before," Hope remarked hatefully. The girl ran upstairs and slammed her bedroom door.

"I'll go talk to her," Allie offered, leaving the adults alone in the living room.

"Maybe we should've waited longer." Joanna hung her head.

"Hey, look at me," Mark insisted. "You'd've been keeping secrets again. She'd be more upset if she came home unexpectedly and found us in a compromising situation." He rubbed his hand on her back. "You deserve to be happy, Joanna."

"She's right. I've made decisions without considerin' the consequences."

"She won't stay mad forever," Mark assured her.

"No, but it's the meantime that worries me. I feel like I'm bein' paid back for givin' my own mother such a hard time."

"I don't think it works that way." He laughed. "Being the parent of a teenager is never easy. You've done a great job. You've sacrificed so much for her. In time, she'll come around."

"So I should look out for my own happiness?" she questioned.

"And mine. It took me too long to tell you how much I need you. I'd be miserable without you now." Mark leaned over and kissed her.

Pressed by unrelenting interrogation, Lenny implicated everyone involved, hoping to get a reduced sentence. The investigation widened to fifteen other cases concerning affluent families linked to baby-brokering deals. His crimes cut much deeper on a personal level for both Mary and Joanna. Joanna called Jessie to fill her in.

"Lenny has a huge gamblin' addiction and he was consortin' with male prostitutes."

"Prison should make him a happy man," Jessie foretold sarcastically. "That explains why he wanted sex in a dark room. How's Mary takin' all this?"

"She's hangin' tough. The Valium she's on helps. She's filin' for divorce. Edith blew a gasket, but her dad's supportive. He knows most of the story. She wants to tell him she's looking for her baby in person this weekend."

"That'll be a sticky conversation," Jessie theorized.

"Lenny knew from the start who I was. He figured out Mary'd been an unwed mother. The bastard told her she was the perfect cover mate for him, because if she ever tried to ruin him for being gay, he'd use the baby she gave away against her. He never loved her or the kids."

"He told her that? What a piece of shit!"

"Lenny also confessed that Wendell Langley paid Dr. White to tie my tubes when he performed my C-section with Hope. There's a carbon copy of a cashier's check as proof."

"Holy shit!" Jessie cried. "You need to sue his ass."

"They've revoked Dr. White's medical license. I'm gonna talk to a lawyer," Joanna relayed. "Oh, and it turns out the Virgin Mary did have Eugenia's notebook. Sister Bridget found it hidden in a crack at the base of the statue in the nuns' hall. It aided the sheriff's department in locating thirty-two infant remains from the woods. Fitch'll be charged with dozens of counts of improper concealment or disposal of the bodies."

"Glad to see our tax dollars at work," Jessie said.

"The big news is, Tommy wants to meet me and his sister," Joanna announced.

"Are you gonna do it?"

"Absolutely. I've thought of little else since I found out he's alive. Hope hasn't agreed to it yet; she's still pretty angry. I think her curiosity will win out, though. They're comin' here this Sunday afternoon. I think I'll feel more comfortable on my own turf."

"Call me after; I wanna hear everythin'." Jessie changed the subject, "So how's Mark?"

"Amazing," Joanna answered.

"Are we talkin' between the sheets or in general?"

"Both." Joanna laughed shyly.

"I knew he'd be, you lucky girl."

"I know I am. But enough about me, what's happenin' with you?"

"Well… I've listed my condo for sale. It's time I head for New York. I've got several club owners out here who're willin' to invest in my nightclub."

"This's so excitin'! You're finally gonna make it happen."

"I'm not gettin' any younger. Now's the time," Jessie agreed.

Catherine drove, with Tommy sitting next to her. The teenager leaned over and switched the fading-out-of-range radio station to a Memphis rock station. Aerosmith's song "Dream On" came in clearly; he turned up the volume and stared out at the passing countryside. Cat's mind bounced with apprehension at meeting the woman who had given her husband two children, one of whom she'd cherished and raised as her own.

When Jack told her the news that Tommy was his own flesh and blood, it felt as if he'd sucked all the air out of the room. They chose to tell Tom the whole story together.

"Nice one, Dad." Tom's face reddened with anger. "You swear you didn't know anything about the switch or the fact that I have a sister?"

"I swear," Jack murmured.

"I know you feel like your whole world is crashing around you. Your father's not living here and finding out the grandfather you admired so much has done some truly dreadful things is a horrible shock." Catherine put her hand to her chest.

"I can't believe Grandfather took it upon himself to have Joanna sterilized; who'd he think he was, Adolf Hitler?" Tom demanded.

"I'm finding out there're a lot of things about my father I'm ashamed of," Cat agreed. She and her son were both grappling with their love for the man they'd adored and the despicable truth of his actions. Tom had requested time to sort out his feelings. After a few weeks, he told Catherine he wanted to meet his birthmother and sister.

Cat's emotions were complicated. At first, she hated Joanna for carrying on with Jack. She forced herself to look at it from Joanna's perspective. She'd been so young. Cat remembered how charming Jack could be and admired Joanna for disassociating her life from Jack's, in 1958.

Catherine also had mixed feelings about Tommy meeting Joanna and Hope. Even before she adopted him, she'd considered the possibility of meeting the birthmother as a variable. However, she'd never imagined she'd be a mistress whom Jack kept a secret.

Catherine eased her Mercedes into the parking space in front of Hollywood Hair. Her heart raced as she turned off the car and asked Tom, "Are you ready?"

Tommy offered, "I'm ready. I'll understand if you don't want to go in with me."

Cat summoned her courage and replied, "If you want me there, I'll come."

Joanna Wilson held open the screen door, inviting them in. Tommy hugged her without reservation. "I'm so glad to finally meet you," he expressed.

Despite the lump in her throat, Joanna managed, "Me too." She took in the sight of the handsome young man. He stood tall, like Jack, but he'd clearly gotten his coloring and facial features from her. Seeing his eyes was surreal; it was like looking in a mirror.

Cat took Joanna's hand. "Thank you for allowing us to come here today."

Joanna nodded and escorted them to the living room. "I'm not sure where Hope is," she explained. "She knew you were comin', but I never got an answer on wanting to meet you. She's still a little upset."

"That's understandable," Tom told her. He didn't let the conversation dangle. He asked her about being a beautician and if she liked living in Memphis. He told her about his baseball team and his plans to attend college at MIT to study environmental engineering. After half an hour, the back door slammed and Hope made her way through the house to the living room. Tom rose from the couch and gave his newly discovered sister a hug.

"Can I get anyone somethin' to drink?" Joanna asked; her own mouth had gone dry.

"That'd be lovely," Catherine replied, blinking at the sight of the girl whose coloring favored Jack, but who shared enough features with Tommy that it was obvious they were siblings.

"I don't want anythin'," Hope told her mother. She turned to Tom. "Come on, I'll show you the backyard." The teenagers disappeared out the back door.

Catherine followed Joanna into the kitchen, where the natural mother poured iced tea.

After a refreshing drink, Cat spoke from her heart. "I'm so sorry for everything my father did to you."

"You're not responsible for your father's actions. We were both in the dark."

"Still, I'd completely understand if you filed a civil suit against my father's estate."

Joanna interrupted her. "That'd be like suin' Tommy, wouldn't it? I don't want anythin'. What's done is done; I'd rather we move on from here." Joanna let Cat think for a moment before she added, "I owe you an apology for gettin' involved with your husband. For as old as I thought I was back then, I made immature decisions."

"I blame Jack more than you. He should've used better judgment."

"Regardless, I'm truly sorry for any pain I've caused you," Joanna admitted.

"I guess there's enough guilt and shame to go around, isn't there?" Catherine smiled, accepting the woman's apology. They observed Joanna's children through the kitchen window as the teenagers talked by the picnic table. "They're the positive side to all of this," Cat pointed out.

"You've been a great mother to Tommy. He's an exceptional young man."

"He made it easy for me," Catherine replied.

"I wish Hope'd make it easier on me. Maybe talkin' to Tom will help," Joanna said.

"She seems like a sweet girl."

"She was, until about twelve. Then teenage angst hit."

"From what I've seen, they tend to grow out of it."

"I'm prayin' she grows out of it soon. Do you wanna know somethin' crazy?" Joanna asked. Catherine nodded. "This doesn't feel as weird as I thought it would. If not for my transgressions, we could've actually been friends."

"Maybe we still can be," Catherine suggested.

"What's he like?" Hope asked Tommy.

"Dad?" Hope nodded. "Distant, I guess. He works a lot."

"You're so calm; aren't you angry?" Hope asked.

"I was at first. I didn't think I'd forgive him for hurting my mom. I was furious with my grandfather. It's not like I can confront him, he's dead."

"I guess if you've got money you can do whatever you want." Hope's jaw tightened.

"No, you can't. What he did was wrong. Catherine didn't raise me with my grandfather's values, and strangely, neither did he. But what he did doesn't wipe out sixteen years of history."

"Well, you're the lucky one. You got ponies and parades while I got hand-me-downs and yard-sale toys. I wish I was the one switched at birth." Her snug shirt, skintight jeans, over-made-up face, and stony attitude indicated to Tom she was hanging with a tough crowd.

"She might be worried you'll become a pregnant teenager."

"Oh, believe me, I won't. I give myself credit for not bein' as stupid as she is." Tom frowned. "Give me a break! Catherine the Great raised you, while Elly May Clampett raised me. I hate Jack for that. I don't want anythin' to do with him," Hope said spitefully. "You seem so willin' to forgive everyone. It doesn't work that way."

"I didn't think it did. But I don't see any point in dragging out a lot of pain when trying to heal wounds would be better. Forgiving Jack hasn't been easy. But if my mother can, I can."

"So they're gonna get back together?" Hope raised her eyebrows.

"I don't know, but at least they're talking. It'd be great if we could all find a place for each other in our lives."

"You want us to be at your high school graduation? And you're gonna pop in here for Thanksgiving and whatnot?" the girl asked, with her hands on her hips.

"I'm not sure if that's possible. I'm glad I got to meet both of you. I always wished I had siblings, growing up. I think it'd be great to get to know you better," Tom offered.

"I wanted a brother or sister, too, but this is all too fucked up for me." Hope shook her head. Finally, she initiated a handshake. "Strange meetin' you, have a nice life." The girl waved behind her as she walked across the yard and climbed behind a tough-looking guy on a motorcycle. Her blond hair blew in the breeze as the couple loudly took off.

Chapter 47

"I take it talking to Hope didn't go too well," Cat stated as she turned the car onto the highway.

"She's pretty hostile," Tommy commented.

"Her whole world's been turned upside down. You know how she feels."

"I do know. It's going to take time." Tom looked out the window. "Did Joanna say anything to you about Dad?"

"She apologized for being involved with him. Why?" Cat asked.

"Hope doesn't want anything to do with him. They've been pretty poor. She resents the fact that I grew up in a family with money and they've struggled."

"I think if Joanna had wanted Jack's help financially, she'd've told him about Hope. I admire her. She made a fine home for them. I'm sad Hope's so angry."

"I understand how she feels," Tommy reasoned. "But today I found myself defending Dad. He didn't know she existed, and he thought I was dead. He was kind of a victim, too."

"Well, now you can see what lies do to people. I hope this lesson keeps you from making mistakes that can haunt you from your past."

"I guess that's the point, Mom. It's the past, ancient history. Hope wanted to know if you're going to get back together with Dad."

Catherine exhaled a deep sigh. "I don't know, son. He kept an affair he knew produced at least one child a secret from me. It's hard to rebuild trust after something like that."

"Yes, it'd take some work, and maybe marriage counseling. But can't you cut him some slack? I mean, he hasn't cheated on you since Joanna, has he?"

"He says he hasn't. I'd like to believe him," Catherine answered honestly.

"Maybe that'd be a good place to start," her son suggested.

"It's much more complicated."

"Only if you let it be," the teenager told her. They drove without conversation for a while. Catherine didn't want to discuss the grown-up issues of her marriage with him. She had enough trouble sorting out her own emotions. Her anger at Jack when she'd initially learned the news of his two illegitimate children had faded to humiliation. Feeling like a fool for being blindsided was harder for her to take than being angry.

Suddenly Tom announced, "Dad asked me to have dinner with him next week. I'm going. He's miserable; he thinks he's lost everything. I'm going to let him know he hasn't lost me."

"I think that's good," Cat said, encouraging him. "He is your father. I'm sure if my father was still alive I'd want to find a way to forgive him, somehow."

Mary sat across the living room from her father. The same white couches, the same clock ticking on the mantel: Everything was identical every time she'd been in that room, discussing life-changing circumstances. Her father sipped his coffee, giving her his full attention.

"You don't know the whole story." She calmly walked across to the fireplace. "The reason I found out about Lenny's crimes was because Tony and I are looking for the baby I gave up for adoption."

"You're in contact with Tony?" Mr. Atherton stiffened.

"Yes. He's been looking for our son for three years, unsuccessfully. He needs my help."

"I thought all that was behind us?" Gerald looked at his shoes.

"How can it be, when there isn't a day that goes by I don't think of my little boy? My mind is too cluttered with *what if* and *if only*. I can't live like that anymore. When you're looking behind you, you're not watching where you're going. In my case, I ended up in a destructive marriage. It'll finally be over when you and I talk."

"I did what I thought was best at the time," her father said.

"I'm not blaming you, Daddy. I need you to understand. It took me years to realize that the day I gave him away, my life stopped. I stayed stuck while my existence went on without me emotionally growing. I did what the nuns said, I pretended like it never happened. A few years ago I almost had a total break-down. That was a wake-up call for me."

Gerald Atherton looked her in the eyes with compassion. "I wish, now, that we'd taken the baby and you home when you were released. I know if I'd seen him, I would've loved him as much as the rest of my grandchildren. If I'd known then what I know now, I'd've let you marry Tony."

"I've played out that scenario in my mind, believe me. It's a dream written in trashy romance novels and doesn't exist. We'd probably be divorced, hating each other."

"You don't have romantic feelings toward him?" her father asked.

"No, I don't. It turns out, the way I had him pictured in my memory isn't who he is. It wasn't him I wanted, it was the adolescent lovesick high, the longing and anguish. It's disturbing when you realize you take comfort in the pain."

"I'm sorry, honey." Her father opened his arms to her. She accepted his embrace. He continued, "I'm so sorry you've had to go through this. I feel responsible for the decisions you've been forced to make. Leonard Hollan fooled me, too. I pushed you toward him; I trusted him completely. He picked the right profession; he's slick as owl shit."

"Yeah, he is," Mary agreed. "All I can do now is try to make things better."

Her father nodded in agreement. She continued, "Lenny's left our finances in a mess. I was thinking, I can sell the house in the suburbs and move back to Memphis. I found a building in an area being renovated for tourism. It has five floors and a storefront on the ground level. I want to hire some employees and open a dress shop. I'll design dresses for weddings, pageants, and proms and hire seamstresses to sew. I can put the sewing room on the second floor, third floor for storage. The top two floors I'll renovate into a large apartment for the kids and me."

"Do you need any money?" he offered.

"No. I have what Grandma left me. That plus the sale of the house will allow me to get started. I want to do this without asking for money. Now, if I fall flat on my face, I may need some money and guidance. I'll need to establish credit. Everything's in Lenny's name."

"You're not going to fall flat on your face. I'll help in any way I can. As for my guidance, you need to follow your own intuition. That's what your grandmother'd tell you."

"She was a wise old bird," Mary remembered fondly.

"I had no idea who she was until after she was gone. I wish I'd known sooner about the baby she relinquished for adoption. It's explained a lot about her," Mr. Atherton admitted.

"How'd you find out?" Mary's voice went higher with surprise.

"I found her journals after she died. It made me realize how you must've felt. But then you met Lenny and got engaged. I'd suspected your marriage was unhappy, but not this bad."

"The hardest part was telling the kids, but I think now they'll understand me better and why I've made such spectacular mistakes. I'm seeing a therapist so I can get rid of all this emotional garbage I've been carrying around."

"That's a wise thing to do. You have my support."

"Even with my decision to find my son?" Mary asked.

"Yes. I think you should. I sometimes wonder about the sister I never knew. It'd be nice if your children didn't have to," Mr. Atherton told her.

"There's a lot of people searching for children they lost to adoption. Tony joined a support group called CUB; it stands for Concerned United Birthparents. Maybe this group and other groups like it can help us find him. They're working to change the law. More girls are keeping their babies and with no shame, not like in 1957. The home violated our rights and didn't tell us about the government programs to help us if we kept our babies. They made us feel ashamed and worthless. But what's even worse, our rights are still being violated because we don't have access to our own records.

"I didn't know Tony and his mother went to a lawyer to get custody of the baby and were told he had no rights to the child. I didn't know I signed away both our rights when I gave him up. When he got paralyzed, Melinda divorced him. He's been a mess. After I agreed to help him find our baby, he enrolled in school and wants to be a special ed teacher."

"You might've saved his life," Mr. Atherton observed.

"In the process, I'm probably saving my own," Mary answered.

To Jessie's surprise, her condo sold quickly, and by late fall of 1974 she was nearing the end stages of opening a new club she namedDiamond's. The grand opening was scheduled for New Year's Eve, and with the help of her California friends and investors, it was sure to be a star-studded event. When Joanna received her invitation, it included plane tickets for her, Mark, and the girls.

"I've made plans for New Year's Eve!" Hope flailed her arms with turbo teenage drama.

"It's New York, someplace you've never been. There'll be movie stars and music legends," Joanna persuaded.

The snotty teen rolled her eyes and growled, "So you spend the New Year with your psycho friends, and I'll be with mine." On her way out the front door Hope shouted, "I'm not goin', you can't make me." Joanna turned to Mark as her shoulders fell in defeat.

"Hope and I can stay with Aunt Jane. You'll have more fun without us," Allie chimed in. She followed Hope.

Mark arranged for the girls to stay with his sister while he and Joanna went to the East Coast. Joanna wasn't comfortable leaving while they were at odds.

Jessie's grand opening exceeded her expectations. The place teemed with celebrities, and Jessie shone brighter than any of them. Joanna watched in amazement as her friend mingled comfortably with the movie-star guests. Exciting energy flowed among the rich and famous. Jessie offered to introduce them to any of their favorite Hollywood stars.

Joanna refused. "No, I'm fine. I'd be mortified if I said somethin' stupid or was so starstruck I'd be tongue-tied." Instead, they hung back at a table with Mary, Prissy, and Will.

"Let me know if you change your mind," Jessie said, leaving an opening. Distracted by an actress Joanna recognized from the soap opera *General Hospital*, Jessie joined the daytime TV crowd. Joanna's skin tingled with goose bumps. The next morning, the excitement soared when the critic from the *New York Times* touted *Diamond's* as the best New Year's Eve party in town and the newest hot spot. Jessie screamed with joy when Joanna read her the review over the phone.

"You're a huge success," Joanna complimented.

"That's all I've ever wanted." Jessie basked in the moment.

Two days later, Mark and Joanna packed their last-minute items in their suitcases and prepared for the cab ride to the airport. Joanna stepped out on the hotel balcony to take one last look at the city. It saddened her to be going home. She'd seen the Statue of Liberty and toured the Metropolitan Museum; the view from the Empire State Building blew her mind, but the horse-drawn-carriage ride in Central Park, with a light snow falling, topped it all. Mark stepped behind her and slid his arms around her waist.

"This has been great," he appraised.

"It really has," she agreed.

"Marry me," he whispered softly in her ear.

Joanna pulled away to see his eyes; he was serious. "This is a little sudden, isn't it?"

"I don't think so; seems like perfect timing to me."

"Mark." She paused. "I don't wanna jump into anythin'. That's been my problem in the past, makin' major life decisions without thinkin' them through."

"So your answer is, you'll consider it?"

"My answer is, I love you and, honestly, I've never been happier. I wanna enjoy things the way they are for a while."

"I understand. I've been happy, too. My thought was marriage'd make it even better." The pad of his thumb traced the line of her cheek tenderly.

"Or, it'd ruin everythin'. I don't wanna take the chance. Let's take it slow."

"I won't pressure you. We'll get married when you're ready. In the meantime, I'm going to make a list of all the reasons we should."

"You're gonna keep askin' till I say yes, aren't you?"

"Yep."

"It's good to know you've got a plan," she concluded, laughing.

Their elation quickly deflated when they came home and learned Hope had refused to sleep at Mark's sister's house. Instead, she invited her boyfriend over to Joanna's and the two of them essentially played house while they were away.

Jane had finally threatened to call Joanna and Hope had begrudgingly followed the curfew while still taking off with her boyfriend during the day. This proved to be the first of many of Hope's defiant acts. She skipped classes her sophomore year and ignored Joanna's groundings. Frightened Hope was sexually active, Joanna took her to a clinic for birth control pills.

"Do you want me to talk to her?" Mark finally suggested.

"No, she'd only consider that fuel for the fire. She's failin' three classes. She's hateful to anyone who loves her. Allie left here in tears this afternoon."

"I know, she told me. I came over to see what's going on," Mark explained. Allie was a good student, stayed active in the school clubs, and considered holding hands with a boy a big deal: the total opposite of Hope.

"Hope's out of control. She won't listen to me. She's as stubborn and bull-headed as I was at her age. Payback's hell!"

Chapter 48

Mary hit several bumps while planning her dress shop. Her house in the suburbs sold fast, forcing her and the children to move while the renovations were incomplete. She pressured the contractor to finish the kitchen and living room the week before the move.

As their belongings were being carried in, the plumber put the finishing touches on the functional bathroom they'd all share. Plastic hung in the doorways to control the construction dust, while hammers and table saws drowned out attempts at conversation, leaving them tense. Peace descended at night when the workers finally went home.

Mary set the children's dinners on the bar area of the kitchen. Seated on tall stools, they ate and shared their experiences of the day.

"I don't like the nuns as much as my teachers at my old school," Luke complained.

"If you weren't pulling pranks all the time, you wouldn't get in trouble," Renee tattled.

"Luke." Mary cocked her head and gave him her mama warning look.

"I'm not doing nothin'." Luke faked innocence.

"Um-hm." Mary's voice betrayed her disbelief.

That evening the kids completed their homework, then watched *The Waltons* on television. When bedtime came, her children climbed into sleeping bags in the living room.

"Get your feet out of my face!" Meg swatted Renee on the legs.

"Mom," the younger girl complained.

"This is totally bogus," her eldest grumbled.

"Marguerite, if you'd be a little more pleasant, it'd be a big help," Mary begged.

"Yeah, Marguerite," Luke chided.

"Buzz off, turkey." Meg threw a pillow, knocking over the lamp. It went dark at the breaking of the bulb.

"Smooth move, Ex-Lax," Luke poked.

Mary left the room to find the broom and a light bulb and Paul whispered, "Take a chill pill." Mary stopped around the corner and eavesdropped. "Mom's working hard to get her business going so she can take care of us. Stop fighting!"

"Who died and made you king of the world?" Luke objected.

"Nobody. But Mom's havin' a rough time. If she fails, we all fail."

"Paul's right," Meg said, backing her brother. "She goes downstairs and works on her designs after we're asleep. Some nights she doesn't sleep at all."

Mary covered her mouth with her hand to suppress a sob. She didn't want them to worry the way she did. She grabbed a workman's broom and a light bulb and returned to clean up the broken glass. Paul sat next to Renee.

Mary expertly swept the glass and dropped it in the waste can. If she had a dime for every mess she'd cleaned, she wouldn't be worried about money.

"I'm sorry, Mama," Meg offered.

"It's all right, baby. I know we're in close quarters." Mary sank into the couch and patted her arm. "We need to band together. I love you kids. Let's make a pact to be kind to one another."

"Okay, Mom," Meg wiped her own tears as she hugged her mother.

Paul nodded his agreement and joined the embrace, as did Renee. Mary motioned to the younger ones, who bounded in for a group hug. "Oh, my love-lies, this adventure's gonna be outta sight. All right! Give me five." They sealed their vow with hand slaps.

A week later Mary and Joanna shivered in their winter coats as they stood across the street from Mary's building watching the sign company installed her lighted MEMPHIS LACE placard. The worker on the scaffolding gave a loud whistle, signaling for the power to go on. The sign glowed warmly against the gray winter day.

"Looks great," Joanna said through chattering teeth.

"This is so exciting, I'm tingly,"

"No, that's the early stages of frostbite," Joanna joked. Mary took the hint.

"Come on, I'll show you the rest." They made a dash for the warmth of her elegant new storefront. Mary led them through: "Over here is the bridal boutique." A three-way mirror anchored a carpeted platform connected to a large dressing room. An enchanting white dress took center stage in the tulle-and-flower-draped display window. "On this side are the prom and pageant dresses for teenagers, and the communion and pageant outfits for the younger ones." Mary pointed at the racks half full of colorful gowns.

"This is amazin'. Your grandma'd be so proud."

"Yeah, I wish she could pull some other strings for me." Joanna raised her eyebrows. "Tony called a week ago, all excited; he was able to get our son's birth certificate number."

"How'd he do that?" Joanna asked, astounded.

"Someone told him to look at the black books behind the counter of the Nashville courthouse, which contain every birth certificate number, even those for the sealed adoptions. He convinced a new girl to let him look at the catalog for 1957. Of course, then he went back to the microfiche. As of yesterday, he hasn't found anything."

"Don't give up hope. He might find him," Joanna encouraged.

"I keep praying." Mary sighed.

Joanna dozed on her living room sofa. The clock chimed 1:00 a.m. and Hope had, once again, broken curfew. At the roar of Jimmy Cochran's motorcycle, Joanna watched out the window as Hope dismounted. The young couple were making out as if they were in the middle of Mardi Gras. Joanna didn't care for Jimmy, an eighteen-year-old high school dropout. As far as Joanna could tell, he spent his time smoking dope, drinking, and fighting.

Having seen enough, Joanna turned on the end-table lamp. Hope broke off the peep show she was giving the neighbors and scampered up the walk. Entering the house, her mother confronted her, arms crossed, standing in the living room archway.

"I know, I'm late, sorry," Hope sang in a snotty tone, stiffening.

"The school called. You skipped again today."

"Big whoop, I'm quitting anyway. Jimmy and I are gettin' married." Hope displayed a ring with a diamond chip in the center.

"What're you thinkin'?" Joanna shouted in disbelief.

"We know what we're doing. You need to sign the consent forms."

"You're pregnant, aren't you?" Joanna deduced.

"Yes, but Jimmy said he'd marry me, even if I wasn't. He loves me, Mama!"

"Oh God," she moaned, shaking her head. Joanna refused her consent and Hope declared all-out war. The disagreements went on for weeks while Hope tried everything from being sweet to screaming and throwing things.

Joanna called Jessie for advice. "You're not gonna like what I tell you," Jessie warned.

"When's that ever stopped you?" Joanna remarked with a laugh.

"If she's so hell-bent on marryin' this guy, let her. You've voiced your objections. If she still insists on gettin' legally bound to the asshole, sign your consent. At least he'll be legally responsible for child support. Prissy will tell you, Hope can petition the court for emancipation; because she's pregnant they'll likely grant it. Then she can get married without your consent and you won't get to be a grandma to the baby."

"Don't tell her," Joanna admonished sarcastically.

"I wouldn't dream of it," Jessie promised.

"It makes me sick that five generations of women in my family have gotten pregnant in their teens," Joanna groaned.

"How'd she get pregnant anyway? I thought you put her on birth control pills last year?"

"I did. She said they made her sick and quit takin' 'em."

"Let's see how she feels about mornin' sickness and givin' birth," Jessie commented.

Less than a month later, Joanna heard Hope banging around in her room. When she investigated, she found her daughter stuffing her belongings into garbage bags. Long blond strands hung from her disheveled ponytail.

"What're you doin'?" Joanna demanded.

"First thing tomorrow, I'm goin' to the principal and blab that I'm knocked up. I'll be expelled. Jimmy and me are moving into a trailer together. You can't stop me because I can get a judge to declare me a mature minor."

"Don't bother," Joanna relented. Sitting on the bed, she continued: "I'll sign my consent. It's against my better judgment, but you've forced my hand. I think you're makin' a big mistake, with a pretty predictable bad outcome."

"I know what you think," Hope whined, exasperated. "We have jobs waiting for us. We know what we're doing. We love each other."

"Please take some time to reconsider your options."

"What, like living here with you? No thanks." Hope continued to bag her clothes.

The next day, Joanna reluctantly accompanied Hope and Jimmy to the courthouse and scribbled her consenting signature.

"The judge isn't gonna have time to marry us for another three hours. You don't have to hang around. I know you don't wanna be here anyway," Hope told her.

"I gave my consent," Joanna offered.

"It'd be nice to have your approval." The girl suddenly hugged Joanna and whispered, "I'm gonna be all right, Mama."

"That's my wish for you," Joanna confessed.

The newlyweds moved into a rented trailer without informing Joanna that it and their jobs were in a small Podunk town an hour away from Memphis.

"I'll bet that was Jimmy's idea," Joanna accused furiously into the phone.

"What difference does it make where we live? You're always bitching at me. I'm tired of it!" Hope hung up and refused to answer when Joanna called back.

Weeks later, Joanna, determined to make peace with Hope, drove out there. Her intentions changed when she parked at the derelict trailer matching Hope's address. Now she wanted to bring her home. That goal intensified when Hope invited her in, exposing conditions worse than her first impression: broken furniture and a musty smell.

"Jimmy's chopper was in front of a bar downtown," Joanna mentioned. "No work today?"

"His boss called off work because of the rain. Jimmy's gonna get with one of his buddies to work a side job." Joanna's gut told her he'd spend the day drinking, with no intention of working. Hope self-consciously cleared a dozen empty beer bottles from the table.

"You can't tell me you're happy livin' this way." Joanna crossed her arms, repulsed by the idea of sitting on the stained sofa.

"The mobile home needs some fixin'," Hope pointed out.

"It needs to be condemned."

"I'm happy at my job and being with Jimmy. I know what you're thinking. Even if you drag me back to Memphis, Jimmy'll come get me tomorrow. We're married now."

"Don't remind me."

"It's my life. If I'm screwing it six ways to Sunday, it's my choice. You've already done a bang-up job fucking up your life and mine in the process!" the girl shouted.

"I didn't come here to argue. But now that I see your livin' conditions, I'm worried this isn't safe for you and a newborn. If I give you the money to move to a clean apartment and buy some new furniture, will you do it?"

Hope abandoned her hostility. "I'll have to talk to Jimmy."

A month later, the couple moved to a two-bedroom ground-floor apartment. Even after Joanna paid for their relocation and bought new furniture, though, her relationship with her daughter remained tense.

The following January, Hope gave birth to a baby girl she named Megan. The fact that Jimmy had been fired from two jobs since they'd married and went long periods without employment multiplied Joanna's concern. She used the money she'd budgeted for Hope's tuition to help with overdue bills.

Joanna dialed Mark's number. "Hey," she began when he answered. "I have to cancel our Sunday movie date. I'm drivin' over to Hope's. Her phone's been disconnected again, and I get nervous when I can't talk to her."

"You want me to go with you?"

"Sure, I'd love the company."

As she pulled onto I-40, Joanna asked Mark, "Do ya think I'm crazy for payin' her bills?"

"No, it's hard being their age and keeping their heads above water."

"I can't help worryin'. Jimmy drinks too much; he reminds me of my father."

"When she gets tired of it, she won't tolerate it anymore," Mark theorized.

"I hope you're right."

When they arrived at the apartment, Jimmy was in the parking lot, tinkering with his motorcycle. Taking a swig of beer, he slurred his greeting: "Hey, Miss W."

"How are ya, Jimmy?" Joanna asked.

"Just keepin' it real."

"Ten thirty in the mornin' and he's drunk on his ass," Joanna whispered to Mark as they approached the open apartment door. A box fan rattled in the front window. Joanna knocked on the doorframe as she entered. On the couch, Hope, wearing cutoff shorts and a halter top, folded a basket of clean baby clothes. Six-month-old Megan ate Cheerios in her high chair. The place was clean; even the dishes were done.

"Hi," Hope acknowledged, continuing her chore.

"Hi. I've been callin' for days, so I know your phone's disconnected."

"We're a little short this month. The bill's on the counter." Hope pointed. Joanna shuffled through the numerous late notices until she found the phone bill. She wrote a check.

"What's wrong with his bike?" Joanna asked.

"Nothing. He bought some fancy new suspension."

"How's that more important than all those past-due bills?"

"Please, Mama, don't start. He's angry because I'm pregnant again."

"Good God, Hope," Joanna exclaimed, disappointed.

"I know," Hope acquiesced miserably. Megan began to fuss, and Hope left off folding to rescue the baby from the high chair. Joanna spotted the Technicolor bruise on her thigh.

"Did Jimmy do that to you?" Joanna demanded.

"I slipped in the shower," Hope lied, poorly.

"I'll take you home right now if he's hittin' you."

"I'm not goin' anywhere. Why do we always come to this?" Hope continued the tirade on why Joanna needed to stay out of her business.

On the drive back to Memphis, Joanna expressed her concern. "That black-and-blue mark looked like it came from the toe of a construction boot to me."

"She's got to admit it before she'll do anything to stop it," Mark said.

"There's the problem. I watched my mother take it until the day my father finally killed her. It truly breaks my heart to see Hope take the same road."

Joanna noticed a card left on her fireplace mantel from Mark. Ever since his first marriage proposal in New York, he'd continued his gentle persuasion by occasionally leaving a card with a reason she should marry him: "Reason 42: I want to wake up next to you every morning." Or "Reason 59: I love the sound of your laughter." After all this time, they were on Reason 132, which said, "My shoulders are strong. I want to help you carry your troubles." Joanna felt as if she'd been lugging a fifty-pound rock around her neck. She called Mark on the phone.

"Yes," she told him, after he answered with, "Hello."

"Yes, what?" he asked, confused.

"Yes, I'll marry you!"

"If I'd known that's the one that'd convince you, I would've used it years ago."

"It's not the last card. It's all the reasons you've given me over the years."

"Well, whatever it was, I'll take it. You're not going to back out tomorrow, are you?"

"Not a chance. You're stuck with me now."

"I was stuck with you the first day I met you."

Mark and Joanna were married by a justice of the peace on a magnificent September day in the backyard of her house. Thirty of their friends and family celebrated at the informal patio reception. Stan played the part of DJ while couples danced barefoot in the grass, while Mrs. Thatcher took the role of caterer. Hundreds of white Christmas lights supplied ambience.

As Joanna and Mark danced in the romantic glow, Prissy, Mary, and Jessie looked on from the picnic table while Hope sat on the porch stairs scowling at Allie and Tom Wyatt, who were sharing a slow dance. Tilley and George Johnson danced in a circle around the bride and groom, stirring laughter from everyone in the yard.

The newlyweds spent the weekend at the Peabody Hotel. Mark rented out his house for extra income and they settled into the new living arrangement at Joanna's. It felt natural for Allie to occupy Hope's bedroom upstairs. Joanna had been her stepdaughter's primary female role model for eight years, so the adjustment was effortless.

In her senior year Allie worked on the school newspaper, where she developed a love for journalism. Before long, she was writing articles covering the energy crisis and environmental concerns. For inspiration, she painted a quote from Joseph Pulitzer on the wall above her typewriter: "The power to mold the future of the Republic will be in the hands of the journalists of future generations." Allie received a scholarship to Columbia University's School of Journalism in New York.

In the springtime of what would've been her senior year, Hope gave birth to a baby boy she named Jason. She bowed out of attending Allie's graduation.

Chapter 49

Things changed drastically a few months later when Hope arrived on their doorstep, Megan by her side, baby Jason squalling in her arms, her right eye swollen shut, her face bruised.

"He beat the hell out of me, Mama. I left him," the girl explained.

Joanna sucked in a breath, pulling them into a hug. "Good God! What happened?"

"I had an abortion. He found the paperwork from Planned Parenthood and lost his mind!"

"An abortion! Oh, Hope…" Joanna hung her head.

"I know, Mama. Please don't lecture me, I already feel bad enough. I seriously couldn't bring another baby into this world of Jimmy's. It's gotten so bad between us." Hope spread a baby blanket on the living room floor to change Jason's soggy diaper.

"I'm sure you did what was best. How'd you pay for it?" Joanna picked up Megan.

"I used the money you sent us for rent."

"Well, I don't give a rat's ass if Jimmy can't pay rent. I'm truly glad you've left him."

Hope took a bottle from the diaper bag and cradled her son. "Ya know, if I'd told Jimmy I was pregnant again, he would've beat me for that, too. I was hopin' he wouldn't find out."

"Promise me ya won't let him talk ya into going back," Joanna pleaded.

"I promise. I have to do right by my kids. With the fightin', they're nervous all the time."

"We're here to help." Joanna kissed Megan's head, then took her to get a cookie.

Joanna called Prissy, and she advised them to take out a restraining order on Jimmy. The more she learned about his behavior and treatment of her daughter, the angrier she got. Joanna wouldn't allow Hope's abusive marriage to continue. The deciding factor for the thirty-eight-year-old grandmother came when she learned Jimmy sold drugs on the side.

Joanna made an anonymous phone call to the police, and by Thanksgiving her good-for-nothing son-in-law was behind bars, facing several years in jail for dealing drugs. The following spring, Hope divorced Jimmy and got her GED. She enrolled in a two-year technical school.

Megan and Jason played happily in the corner of the salon with Hot Wheels cars while Joanna trimmed Mary's hair.

"So I guess Hope and the kids living here is working out?" Mary asked.

"Yeah, it's been fine. She's done a lot of maturing of late." Joanna cut Mary's bangs.

"It's amazing how smart we become when they have to be adults."

Joanna laughed. "It's no trouble havin' the babies with me while I work. They're good kids. She's enjoyin' school."

"Speaking of school, Tony graduated. He's taken a job in Lexington as a gym teacher for disabled kids. He's also getting married to a gal he met at a birthparents' support group. She's looking for a daughter she surrendered and supports his search." Mary brushed hair off her nose.

"How's his quest goin'?"

"Nothing encouraging. Unless the laws change, I'm afraid we'll never find him."

"Prissy is workin' on that with the group she belongs to," Joanna encouraged. "Maybe you'll get lucky and he's lookin' for you too."

"That'd be nice. Tony's going to keep looking. I'm glad he's getting on with his life."

"So no jealousy over him gettin' married?"

"No. I'm too busy with my shop and the kids to bother with a man."

"Never say never," Joanna teased.

"I'm saying never!" Mary corrected. Joanna smiled at her in the mirror.

When Hope earned her associate's degree, she and the children moved to Huntsville, Alabama, where she took a well-paying job with a contract manufacturing company. Mark and Joanna enjoyed the peacefulness of their home and the time they were able to spend together. Unfortunately, this only lasted a short time before the next crisis came along.

Jessie's frantic voice came through, long-distance: "I need you to do somethin' for me."

"What's wrong?"

"I got a call from the New Orleans Coroner's Office. My mama's dead and I've got to go back and handle the details." Jessie paused. "I don't wanna do this alone." Within twelve hours, they met at the airport in Louisiana. Jessie had already identified her mother's body at the morgue. To Joanna, she looked tired, but levelheaded.

It felt voyeuristic, entering Jessie's mom's apartment. A cup of tea and a half-eaten biscuit waited for Mrs. Devereaux; an ashtray with two extinguished butts rested on the living room coffee table. The apartment was neat except for the unmade bed with the crumpled nightgown on the pillows. Jessie tiptoed through the rooms, stopping briefly to look around without speaking. Halting suddenly, she opened a closed door and entered a bedroom occupied by a single bed and polished furniture, fit for a guest, yet void of personal treasures. Jessie opened the closet and pulled out boxes of belongings she'd left behind.

"I'm surprised she held on to this shit. It's like she expected me to return." Jessie spoke for the first time since they'd crossed the threshold. "I swore I'd never come back."

Suddenly someone knocked on the front door. Responding, Jessie met a white-haired woman in a housedress, with a long-haired orange cat wiggling for an escape.

"I'm Nona Bailey, I'm guessin' you're Jessica, Ms. Devereaux's daughter."

"That's right," Jessie answered.

"This here's your mama's cat. She's well trained, doesn't need a litter box. Let her out twice a day and she takes care of business in the flower bed, then comes right back in." Mrs. Bailey held out the animal to Jessie, who took two steps backward. Joanna took the cat from the neighbor. She stroked it softly and the puss nuzzled her chin and purred loudly.

"What a sweet kitty; what's her name?" Joanna asked.

"Diamond," Mrs. Bailey answered. "The auction house came by and dropped off boxes here in the hallway. If ya need anythin', just holler."

"Well, thank you for takin' care of her cat. You're the one who called the ambulance?"

The white-haired lady nodded. "Did the coroner say it was a heart attack?"

"Yes," Jessie confirmed.

"I'm so sorry. If there's anythin' I can do…" The woman squeezed Jessie's hand.

"Thanks," Jessie replied.

The elderly woman cautiously descended the stairs and Jessie dragged in the first stack of unassembled boxes. Joanna sat on the sofa, petting the cat with the crystal-green eyes.

"A cat named Diamond, with red hair and green eyes? Sounds like she followed your career," Joanna commented.

"That goes to show you how fucked up she was. What the hell am I supposed to do with a goddamn cat? I suck with living things. I kill houseplants."

"She's a sweet cat," Joanna evaluated.

"We'll worry about her later. I've hired an auction house to dispose of all this shit. But I wanna go through it myself. Mama was notorious for hidin' money, a product of the Depression, I guess. Every towel needs to be unfolded, every sock searched. She was crazy."

Joanna emptied the kitchen cabinets, taking inventory of the dishes as she wrapped them in paper while Jessie boxed all food items for donation to a local soup kitchen.

"Look at this, two hundred dollars in the Quaker Oats and another fifty in the sugar. Check everythin'."

Joanna turned over a cup and found a $10 bill. "I see what you mean." Jessie spied liquor on the top shelf of the cabinet and retrieved a full bottle of tequila and two shot glasses. She poured for both of them.

"Thanks for the scavenger hunt, Mama!" she jeered sarcastically in a toast. They swallowed the intoxicating liquid.

Quickly they went back to work. Jessie grabbed the bottle of tequila and sipped on it while inspecting a bookcase full of romance novels, fanning the pages and retrieving her mother's hidden bank account. At dinnertime Joanna went out for jambalaya from the French Quarter, which they doused with several more shots of tequila.

Shortly before dusk, a priest came by to discuss the funeral arrangements. "There won't be a funeral. She'll be cremated and her urn placed at my dad's grave."

"Don't you at least want me to offer a final prayer for her soul?" he asked, stunned.

"Look, Padre, if she didn't get the last rites, that's her problem. I guarantee you, she's already in hell. Don't waste your breath," Jessie announced.

Shocked, the priest retreated as if a tornado siren had sounded. Diamond the cat followed the priest out to the street.

"With any luck, she won't come back," Jessie hoped.

Twenty minutes later the cat pawed the back door, meowing. Joanna let her in and the animal stuck close to her the rest of the evening. By nine o'clock Joanna yawned, exhausted. The pair had discovered $10,000 stashed away in strange places and had reduced Jessie's childhood home to stacks of boxes.

"Why don't you take my old bedroom? There's only my mama's bedroom left. I'll get it finished and crash on the couch," Jessie told her. Joanna didn't argue as she shuffled off to the smaller bedroom with the cat purring at her heels. In the middle of the night, Joanna was jolted from a heavy sleep by the sound of Jessie shrieking and glass breaking.

Joanna flew from her bed to the mother's bedroom, where she found Jessie smashing the dresser accessories, using a photo album as if it were a baseball bat.

"Why couldn't you love me?" Jessie screamed. She smashed the second table lamp, breathing hard and crying hysterically.

"Jessie! It's okay!" Avoiding the broken glass, Joanna pulled Jessie into a hug.

"Why couldn't she love me? Why did she treat me like I was nothin' but a burden to her?" Jessie cried. "Why couldn't she be a good mom when I needed her?"

"I don't know, Jess," Joanna comforted, leading her to sit on the bed.

"Look what I found," Jessie labored between her sobs. She handed Joanna a scrapbook containing baby pictures. In them, her proud, young parents were holding her; her father, handsome, dressed in an army uniform. Jessie flipped to the pages toward the back of the album, displaying flyers with her as the head-liner.

"All the time I was growin' up, she told me I was wastin' my time with music. She used to say I'd never amount to anythin'! Look on the last page; the article from the *New York Times*, about the opening night of Diamonds, and a coaster. You're right, she followed my career. She came to New York and never tried to talk to me. Who does that?"

Joanna softly reasoned, "Maybe losing your dad devastated her. Maybe she felt if she loved you, she'd lose you, too."

"Well? She did lose me, didn't she?" Jessie heaved spasm breaths. "I let it get to me. She said I was a slut, so I drank myself to oblivion and whored around the way she did! I'm always afraid people are gonna realize I'm a fake. Because of her, I don't let anyone close."

"That's not true Jessie. I'm close to you."

"You're the exception." Jessie blew her nose.

"As for the fakin' it part, you're the most genuine person I know. At least I never have to guess what you're thinkin'—you always call it the way you see it."

Jessie chuckled, tears running. "Yeah, even when you don't wanna hear it."

Joanna laughed, too, then advised seriously, "Don't do this to yourself. You've got to shut off the voices from the past; they're lying to you. You aren't worthless, honey, you're fabulous."

"I don't wanna end up like her. With no one to love me or care when I'm gone."

"You're not gonna end up that way."

"If I don't change, I will. I met someone, his name is Russell Detrick. He's a talented artist; wealthy, gorgeous. He wants to marry me."

"So, what's the problem?" Joanna asked.

"I'm the problem! He wants kids. I keep tellin' him I'd fuck it up."

"How long've you been seein' him?"

"Over a year, exclusively."

"Why'd you keep it to yourself all this time?"

"I was afraid I'd jinx it. Let's face it: I don't even know if I can get pregnant again. I've been on birth control pills for years. And even if I could, can you imagine me as a parent?"

"Have you told him this?"

"Yes! I've told him everythin' and he still wants me. He says there's no set rules on parentin'. He wants me to move into his Manhattan apartment."

"Sounds like he has it worked out." Joanna shrugged, not seeing the problem.

"You don't get it."

"I get it. You're the one who has a distorted view. No one else sees you that way."

"Really?"

"Really." Joanna tousled her friend's thick red hair.

"I've got a bad tequila headache," Jessie admitted.

"I'll bet." Joanna looked at the shards of the liquor bottle she'd thrown against the wall.

A few days later, the two women were on their way to the airport to return to their homes. Diamond meowed loudly from the critter carrier in the backseat. Joanna had agreed to adopt the cat, since the creature seemed to have picked her as family.

"I've made a decision," Jessie announced.

"Should I brace myself?" Joanna asked, joking.

Jessie smiled, "I'm gonna tell Russ if I get pregnant, we'll get married. In the meantime I'll move in with him." When Joanna didn't respond, Jessie questioned, "I've shocked you?"

"Yeah, a little. You were so against the idea. What changed your mind?"

"A lot of soul searchin'. In the right circumstances I might be an outstandin' mother."

"I think that's true," Joanna agreed, encouraged by the conviction in Jessie's voice.

"Russ is the only man whose made me even entertain the idea of marriage and a child. When you meet him, you'll understand. He's kind, sweet, and so funny. He loves me in a way I didn't expect to ever be loved. He encourages my strengths, but at the same time he accepts my weaknesses. He's incredible."

"You sound like a woman in love," Joanna pointed out.

"I am. For the first time in my life, I really am."

Jessie called Joanna three months later to tell her she'd gotten married. She and Russell were blessed with a baby boy in November 1979. They named him Zackary.

As she vowed, Jessie turned out to be an excellent mother. She confessed to Joanna that until Zack, she didn't know it was possible to love someone so much.

Chapter 50

Joanna and Mark were thrilled Allie, in her senior year at Columbia, planned to come home for Thanksgiving. The biggest surprise was the phone call from Tom Wyatt, wondering if he could spend Thanksgiving with them. Joanna expressed concern over how Catherine and Jack might feel. Tom explained they were vacationing in Europe.

Hope's crew, along with her boyfriend, arrived on Wednesday at lunchtime, and Joanna delighted in the hugs from her five-year-old granddaughter and four-year-old grandson. Hope appeared to be healthy and happy and Joanna instantly liked her new boyfriend. Brian Tipton worked as a manager in the shipping department at Hope's job. He was quiet and, in Joanna's opinion, needed a haircut. His dry wit and laid-back disposition made it okay for her to tease him about giving him a trim before they went home.

Mark met Allie and Tom at the Memphis International Airport that evening. The long-distance travelers coordinated their flights to require only one trip to the busy airport.

The house on Hollywood Avenue was, once again, filled with the exuberant sounds of young people. Lively and sometimes passionate conversation arose, especially when the topic turned to the environment and energy alternatives.

"The reason we're in an energy crisis is because Americans want to drive their gas-guzzler cars, when what we should be doing is working on alternative energy sources," Tom explained.

"Cleaner sources, like solar, electric, and wind power," Allie put in.

"You're aware, a few years ago scientists found a hole in our ozone layer? This is caused by hydrocarbons and toxic garbage pumped into the environment the last hundred years."

"Don't even get me started on the subject of the ozone and garbage or we'll be talking about recycling for the next hour," Allie warned, laughing.

"I guess the bottom line is, if people don't change, my great-grandchildren won't have a planet fit to sustain life," Tom theorized.

"Nothing'll change if people aren't informed," Allie advised.

Hope's boyfriend, Brian, entered the conversation. "If you think about it, human beings have caused the damage to this planet, almost like a parasite invasion. I know it sounds like science fiction, but my neighbor, who works at NASA, is searching for inhabitable planets so when humans trash this one, we have another one to go to."

"If scientists can figure out a way to do it, they will," Joanna speculated.

"It isn't even a matter of if, it's more like when, Mama. Where we live, so many companies are inventing new technologies that remind me of *The Jetson's* and *Star Trek*. I heard an engineer say within ten years everyone'll have phones in their cars," Hope told them.

"I can't imagine all the changes these little ones will see in their lifetime," Joanna mused, rocking sleeping Jason. "And to think, when I was growin' up on the farm, we didn't have indoor plumbin' till I was seven."

"I know, I know!" Hope teased laughing. "And you had to walk ten miles to school, in the snow, and it was uphill both ways!" Hope had them all laughing.

It comforted Joanna to witness the lack of tension in her home that weekend. Even Hope and Tom were joking with each other. She was also glad that Allie and Hope had mended their friendship.

At one point on Saturday afternoon, Joanna noticed Mark and Tom out by the roses, in a serious conversation. Later, Mark told her Tom had asked for some advice regarding women.

"It seems he's met someone he's crazy about," Mark confided.

"I hope you didn't tell him to wait years to tell her he's in love with her." Joanna smiled, swatting him with the tea towel.

"No! I told him to spend time with her. Get to know her. If there's something there and the timing's right, it'll be apparent fairly quickly to both of them."

"Sound advice," Joanna complimented.

The real surprise came a few weeks later when they learned Tom made regular trips from Boston to New York to visit Allie. By New Year's, they'd made it known they were dating. When Allie graduated in 1981, the couple announced their engagement.

Allie'd always dreamed of a fairy-tale wedding, and Mark as a proud father saw to it she'd have it. The ceremony took place at a Catholic church in Memphis, with the reception at the newly restored Peabody Hotel.

Joanna found it humorous that she was both the mother of the bride and the mother of the groom, albeit stepmother to the bride and birthmother to the groom, as well as the mother-in-law to her own son. Jessie quipped there must be a southern joke in there somewhere.

It felt odd to Joanna to be in the same room with the Wyatts. Catherine and Jack seemed happy and Joanna was glad. She limited conversation with Jack to pleasantries.

At the reception, Joanna's breath quickened when she noticed Hope sit alone with Jack at a table. Joanna watched out of the corner of her eye to make sure the exchange remained civil. Her fears were abated when Hope got up and Jack handed her a piece of paper that she assumed contained his phone number.

The band played "Endless Love" for the bride and the groom's first dance. Joanna stood off to the side, tears in her eyes, touched by how happy they looked. Her concentration broke when Catherine's arm slipped around her shoulder. She too, had the look of a proud mother.

"Thank you for bringing these wonderful children into my life. Without you I never would've known Tom, and without you Tom never would've met Allie."

"Bizarre, isn't it?" Joanna patted Catherine's hand.

"We're going to be grandparents together someday," Catherine pointed out.

"I'm lookin' forward to it," Joanna responded.

"Me too."

The band ended the song and their children sealed the tradition with a kiss that held the hopes and promises of the years to come. The two women gave each other an understanding squeeze. If anyone witnessed the touching moment between the mothers, it was never mentioned.

A few years later, when Allie became pregnant, Tom secured a job in Memphis, at a solar energy company. Allie eventually got a column in an environmental magazine, which she wrote from home, and had two more babies. When they traveled, Mark and Joanna were thrilled to watch the grandchildren.

Around the same time, Hope married Brian Tipton. He took a manager's position with FedEx in Memphis and Joanna had her children close by; her house became the center of family activity. She adored and spoiled her five grandchildren and was content with her life.

On a sweltering summer day in 1990, Mary finally got the phone call from Tony she'd waited a lifetime for. He'd found their son.

"A woman from CUB put me in touch with computer hackers. I paid eight hundred dollars and within three days they found our son," Mary's high school sweetheart explained.

"Is that legal?"

"No, but I don't care! They found our son! His name is Randy Ayers. He lives in Atlanta with his wife and two sons. He's a middle school gym teacher and football coach. I just got off the phone with him. He's eager to meet us. He wants you to call him."

Through blurry eyes, Mary wrote down the numbers Tony called out to her. Within two weeks, the child she'd given away thirty-three years earlier made a trip to Memphis to meet her. She marked the occasion as bittersweet, when she learned Randy's childhood hadn't been the best. He'd been the second child adopted by Tracy and David Ayers. When he was eight years old, his adoptive mother became pregnant with a little boy. It seemed Mrs. and Mr. Ayers favored their natural child over the two boys they'd adopted and treated them unequally. As hard as the boy tried, he couldn't get them to notice him anymore. This led to defiant and reckless behavior as a teenager. Eventually he accepted the injustice of their behavior, but still struggled with the bitterness.

His attitude toward Mary and Tony was warm and understanding. Being a schoolteacher gave him firsthand knowledge of the problems of teen pregnancy. It touched him that the couple had spent the last seventeen years trying to find him. Randy was also grateful for the brothers and sisters who welcomed him without reservation.

In the perfect culmination for Mary, her long-lost son told her, "For the first time in my life I feel like I have a family."

She told him, "You do, and this is exactly how it should be."

A year later, Joanna got a phone call from Jessie's husband, Russell, with devastating news: Her friend was quite ill and asking for her to come to see her.

Joanna flew into JFK airport on a blustery winter morning and took a cab to the apartment Jessie called home with her husband and son. Russell tried to brace Joanna for Jessie's condition, explaining she'd refused to go to the hospital weeks ago. Against Russell's wishes, she'd signed a Do Not Resuscitate form and insisted he call in hospice.

"The chemo has weakened her heart. The doctors say it could give out at any time," Jessie's husband explained.

At first glance, Joanna would've guessed Jessie was already gone. Her transparent, pale skin seemed magnified by the bright-red turban on her head. Her sunken eyes fluttered, and she smiled when she saw Joanna.

"Well, there you are," she said with labored breath, removing her oxygen mask.

"Here I am, girl." Joanna smiled back, suppressing the lump in her throat. In those green eyes, Joanna saw the Jessie she loved so much.

"I fired my hairdresser," Jessie joked, trying to lighten the moment.

"I never understood why you let someone other than me do your hair in the first place," Joanna quipped. She sat on the bed and took Jessie's hand. Jessie winced, with pain.

"Can I call the nurse? Do you want somethin' for the pain?" Joanna asked.

"No, it'll only gork me out. I have things I wanna say to you. Things I meant to say. I wanna tell you I'm sorry." Jessie's eyes glistened with tears.

"Sorry? Sorry for what?" Joanna's hot tears ran down her cheeks.

"For what I'm gonna ask you to do. I want you to talk sense into Russ. He has to let me go." Jessie put the mask on and took several deep breaths. "I've fought so hard. He and Zack won't accept I can't fight anymore."

Joanna tried to calm her, rubbing her arm, "Shhhh now, you're tired."

"Yes! I'm tired! I'm dyin'. I have to explain why I wouldn't let Russ tell you I was sick."

"You don't have to explain anythin' to me."

"Yes I do!" Jessie spoke quickly, with renewed strength. "The odds for me weren't good from the beginnin'. I did this to myself by livin' a reckless life. I didn't want everyone hangin' around with long faces for months. It's so ironic, now that I have everythin' I've dreamed of, I get my non-refundable ticket punched. I've only gone through the treatments for Russ and Zack. I didn't want everyone to remember me the way I look now." Jessie weakly laid her head back.

"The way you look now?" Joanna whispered, "All I see is my friend Jessie. It's gonna be so hard for me to let you go, too."

"You've been my rock, my safe harbor. You were always there for me," Jessie whispered.

"You've always been my voice of reason, as crazy as that sounds!" Joanna told her.

"That is crazy." Jessie's eyes were getting heavy. "Will you do this for me?"

"Yes, of course. But, as long as I've known you, you've always done things on your own terms. I doubt this time will be any different. Sleep now; put your mind at ease," Joanna assured.

Prissy and Mary arrived the next morning. Both women had their own private time with Jessie and came out crying the way Joanna had. That evening Jessie was surrounded by her closest friends. Joanna painted Jessie's fingernails her favorite shade of red, while Prissy gave an overview of the cases she'd observed involving adopted children or birthparents who were challenging the laws that kept their records sealed.

"It's only a matter of time before a case sets the precedent and overturns the law."

"Keep pushin' them. You'll get there," Jessie told her.

"Even though I've found my son, I still want to see what Mrs. Lewis wrote about me and what the caseworker wrote about Randy's adoptive parents," Mary asserted.

"What was it you said, Mary? That you were tired of lookin' behind you?" Jessie asked.

Mary nodded. "I think we've all overcome that syndrome and we're wiser because of it."

"Well, if experience from makin' major mistakes produces wisdom, I must be a genius at this point!" Jessie announced, laughing along with her friends. In a moment, the hospice nurse came in to get Jessie settled for the night.

"Your color looks better this evening, Jessie."

"These gals cheered me up."

"Well, I'm going to have to hustle all of you out so my patient can sleep. That way she'll have the energy for more of this tomorrow."

The visitors obeyed and went out to the living room where Russell read the *New York Times* while Zack sorted through Lego spaceship pieces.

Russ smiled. "It's so refreshing to hear her laugh. I don't know how she maintains her sense of humor. She's never complained or been short with us or the health-care people."

"Thanks for callin' us," Joanna offered.

"I figured it was time. They keep telling me it won't be long." His voice cracked a little.

The nurse came out to the living room and announced, "Jessie wants to say good night to Zack." The boy went running to his mother's bedroom.

"I think we'll say good night, too, and head over to the hotel," Joanna told him. "Is around eleven okay for us to come by tomorrow morning?"

"That'll be fine. Thanks for being here; you don't know how much it helps," Russ said.

Sometime during the night, Jessie passed away peacefully in her sleep. Her best friends received the call from Russ at eight the next morning. Hundreds attended the visitation. A private funeral was reserved for family and close friends. Then a public party was held at Diamonds, with music and laughter as people remembered the fiery redhead with stories about her life.

At six fifty in the evening, the club hushed when Russ turned on the closing of the national news. Peter Jennings's voice filled the silence: "Finally, tonight, we say goodbye to one of New York's best loved entrepreneurs. Most people knew her as Jessie Diamond, the owner of the famous *Diamonds* nightclub. She was born Jessica Devereaux in 1939, in New Orleans. Even as a child, she possessed a remarkable talent as a pianist. By the age of twenty, she changed her name to Jessie Diamond and moved out to California, where her music was heard in blockbuster movies and commercials. In 1974 she opened Diamonds in New York and began the fundraising work she said enriched her life. She founded an assistance center for single mothers, which offered job training and child care, as well as aid with the basics. Her greatest work, perhaps, came in the last few years: establishing a foundation to provide free music lessons to young musicians, who otherwise couldn't afford professional training. Tonight at her nightclub, there is a celebration in her honor. She leaves behind a husband, well-known artist Russell Detrick, and their twelve-year-old son, Zack. Jessica Devereaux was fifty-two years old. That's our report on *World News Tonight*. I'm Peter Jennings, good night." A cheer exploded from the crowd as the TV was turned off.

Prissy leaned over to Mary and Joanna, "Jessie would've loved that!"

"She would've laughed her ass off!" Mary imagined, wiping the tears she couldn't help.

"Yeah! She would've!" Joanna agreed.

In September 1999, the Supreme Court of Tennessee at Nashville issued an opinion in the case of *Promise Doe, et al., v. Donald Sundquist, et al.*, upholding a new adoption records law stating that the disclosure of adoption records does not violate the right to privacy, giving those who desired it access to their adoption records.

Since 2005, home DNA kits have grown in popularity. To date twenty-six million people have submitted their DNA to various companies, making it easier for adoptees to connect with their birth families.

As of 2020, nineteen states have not unsealed the adoption records from the Baby Scoop Era.

Acknowledgments

Ten years ago, a friend asked me to do an internet search for the mother who gave her up for adoption while residing in a home for unwed mothers. During my research I was fascinated and appalled by these seemingly benevolent institutions whose goal was to convince the young women to surrender their babies to closed adoptions. The more I learned about what is now known as the Baby Scoop Era, the more I felt compelled to write a fictional account of what took place in this country when between 1950 and 1980 1.5 million girls were sent to these homes. I'm indebted to my friend Melissa who put me on this path.

I thank the women in my writer's group at the Murphy Library who were the first to hear the book and encouraged me to publish.

This book would not have happened without the opportunity for me to present this manuscript during Pitch week 19 at When Words Count writer's retreat in Rochester Vermont. Thanks to Steve Eisner, Amber Griffith, and everyone there for the experience that profoundly changed my life.

I'm grateful to Laura Tippy and Lynell Aycock for being my first editors and awesome enthusiasts of the story. I have to thank Peggy Collings with Concerned United Birthparents for being a great cheerleader as well as Fran Gruss Levin, Rickie Solinger, and Pamela Karanova the founder of Adoptees Connect for their endorsements.

A huge thank you goes to David LeGere and the team at Woodhall Press for believing in this project and for walking me through the process.

Last but not least, I am grateful to my husband and kids. Your love and support means the world to me.

About the Author

D.W. Hogan is a lifelong writer having majored in English at the University of Alabama in Huntsville. She's the mother of four grown children and grandmother to two. She is a full-time author and lives in Huntsville, Alabama with her husband. *Unbroken Bonds* is her Debut novel. Check out DWHogan.com for more information. You can follow her on Facebook D.W. Hogan author and on Instagram dawnhoganauthor.